THE RED PYRAMID

THE GRAPHIC NOVEL

RICK RIORDAN

ADAPTED BY
ORPHEUS COLLAR

LETTERED BY
JARED FLETCHER

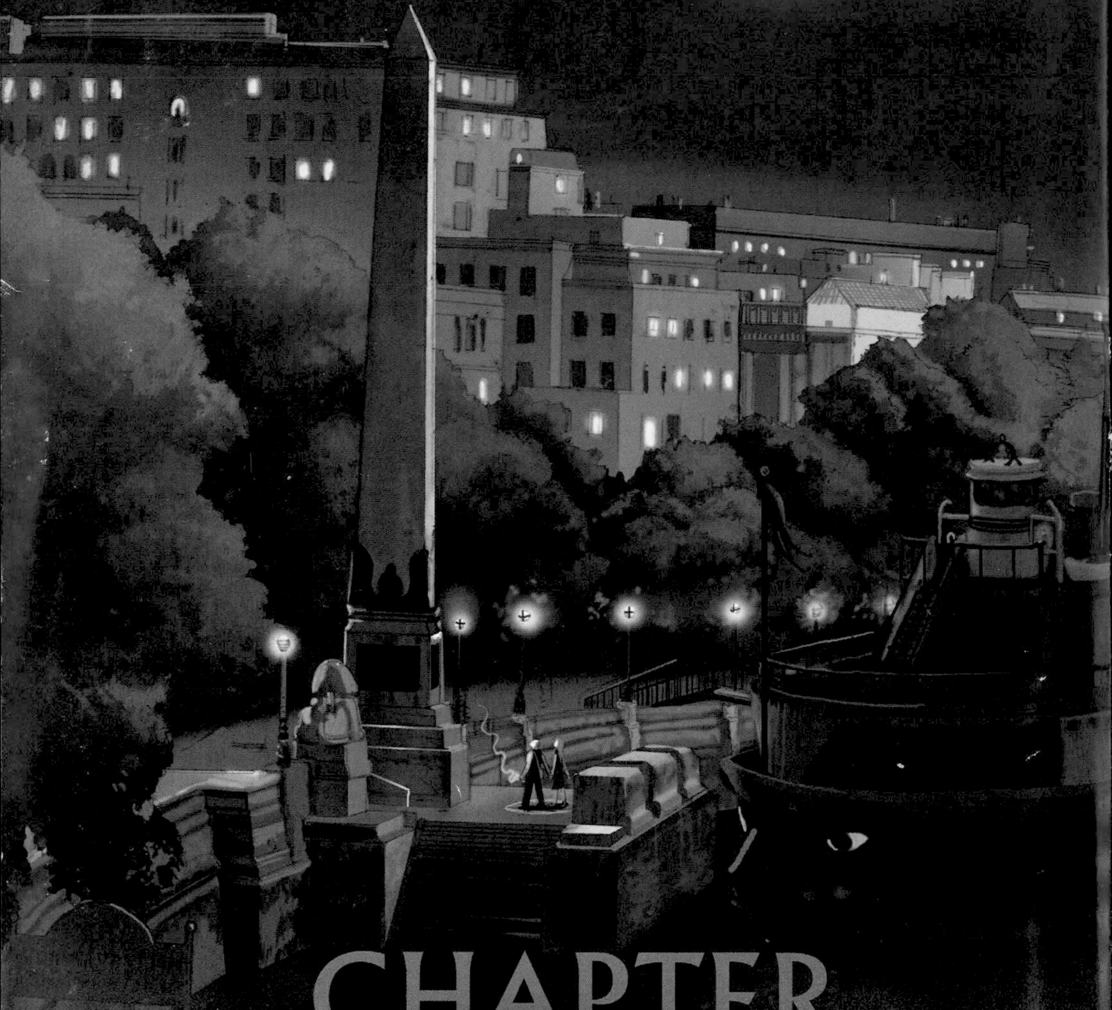

CHAPTER 1

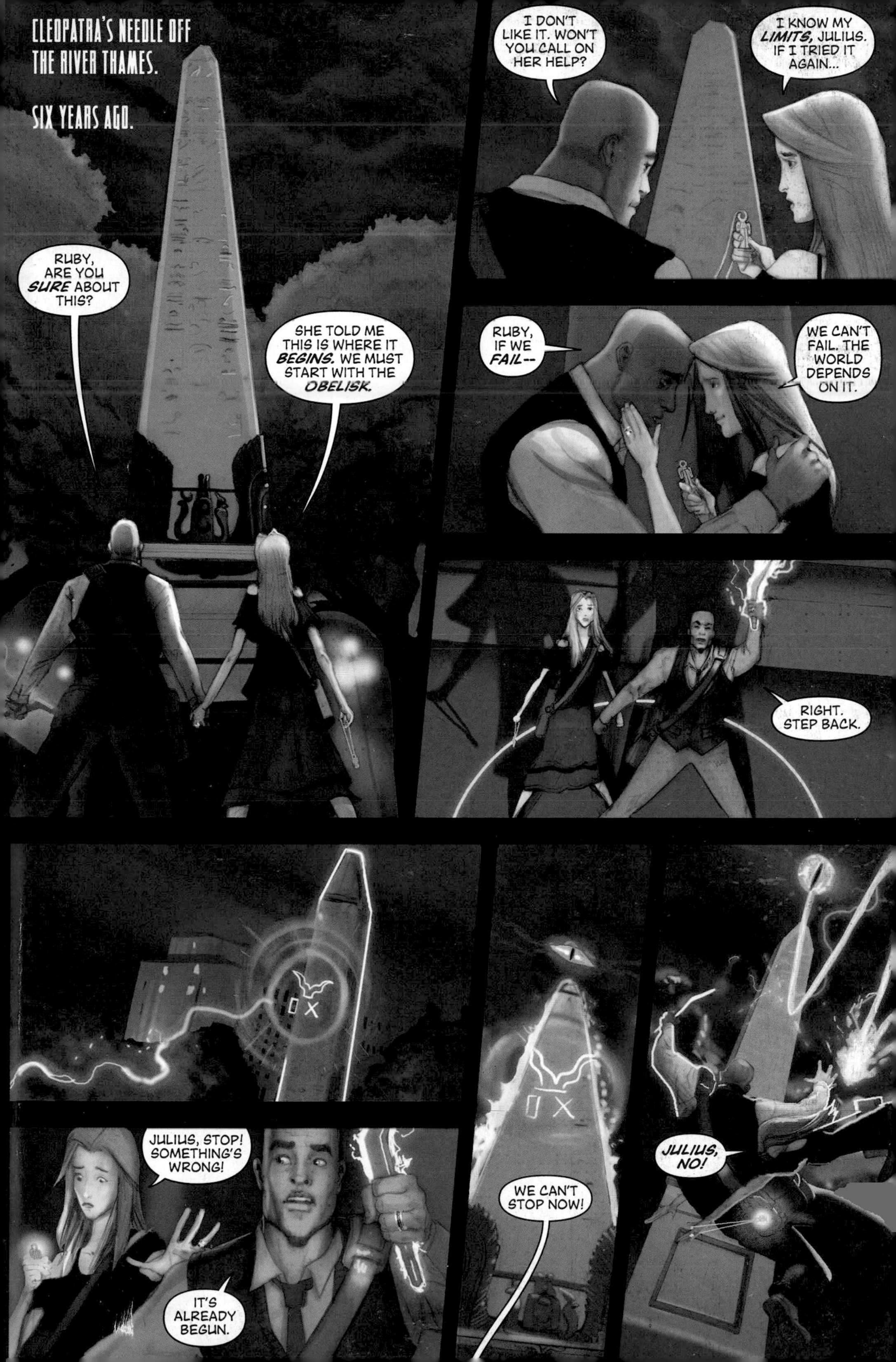
CLEOPATRA'S NEEDLE OFF THE RIVER THAMES.
SIX YEARS AGO.
RUBY, ARE YOU SURE ABOUT THIS?
SHE TOLD ME THIS IS WHERE IT BEGINS. WE MUST START WITH THE OBELISK.
I DON'T LIKE IT. WON'T YOU CALL ON HER HELP?
I KNOW MY LIMITS, JULIUS. IF I TRIED IT AGAIN...
RUBY, IF WE FAIL--
WE CAN'T FAIL. THE WORLD DEPENDS ON IT.
RIGHT. STEP BACK.
JULIUS, STOP! SOMETHING'S WRONG!
IT'S ALREADY BEGUN.
WE CAN'T STOP NOW!
JULIUS, NO!

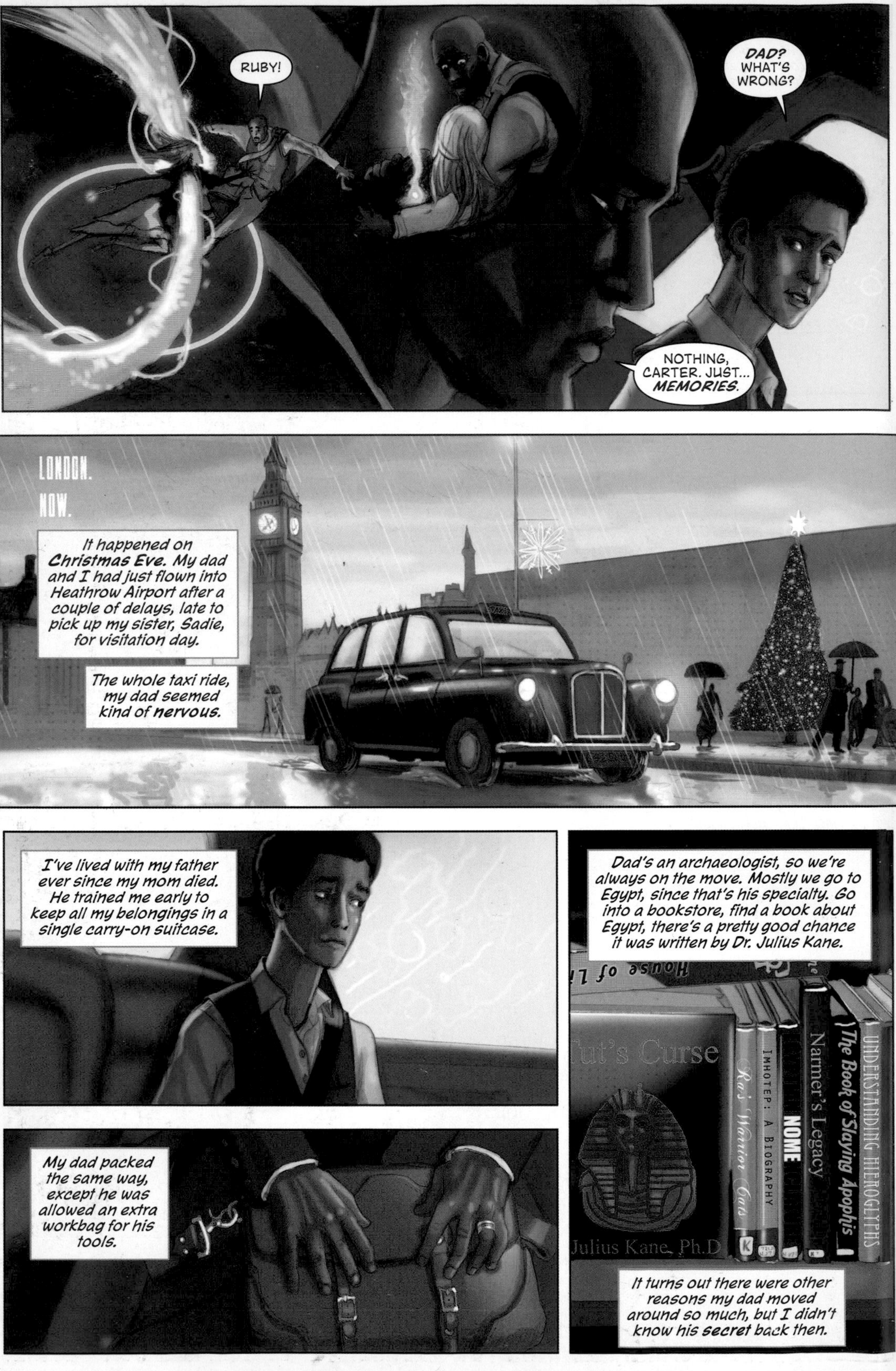

RUBY!
DAD? WHAT'S WRONG?
NOTHING, CARTER. JUST... MEMORIES.
LONDON.
NOW.
It happened on Christmas Eve. My dad and I had just flown into Heathrow Airport after a couple of delays, late to pick up my sister, Sadie, for visitation day.
The whole taxi ride, my dad seemed kind of nervous.
I've lived with my father ever since my mom died. He trained me early to keep all my belongings in a single carry-on suitcase.
My dad packed the same way, except he was allowed an extra workbag for his tools.
Dad's an archaeologist, so we're always on the move. Mostly we go to Egypt, since that's his specialty. Go into a bookstore, find a book about Egypt, there's a pretty good chance it was written by Dr. Julius Kane.
Tut's Curse
Julius Kane, Ph.D
IMHOTEP: A BIOGRAPHY
NOME
Narmer's Legacy
The Book of Slaying Apophis
UNDERSTANDING HIEROGLYPHS
It turns out there were other reasons my dad moved around so much, but I didn't know his secret back then.

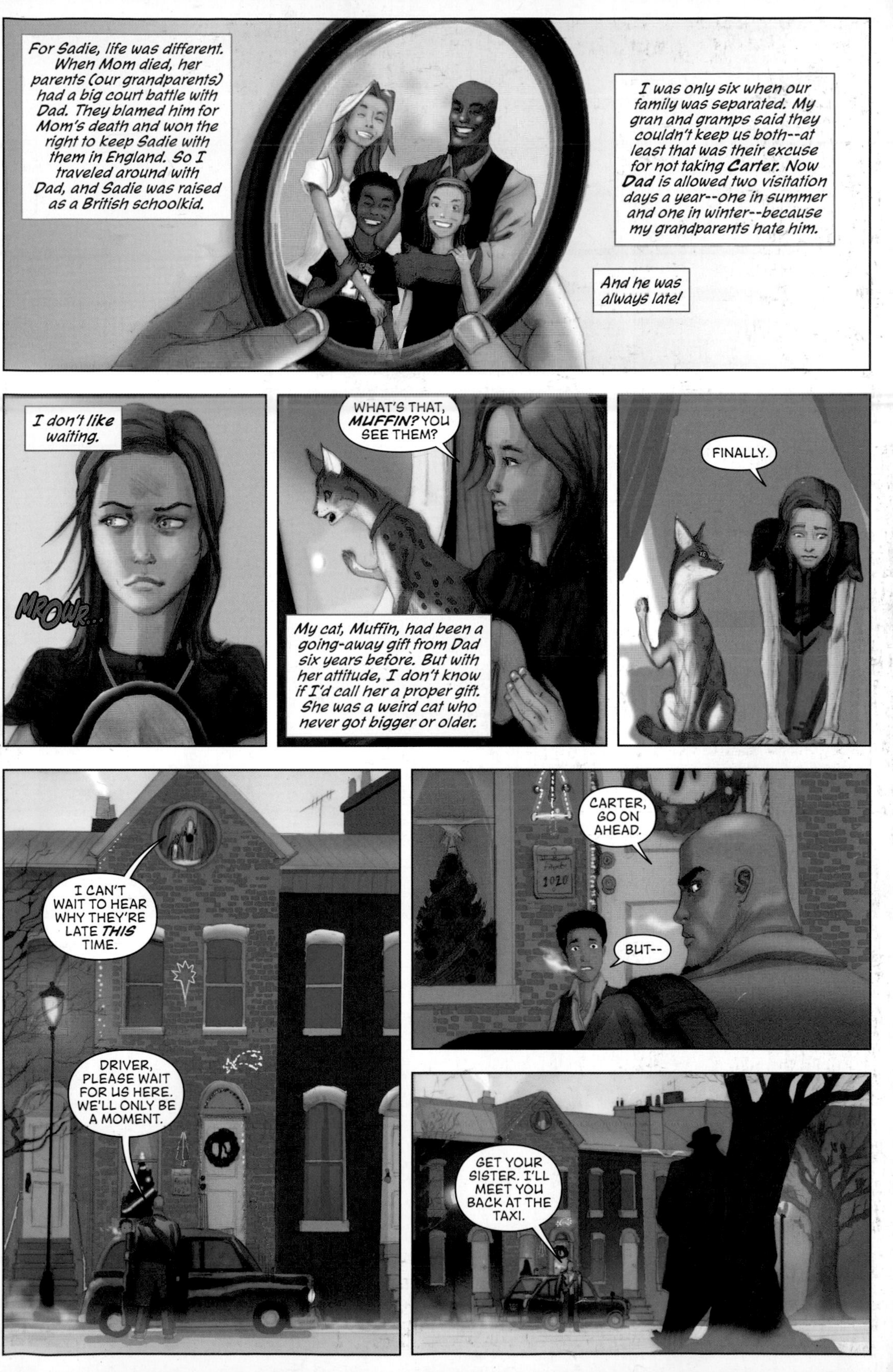
For Sadie, life was different. When Mom died, her parents (our grandparents) had a big court battle with Dad. They blamed him for Mom's death and won the right to keep Sadie with them in England. So I traveled around with Dad, and Sadie was raised as a British schoolkid.
I was only six when our family was separated. My gran and gramps said they couldn't keep us both--at least that was their excuse for not taking Carter. Now Dad is allowed two visitation days a year--one in summer and one in winter--because my grandparents hate him.
And he was always late!
I don't like waiting.
MROWR...
WHAT'S THAT, MUFFIN? YOU SEE THEM?
My cat, Muffin, had been a going-away gift from Dad six years before. But with her attitude, I don't know if I'd call her a proper gift. She was a weird cat who never got bigger or older.
FINALLY.
I CAN'T WAIT TO HEAR WHY THEY'RE LATE THIS TIME.
DRIVER, PLEASE WAIT FOR US HERE. WE'LL ONLY BE A MOMENT.
CARTER, GO ON AHEAD.
BUT--
GET YOUR SISTER. I'LL MEET YOU BACK AT THE TAXI.

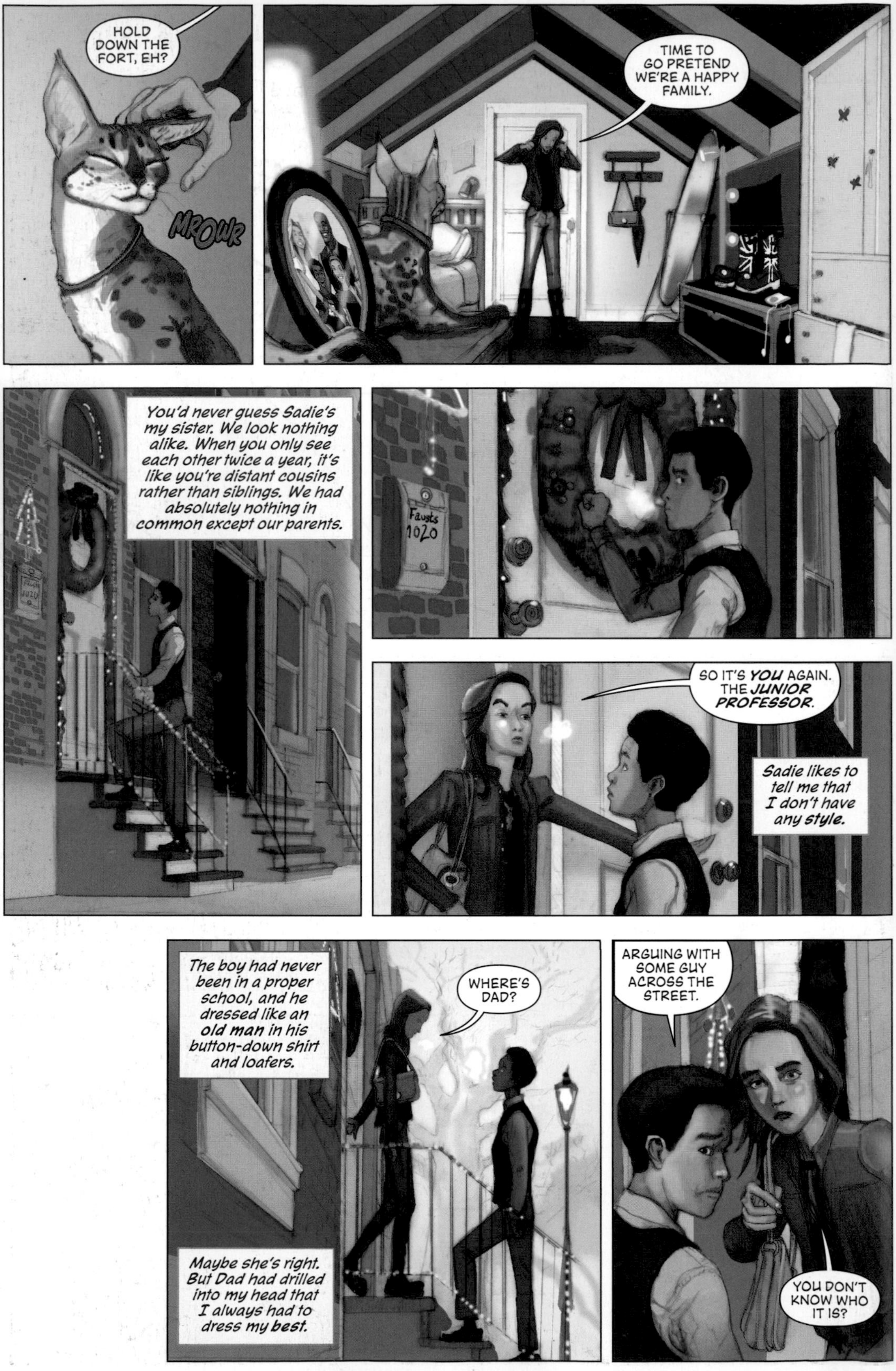
HOLD DOWN THE FORT, EH?
MROWR
TIME TO GO PRETEND WE'RE A HAPPY FAMILY.
You'd never guess Sadie's my sister. We look nothing alike. When you only see each other twice a year, it's like you're distant cousins rather than siblings. We had absolutely nothing in common except our parents.
Fausts 1020
SO IT'S YOU AGAIN. THE JUNIOR PROFESSOR.
Sadie likes to tell me that I don't have any style.
The boy had never been in a proper school, and he dressed like an old man in his button-down shirt and loafers.
WHERE'S DAD?
Maybe she's right. But Dad had drilled into my head that I always had to dress my best.
ARGUING WITH SOME GUY ACROSS THE STREET.
YOU DON'T KNOW WHO IT IS?

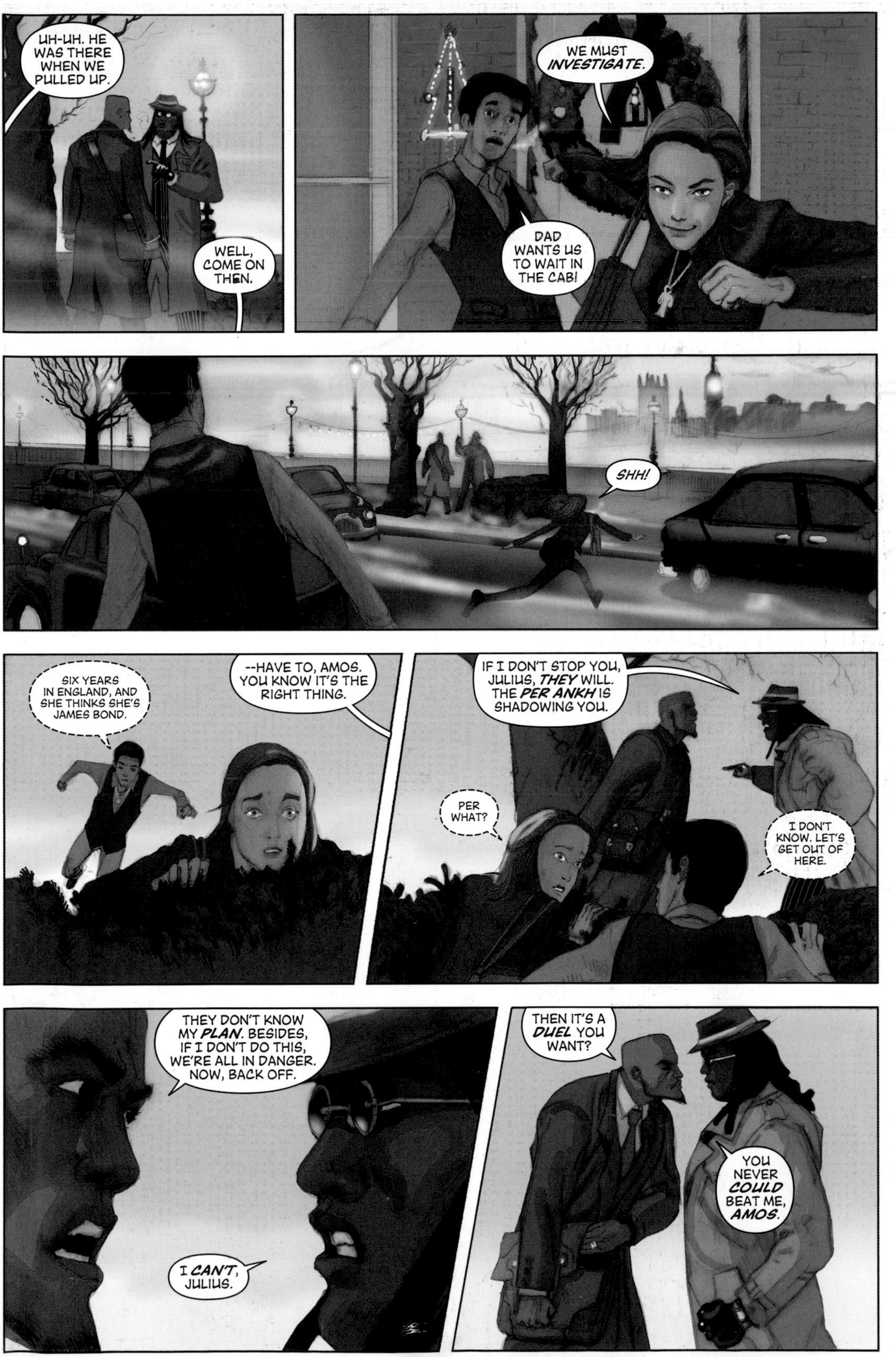
UH-UH. HE WAS THERE WHEN WE PULLED UP.
WELL, COME ON THEN.
WE MUST *INVESTIGATE*.
DAD WANTS US TO WAIT IN THE CAB!
SHH!
SIX YEARS IN ENGLAND, AND SHE THINKS SHE'S JAMES BOND.
--HAVE TO, AMOS. YOU KNOW IT'S THE RIGHT THING.
IF I DON'T STOP YOU, JULIUS, *THEY* WILL. THE *PER ANKH* IS SHADOWING YOU.
PER WHAT?
I DON'T KNOW. LET'S GET OUT OF HERE.
THEY DON'T KNOW MY *PLAN*. BESIDES, IF I DON'T DO THIS, WE'RE ALL IN DANGER. NOW, BACK OFF.
I *CAN'T*, JULIUS.
THEN IT'S A *DUEL* YOU WANT?
YOU NEVER *COULD* BEAT ME, *AMOS*.

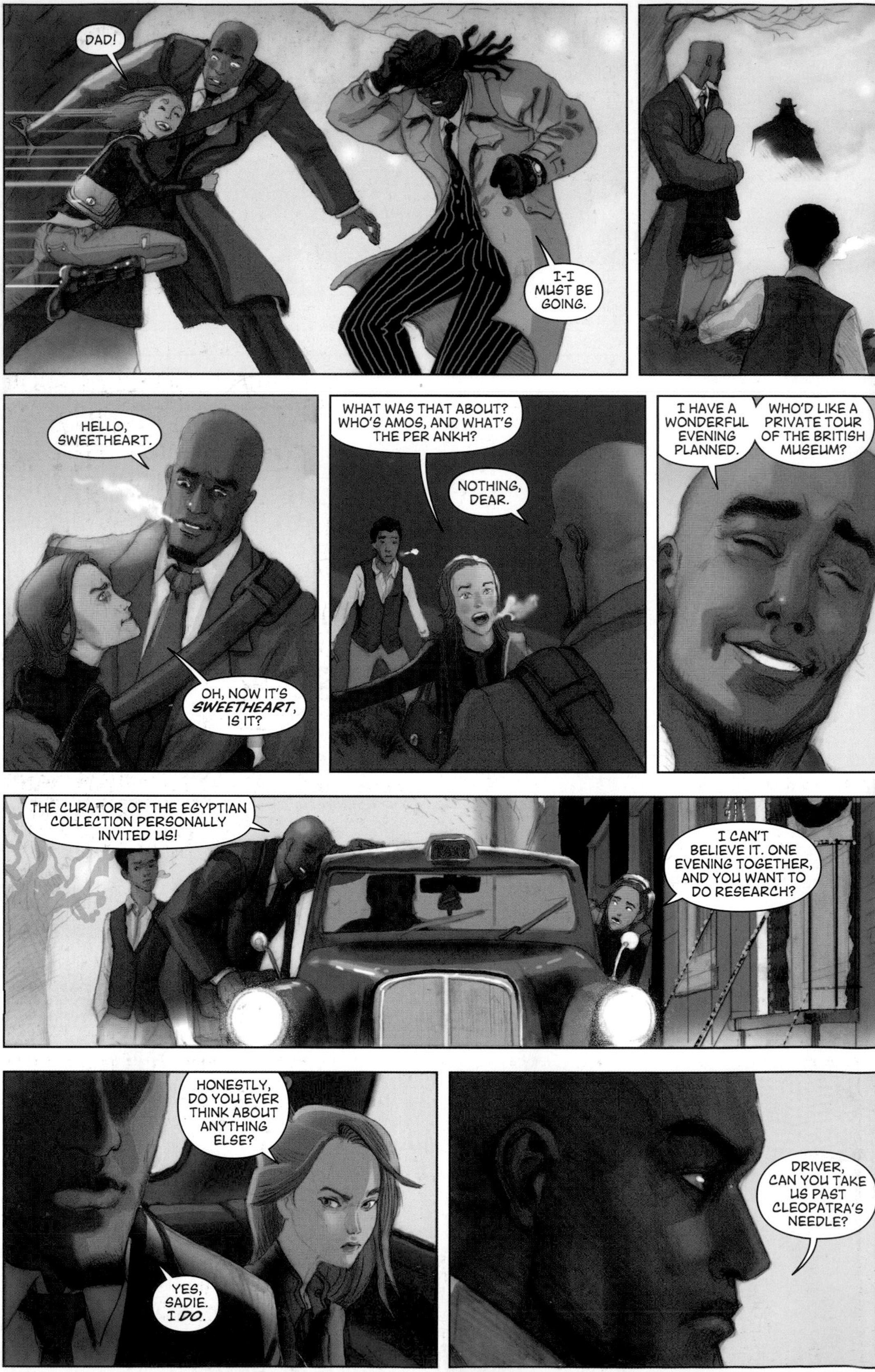
DAD!
I-I MUST BE GOING.
HELLO, SWEETHEART.
OH, NOW IT'S *SWEETHEART*, IS IT?
WHAT WAS THAT ABOUT? WHO'S AMOS, AND WHAT'S THE PER ANKH?
NOTHING, DEAR.
I HAVE A WONDERFUL EVENING PLANNED.
WHO'D LIKE A PRIVATE TOUR OF THE BRITISH MUSEUM?
THE CURATOR OF THE EGYPTIAN COLLECTION PERSONALLY INVITED US!
I CAN'T BELIEVE IT. ONE EVENING TOGETHER, AND YOU WANT TO DO RESEARCH?
HONESTLY, DO YOU EVER THINK ABOUT ANYTHING ELSE?
YES, SADIE. I *DO*.
DRIVER, CAN YOU TAKE US PAST CLEOPATRA'S NEEDLE?

DO WE HAVE TO STOP FOR *EVERY* MONUMENT?

I HAD TO SEE IT AGAIN, WHERE IT HAPPENED... THE LAST PLACE I SAW YOUR *MOTHER.*

ARE YOU TELLING US SHE DIED HERE? AT CLEOPATRA'S NEEDLE? WHAT HAPPENED?

DAD! I GO PAST THIS EVERY DAY. YOU MEAN TO SAY-- ALL THIS TIME-- I DIDN'T EVEN KNOW?

DO YOU STILL HAVE YOUR CAT?

MUFFIN? OF COURSE I DO! WHAT DOES THAT HAVE TO DO WITH ANYTHING?

AND YOUR *AMULET?* LET ME SEE IT.

Right before we were separated, Dad gave us both Egyptian amulets.

Mine had been Mom's. It looked a bit like an angel, or perhaps a killer alien robot.

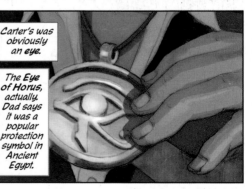

Carter's was obviously an *eye.*

The *Eye of Horus,* actually. Dad says it was a popular protection symbol in Ancient Egypt.

HAPPY NOW? BUT DON'T CHANGE THE SUBJECT. GRAN'S ALWAYS SAYING YOU CAUSED MUM'S DEATH. THAT'S NOT *TRUE,* IS IT?

DRIVER, PLEASE CONTINUE TO THE MUSEUM.

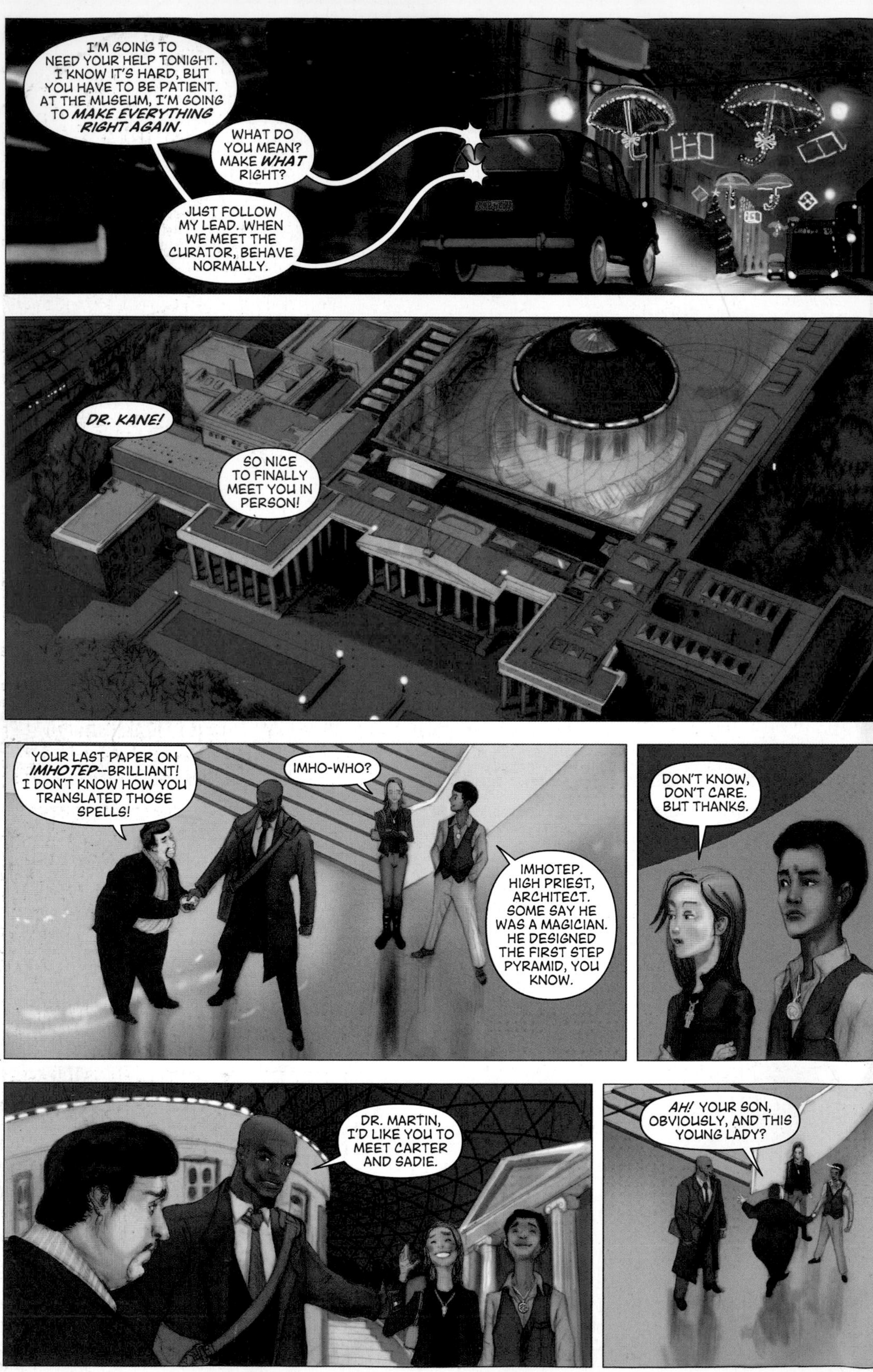
I'M GOING TO NEED YOUR HELP TONIGHT. I KNOW IT'S HARD, BUT YOU HAVE TO BE PATIENT. AT THE MUSEUM, I'M GOING TO MAKE EVERYTHING RIGHT AGAIN.
WHAT DO YOU MEAN? MAKE WHAT RIGHT?
JUST FOLLOW MY LEAD. WHEN WE MEET THE CURATOR, BEHAVE NORMALLY.
DR. KANE!
SO NICE TO FINALLY MEET YOU IN PERSON!
YOUR LAST PAPER ON IMHOTEP--BRILLIANT! I DON'T KNOW HOW YOU TRANSLATED THOSE SPELLS!
IMHO-WHO?
IMHOTEP. HIGH PRIEST, ARCHITECT. SOME SAY HE WAS A MAGICIAN. HE DESIGNED THE FIRST STEP PYRAMID, YOU KNOW.
DON'T KNOW, DON'T CARE. BUT THANKS.
DR. MARTIN, I'D LIKE YOU TO MEET CARTER AND SADIE.
AH! YOUR SON, OBVIOUSLY, AND THIS YOUNG LADY?

MY DAUGHTER.

WHY YES, YES, OF COURSE!

SO, THE STONE.

YES! RIGHT THIS WAY, DR. KANE. WE'RE VERY HONORED.

THOUGH I CAN'T IMAGINE WHAT NEW INFORMATION YOU COULD GLEAN FROM IT. IT'S BEEN STUDIED TO DEATH--OUR MOST FAMOUS ARTIFACT.

YOU MAY BE SURPRISED.

There's always that flash of confusion across people's faces when they realize I'm part of the family.

It doesn't matter how open-minded people think they are. I hate it, but over the years, we've come to expect it.

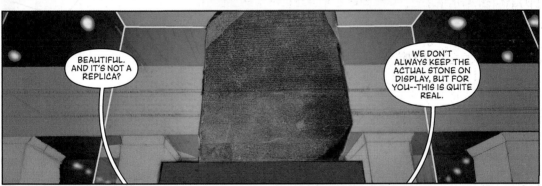

BEAUTIFUL. AND IT'S NOT A REPLICA?

WE DON'T ALWAYS KEEP THE ACTUAL STONE ON DISPLAY, BUT FOR YOU--THIS IS QUITE REAL.

THE ROSETTA STONE!

ISN'T THAT A COMPUTER PROGRAM?

YOUNG LADY, THE ROSETTA STONE WAS THE KEY TO DECIPHERING HIEROGLYPHICS! IT WAS DISCOVERED BY NAPOLEON'S ARMY IN 1799 AND--

OH, RIGHT. I REMEMBER NOW.

SADIE, UNTIL THIS STONE WAS DISCOVERED, NO ONE WAS ABLE TO READ HIEROGLYPHICS. THE WRITTEN LANGUAGE OF EGYPT HAD BEEN *FORGOTTEN*.

THEN, AN ENGLISHMAN NAMED THOMAS YOUNG PROVED THAT THE ROSETTA STONE'S THREE LANGUAGES ALL TOLD THE SAME MESSAGE.

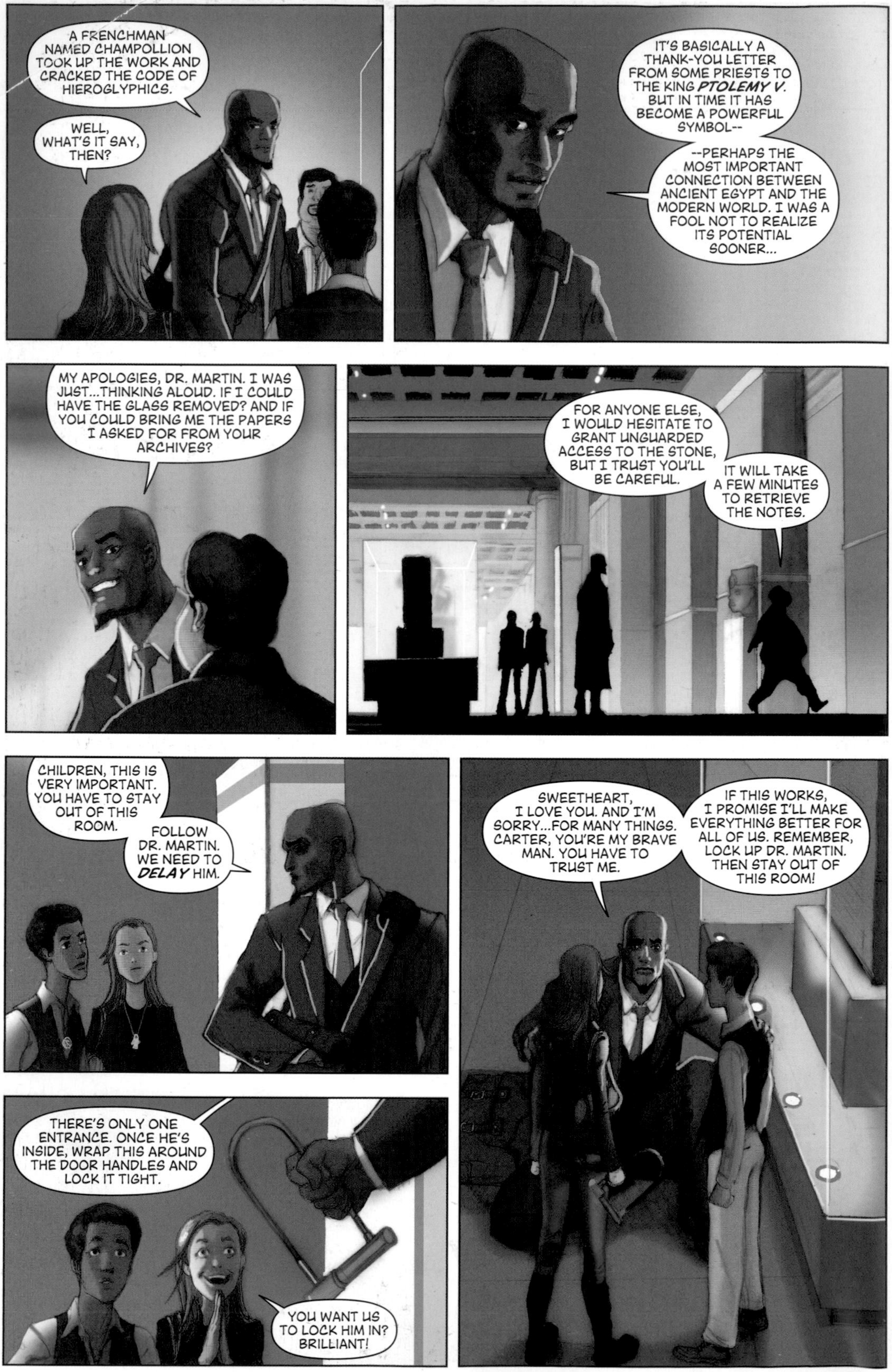
A FRENCHMAN NAMED CHAMPOLLION TOOK UP THE WORK AND CRACKED THE CODE OF HIEROGLYPHICS.
WELL, WHAT'S IT SAY, THEN?
IT'S BASICALLY A THANK-YOU LETTER FROM SOME PRIESTS TO THE KING *PTOLEMY V.* BUT IN TIME IT HAS BECOME A POWERFUL SYMBOL--
--PERHAPS THE MOST IMPORTANT CONNECTION BETWEEN ANCIENT EGYPT AND THE MODERN WORLD. I WAS A FOOL NOT TO REALIZE ITS POTENTIAL SOONER...
MY APOLOGIES, DR. MARTIN. I WAS JUST...THINKING ALOUD. IF I COULD HAVE THE GLASS REMOVED? AND IF YOU COULD BRING ME THE PAPERS I ASKED FOR FROM YOUR ARCHIVES?
FOR ANYONE ELSE, I WOULD HESITATE TO GRANT UNGUARDED ACCESS TO THE STONE, BUT I TRUST YOU'LL BE CAREFUL.
IT WILL TAKE A FEW MINUTES TO RETRIEVE THE NOTES.
CHILDREN, THIS IS VERY IMPORTANT. YOU HAVE TO STAY OUT OF THIS ROOM.
FOLLOW DR. MARTIN. WE NEED TO *DELAY* HIM.
THERE'S ONLY ONE ENTRANCE. ONCE HE'S INSIDE, WRAP THIS AROUND THE DOOR HANDLES AND LOCK IT TIGHT.
YOU WANT US TO LOCK HIM IN? BRILLIANT!
SWEETHEART, I LOVE YOU. AND I'M SORRY...FOR MANY THINGS. CARTER, YOU'RE MY BRAVE MAN. YOU HAVE TO TRUST ME.
IF THIS WORKS, I PROMISE I'LL MAKE EVERYTHING BETTER FOR ALL OF US. REMEMBER, LOCK UP DR. MARTIN. THEN STAY OUT OF THIS ROOM!

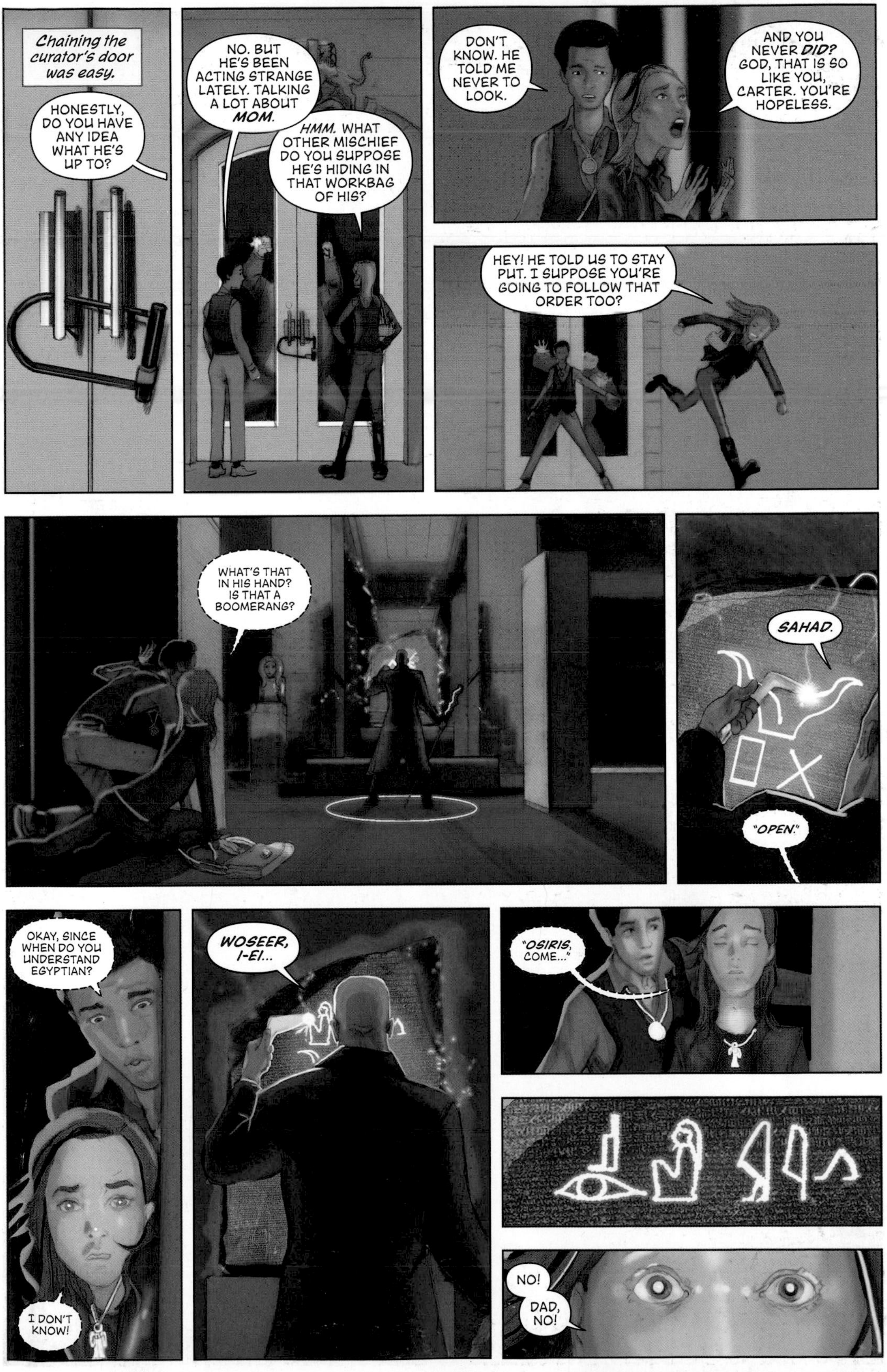
Chaining the curator's door was easy.
HONESTLY, DO YOU HAVE ANY IDEA WHAT HE'S UP TO?
NO. BUT HE'S BEEN ACTING STRANGE LATELY. TALKING A LOT ABOUT MOM.
HMM. WHAT OTHER MISCHIEF DO YOU SUPPOSE HE'S HIDING IN THAT WORKBAG OF HIS?
DON'T KNOW. HE TOLD ME NEVER TO LOOK.
AND YOU NEVER DID? GOD, THAT IS SO LIKE YOU, CARTER. YOU'RE HOPELESS.
HEY! HE TOLD US TO STAY PUT. I SUPPOSE YOU'RE GOING TO FOLLOW THAT ORDER TOO?
WHAT'S THAT IN HIS HAND? IS THAT A BOOMERANG?
SAHAD.
"OPEN."
OKAY, SINCE WHEN DO YOU UNDERSTAND EGYPTIAN?
I DON'T KNOW!
WOSEER, I-EI...
"OSIRIS, COME..."
NO!
DAD, NO!

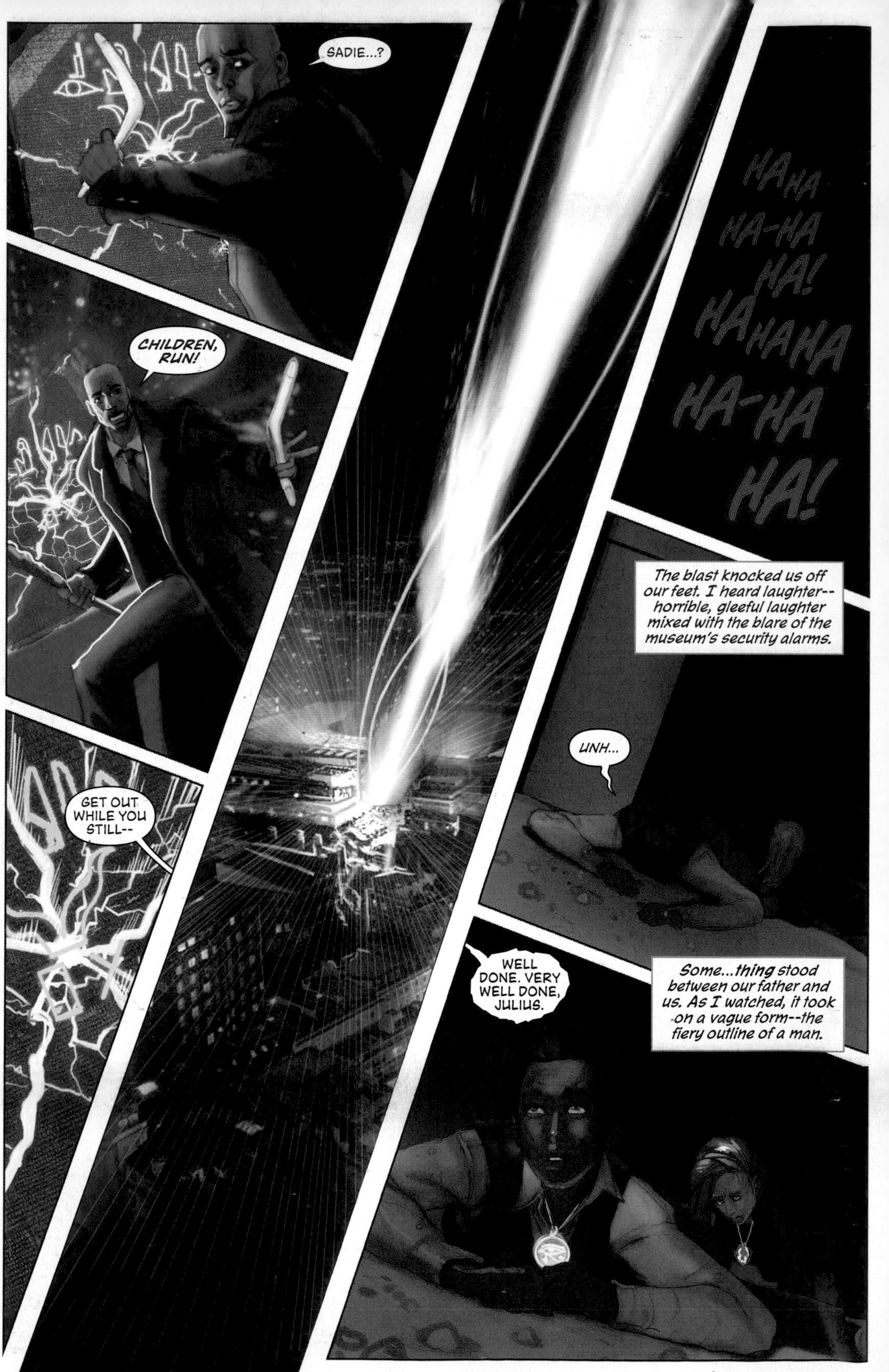
SADIE...?
CHILDREN, RUN!
GET OUT WHILE YOU STILL--
HA HA HA-HA HA! HA HA HA HA HA-HA HA!
The blast knocked us off our feet. I heard laughter--horrible, gleeful laughter mixed with the blare of the museum's security alarms.
UNH...
WELL DONE. VERY WELL DONE, JULIUS.
Some...thing stood between our father and us. As I watched, it took on a vague form--the fiery outline of a man.

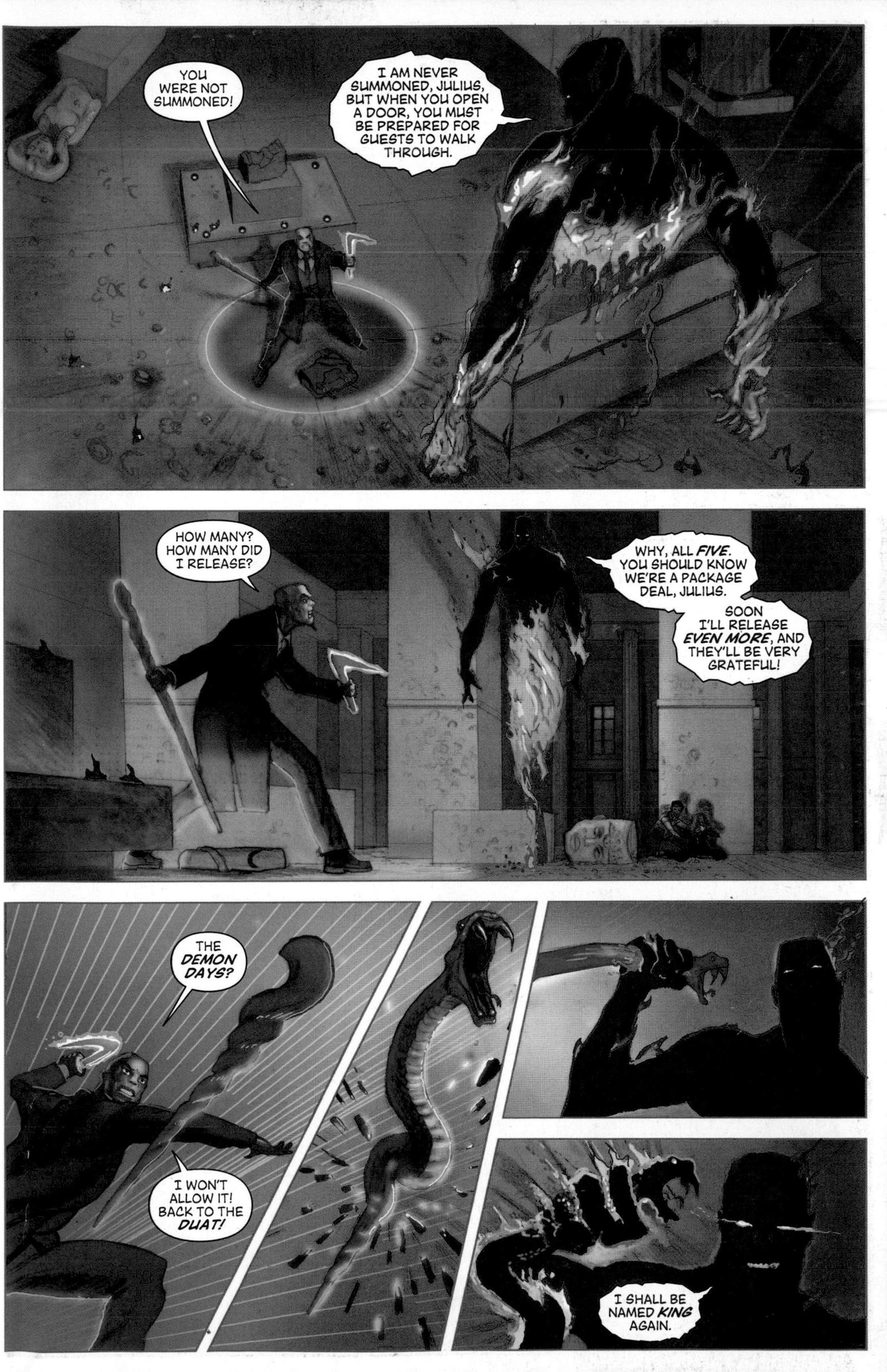

YOU WERE NOT SUMMONED!
I AM NEVER SUMMONED, JULIUS, BUT WHEN YOU OPEN A DOOR, YOU MUST BE PREPARED FOR GUESTS TO WALK THROUGH.
HOW MANY? HOW MANY DID I RELEASE?
WHY, ALL *FIVE*. YOU SHOULD KNOW WE'RE A PACKAGE DEAL, JULIUS.
SOON I'LL RELEASE *EVEN MORE*, AND THEY'LL BE VERY GRATEFUL!
THE *DEMON DAYS*?
I WON'T ALLOW IT! BACK TO THE *DUAT!*
I SHALL BE NAMED *KING* AGAIN.

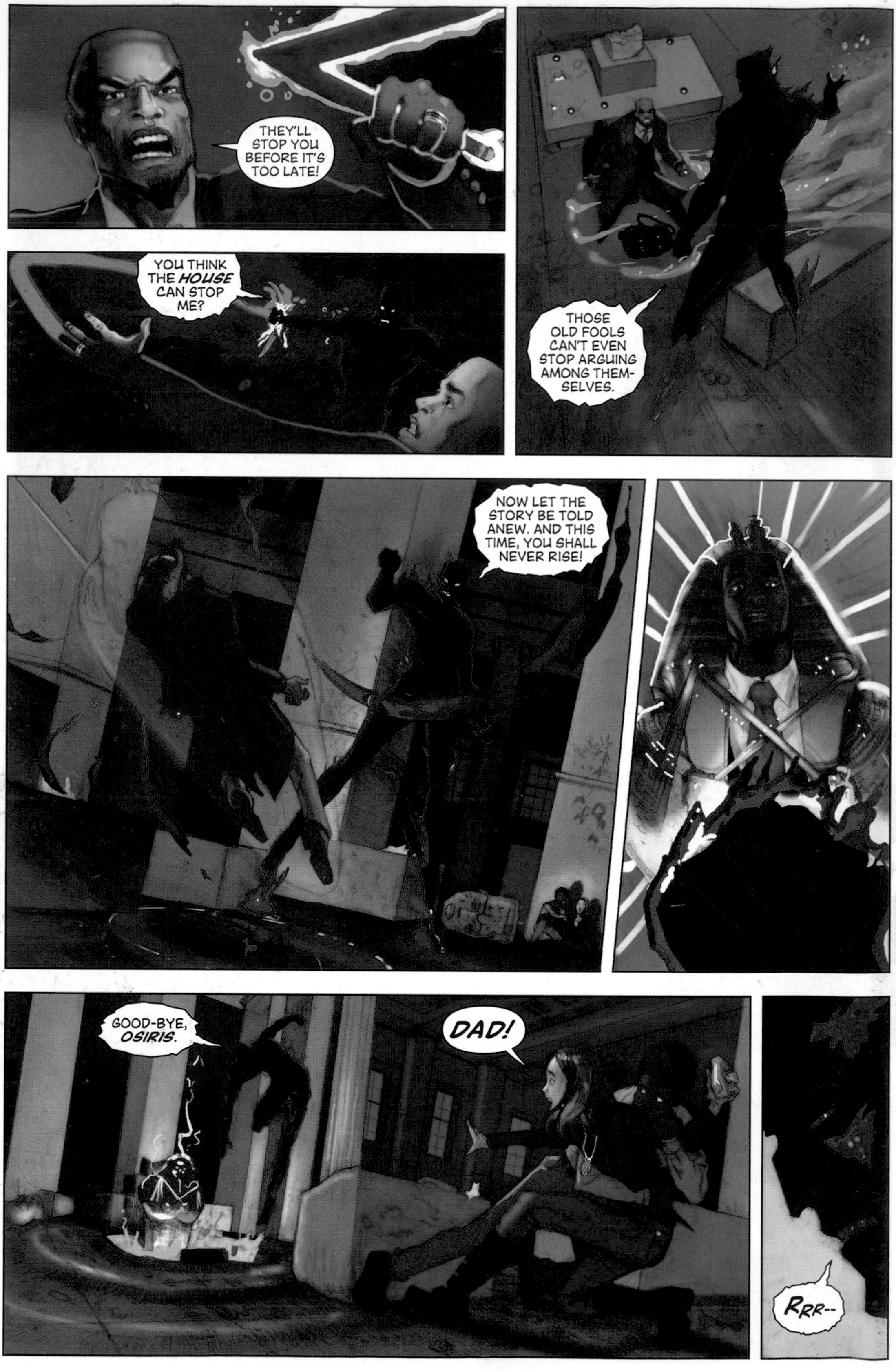
THEY'LL STOP YOU BEFORE IT'S TOO LATE!
YOU THINK THE *HOUSE* CAN STOP ME?
THOSE OLD FOOLS CAN'T EVEN STOP ARGUING AMONG THEM-SELVES.
NOW LET THE STORY BE TOLD ANEW. AND THIS TIME, YOU SHALL NEVER RISE!
GOOD-BYE, *OSIRIS*.
DAD!
RRR--

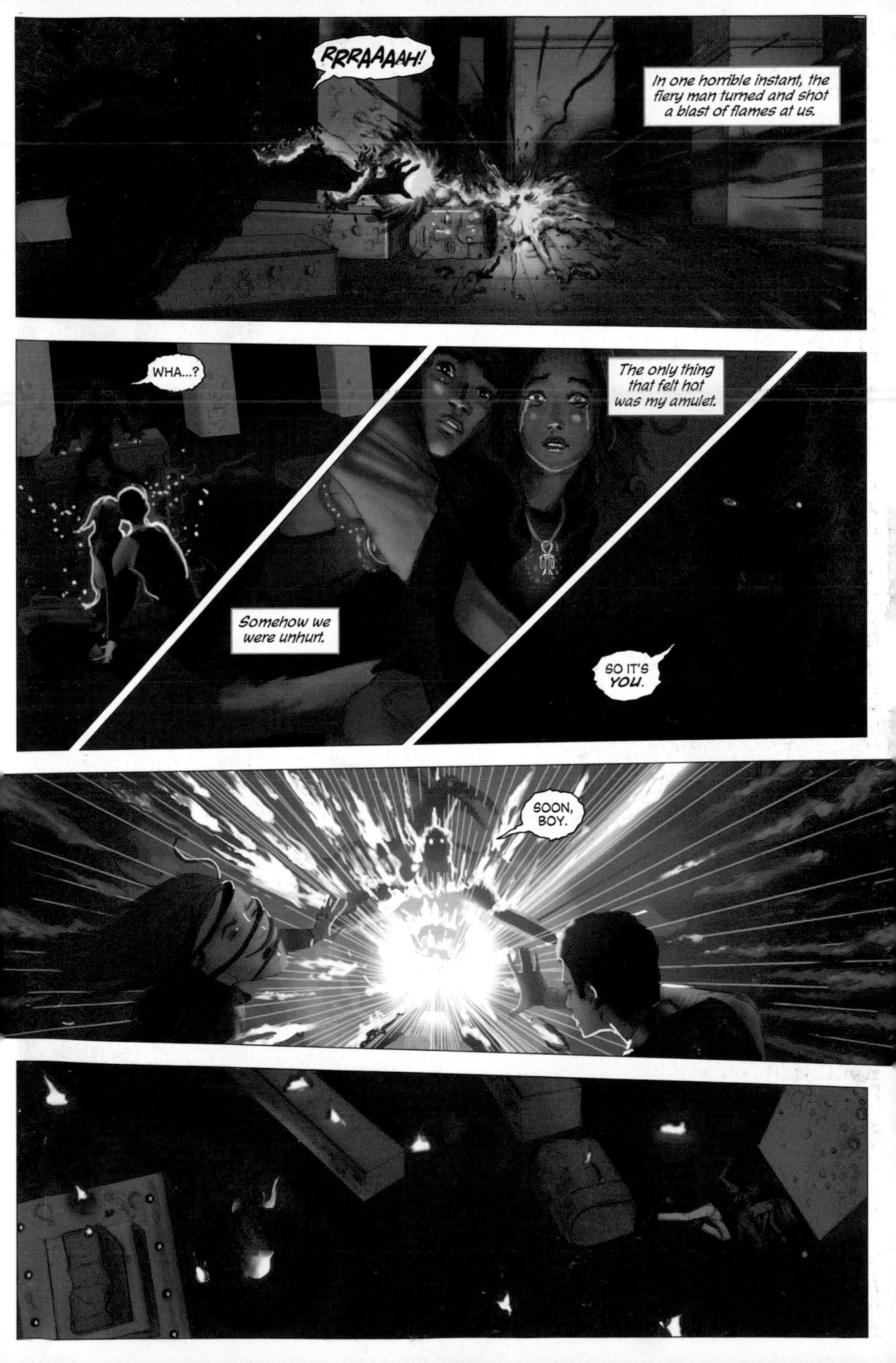
RRRAAAAH!
In one horrible instant, the fiery man turned and shot a blast of flames at us.
WHA...?
Somehow we were unhurt.
The only thing that felt hot was my amulet.
SO IT'S YOU.
SOON, BOY.

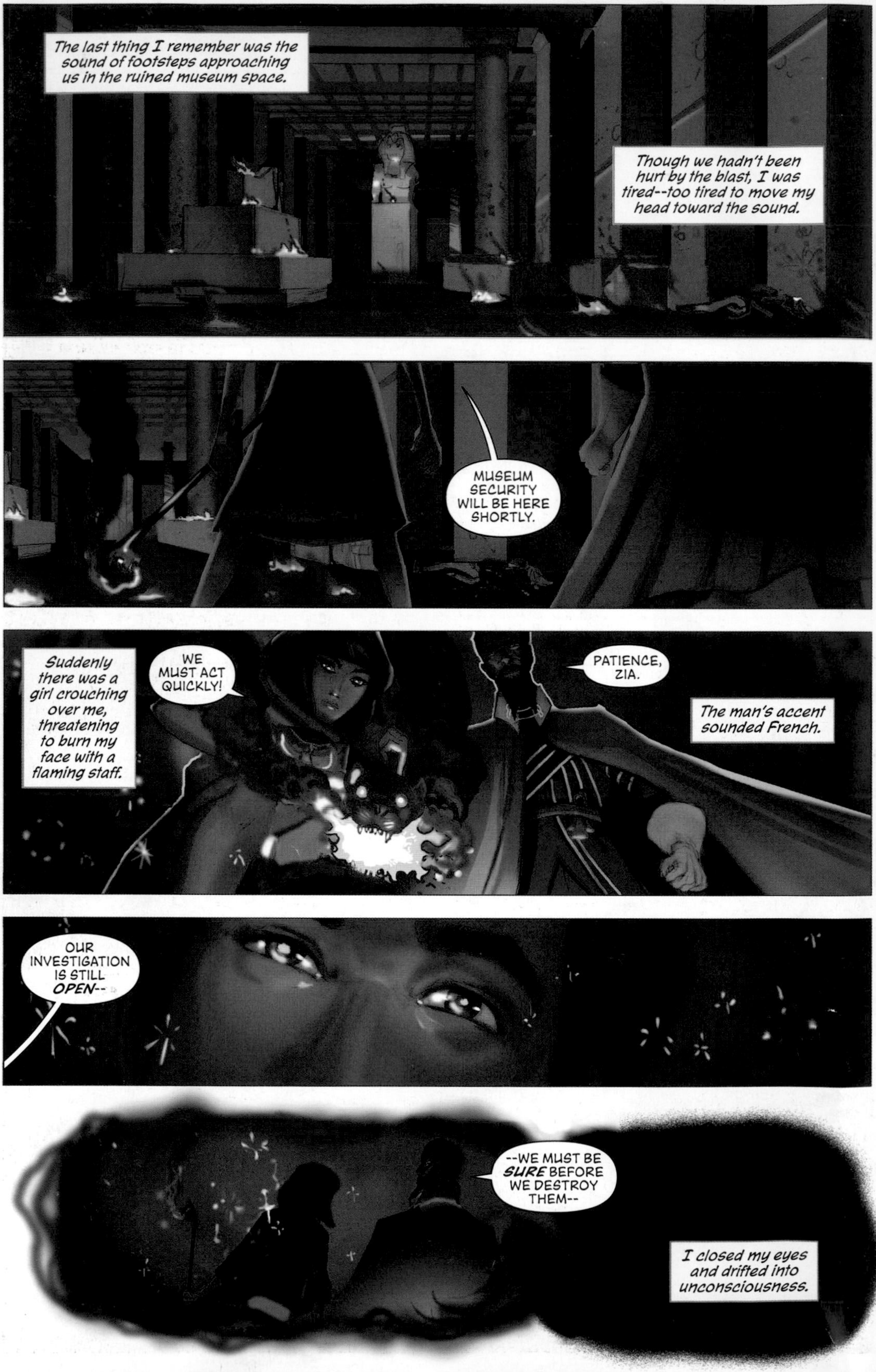
The last thing I remember was the sound of footsteps approaching us in the ruined museum space.
Though we hadn't been hurt by the blast, I was tired--too tired to move my head toward the sound.
MUSEUM SECURITY WILL BE HERE SHORTLY.
Suddenly there was a girl crouching over me, threatening to burn my face with a flaming staff.
WE MUST ACT QUICKLY!
PATIENCE, ZIA.
The man's accent sounded French.
OUR INVESTIGATION IS STILL OPEN--
--WE MUST BE SURE BEFORE WE DESTROY THEM--
I closed my eyes and drifted into unconsciousness.

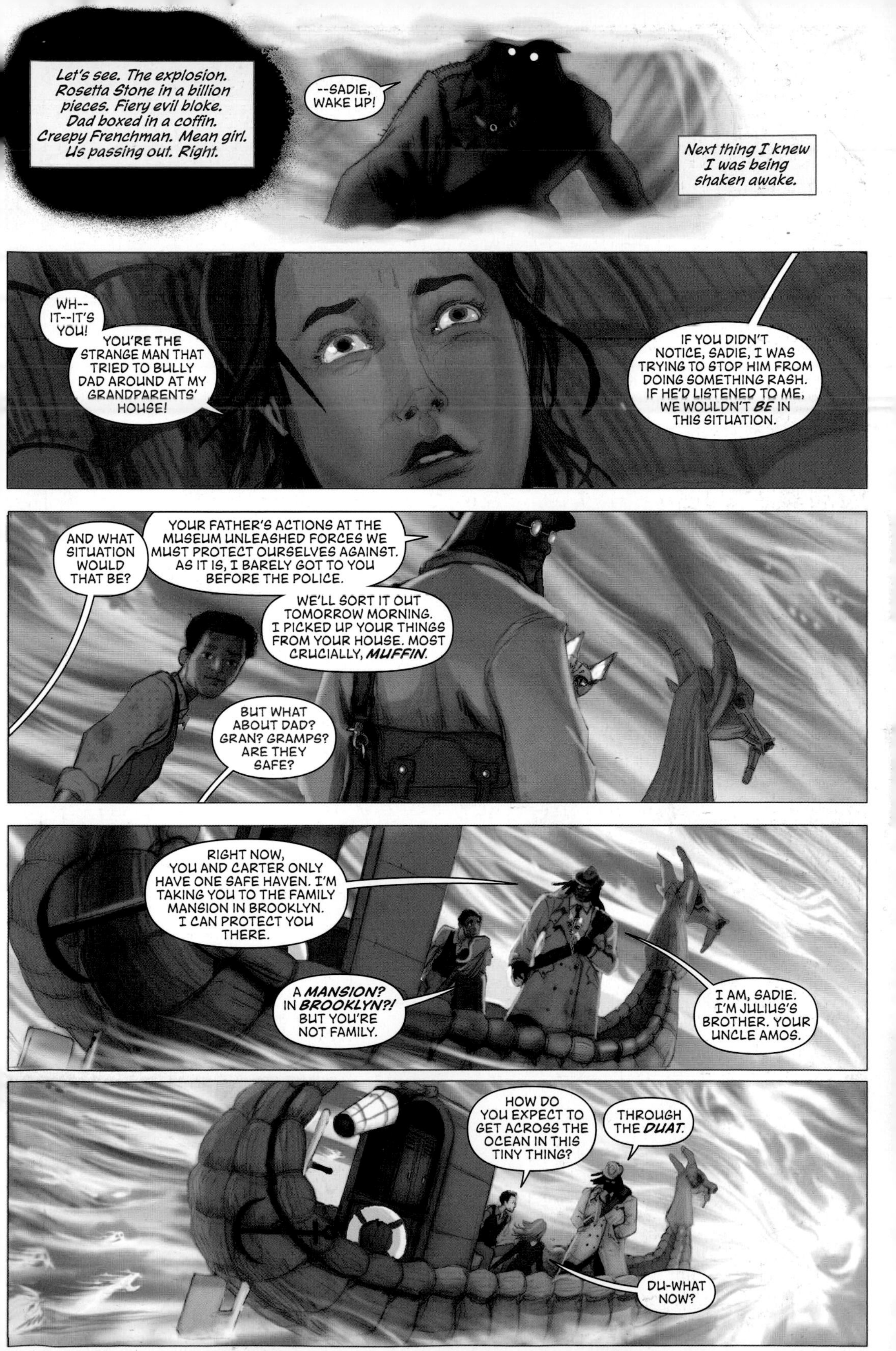
Let's see. The explosion. Rosetta Stone in a billion pieces. Fiery evil bloke. Dad boxed in a coffin. Creepy Frenchman. Mean girl. Us passing out. Right.
--SADIE, WAKE UP!
Next thing I knew I was being shaken awake.
WH-- IT--IT'S YOU!
YOU'RE THE STRANGE MAN THAT TRIED TO BULLY DAD AROUND AT MY GRANDPARENTS' HOUSE!
IF YOU DIDN'T NOTICE, SADIE, I WAS TRYING TO STOP HIM FROM DOING SOMETHING RASH. IF HE'D LISTENED TO ME, WE WOULDN'T *BE* IN THIS SITUATION.
AND WHAT SITUATION WOULD THAT BE?
YOUR FATHER'S ACTIONS AT THE MUSEUM UNLEASHED FORCES WE MUST PROTECT OURSELVES AGAINST. AS IT IS, I BARELY GOT TO YOU BEFORE THE POLICE.
WE'LL SORT IT OUT TOMORROW MORNING. I PICKED UP YOUR THINGS FROM YOUR HOUSE. MOST CRUCIALLY, *MUFFIN*.
BUT WHAT ABOUT DAD? GRAN? GRAMPS? ARE THEY SAFE?
RIGHT NOW, YOU AND CARTER ONLY HAVE ONE SAFE HAVEN. I'M TAKING YOU TO THE FAMILY MANSION IN BROOKLYN. I CAN PROTECT YOU THERE.
A *MANSION?* IN *BROOKLYN?!* BUT YOU'RE NOT FAMILY.
I AM, SADIE. I'M JULIUS'S BROTHER. YOUR UNCLE AMOS.
HOW DO YOU EXPECT TO GET ACROSS THE OCEAN IN THIS TINY THING?
THROUGH THE *DUAT*.
DU-WHAT NOW?

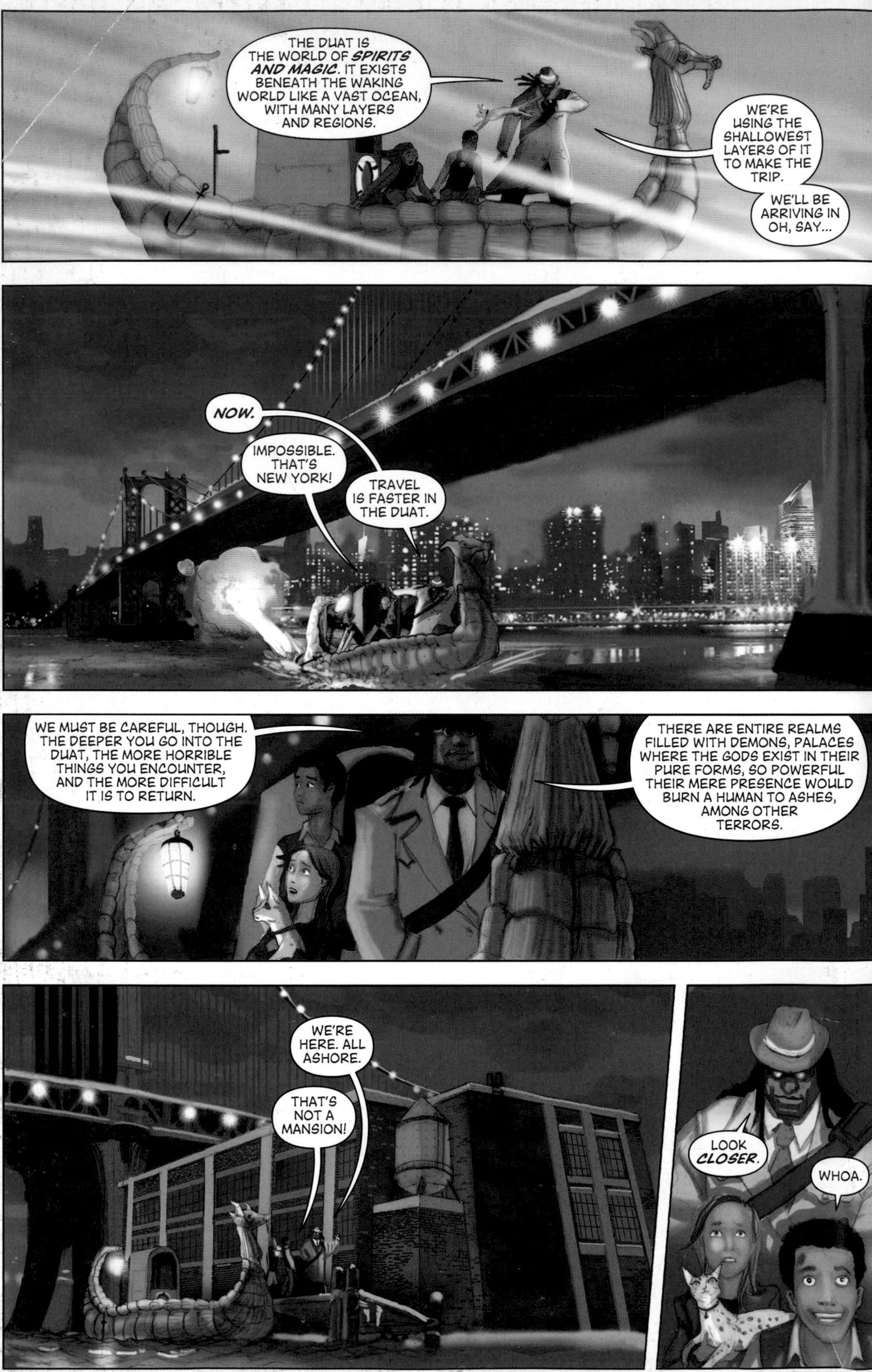
THE DUAT IS THE WORLD OF SPIRITS AND MAGIC. IT EXISTS BENEATH THE WAKING WORLD LIKE A VAST OCEAN, WITH MANY LAYERS AND REGIONS.
WE'RE USING THE SHALLOWEST LAYERS OF IT TO MAKE THE TRIP.
WE'LL BE ARRIVING IN OH, SAY...
NOW.
IMPOSSIBLE. THAT'S NEW YORK!
TRAVEL IS FASTER IN THE DUAT.
WE MUST BE CAREFUL, THOUGH. THE DEEPER YOU GO INTO THE DUAT, THE MORE HORRIBLE THINGS YOU ENCOUNTER, AND THE MORE DIFFICULT IT IS TO RETURN.
THERE ARE ENTIRE REALMS FILLED WITH DEMONS, PALACES WHERE THE GODS EXIST IN THEIR PURE FORMS, SO POWERFUL THEIR MERE PRESENCE WOULD BURN A HUMAN TO ASHES, AMONG OTHER TERRORS.
WE'RE HERE. ALL ASHORE.
THAT'S NOT A MANSION!
LOOK CLOSER.
WHOA.

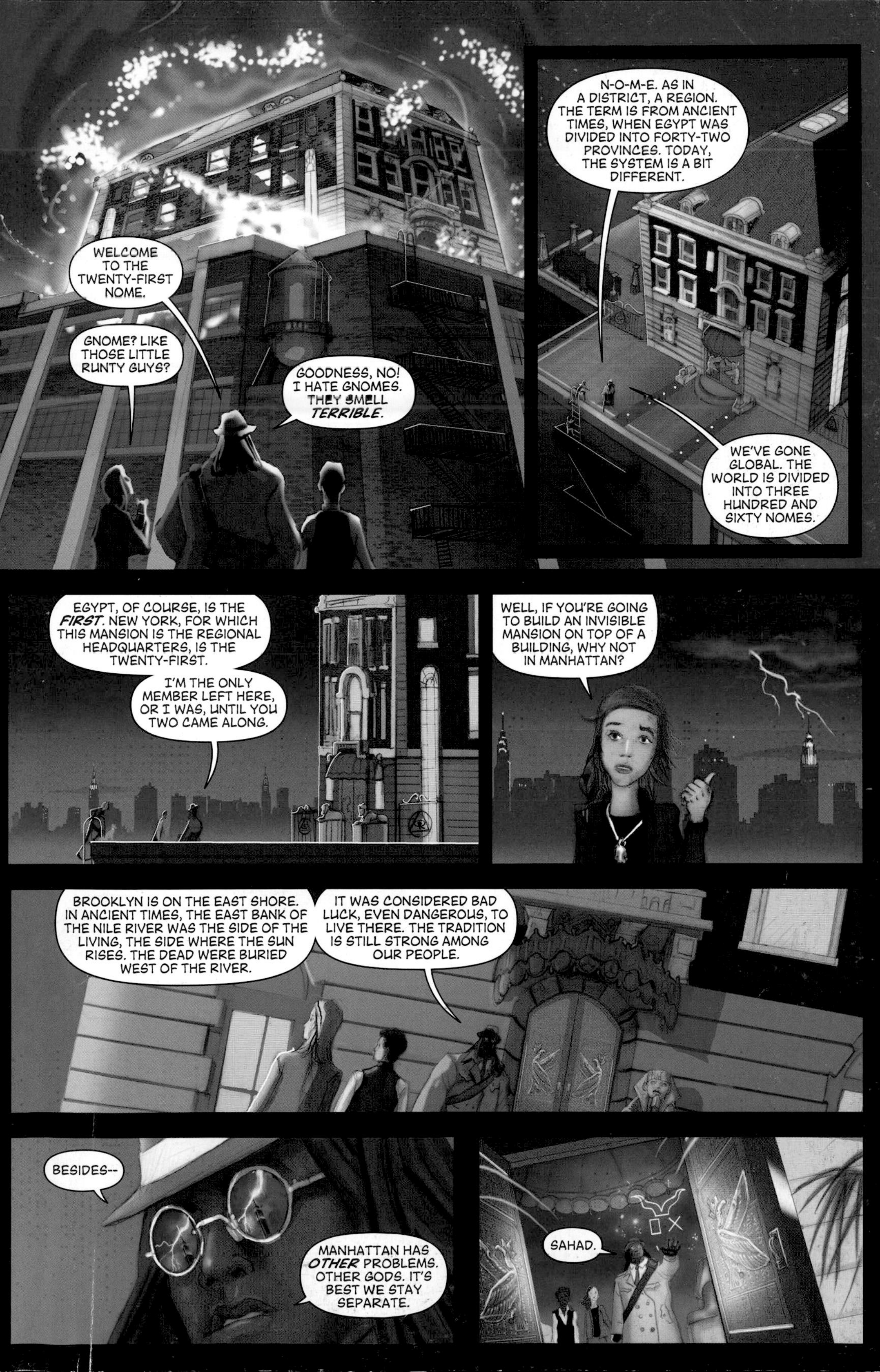
WELCOME TO THE TWENTY-FIRST NOME.
GNOME? LIKE THOSE LITTLE RUNTY GUYS?
GOODNESS, NO! I HATE GNOMES. THEY SMELL TERRIBLE.
N-O-M-E. AS IN A DISTRICT, A REGION. THE TERM IS FROM ANCIENT TIMES, WHEN EGYPT WAS DIVIDED INTO FORTY-TWO PROVINCES. TODAY, THE SYSTEM IS A BIT DIFFERENT.
WE'VE GONE GLOBAL. THE WORLD IS DIVIDED INTO THREE HUNDRED AND SIXTY NOMES.
EGYPT, OF COURSE, IS THE FIRST. NEW YORK, FOR WHICH THIS MANSION IS THE REGIONAL HEADQUARTERS, IS THE TWENTY-FIRST.
I'M THE ONLY MEMBER LEFT HERE, OR I WAS, UNTIL YOU TWO CAME ALONG.
WELL, IF YOU'RE GOING TO BUILD AN INVISIBLE MANSION ON TOP OF A BUILDING, WHY NOT IN MANHATTAN?
BROOKLYN IS ON THE EAST SHORE. IN ANCIENT TIMES, THE EAST BANK OF THE NILE RIVER WAS THE SIDE OF THE LIVING, THE SIDE WHERE THE SUN RISES. THE DEAD WERE BURIED WEST OF THE RIVER.
IT WAS CONSIDERED BAD LUCK, EVEN DANGEROUS, TO LIVE THERE. THE TRADITION IS STILL STRONG AMONG OUR PEOPLE.
BESIDES--
MANHATTAN HAS OTHER PROBLEMS. OTHER GODS. IT'S BEST WE STAY SEPARATE.
SAHAD.

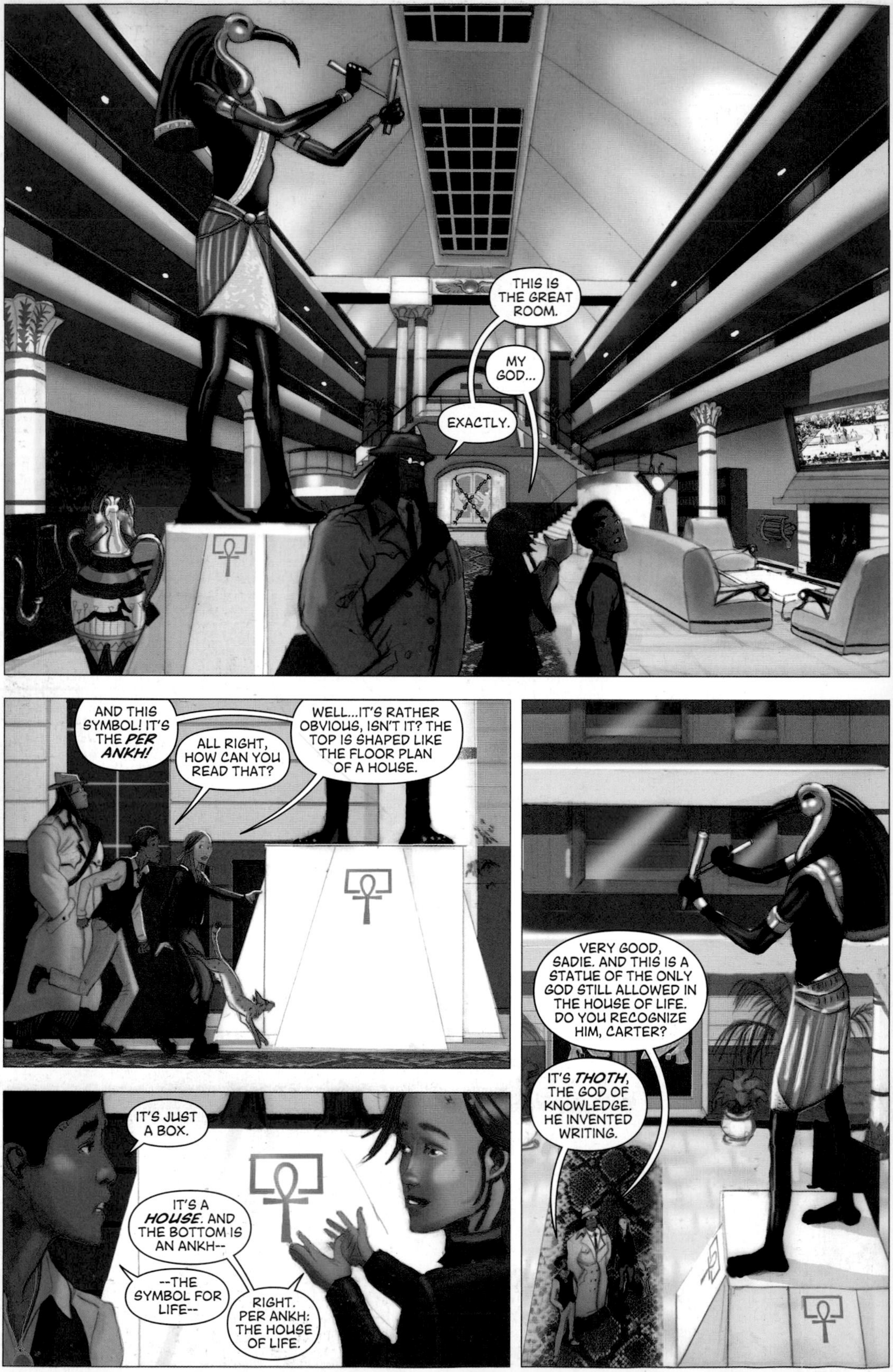
THIS IS THE GREAT ROOM.
MY GOD...
EXACTLY.
AND THIS SYMBOL! IT'S THE *PER ANKH!*
ALL RIGHT, HOW CAN YOU READ THAT?
WELL...IT'S RATHER OBVIOUS, ISN'T IT? THE TOP IS SHAPED LIKE THE FLOOR PLAN OF A HOUSE.
IT'S JUST A BOX.
IT'S A *HOUSE*. AND THE BOTTOM IS AN ANKH--
--THE SYMBOL FOR LIFE--
RIGHT. PER ANKH: THE HOUSE OF LIFE.
VERY GOOD, SADIE. AND THIS IS A STATUE OF THE ONLY GOD STILL ALLOWED IN THE HOUSE OF LIFE. DO YOU RECOGNIZE HIM, CARTER?
IT'S *THOTH*, THE GOD OF KNOWLEDGE. HE INVENTED WRITING.

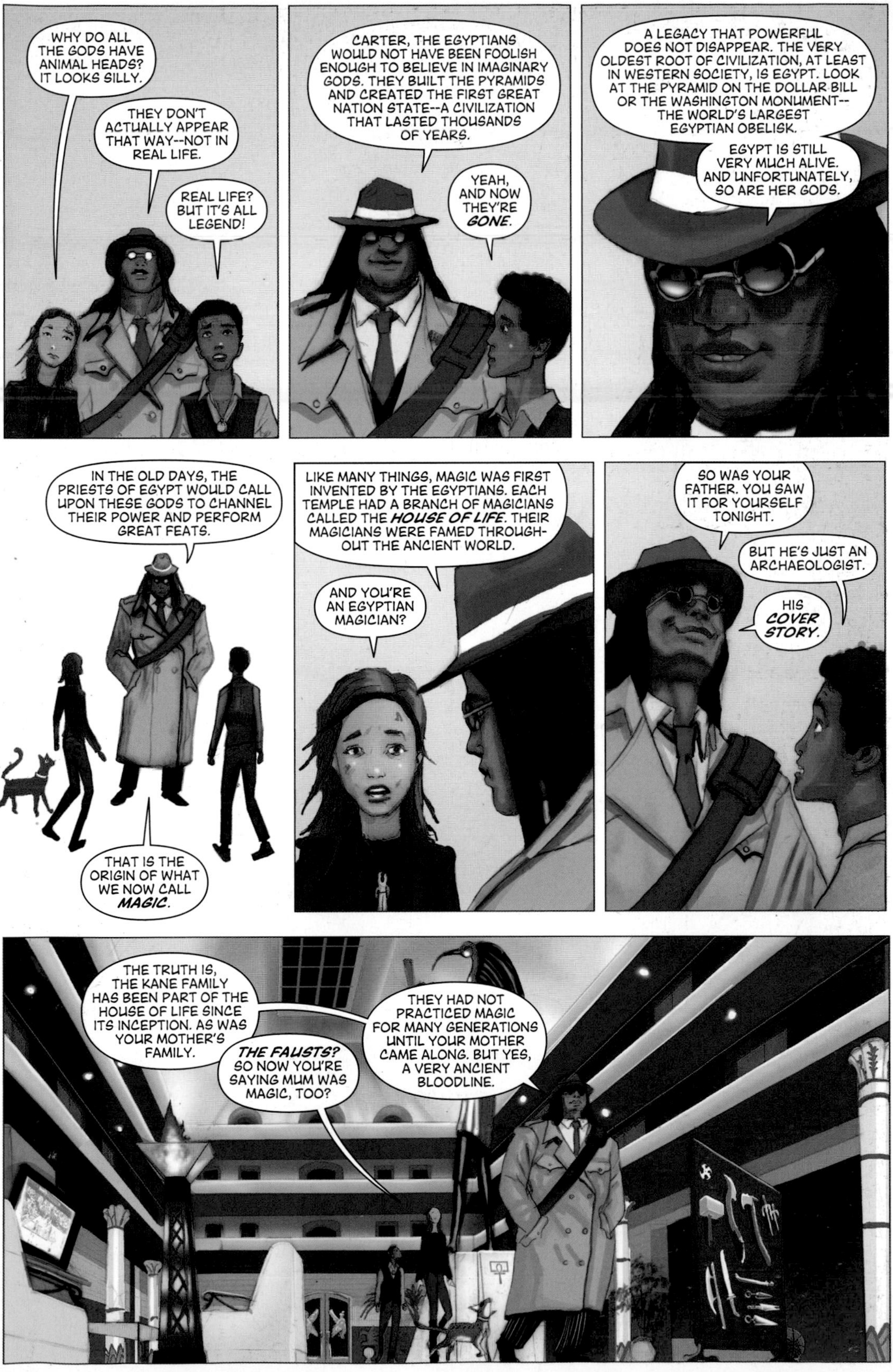
WHY DO ALL THE GODS HAVE ANIMAL HEADS? IT LOOKS SILLY.
THEY DON'T ACTUALLY APPEAR THAT WAY--NOT IN REAL LIFE.
REAL LIFE? BUT IT'S ALL LEGEND!
CARTER, THE EGYPTIANS WOULD NOT HAVE BEEN FOOLISH ENOUGH TO BELIEVE IN IMAGINARY GODS. THEY BUILT THE PYRAMIDS AND CREATED THE FIRST GREAT NATION STATE--A CIVILIZATION THAT LASTED THOUSANDS OF YEARS.
YEAH, AND NOW THEY'RE GONE.
A LEGACY THAT POWERFUL DOES NOT DISAPPEAR. THE VERY OLDEST ROOT OF CIVILIZATION, AT LEAST IN WESTERN SOCIETY, IS EGYPT. LOOK AT THE PYRAMID ON THE DOLLAR BILL OR THE WASHINGTON MONUMENT-- THE WORLD'S LARGEST EGYPTIAN OBELISK.
EGYPT IS STILL VERY MUCH ALIVE. AND UNFORTUNATELY, SO ARE HER GODS.
IN THE OLD DAYS, THE PRIESTS OF EGYPT WOULD CALL UPON THESE GODS TO CHANNEL THEIR POWER AND PERFORM GREAT FEATS.
THAT IS THE ORIGIN OF WHAT WE NOW CALL MAGIC.
LIKE MANY THINGS, MAGIC WAS FIRST INVENTED BY THE EGYPTIANS. EACH TEMPLE HAD A BRANCH OF MAGICIANS CALLED THE HOUSE OF LIFE. THEIR MAGICIANS WERE FAMED THROUGHOUT THE ANCIENT WORLD.
AND YOU'RE AN EGYPTIAN MAGICIAN?
SO WAS YOUR FATHER. YOU SAW IT FOR YOURSELF TONIGHT.
BUT HE'S JUST AN ARCHAEOLOGIST.
HIS COVER STORY.
THE TRUTH IS, THE KANE FAMILY HAS BEEN PART OF THE HOUSE OF LIFE SINCE ITS INCEPTION. AS WAS YOUR MOTHER'S FAMILY.
THE FAUSTS? SO NOW YOU'RE SAYING MUM WAS MAGIC, TOO?
THEY HAD NOT PRACTICED MAGIC FOR MANY GENERATIONS UNTIL YOUR MOTHER CAME ALONG. BUT YES, A VERY ANCIENT BLOODLINE.

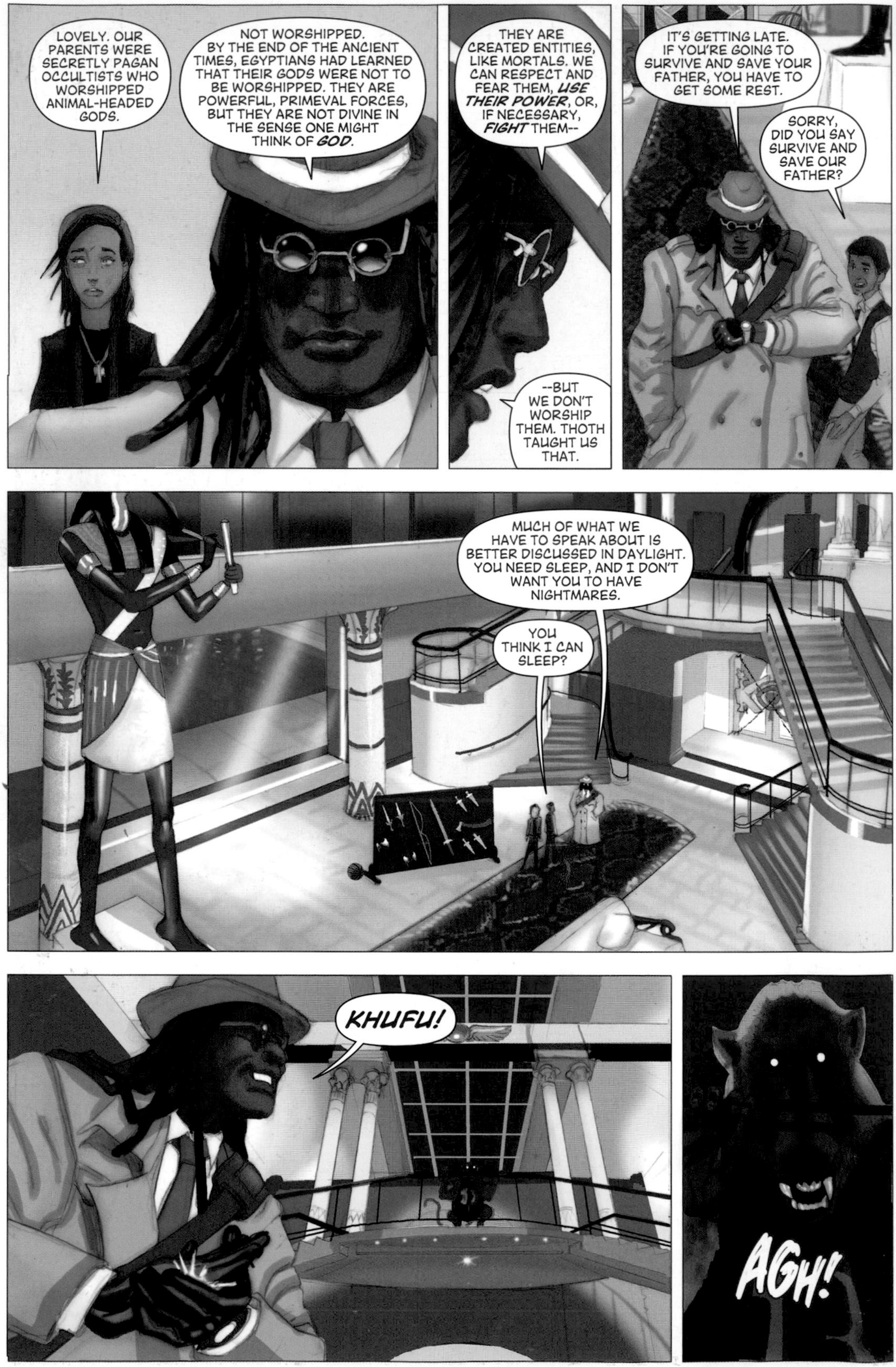
LOVELY. OUR PARENTS WERE SECRETLY PAGAN OCCULTISTS WHO WORSHIPPED ANIMAL-HEADED GODS.
NOT WORSHIPPED. BY THE END OF THE ANCIENT TIMES, EGYPTIANS HAD LEARNED THAT THEIR GODS WERE NOT TO BE WORSHIPPED. THEY ARE POWERFUL, PRIMEVAL FORCES, BUT THEY ARE NOT DIVINE IN THE SENSE ONE MIGHT THINK OF *GOD*.
THEY ARE CREATED ENTITIES, LIKE MORTALS. WE CAN RESPECT AND FEAR THEM, ***USE THEIR POWER***, OR, IF NECESSARY, ***FIGHT*** THEM--
--BUT WE DON'T WORSHIP THEM. THOTH TAUGHT US THAT.
IT'S GETTING LATE. IF YOU'RE GOING TO SURVIVE AND SAVE YOUR FATHER, YOU HAVE TO GET SOME REST.
SORRY, DID YOU SAY SURVIVE AND SAVE OUR FATHER?
MUCH OF WHAT WE HAVE TO SPEAK ABOUT IS BETTER DISCUSSED IN DAYLIGHT. YOU NEED SLEEP, AND I DON'T WANT YOU TO HAVE NIGHTMARES.
YOU THINK I CAN SLEEP?
KHUFU!
AGH!

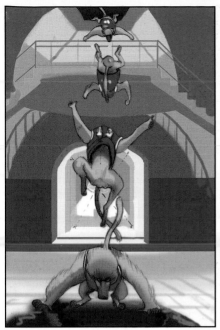

URP!

RIGHT. YOU'VE GOT A MONKEY BUTLER. WHY NOT?

KHUFU WILL SHOW YOU TO YOUR ROOMS.

TOMORROW MORNING, MEET ME OUTSIDE ON THE TERRACE.

WE'LL BEGIN YOUR ORIENTATION OVER BREAKFAST. WE HAVE MUCH TRAINING TO DO.

UM, AMOS?

DO YOU THINK I COULD HAVE MY FATHER'S WORKBAG BACK? I REALLY APPRECIATE YOUR SAVING IT FROM THE MUSEUM, BUT--

SORRY, CARTER. FOR NOW, IT'S BEST IF I LOCK IT IN THE LIBRARY.

YOU'LL GET IT BACK WHEN THE TIME IS RIGHT.

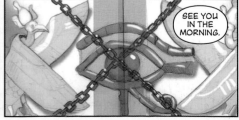

SEE YOU IN THE MORNING.

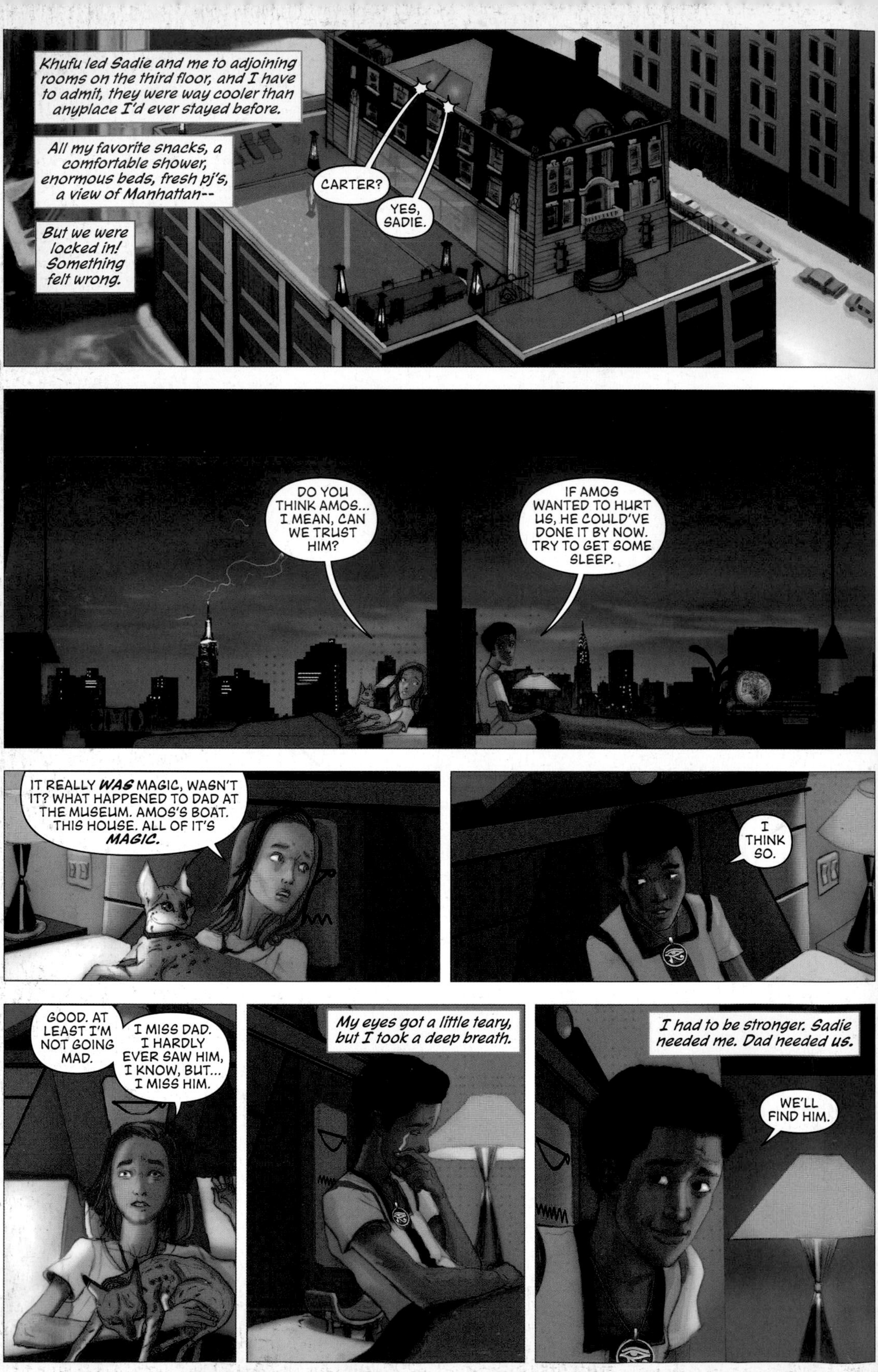

Khufu led Sadie and me to adjoining rooms on the third floor, and I have to admit, they were way cooler than anyplace I'd ever stayed before.
All my favorite snacks, a comfortable shower, enormous beds, fresh pj's, a view of Manhattan--
But we were locked in! Something felt wrong.
CARTER?
YES, SADIE.
DO YOU THINK AMOS... I MEAN, CAN WE TRUST HIM?
IF AMOS WANTED TO HURT US, HE COULD'VE DONE IT BY NOW. TRY TO GET SOME SLEEP.
IT REALLY WAS MAGIC, WASN'T IT? WHAT HAPPENED TO DAD AT THE MUSEUM. AMOS'S BOAT. THIS HOUSE. ALL OF IT'S MAGIC.
I THINK SO.
GOOD. AT LEAST I'M NOT GOING MAD.
I MISS DAD. I HARDLY EVER SAW HIM, I KNOW, BUT... I MISS HIM.
My eyes got a little teary, but I took a deep breath.
I had to be stronger. Sadie needed me. Dad needed us.
WE'LL FIND HIM.

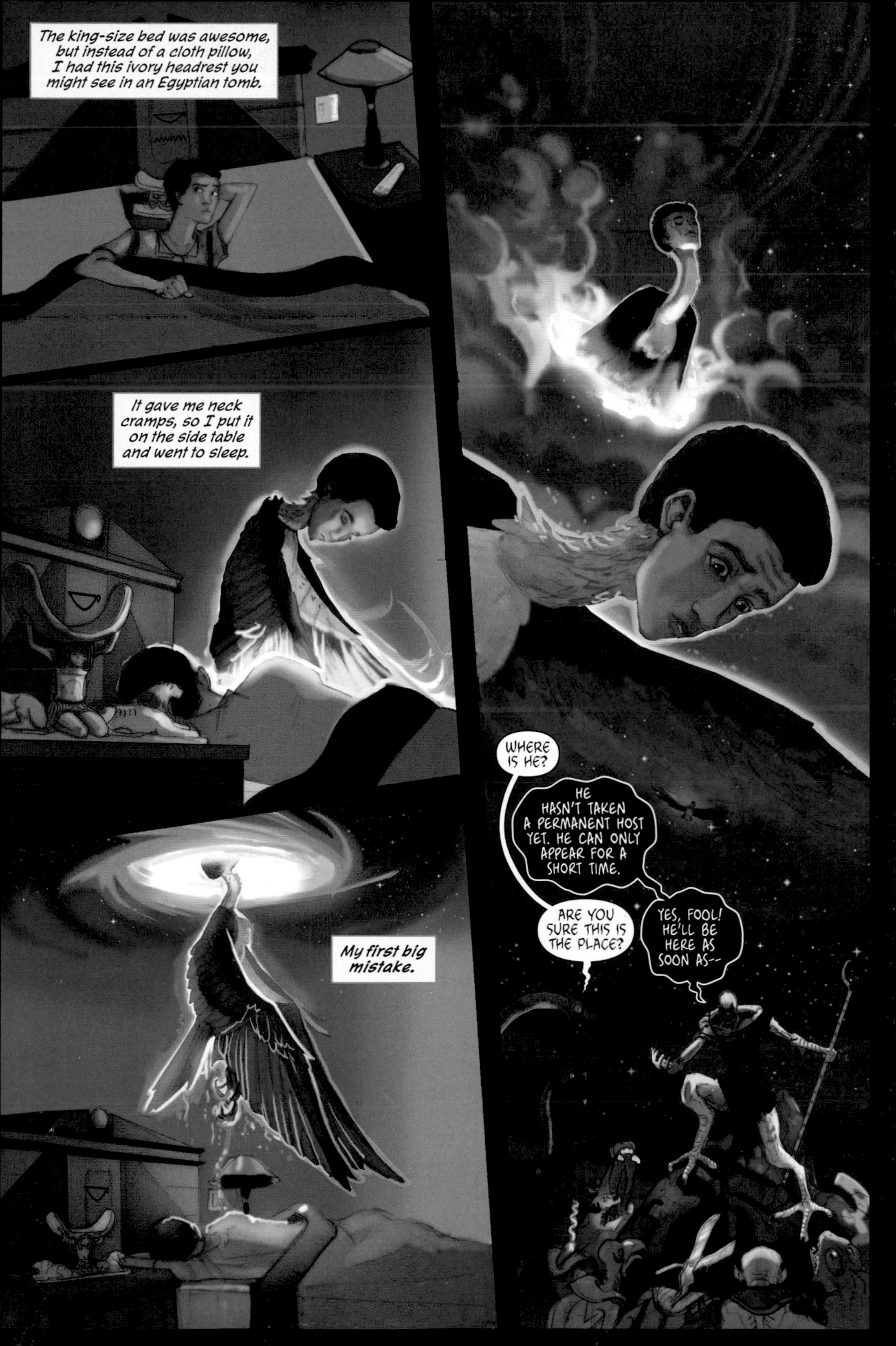
The king-size bed was awesome, but instead of a cloth pillow, I had this ivory headrest you might see in an Egyptian tomb.
It gave me neck cramps, so I put it on the side table and went to sleep.
My first big mistake.
WHERE IS HE?
HE HASN'T TAKEN A PERMANENT HOST YET. HE CAN ONLY APPEAR FOR A SHORT TIME.
ARE YOU SURE THIS IS THE PLACE?
YES, FOOL! HE'LL BE HERE AS SOON AS--

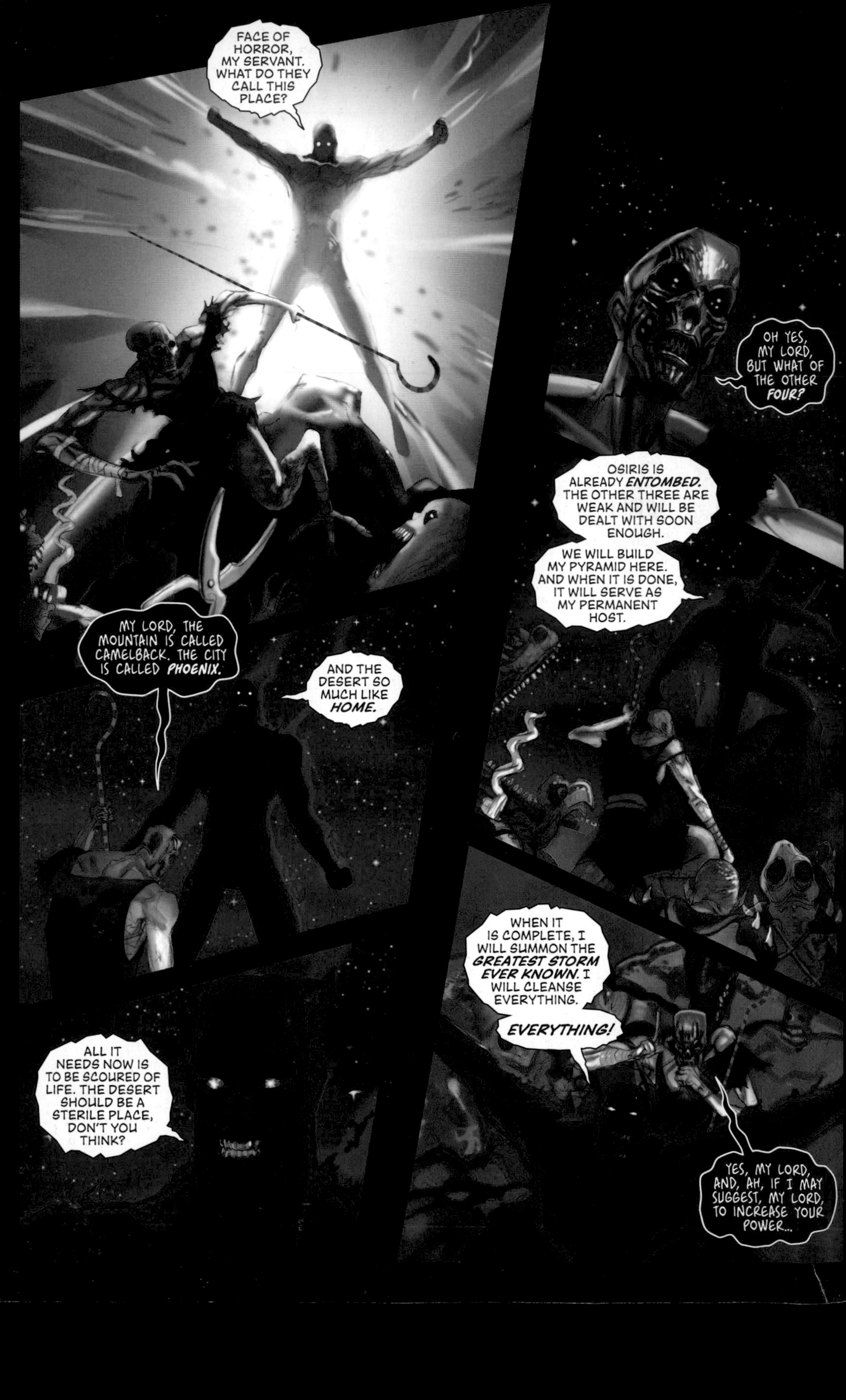
FACE OF HORROR, MY SERVANT. WHAT DO THEY CALL THIS PLACE?
OH YES, MY LORD, BUT WHAT OF THE OTHER FOUR?
OSIRIS IS ALREADY ENTOMBED. THE OTHER THREE ARE WEAK AND WILL BE DEALT WITH SOON ENOUGH.
WE WILL BUILD MY PYRAMID HERE. AND WHEN IT IS DONE, IT WILL SERVE AS MY PERMANENT HOST.
MY LORD, THE MOUNTAIN IS CALLED CAMELBACK. THE CITY IS CALLED PHOENIX.
AND THE DESERT SO MUCH LIKE HOME.
WHEN IT IS COMPLETE, I WILL SUMMON THE GREATEST STORM EVER KNOWN. I WILL CLEANSE EVERYTHING.
EVERYTHING!
ALL IT NEEDS NOW IS TO BE SCOURED OF LIFE. THE DESERT SHOULD BE A STERILE PLACE, DON'T YOU THINK?
YES, MY LORD, AND, AH, IF I MAY SUGGEST, MY LORD, TO INCREASE YOUR POWER...

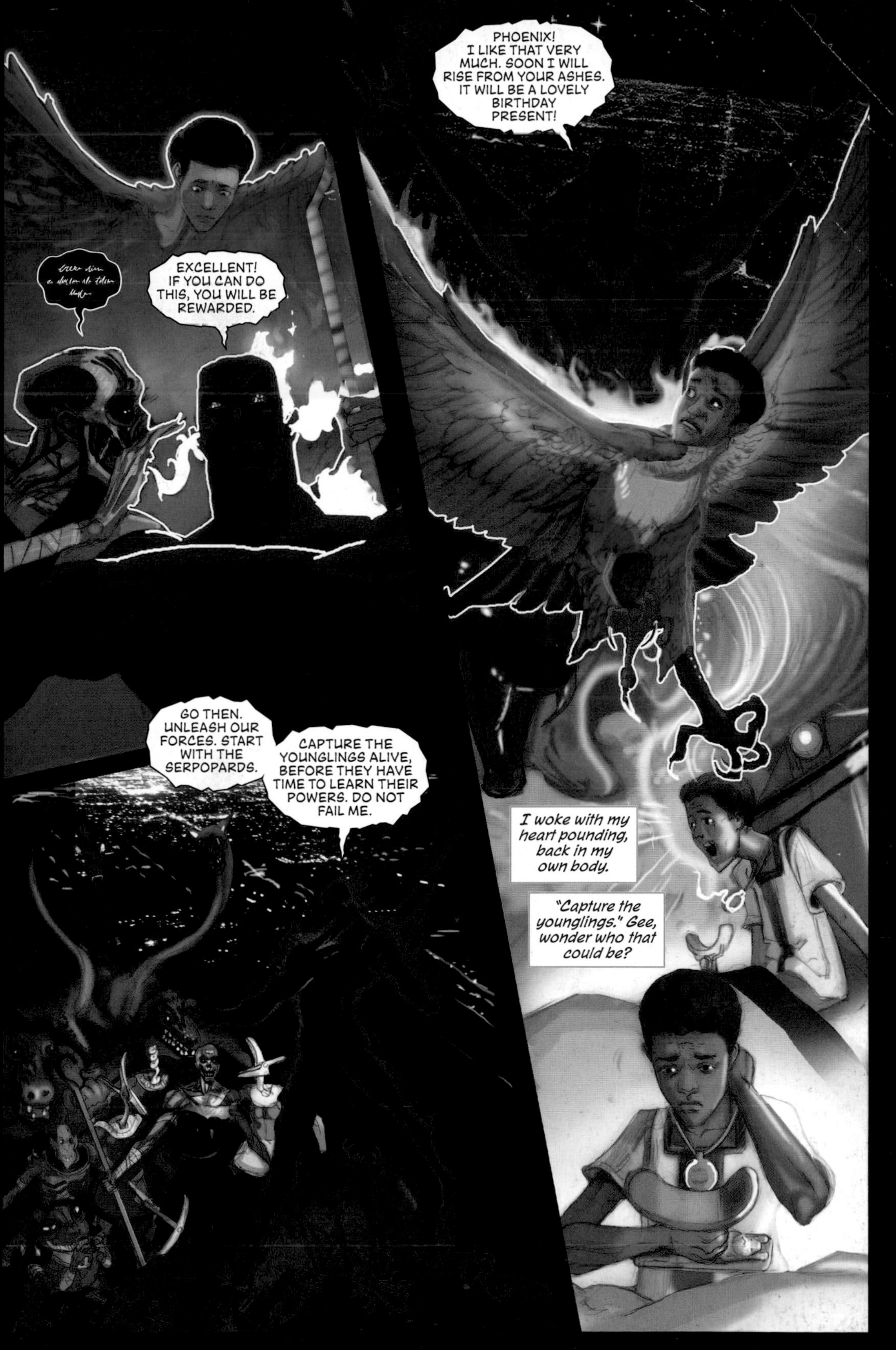
EXCELLENT! IF YOU CAN DO THIS, YOU WILL BE REWARDED.
PHOENIX! I LIKE THAT VERY MUCH. SOON I WILL RISE FROM YOUR ASHES. IT WILL BE A LOVELY BIRTHDAY PRESENT!
GO THEN. UNLEASH OUR FORCES. START WITH THE SERPOPARDS.
CAPTURE THE YOUNGLINGS ALIVE, BEFORE THEY HAVE TIME TO LEARN THEIR POWERS. DO NOT FAIL ME.
I woke with my heart pounding, back in my own body.
"Capture the younglings." Gee, wonder who that could be?

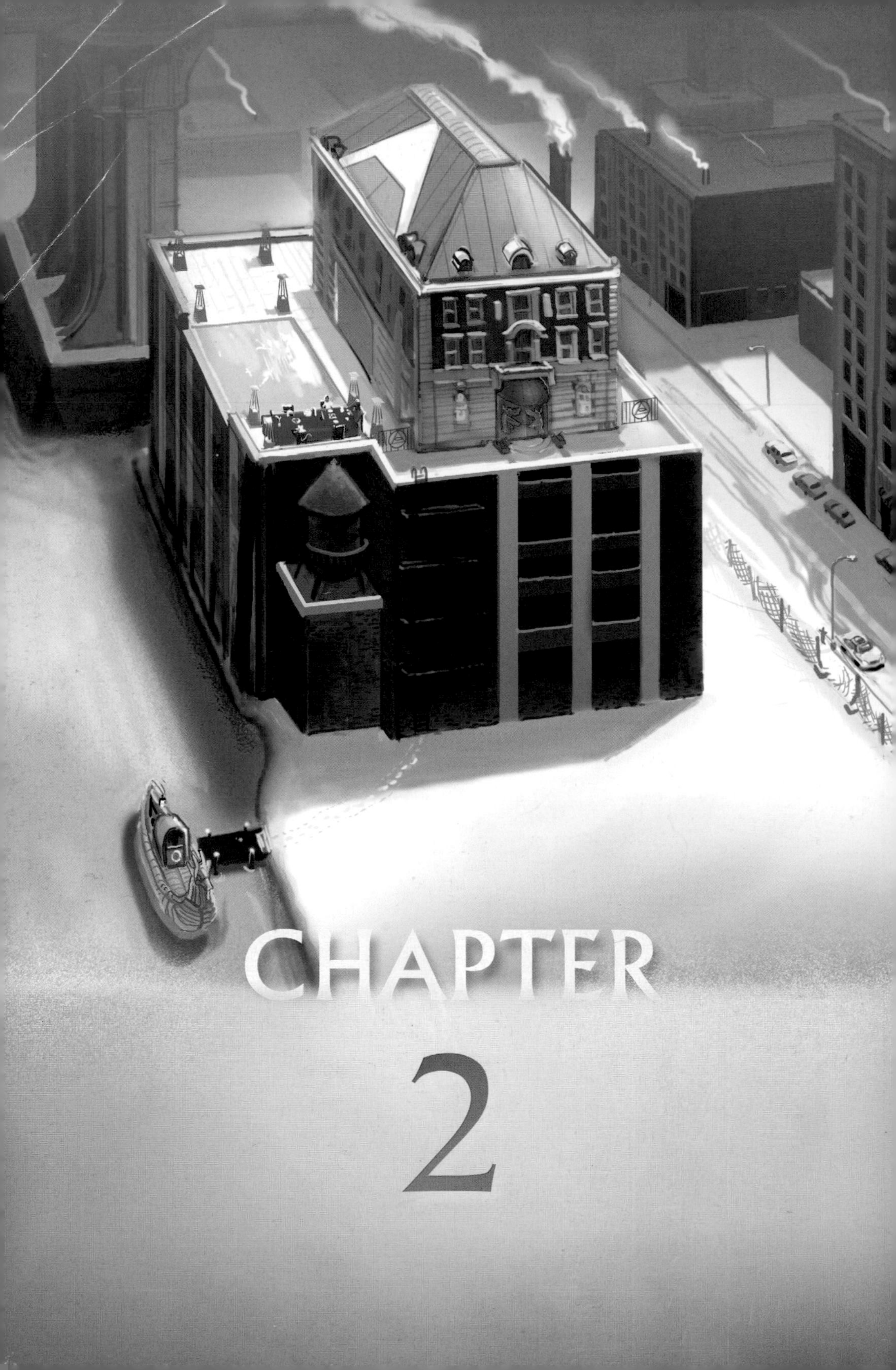

CHAPTER 2

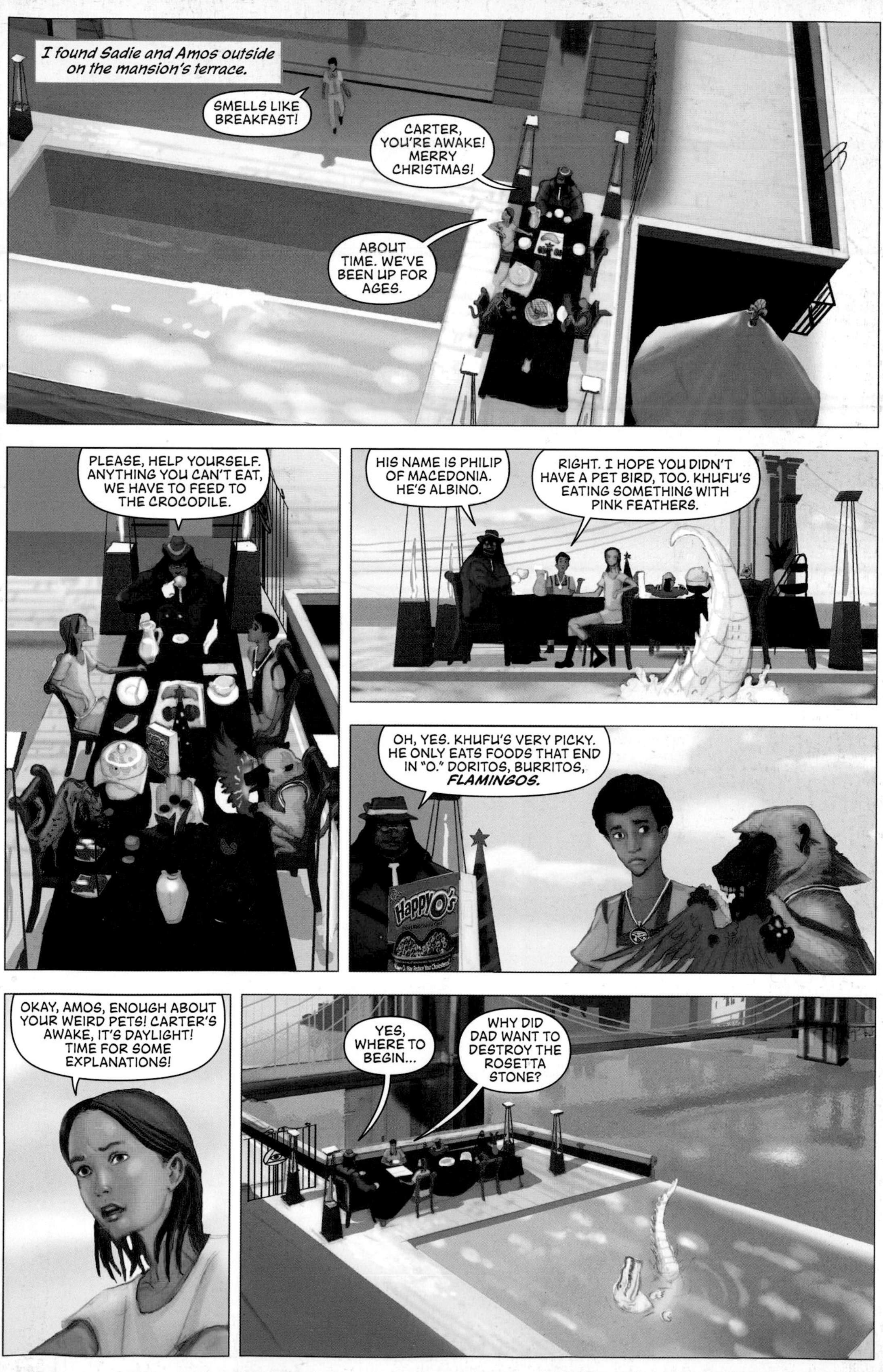
I found Sadie and Amos outside on the mansion's terrace.
SMELLS LIKE BREAKFAST!
CARTER, YOU'RE AWAKE! MERRY CHRISTMAS!
ABOUT TIME. WE'VE BEEN UP FOR AGES.
PLEASE, HELP YOURSELF. ANYTHING YOU CAN'T EAT, WE HAVE TO FEED TO THE CROCODILE.
HIS NAME IS PHILIP OF MACEDONIA. HE'S ALBINO.
RIGHT. I HOPE YOU DIDN'T HAVE A PET BIRD, TOO. KHUFU'S EATING SOMETHING WITH PINK FEATHERS.
OH, YES. KHUFU'S VERY PICKY. HE ONLY EATS FOODS THAT END IN "O." DORITOS, BURRITOS, ***FLAMINGOS.***
Happy O's
OKAY, AMOS, ENOUGH ABOUT YOUR WEIRD PETS! CARTER'S AWAKE, IT'S DAYLIGHT! TIME FOR SOME EXPLANATIONS!
YES, WHERE TO BEGIN...
WHY DID DAD WANT TO DESTROY THE ROSETTA STONE?

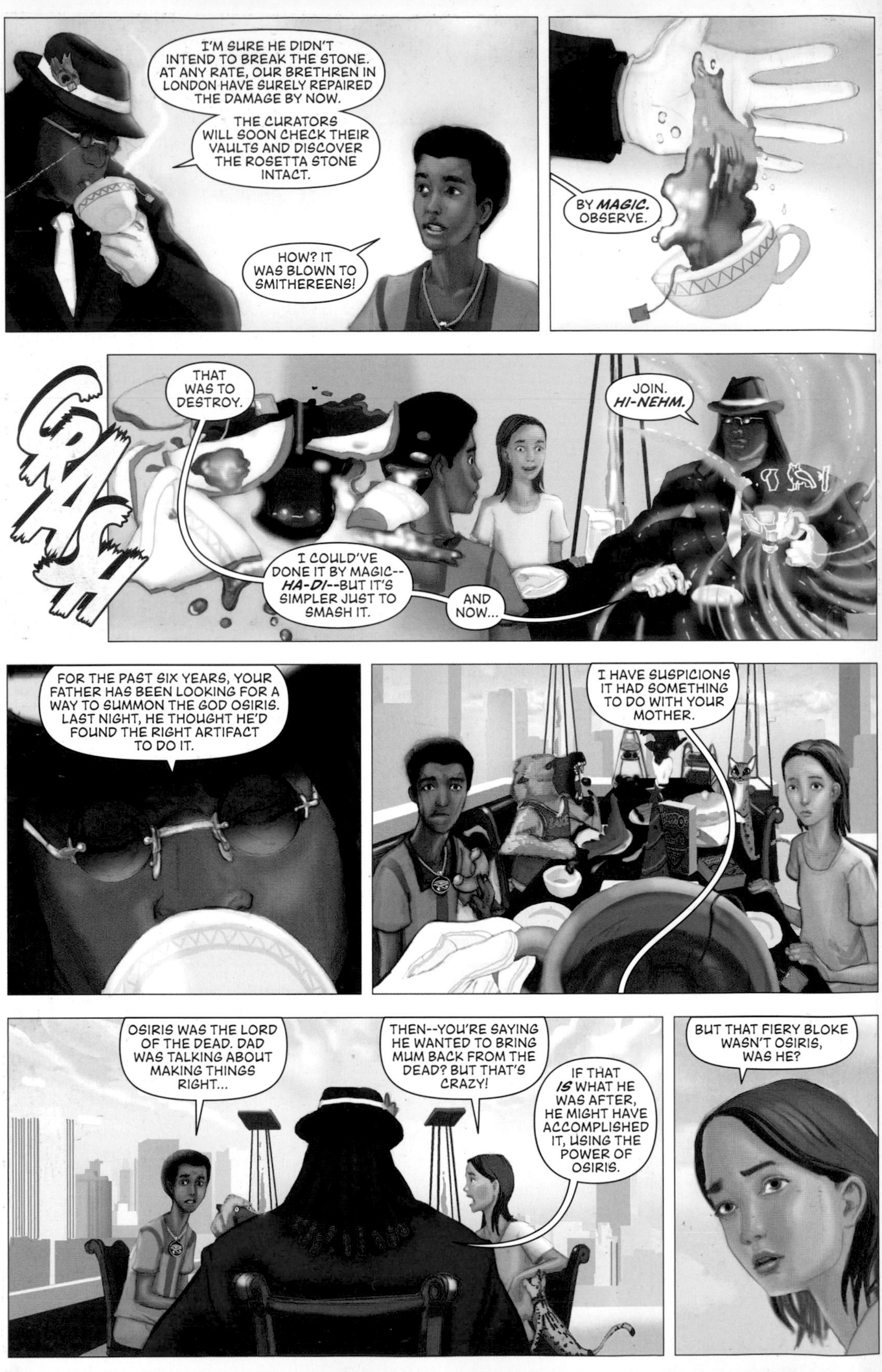
I'M SURE HE DIDN'T INTEND TO BREAK THE STONE. AT ANY RATE, OUR BRETHREN IN LONDON HAVE SURELY REPAIRED THE DAMAGE BY NOW.
THE CURATORS WILL SOON CHECK THEIR VAULTS AND DISCOVER THE ROSETTA STONE INTACT.
HOW? IT WAS BLOWN TO SMITHEREENS!
BY MAGIC. OBSERVE.
CRASH
THAT WAS TO DESTROY.
I COULD'VE DONE IT BY MAGIC--HA-DI--BUT IT'S SIMPLER JUST TO SMASH IT.
AND NOW...
JOIN. HI-NEHM.
FOR THE PAST SIX YEARS, YOUR FATHER HAS BEEN LOOKING FOR A WAY TO SUMMON THE GOD OSIRIS. LAST NIGHT, HE THOUGHT HE'D FOUND THE RIGHT ARTIFACT TO DO IT.
I HAVE SUSPICIONS IT HAD SOMETHING TO DO WITH YOUR MOTHER.
OSIRIS WAS THE LORD OF THE DEAD. DAD WAS TALKING ABOUT MAKING THINGS RIGHT...
THEN--YOU'RE SAYING HE WANTED TO BRING MUM BACK FROM THE DEAD? BUT THAT'S CRAZY!
IF THAT IS WHAT HE WAS AFTER, HE MIGHT HAVE ACCOMPLISHED IT, USING THE POWER OF OSIRIS.
BUT THAT FIERY BLOKE WASN'T OSIRIS, WAS HE?

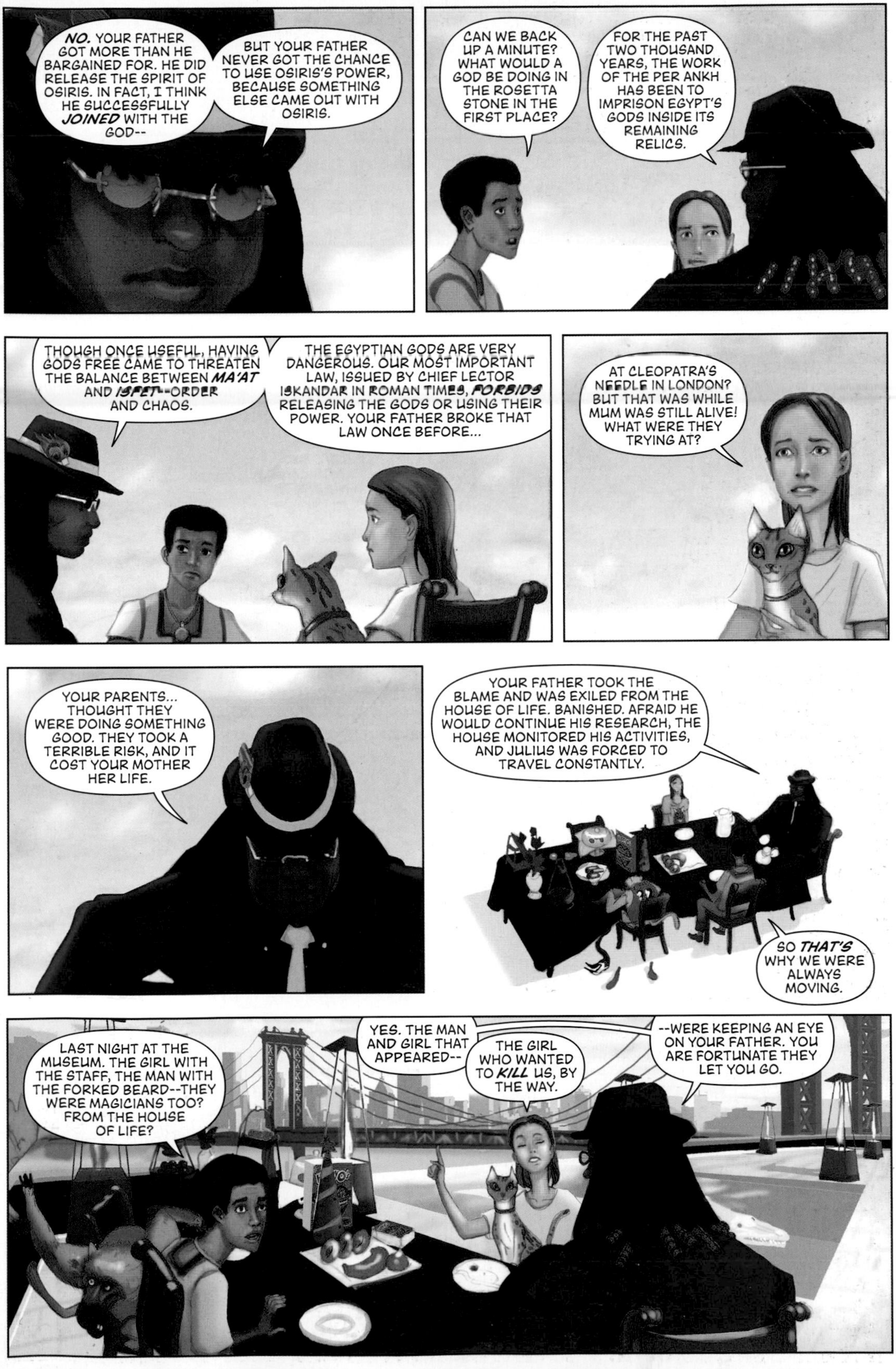
NO. YOUR FATHER GOT MORE THAN HE BARGAINED FOR. HE DID RELEASE THE SPIRIT OF OSIRIS. IN FACT, I THINK HE SUCCESSFULLY JOINED WITH THE GOD--
BUT YOUR FATHER NEVER GOT THE CHANCE TO USE OSIRIS'S POWER, BECAUSE SOMETHING ELSE CAME OUT WITH OSIRIS.
CAN WE BACK UP A MINUTE? WHAT WOULD A GOD BE DOING IN THE ROSETTA STONE IN THE FIRST PLACE?
FOR THE PAST TWO THOUSAND YEARS, THE WORK OF THE PER ANKH HAS BEEN TO IMPRISON EGYPT'S GODS INSIDE ITS REMAINING RELICS.
THOUGH ONCE USEFUL, HAVING GODS FREE CAME TO THREATEN THE BALANCE BETWEEN MA'AT AND ISFET--ORDER AND CHAOS.
THE EGYPTIAN GODS ARE VERY DANGEROUS. OUR MOST IMPORTANT LAW, ISSUED BY CHIEF LECTOR ISKANDAR IN ROMAN TIMES, FORBIDS RELEASING THE GODS OR USING THEIR POWER. YOUR FATHER BROKE THAT LAW ONCE BEFORE...
AT CLEOPATRA'S NEEDLE IN LONDON? BUT THAT WAS WHILE MUM WAS STILL ALIVE! WHAT WERE THEY TRYING AT?
YOUR PARENTS... THOUGHT THEY WERE DOING SOMETHING GOOD. THEY TOOK A TERRIBLE RISK, AND IT COST YOUR MOTHER HER LIFE.
YOUR FATHER TOOK THE BLAME AND WAS EXILED FROM THE HOUSE OF LIFE. BANISHED. AFRAID HE WOULD CONTINUE HIS RESEARCH, THE HOUSE MONITORED HIS ACTIVITIES, AND JULIUS WAS FORCED TO TRAVEL CONSTANTLY.
SO THAT'S WHY WE WERE ALWAYS MOVING.
LAST NIGHT AT THE MUSEUM. THE GIRL WITH THE STAFF, THE MAN WITH THE FORKED BEARD--THEY WERE MAGICIANS TOO? FROM THE HOUSE OF LIFE?
YES. THE MAN AND GIRL THAT APPEARED--
THE GIRL WHO WANTED TO KILL US, BY THE WAY.
--WERE KEEPING AN EYE ON YOUR FATHER. YOU ARE FORTUNATE THEY LET YOU GO.

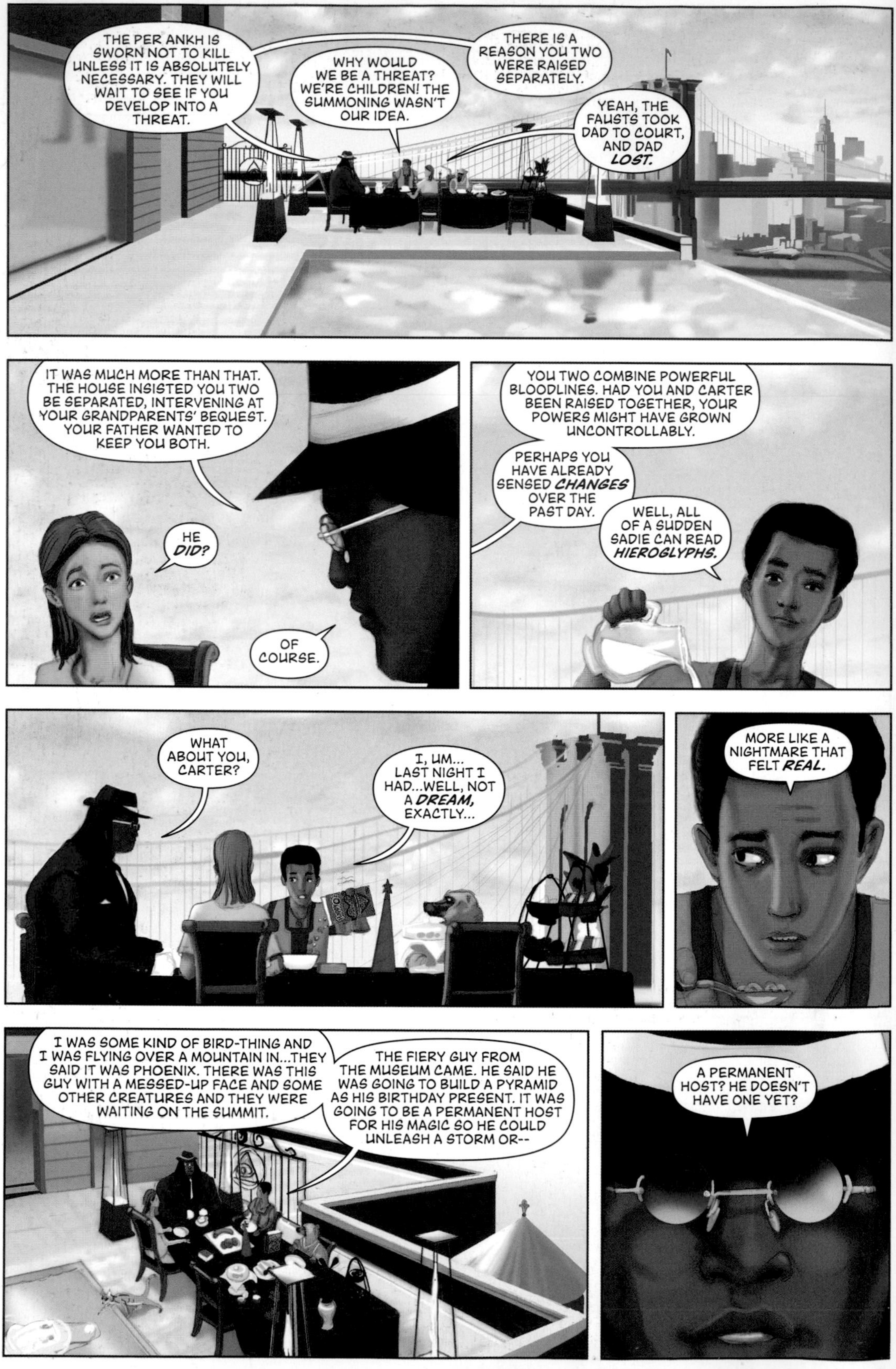
THE PER ANKH IS SWORN NOT TO KILL UNLESS IT IS ABSOLUTELY NECESSARY. THEY WILL WAIT TO SEE IF YOU DEVELOP INTO A THREAT.
WHY WOULD WE BE A THREAT? WE'RE CHILDREN! THE SUMMONING WASN'T OUR IDEA.
THERE IS A REASON YOU TWO WERE RAISED SEPARATELY.
YEAH, THE FAUSTS TOOK DAD TO COURT, AND DAD *LOST.*
IT WAS MUCH MORE THAN THAT. THE HOUSE INSISTED YOU TWO BE SEPARATED, INTERVENING AT YOUR GRANDPARENTS' BEQUEST. YOUR FATHER WANTED TO KEEP YOU BOTH.
HE *DID?*
OF COURSE.
YOU TWO COMBINE POWERFUL BLOODLINES. HAD YOU AND CARTER BEEN RAISED TOGETHER, YOUR POWERS MIGHT HAVE GROWN UNCONTROLLABLY.
PERHAPS YOU HAVE ALREADY SENSED *CHANGES* OVER THE PAST DAY.
WELL, ALL OF A SUDDEN SADIE CAN READ *HIEROGLYPHS.*
WHAT ABOUT YOU, CARTER?
I, UM... LAST NIGHT I HAD...WELL, NOT A *DREAM,* EXACTLY...
MORE LIKE A NIGHTMARE THAT FELT *REAL.*
I WAS SOME KIND OF BIRD-THING AND I WAS FLYING OVER A MOUNTAIN IN...THEY SAID IT WAS PHOENIX. THERE WAS THIS GUY WITH A MESSED-UP FACE AND SOME OTHER CREATURES AND THEY WERE WAITING ON THE SUMMIT.
THE FIERY GUY FROM THE MUSEUM CAME. HE SAID HE WAS GOING TO BUILD A PYRAMID AS HIS BIRTHDAY PRESENT. IT WAS GOING TO BE A PERMANENT HOST FOR HIS MAGIC SO HE COULD UNLEASH A STORM OR--
A PERMANENT HOST? HE DOESN'T HAVE ONE YET?

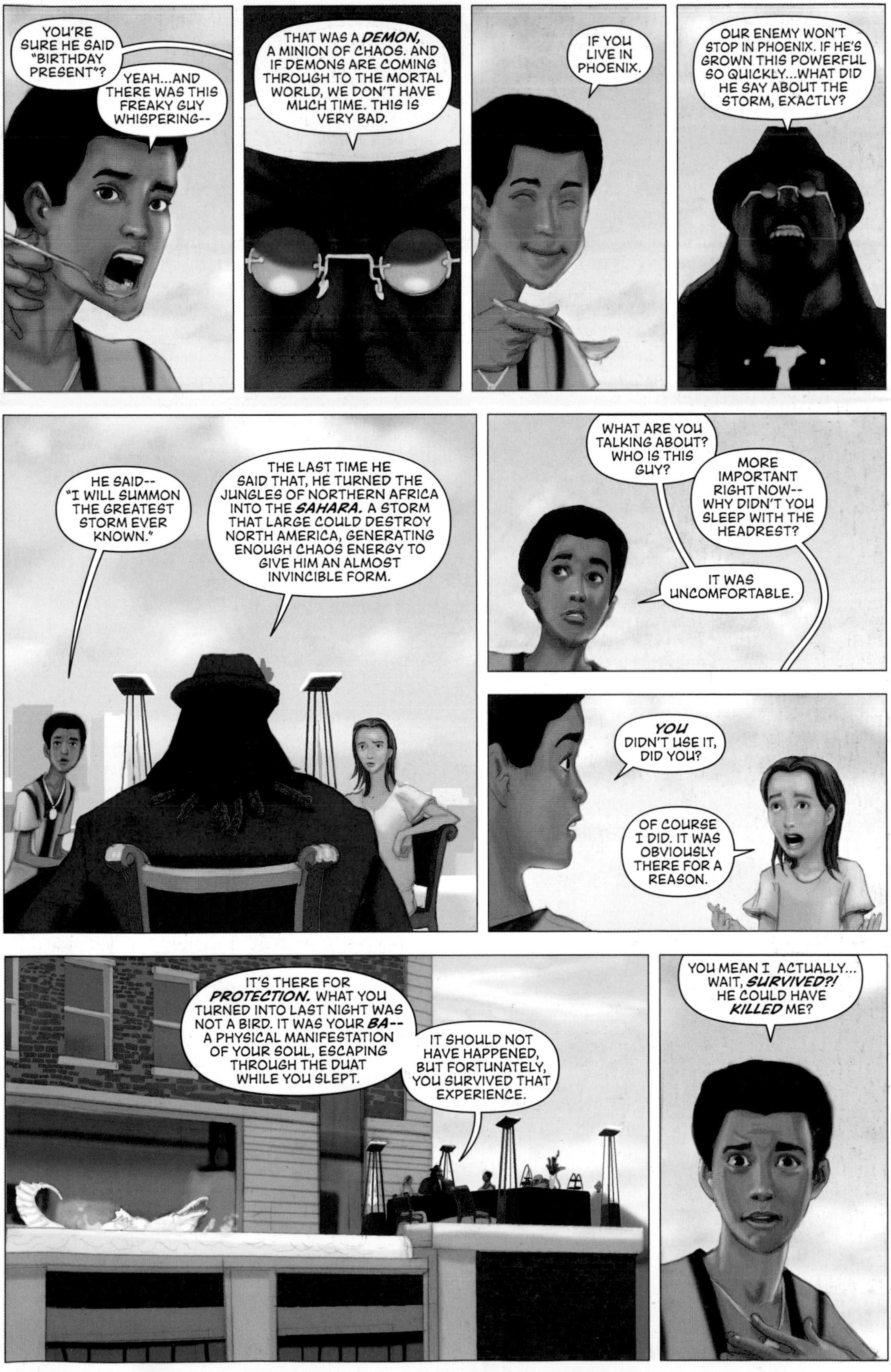
YOU'RE SURE HE SAID "BIRTHDAY PRESENT"?
YEAH...AND THERE WAS THIS FREAKY GUY WHISPERING--
THAT WAS A DEMON, A MINION OF CHAOS. AND IF DEMONS ARE COMING THROUGH TO THE MORTAL WORLD, WE DON'T HAVE MUCH TIME. THIS IS VERY BAD.
IF YOU LIVE IN PHOENIX.
OUR ENEMY WON'T STOP IN PHOENIX. IF HE'S GROWN THIS POWERFUL SO QUICKLY...WHAT DID HE SAY ABOUT THE STORM, EXACTLY?
HE SAID-- "I WILL SUMMON THE GREATEST STORM EVER KNOWN."
THE LAST TIME HE SAID THAT, HE TURNED THE JUNGLES OF NORTHERN AFRICA INTO THE SAHARA. A STORM THAT LARGE COULD DESTROY NORTH AMERICA, GENERATING ENOUGH CHAOS ENERGY TO GIVE HIM AN ALMOST INVINCIBLE FORM.
WHAT ARE YOU TALKING ABOUT? WHO IS THIS GUY?
MORE IMPORTANT RIGHT NOW-- WHY DIDN'T YOU SLEEP WITH THE HEADREST?
IT WAS UNCOMFORTABLE.
YOU DIDN'T USE IT, DID YOU?
OF COURSE I DID. IT WAS OBVIOUSLY THERE FOR A REASON.
IT'S THERE FOR PROTECTION. WHAT YOU TURNED INTO LAST NIGHT WAS NOT A BIRD. IT WAS YOUR BA-- A PHYSICAL MANIFESTATION OF YOUR SOUL, ESCAPING THROUGH THE DUAT WHILE YOU SLEPT.
IT SHOULD NOT HAVE HAPPENED, BUT FORTUNATELY, YOU SURVIVED THAT EXPERIENCE.
YOU MEAN I ACTUALLY... WAIT, SURVIVED?! HE COULD HAVE KILLED ME?

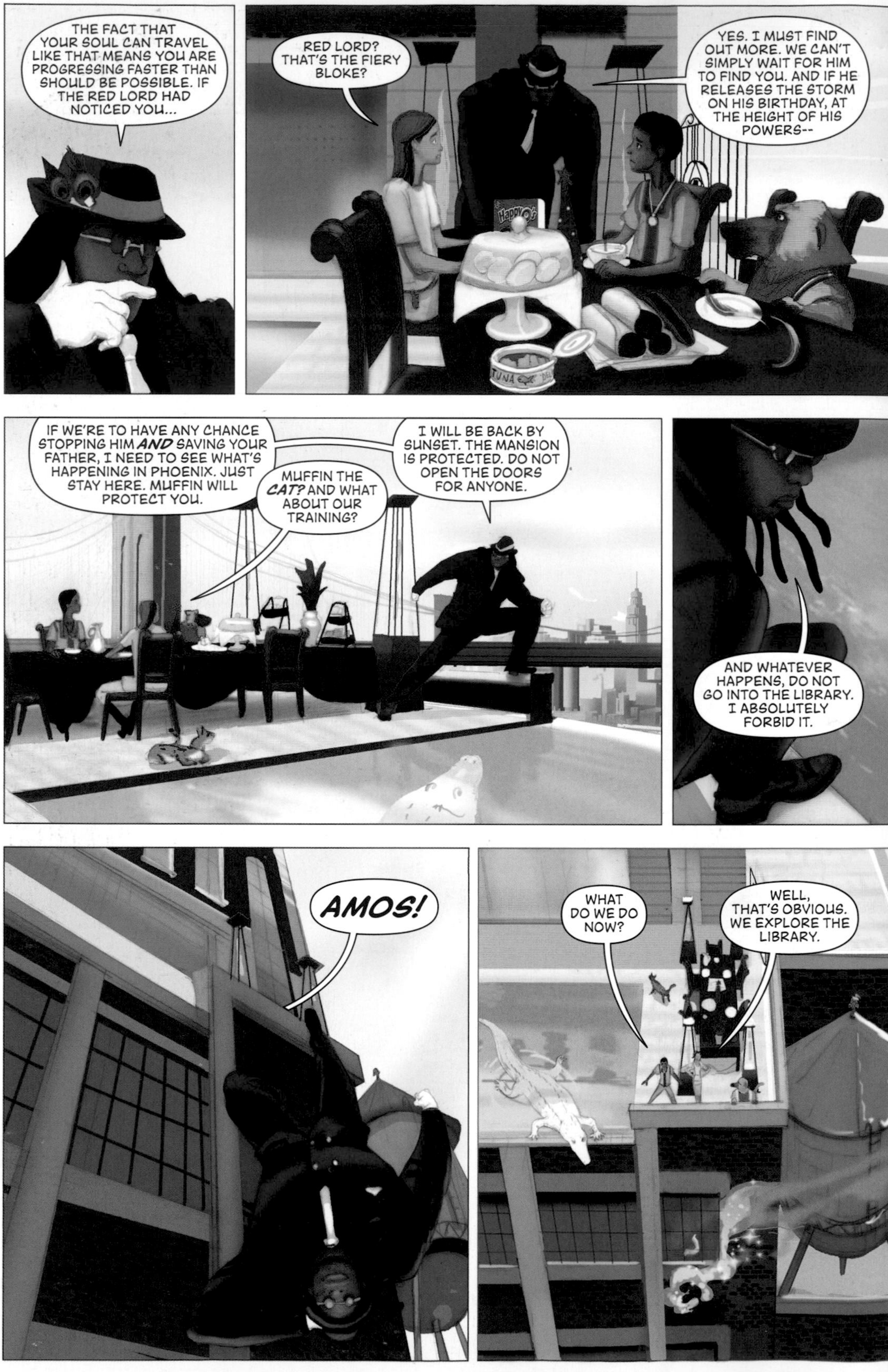
THE FACT THAT YOUR SOUL CAN TRAVEL LIKE THAT MEANS YOU ARE PROGRESSING FASTER THAN SHOULD BE POSSIBLE. IF THE RED LORD HAD NOTICED YOU...
RED LORD? THAT'S THE FIERY BLOKE?
YES. I MUST FIND OUT MORE. WE CAN'T SIMPLY WAIT FOR HIM TO FIND YOU. AND IF HE RELEASES THE STORM ON HIS BIRTHDAY, AT THE HEIGHT OF HIS POWERS--
Happy O's
TUNA
IF WE'RE TO HAVE ANY CHANCE STOPPING HIM AND SAVING YOUR FATHER, I NEED TO SEE WHAT'S HAPPENING IN PHOENIX. JUST STAY HERE. MUFFIN WILL PROTECT YOU.
MUFFIN THE CAT? AND WHAT ABOUT OUR TRAINING?
I WILL BE BACK BY SUNSET. THE MANSION IS PROTECTED. DO NOT OPEN THE DOORS FOR ANYONE.
AND WHATEVER HAPPENS, DO NOT GO INTO THE LIBRARY. I ABSOLUTELY FORBID IT.
AMOS!
WHAT DO WE DO NOW?
WELL, THAT'S OBVIOUS. WE EXPLORE THE LIBRARY.

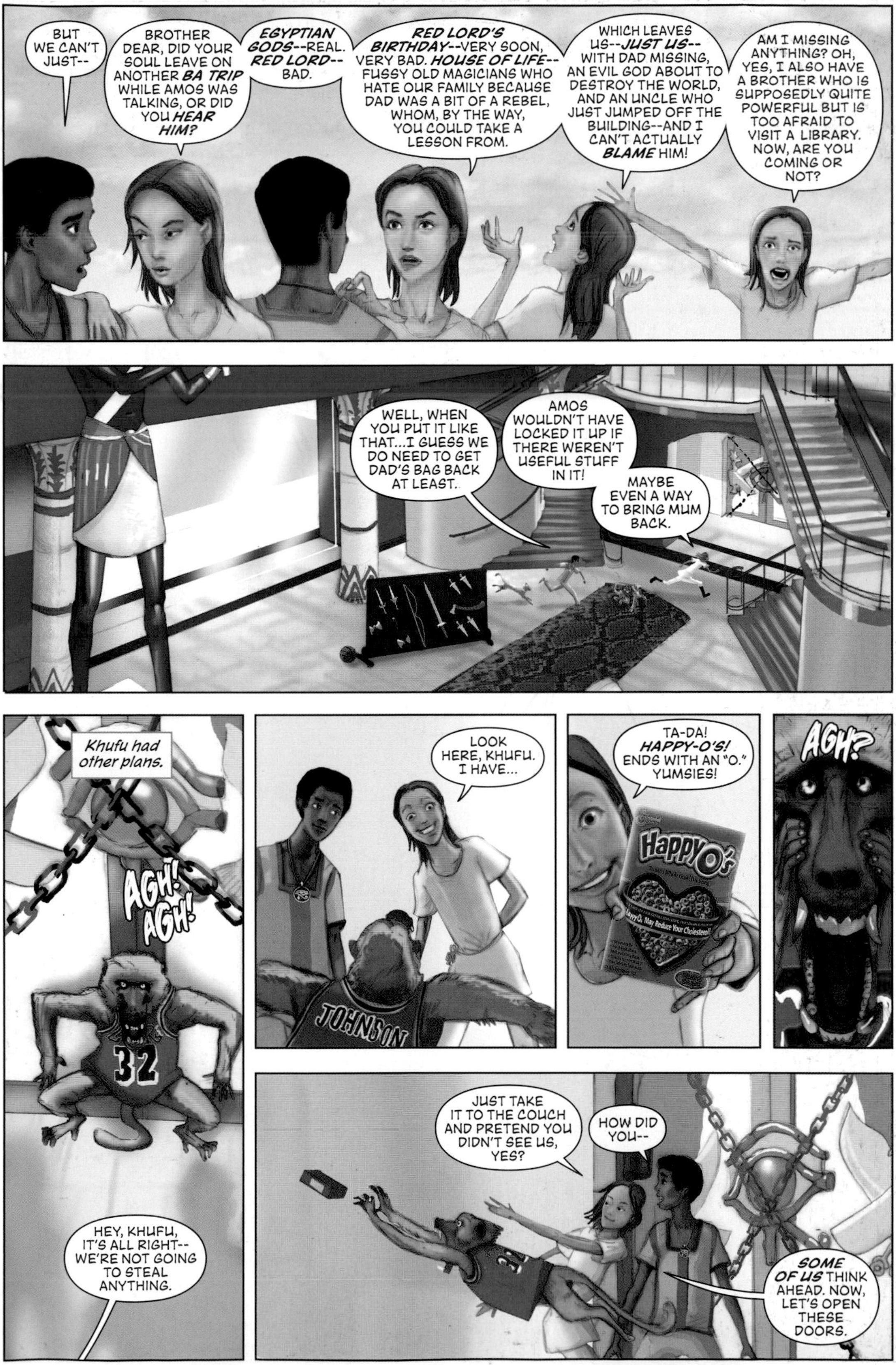
BUT WE CAN'T JUST--
BROTHER DEAR, DID YOUR SOUL LEAVE ON ANOTHER BA TRIP WHILE AMOS WAS TALKING, OR DID YOU HEAR HIM?
EGYPTIAN GODS--REAL. RED LORD--BAD.
RED LORD'S BIRTHDAY--VERY SOON, VERY BAD. HOUSE OF LIFE--FUSSY OLD MAGICIANS WHO HATE OUR FAMILY BECAUSE DAD WAS A BIT OF A REBEL, WHOM, BY THE WAY, YOU COULD TAKE A LESSON FROM.
WHICH LEAVES US--JUST US--WITH DAD MISSING, AN EVIL GOD ABOUT TO DESTROY THE WORLD, AND AN UNCLE WHO JUST JUMPED OFF THE BUILDING--AND I CAN'T ACTUALLY BLAME HIM!
AM I MISSING ANYTHING? OH, YES, I ALSO HAVE A BROTHER WHO IS SUPPOSEDLY QUITE POWERFUL BUT IS TOO AFRAID TO VISIT A LIBRARY. NOW, ARE YOU COMING OR NOT?
WELL, WHEN YOU PUT IT LIKE THAT...I GUESS WE DO NEED TO GET DAD'S BAG BACK AT LEAST.
AMOS WOULDN'T HAVE LOCKED IT UP IF THERE WEREN'T USEFUL STUFF IN IT!
MAYBE EVEN A WAY TO BRING MUM BACK.
Khufu had other plans.
AGH! AGH!
HEY, KHUFU, IT'S ALL RIGHT--WE'RE NOT GOING TO STEAL ANYTHING.
LOOK HERE, KHUFU. I HAVE...
JOHNSON
TA-DA! HAPPY-O'S! ENDS WITH AN "O." YUMSIES!
Happy O's
Happy O's May Reduce Your Cholesterol!
AGH?
JUST TAKE IT TO THE COUCH AND PRETEND YOU DIDN'T SEE US, YES?
HOW DID YOU--
SOME OF US THINK AHEAD. NOW, LET'S OPEN THESE DOORS.

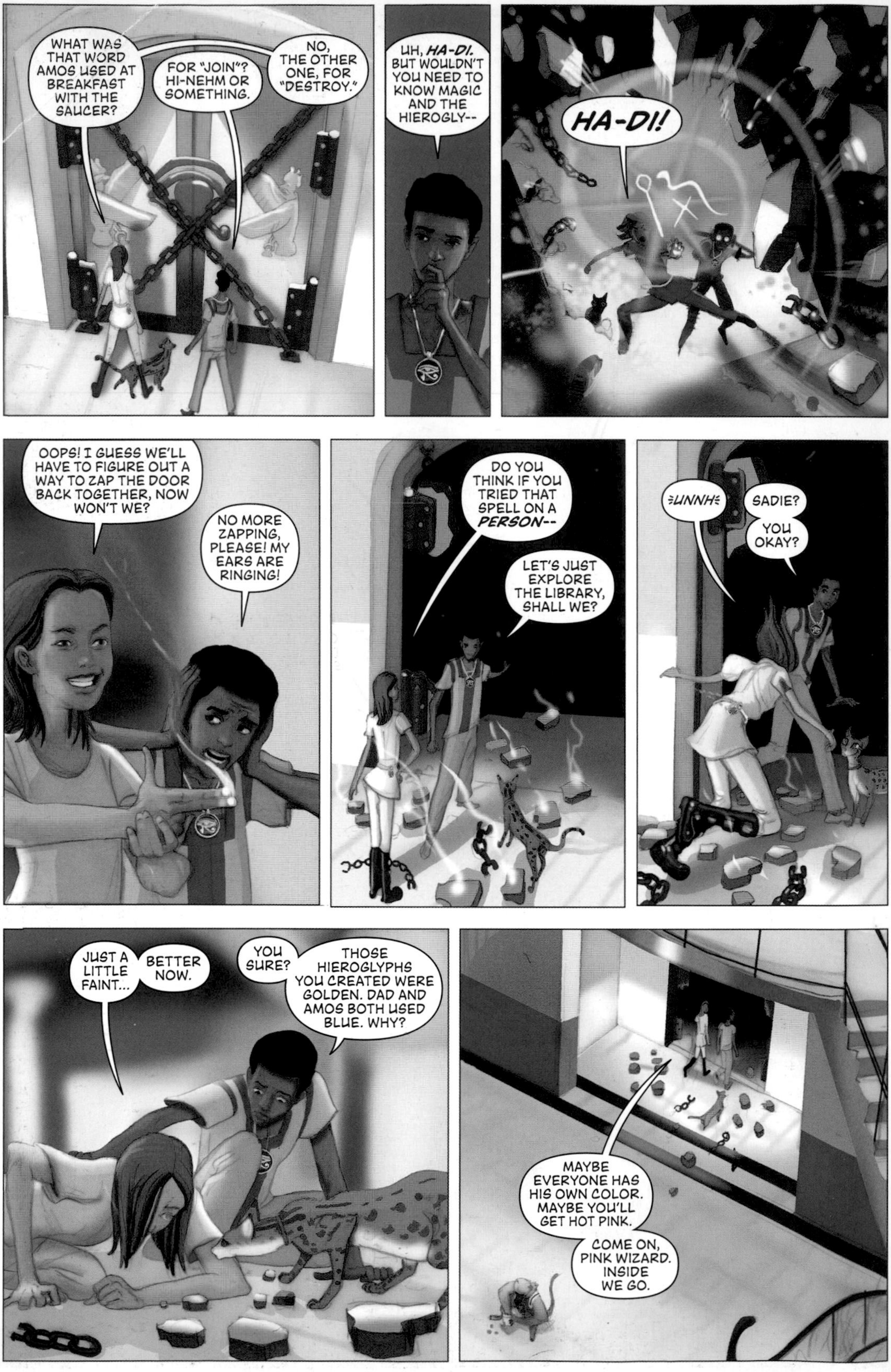
WHAT WAS THAT WORD AMOS USED AT BREAKFAST WITH THE SAUCER?
FOR "JOIN"? HI-NEHM OR SOMETHING.
NO, THE OTHER ONE, FOR "DESTROY."
UH, *HA-DI.* BUT WOULDN'T YOU NEED TO KNOW MAGIC AND THE HIEROGLY--
HA-DI!
OOPS! I GUESS WE'LL HAVE TO FIGURE OUT A WAY TO ZAP THE DOOR BACK TOGETHER, NOW WON'T WE?
NO MORE ZAPPING, PLEASE! MY EARS ARE RINGING!
DO YOU THINK IF YOU TRIED THAT SPELL ON A *PERSON*--
LET'S JUST EXPLORE THE LIBRARY, SHALL WE?
UNNH
SADIE?
YOU OKAY?
JUST A LITTLE FAINT...
BETTER NOW.
YOU SURE?
THOSE HIEROGLYPHS YOU CREATED WERE GOLDEN. DAD AND AMOS BOTH USED BLUE. WHY?
MAYBE EVERYONE HAS HIS OWN COLOR. MAYBE YOU'LL GET HOT PINK.
COME ON, PINK WIZARD. INSIDE WE GO.

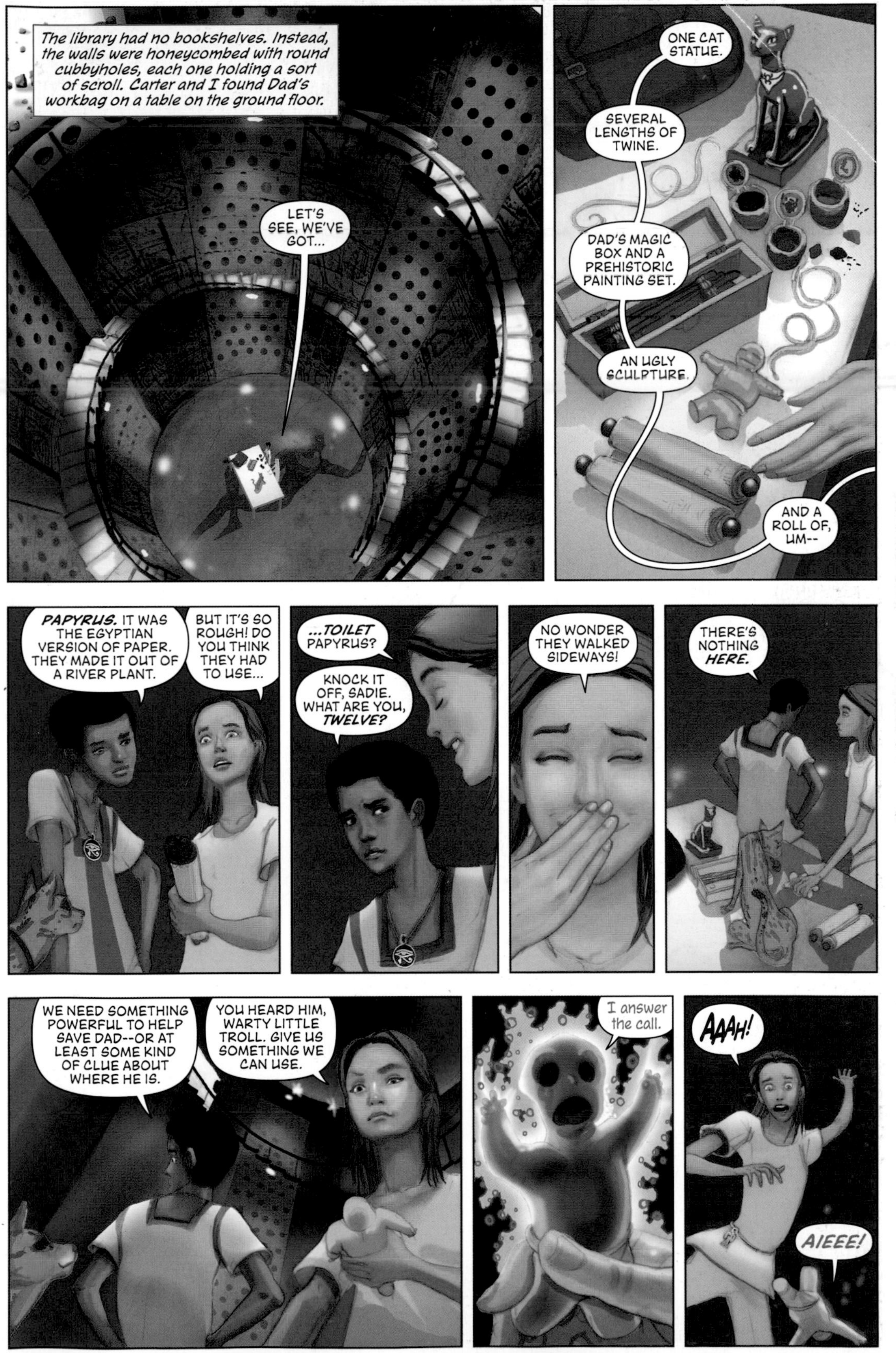
The library had no bookshelves. Instead, the walls were honeycombed with round cubbyholes, each one holding a sort of scroll. Carter and I found Dad's workbag on a table on the ground floor.
LET'S SEE, WE'VE GOT...
ONE CAT STATUE.
SEVERAL LENGTHS OF TWINE.
DAD'S MAGIC BOX AND A PREHISTORIC PAINTING SET.
AN UGLY SCULPTURE.
AND A ROLL OF, UM--
PAPYRUS. IT WAS THE EGYPTIAN VERSION OF PAPER. THEY MADE IT OUT OF A RIVER PLANT.
BUT IT'S SO ROUGH! DO YOU THINK THEY HAD TO USE...
...TOILET PAPYRUS?
KNOCK IT OFF, SADIE. WHAT ARE YOU, TWELVE?
NO WONDER THEY WALKED SIDEWAYS!
THERE'S NOTHING HERE.
WE NEED SOMETHING POWERFUL TO HELP SAVE DAD--OR AT LEAST SOME KIND OF CLUE ABOUT WHERE HE IS.
YOU HEARD HIM, WARTY LITTLE TROLL. GIVE US SOMETHING WE CAN USE.
I answer the call.
AAAH!
AIEEE!

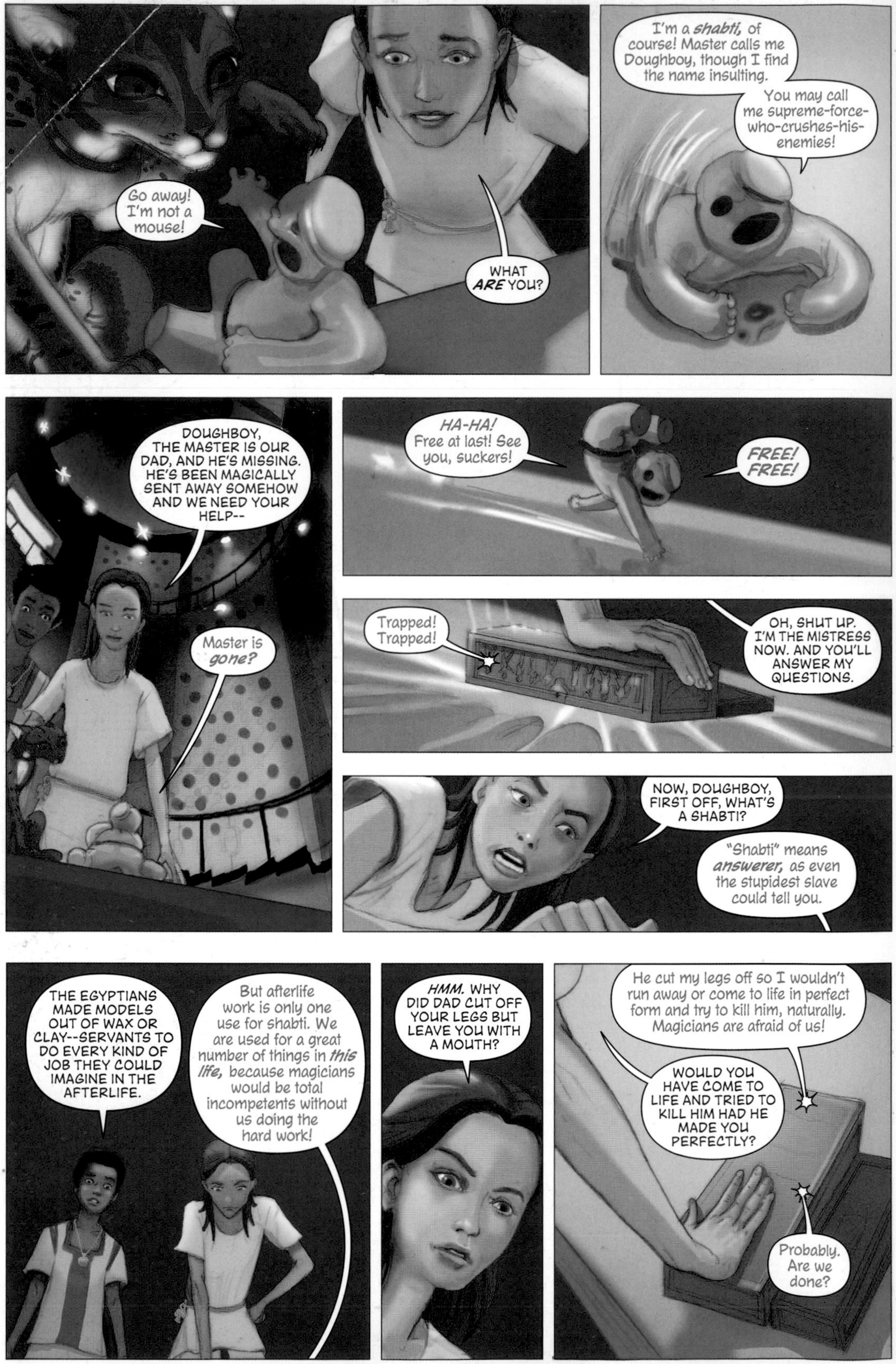
Go away! I'm not a mouse!
WHAT *ARE* YOU?
I'm a *shabti,* of course! Master calls me Doughboy, though I find the name insulting.
You may call me supreme-force-who-crushes-his-enemies!
DOUGHBOY, THE MASTER IS OUR DAD, AND HE'S MISSING. HE'S BEEN MAGICALLY SENT AWAY SOMEHOW AND WE NEED YOUR HELP--
Master is *gone?*
HA-HA! Free at last! See you, suckers!
FREE! FREE!
Trapped! Trapped!
OH, SHUT UP. I'M THE MISTRESS NOW. AND YOU'LL ANSWER MY QUESTIONS.
NOW, DOUGHBOY, FIRST OFF, WHAT'S A SHABTI?
"Shabti" means *answerer,* as even the stupidest slave could tell you.
THE EGYPTIANS MADE MODELS OUT OF WAX OR CLAY--SERVANTS TO DO EVERY KIND OF JOB THEY COULD IMAGINE IN THE AFTERLIFE.
But afterlife work is only one use for shabti. We are used for a great number of things in *this life,* because magicians would be total incompetents without us doing the hard work!
HMM. WHY DID DAD CUT OFF YOUR LEGS BUT LEAVE YOU WITH A MOUTH?
He cut my legs off so I wouldn't run away or come to life in perfect form and try to kill him, naturally. Magicians are afraid of us!
WOULD YOU HAVE COME TO LIFE AND TRIED TO KILL HIM HAD HE MADE YOU PERFECTLY?
Probably. Are we done?

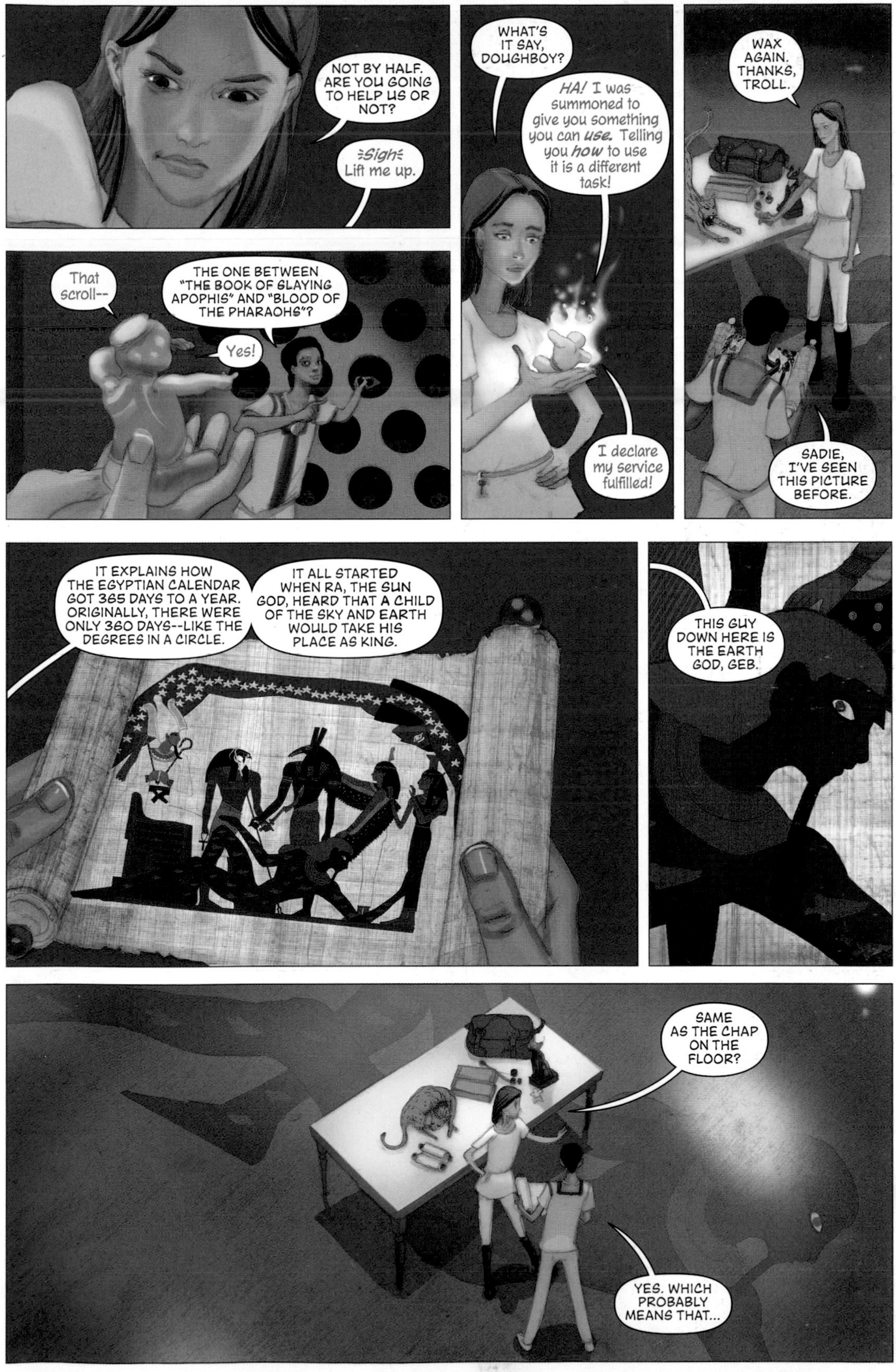
NOT BY HALF. ARE YOU GOING TO HELP US OR NOT?
Sigh Lift me up.
WHAT'S IT SAY, DOUGHBOY?
HA! I was summoned to give you something you can use. Telling you how to use it is a different task!
WAX AGAIN. THANKS, TROLL.
That scroll--
THE ONE BETWEEN "THE BOOK OF SLAYING APOPHIS" AND "BLOOD OF THE PHARAOHS"?
Yes!
I declare my service fulfilled!
SADIE, I'VE SEEN THIS PICTURE BEFORE.
IT EXPLAINS HOW THE EGYPTIAN CALENDAR GOT 365 DAYS TO A YEAR. ORIGINALLY, THERE WERE ONLY 360 DAYS--LIKE THE DEGREES IN A CIRCLE.
IT ALL STARTED WHEN RA, THE SUN GOD, HEARD THAT A CHILD OF THE SKY AND EARTH WOULD TAKE HIS PLACE AS KING.
THIS GUY DOWN HERE IS THE EARTH GOD, GEB.
SAME AS THE CHAP ON THE FLOOR?
YES. WHICH PROBABLY MEANS THAT...

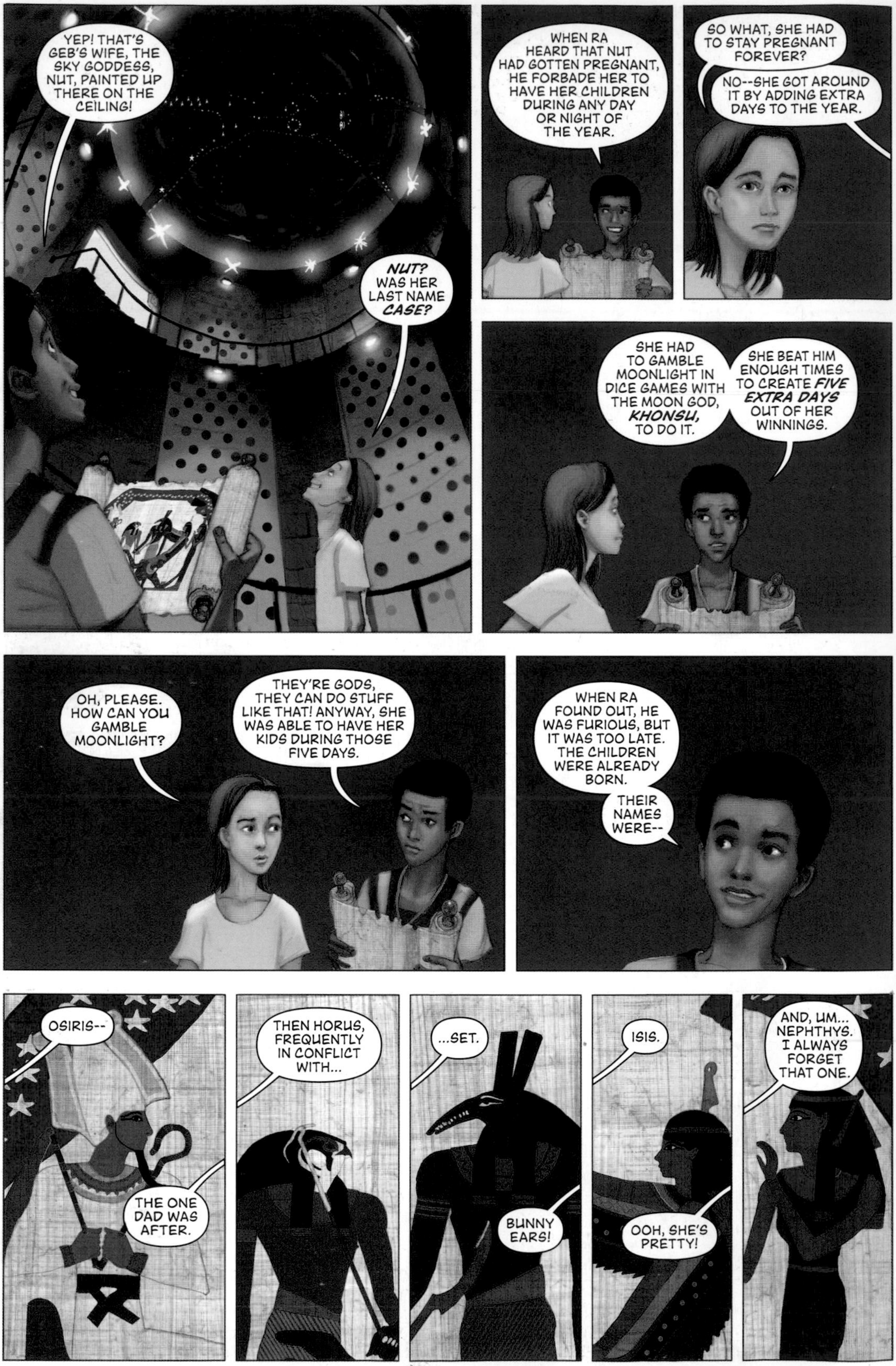

YEP! THAT'S GEB'S WIFE, THE SKY GODDESS, NUT, PAINTED UP THERE ON THE CEILING!
NUT? WAS HER LAST NAME *CASE?*
WHEN RA HEARD THAT NUT HAD GOTTEN PREGNANT, HE FORBADE HER TO HAVE HER CHILDREN DURING ANY DAY OR NIGHT OF THE YEAR.
SO WHAT, SHE HAD TO STAY PREGNANT FOREVER?
NO--SHE GOT AROUND IT BY ADDING EXTRA DAYS TO THE YEAR.
SHE HAD TO GAMBLE MOONLIGHT IN DICE GAMES WITH THE MOON GOD, *KHONSU,* TO DO IT.
SHE BEAT HIM ENOUGH TIMES TO CREATE *FIVE EXTRA DAYS* OUT OF HER WINNINGS.
OH, PLEASE. HOW CAN YOU GAMBLE MOONLIGHT?
THEY'RE GODS, THEY CAN DO STUFF LIKE THAT! ANYWAY, SHE WAS ABLE TO HAVE HER KIDS DURING THOSE FIVE DAYS.
WHEN RA FOUND OUT, HE WAS FURIOUS, BUT IT WAS TOO LATE. THE CHILDREN WERE ALREADY BORN.
THEIR NAMES WERE--
OSIRIS--
THE ONE DAD WAS AFTER.
THEN HORUS, FREQUENTLY IN CONFLICT WITH...
...SET.
BUNNY EARS!
ISIS.
OOH, SHE'S PRETTY!
AND, UM... NEPHTHYS. I ALWAYS FORGET THAT ONE.

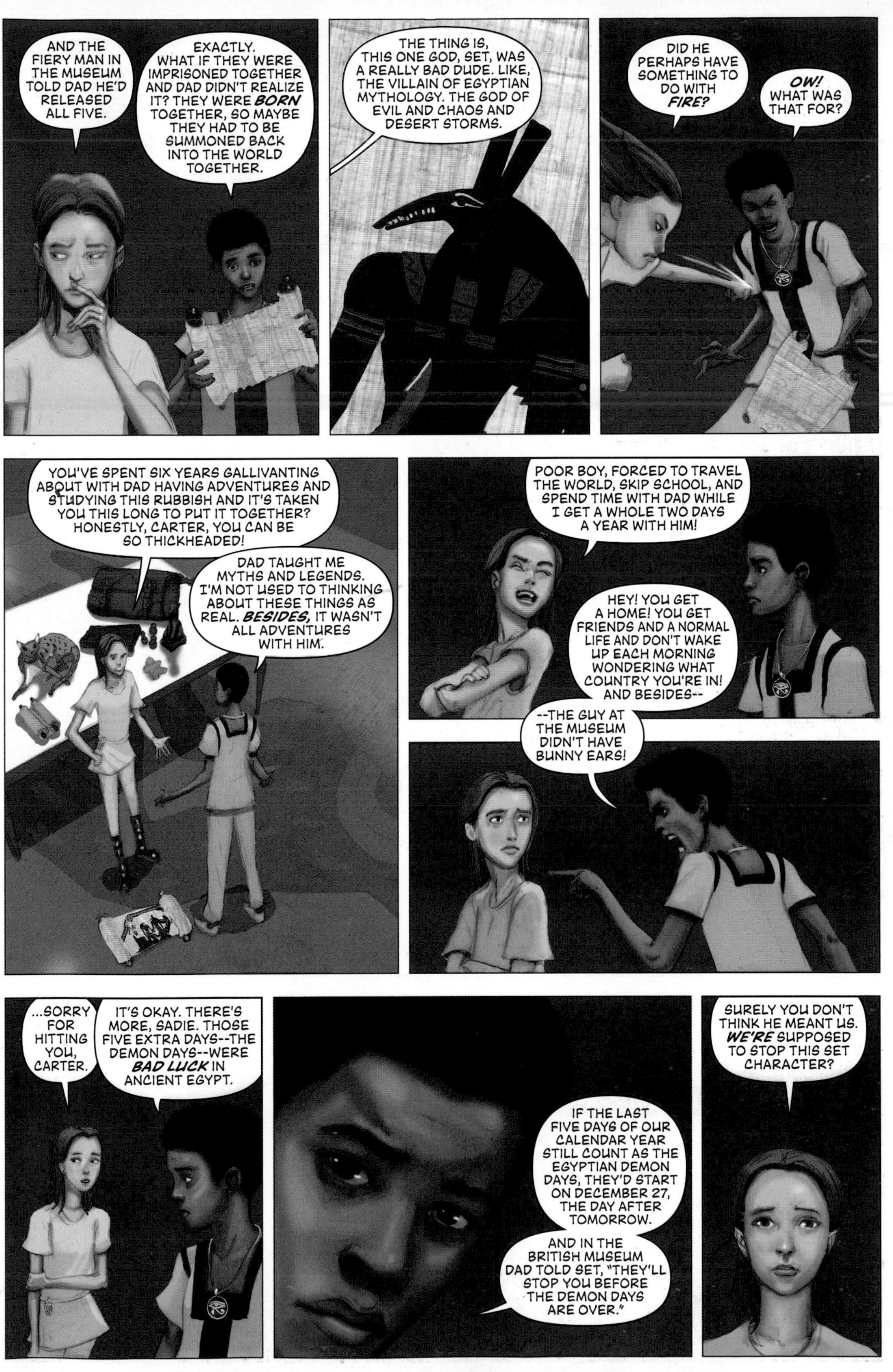
AND THE FIERY MAN IN THE MUSEUM TOLD DAD HE'D RELEASED ALL FIVE.
EXACTLY. WHAT IF THEY WERE IMPRISONED TOGETHER AND DAD DIDN'T REALIZE IT? THEY WERE BORN TOGETHER, SO MAYBE THEY HAD TO BE SUMMONED BACK INTO THE WORLD TOGETHER.
THE THING IS, THIS ONE GOD, SET, WAS A REALLY BAD DUDE. LIKE, THE VILLAIN OF EGYPTIAN MYTHOLOGY. THE GOD OF EVIL AND CHAOS AND DESERT STORMS.
DID HE PERHAPS HAVE SOMETHING TO DO WITH FIRE?
OW! WHAT WAS THAT FOR?
YOU'VE SPENT SIX YEARS GALLIVANTING ABOUT WITH DAD HAVING ADVENTURES AND STUDYING THIS RUBBISH AND IT'S TAKEN YOU THIS LONG TO PUT IT TOGETHER? HONESTLY, CARTER, YOU CAN BE SO THICKHEADED!
DAD TAUGHT ME MYTHS AND LEGENDS. I'M NOT USED TO THINKING ABOUT THESE THINGS AS REAL. BESIDES, IT WASN'T ALL ADVENTURES WITH HIM.
POOR BOY, FORCED TO TRAVEL THE WORLD, SKIP SCHOOL, AND SPEND TIME WITH DAD WHILE I GET A WHOLE TWO DAYS A YEAR WITH HIM!
HEY! YOU GET A HOME! YOU GET FRIENDS AND A NORMAL LIFE AND DON'T WAKE UP EACH MORNING WONDERING WHAT COUNTRY YOU'RE IN! AND BESIDES--
--THE GUY AT THE MUSEUM DIDN'T HAVE BUNNY EARS!
...SORRY FOR HITTING YOU, CARTER.
IT'S OKAY. THERE'S MORE, SADIE. THOSE FIVE EXTRA DAYS--THE DEMON DAYS--WERE BAD LUCK IN ANCIENT EGYPT.
IF THE LAST FIVE DAYS OF OUR CALENDAR YEAR STILL COUNT AS THE EGYPTIAN DEMON DAYS, THEY'D START ON DECEMBER 27, THE DAY AFTER TOMORROW.
AND IN THE BRITISH MUSEUM DAD TOLD SET, "THEY'LL STOP YOU BEFORE THE DEMON DAYS ARE OVER."
SURELY YOU DON'T THINK HE MEANT US. WE'RE SUPPOSED TO STOP THIS SET CHARACTER?

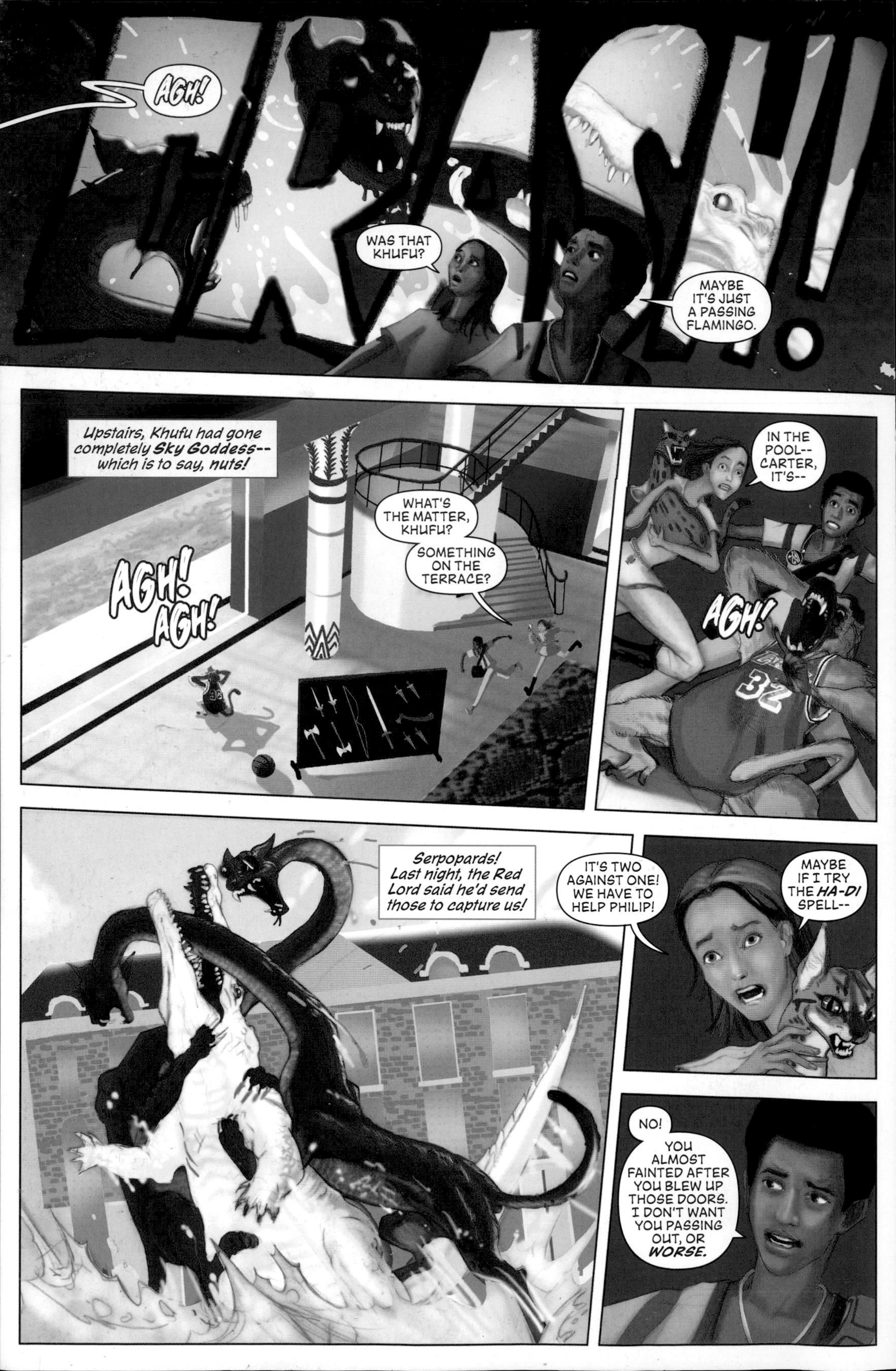
AGH!
WAS THAT KHUFU?
MAYBE IT'S JUST A PASSING FLAMINGO.
Upstairs, Khufu had gone completely Sky Goddess-- which is to say, nuts!
WHAT'S THE MATTER, KHUFU?
SOMETHING ON THE TERRACE?
AGH! AGH!
IN THE POOL-- CARTER, IT'S--
AGH!
Serpopards! Last night, the Red Lord said he'd send those to capture us!
IT'S TWO AGAINST ONE! WE HAVE TO HELP PHILIP!
MAYBE IF I TRY THE HA-DI SPELL--
NO!
YOU ALMOST FAINTED AFTER YOU BLEW UP THOSE DOORS. I DON'T WANT YOU PASSING OUT, OR WORSE.

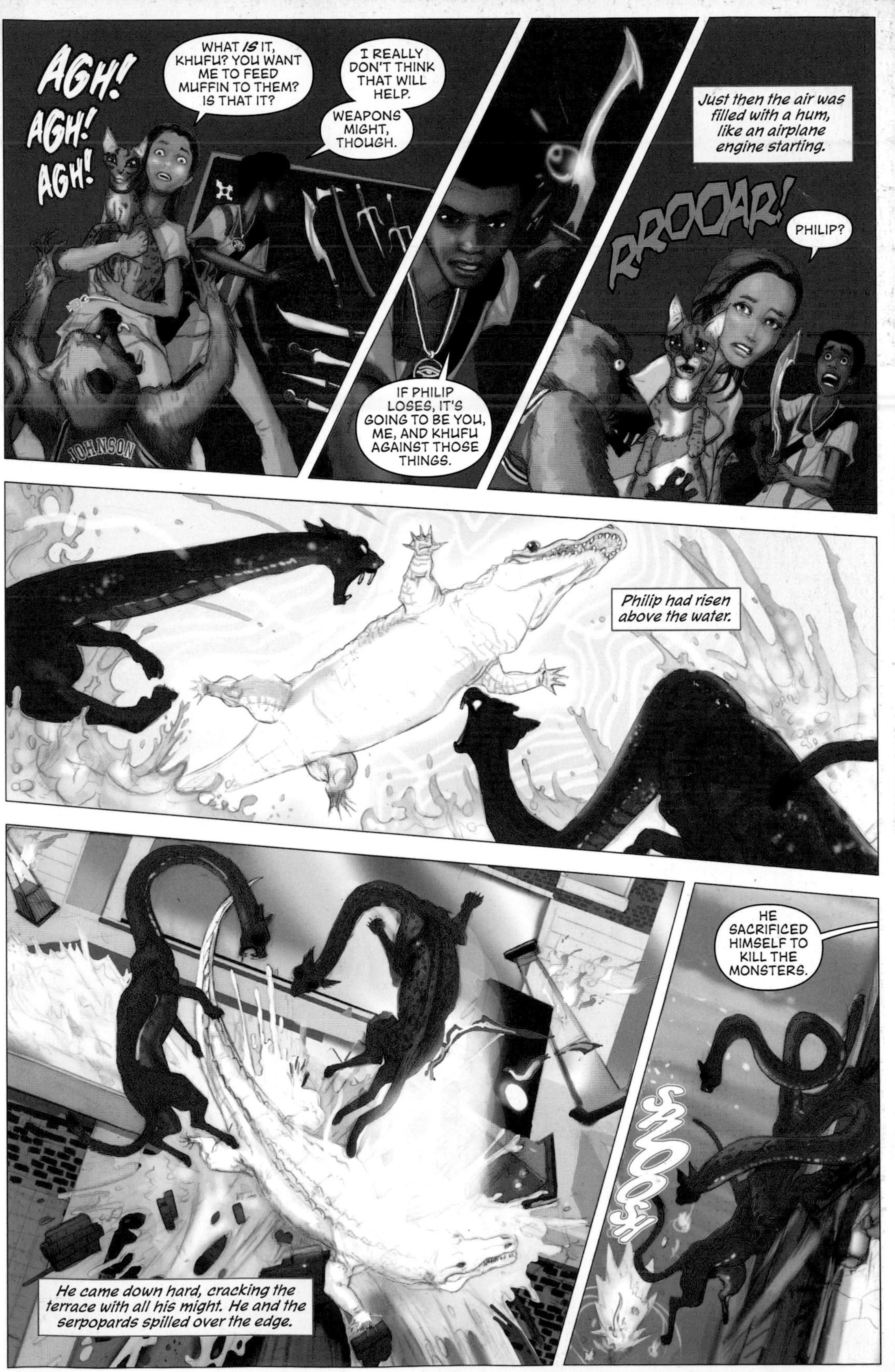
AGH! AGH! AGH!
WHAT IS IT, KHUFU? YOU WANT ME TO FEED MUFFIN TO THEM? IS THAT IT?
I REALLY DON'T THINK THAT WILL HELP.
WEAPONS MIGHT, THOUGH.
JOHNSON
IF PHILIP LOSES, IT'S GOING TO BE YOU, ME, AND KHUFU AGAINST THOSE THINGS.
Just then the air was filled with a hum, like an airplane engine starting.
RROOAR!
PHILIP?
Philip had risen above the water.
He came down hard, cracking the terrace with all his might. He and the serpopards spilled over the edge.
HE SACRIFICED HIMSELF TO KILL THE MONSTERS.
SPLOOSH

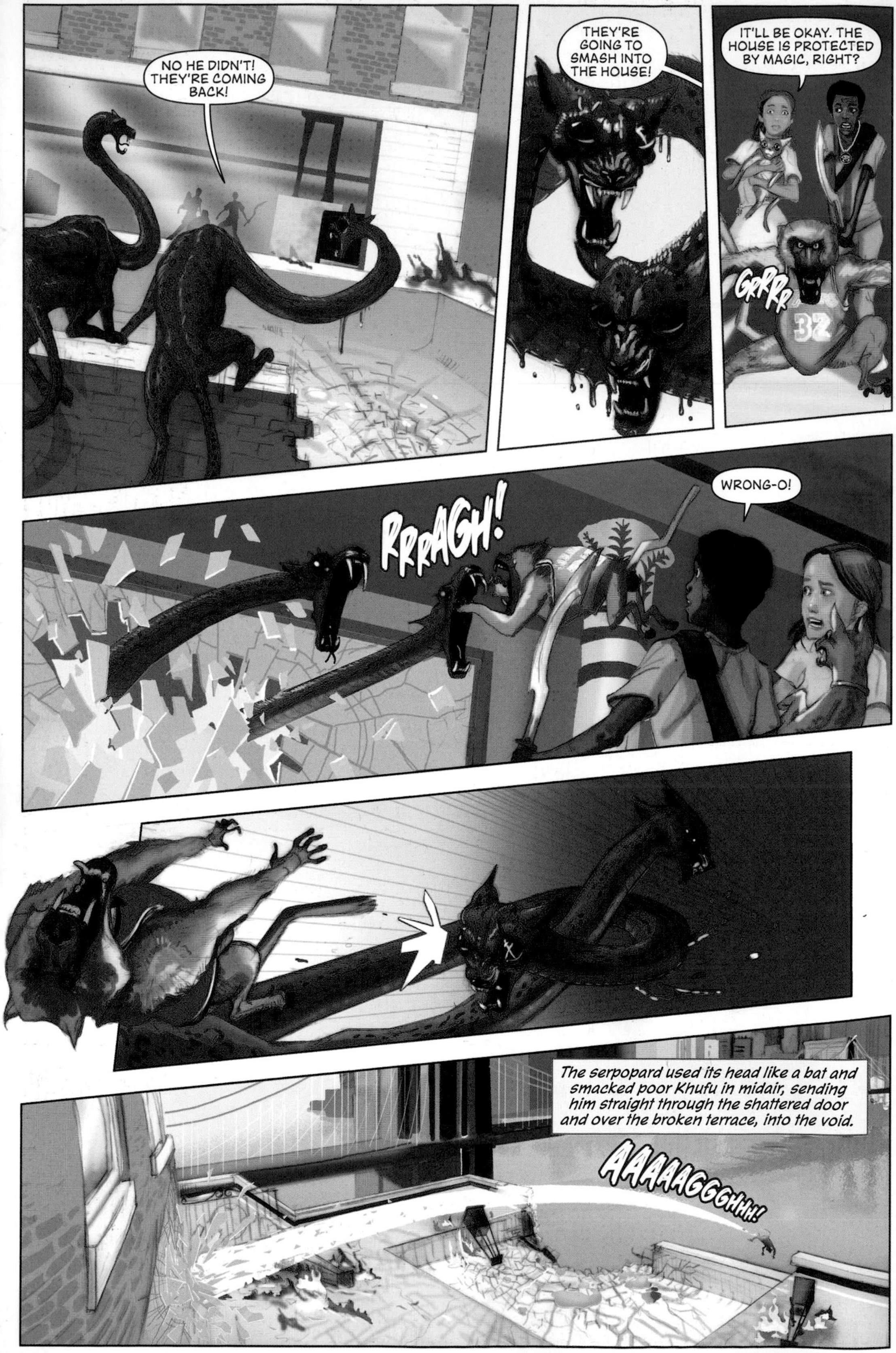
NO HE DIDN'T! THEY'RE COMING BACK!
THEY'RE GOING TO SMASH INTO THE HOUSE!
IT'LL BE OKAY. THE HOUSE IS PROTECTED BY MAGIC, RIGHT?
GRRRR
RRRAGH!
WRONG-O!
The serpopard used its head like a bat and smacked poor Khufu in midair, sending him straight through the shattered door and over the broken terrace, into the void.
AAAAAGGGHHH!

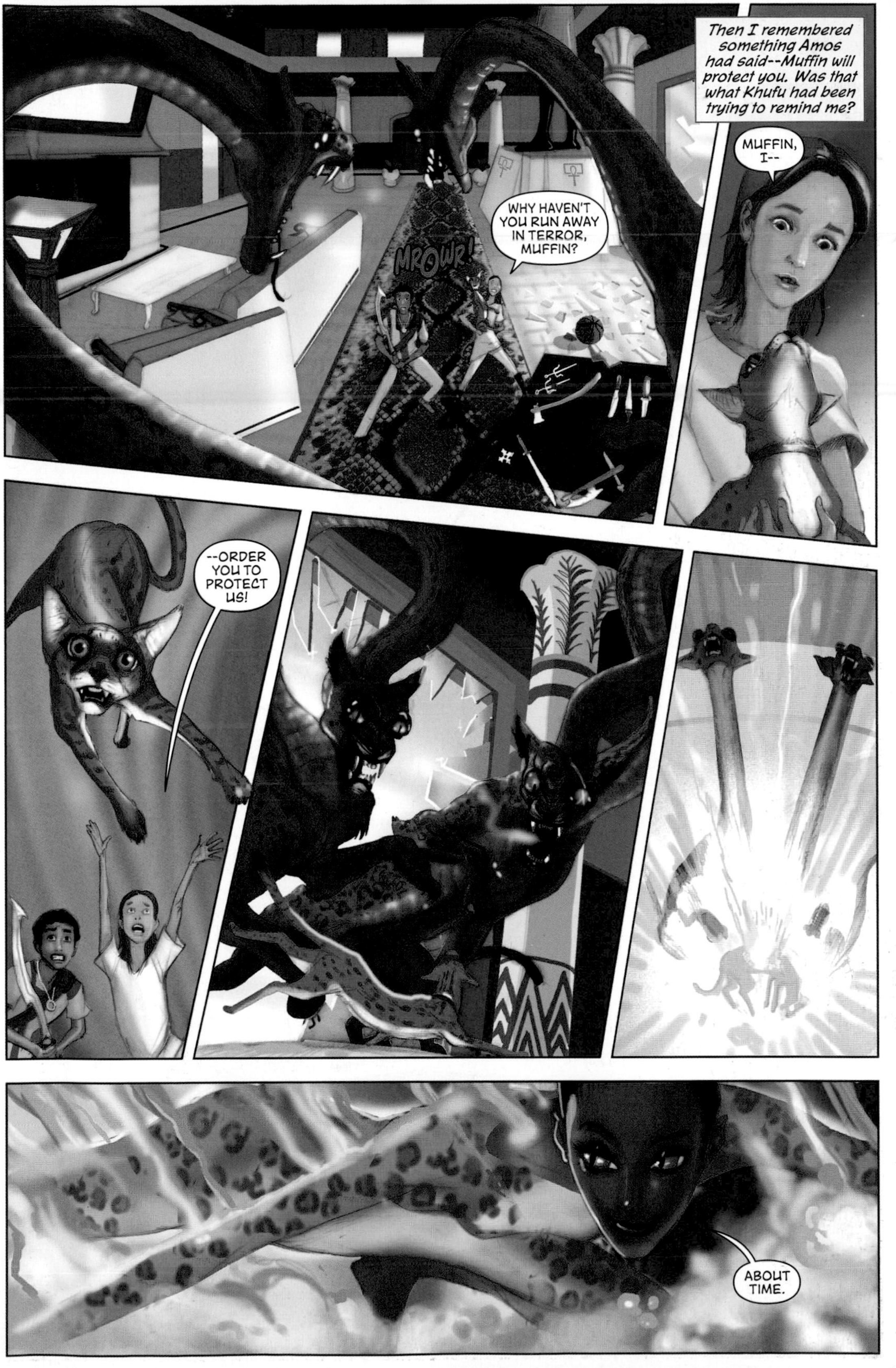
MROWR!
WHY HAVEN'T YOU RUN AWAY IN TERROR, MUFFIN?
Then I remembered something Amos had said--Muffin will protect you. Was that what Khufu had been trying to remind me?
MUFFIN, I--
--ORDER YOU TO PROTECT US!
ABOUT TIME.

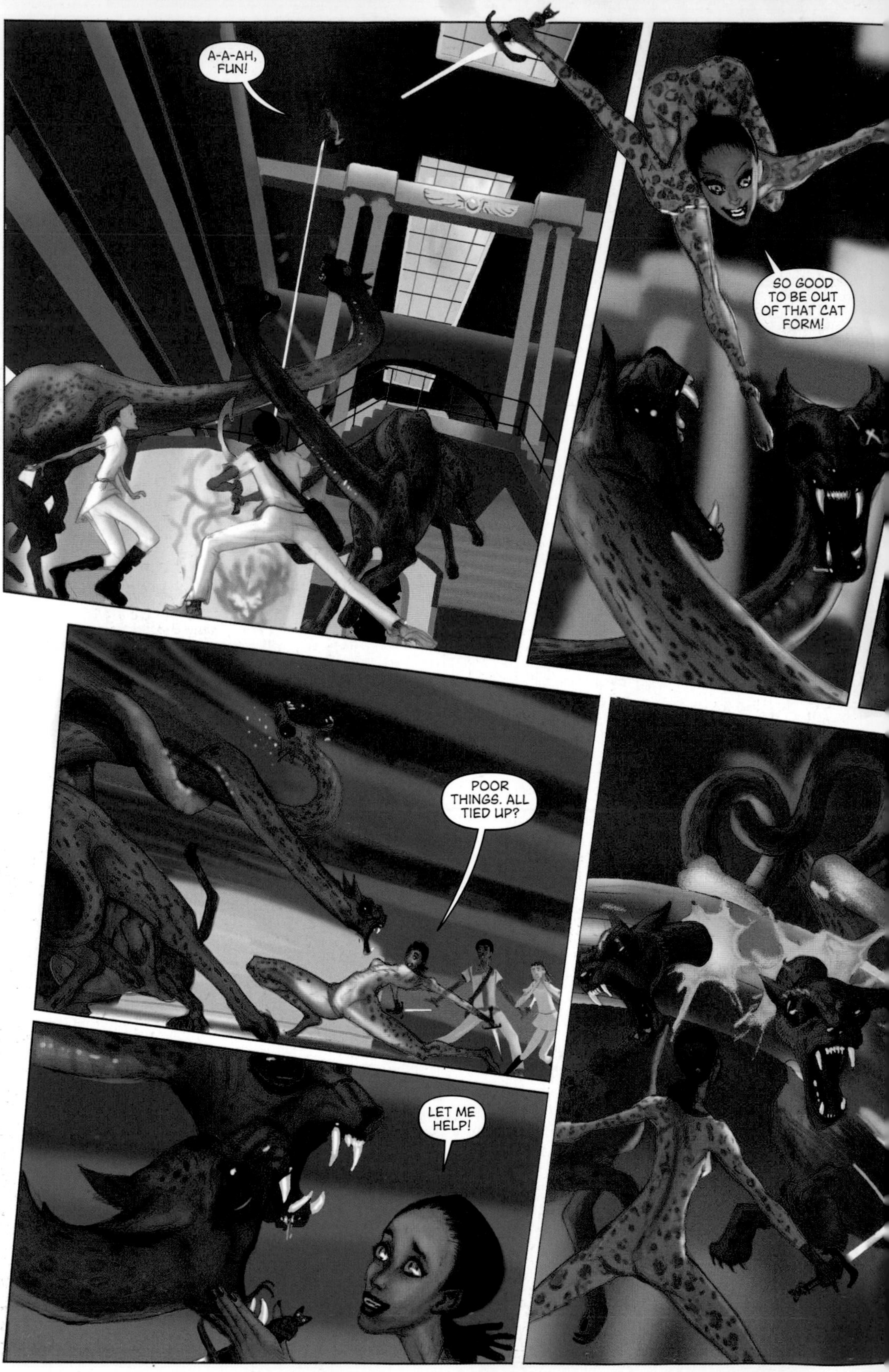
A-A-AH, FUN!
SO GOOD TO BE OUT OF THAT CAT FORM!
POOR THINGS. ALL TIED UP?
LET ME HELP!

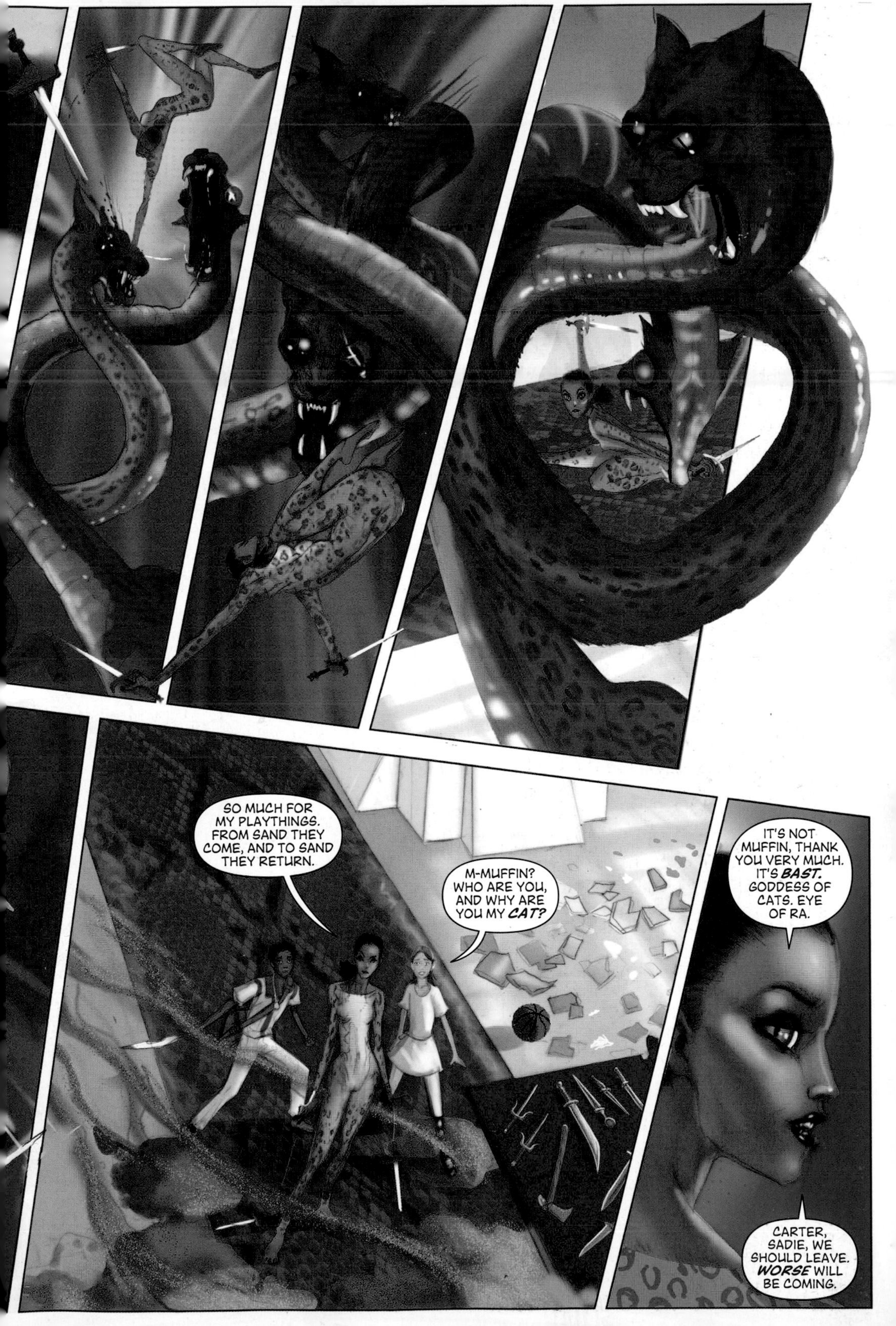
SO MUCH FOR MY PLAYTHINGS. FROM SAND THEY COME, AND TO SAND THEY RETURN.
M-MUFFIN? WHO ARE YOU, AND WHY ARE YOU MY *CAT?*
IT'S NOT MUFFIN, THANK YOU VERY MUCH. IT'S ***BAST.*** GODDESS OF CATS. EYE OF RA.
CARTER, SADIE, WE SHOULD LEAVE. ***WORSE*** WILL BE COMING.

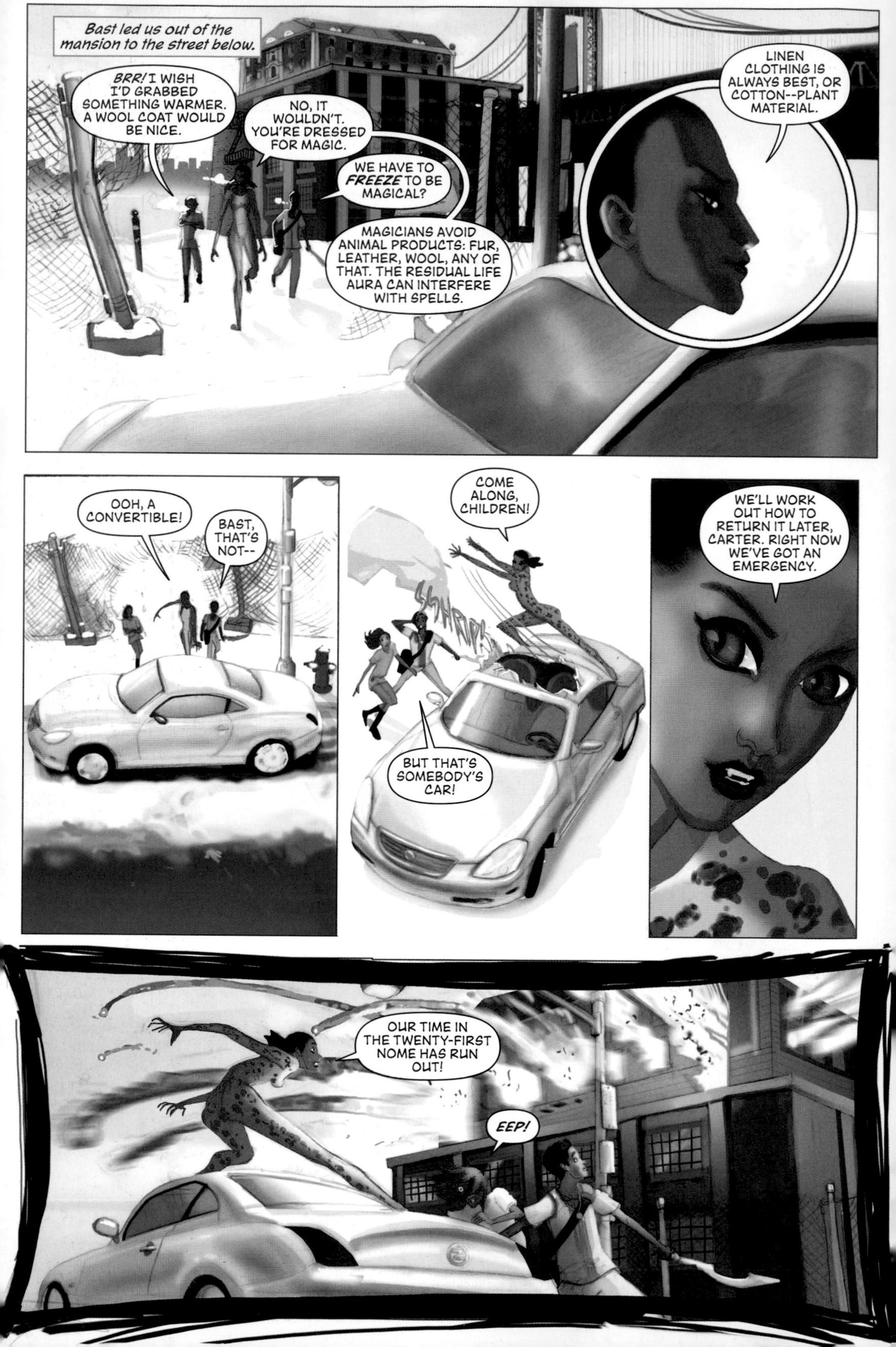
Bast led us out of the mansion to the street below.
BRR! I WISH I'D GRABBED SOMETHING WARMER. A WOOL COAT WOULD BE NICE.
NO, IT WOULDN'T. YOU'RE DRESSED FOR MAGIC.
WE HAVE TO FREEZE TO BE MAGICAL?
MAGICIANS AVOID ANIMAL PRODUCTS: FUR, LEATHER, WOOL, ANY OF THAT. THE RESIDUAL LIFE AURA CAN INTERFERE WITH SPELLS.
LINEN CLOTHING IS ALWAYS BEST, OR COTTON--PLANT MATERIAL.
OOH, A CONVERTIBLE!
BAST, THAT'S NOT--
COME ALONG, CHILDREN!
SHHRIP!
BUT THAT'S SOMEBODY'S CAR!
WE'LL WORK OUT HOW TO RETURN IT LATER, CARTER. RIGHT NOW WE'VE GOT AN EMERGENCY.
OUR TIME IN THE TWENTY-FIRST NOME HAS RUN OUT!
EEP!

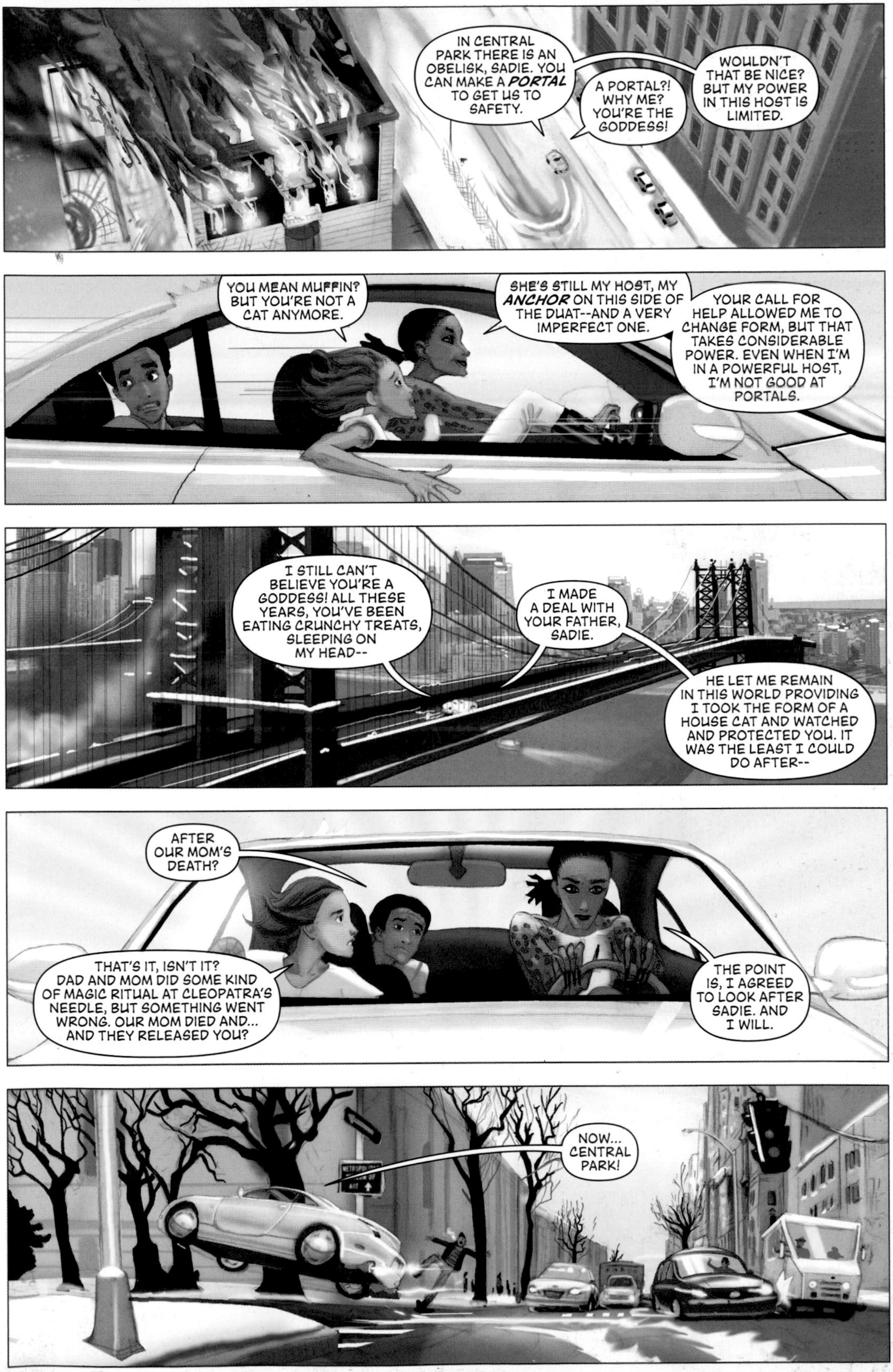
IN CENTRAL PARK THERE IS AN OBELISK, SADIE. YOU CAN MAKE A PORTAL TO GET US TO SAFETY.
A PORTAL?! WHY ME? YOU'RE THE GODDESS!
WOULDN'T THAT BE NICE? BUT MY POWER IN THIS HOST IS LIMITED.
YOU MEAN MUFFIN? BUT YOU'RE NOT A CAT ANYMORE.
SHE'S STILL MY HOST, MY ANCHOR ON THIS SIDE OF THE DUAT--AND A VERY IMPERFECT ONE.
YOUR CALL FOR HELP ALLOWED ME TO CHANGE FORM, BUT THAT TAKES CONSIDERABLE POWER. EVEN WHEN I'M IN A POWERFUL HOST, I'M NOT GOOD AT PORTALS.
I STILL CAN'T BELIEVE YOU'RE A GODDESS! ALL THESE YEARS, YOU'VE BEEN EATING CRUNCHY TREATS, SLEEPING ON MY HEAD--
I MADE A DEAL WITH YOUR FATHER, SADIE.
HE LET ME REMAIN IN THIS WORLD PROVIDING I TOOK THE FORM OF A HOUSE CAT AND WATCHED AND PROTECTED YOU. IT WAS THE LEAST I COULD DO AFTER--
AFTER OUR MOM'S DEATH?
THAT'S IT, ISN'T IT? DAD AND MOM DID SOME KIND OF MAGIC RITUAL AT CLEOPATRA'S NEEDLE, BUT SOMETHING WENT WRONG. OUR MOM DIED AND... AND THEY RELEASED YOU?
THE POINT IS, I AGREED TO LOOK AFTER SADIE. AND I WILL.
NOW... CENTRAL PARK!

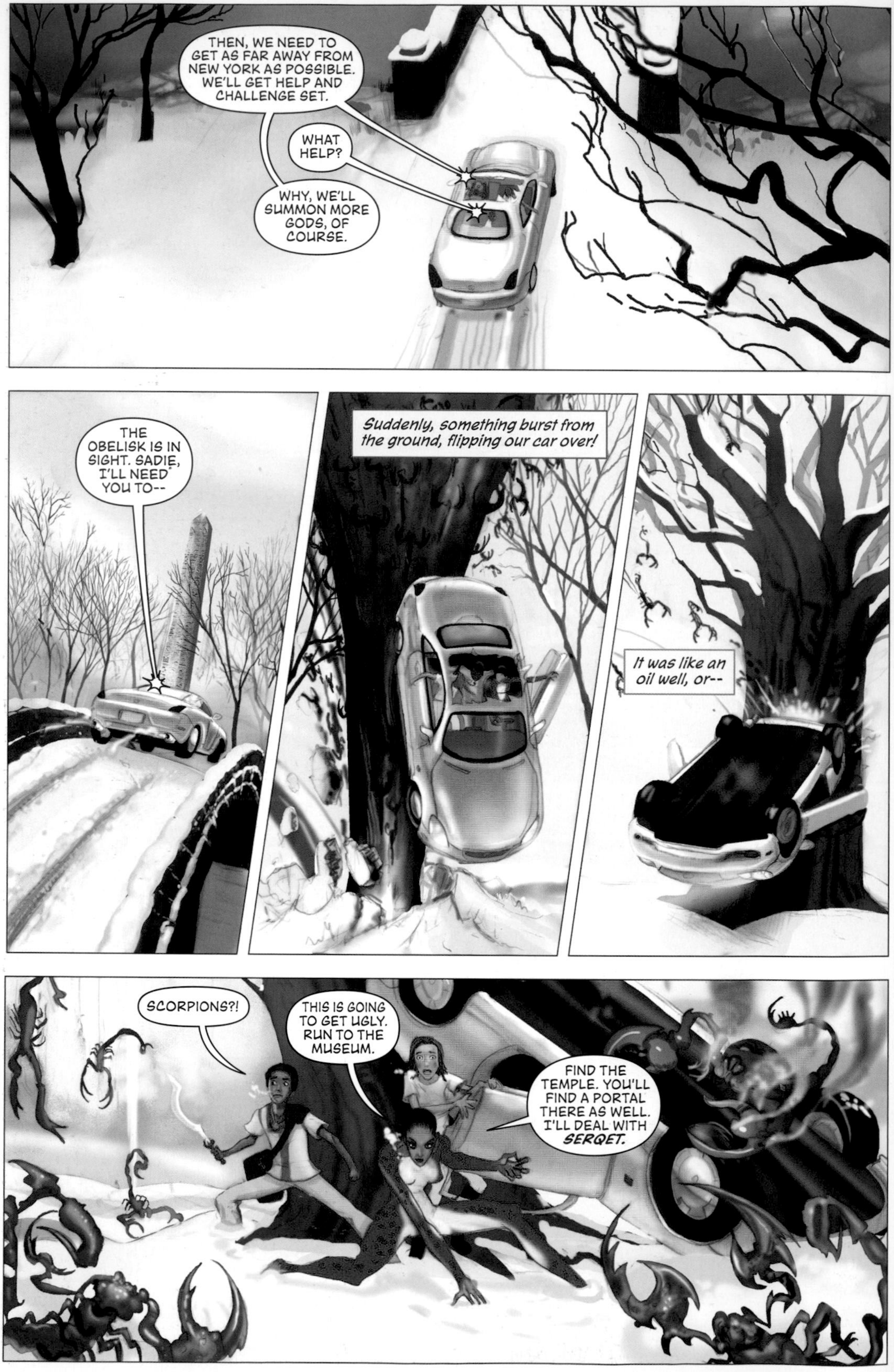
THEN, WE NEED TO GET AS FAR AWAY FROM NEW YORK AS POSSIBLE. WE'LL GET HELP AND CHALLENGE SET.
WHAT HELP?
WHY, WE'LL SUMMON MORE GODS, OF COURSE.
THE OBELISK IS IN SIGHT. SADIE, I'LL NEED YOU TO--
Suddenly, something burst from the ground, flipping our car over!
It was like an oil well, or--
SCORPIONS?!
THIS IS GOING TO GET UGLY. RUN TO THE MUSEUM.
FIND THE TEMPLE. YOU'LL FIND A PORTAL THERE AS WELL. I'LL DEAL WITH SERQET.

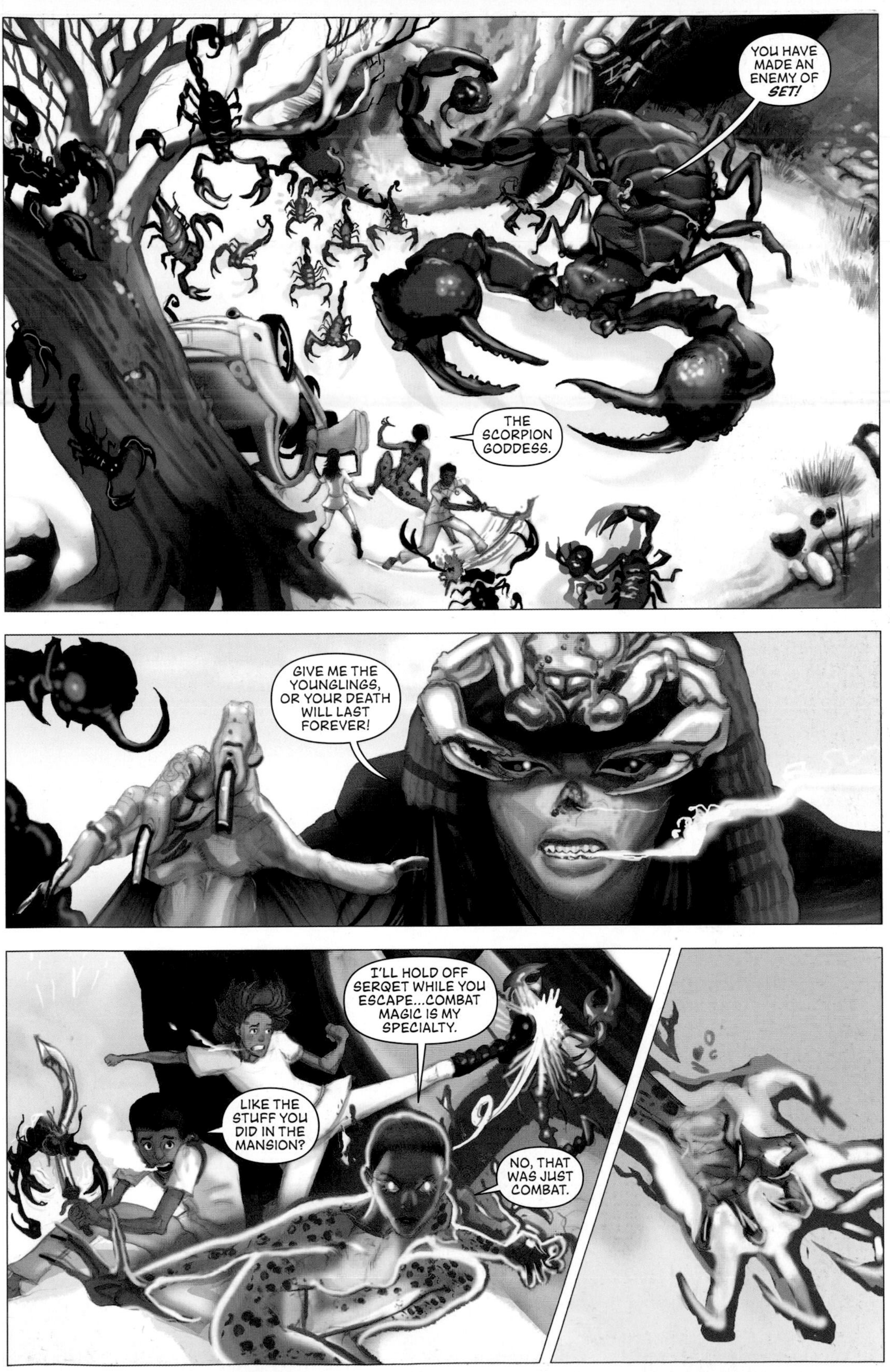
YOU HAVE MADE AN ENEMY OF SET!
THE SCORPION GODDESS.
GIVE ME THE YOUNGLINGS, OR YOUR DEATH WILL LAST FOREVER!
I'LL HOLD OFF SERQET WHILE YOU ESCAPE...COMBAT MAGIC IS MY SPECIALTY.
LIKE THE STUFF YOU DID IN THE MANSION?
NO, THAT WAS JUST COMBAT.

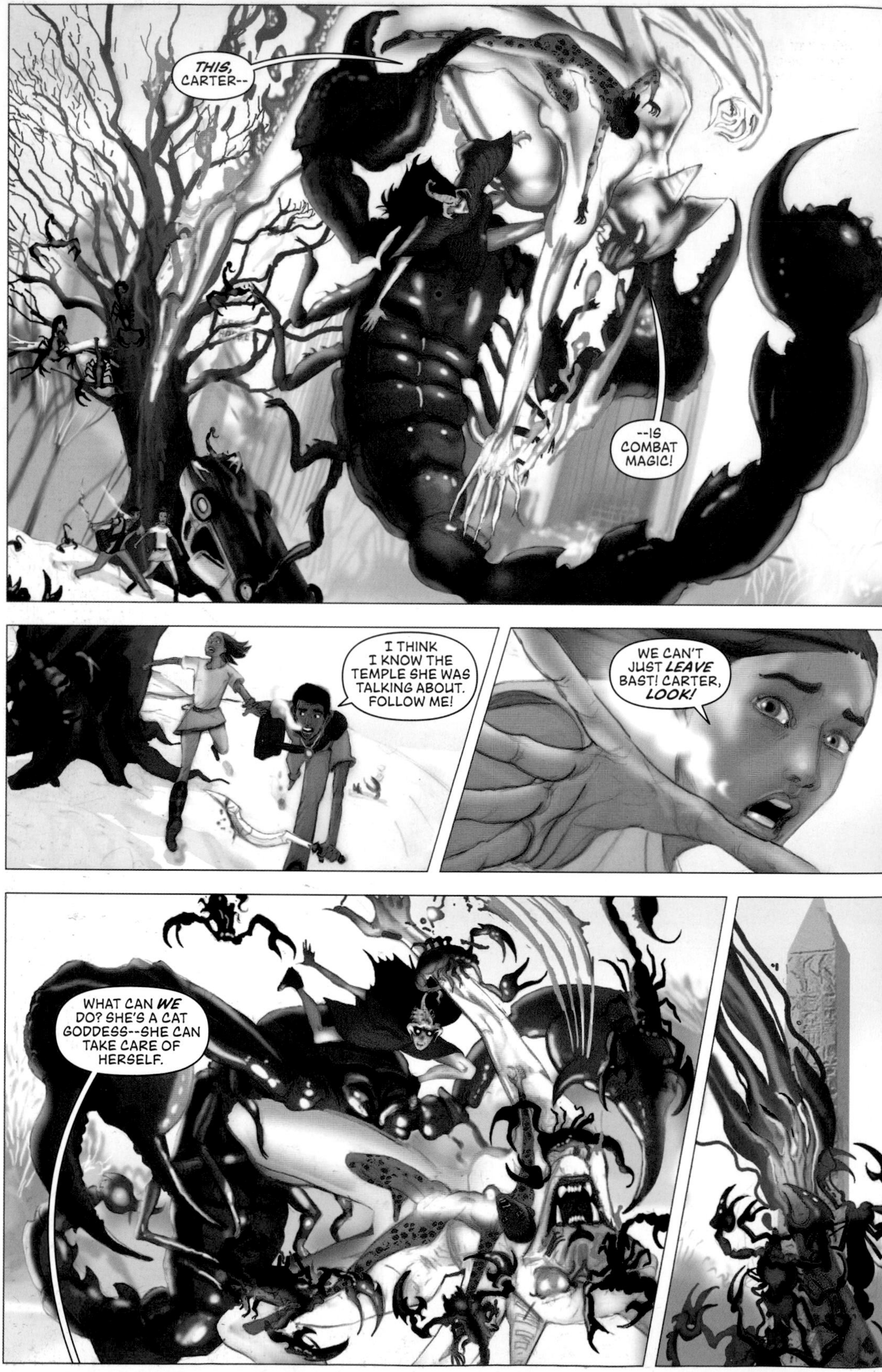
THIS, CARTER--
--IS COMBAT MAGIC!
I THINK I KNOW THE TEMPLE SHE WAS TALKING ABOUT. FOLLOW ME!
WE CAN'T JUST LEAVE BAST! CARTER, LOOK!
WHAT CAN WE DO? SHE'S A CAT GODDESS--SHE CAN TAKE CARE OF HERSELF.

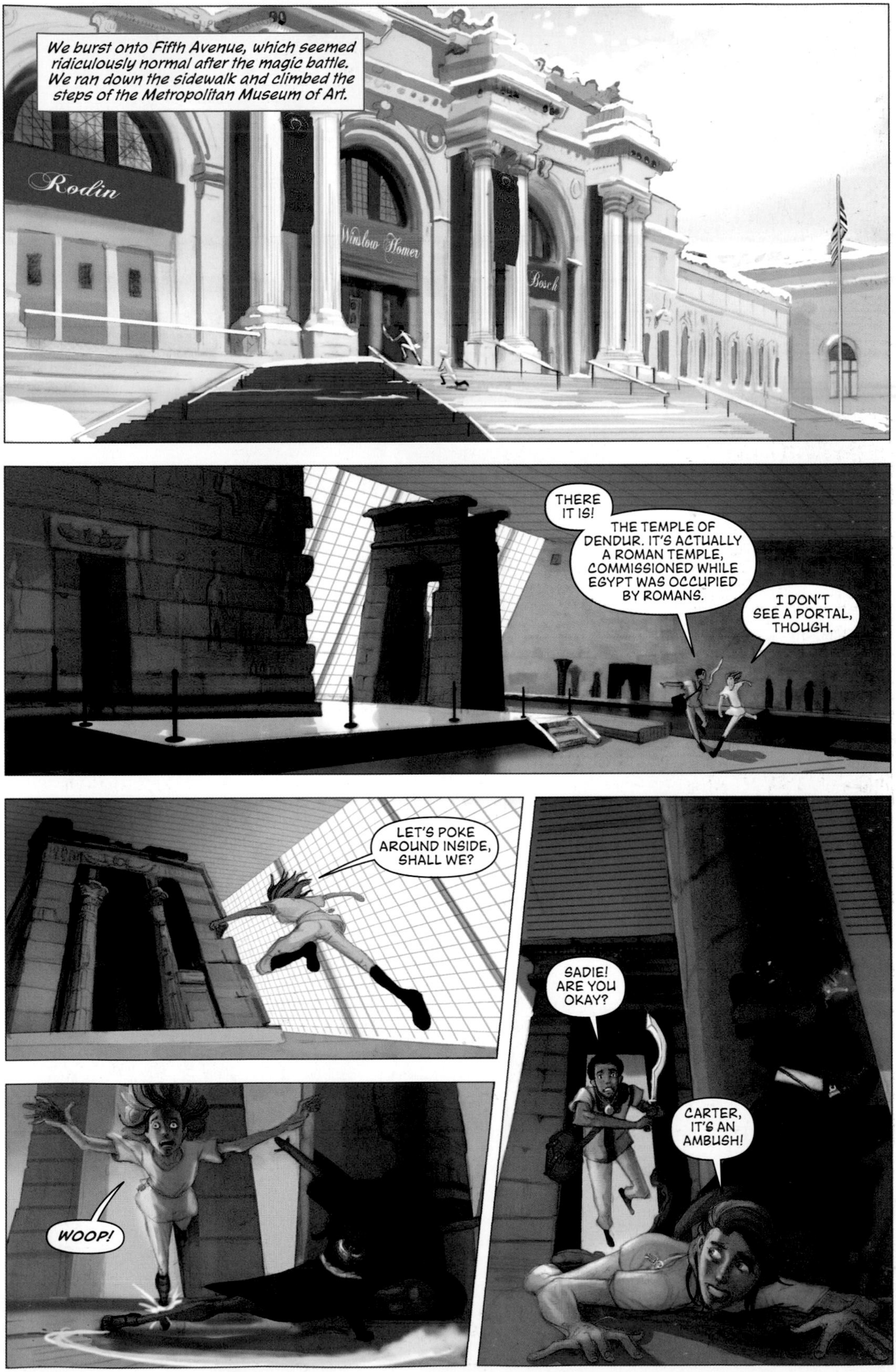
We burst onto Fifth Avenue, which seemed ridiculously normal after the magic battle. We ran down the sidewalk and climbed the steps of the Metropolitan Museum of Art.
Rodin
Winslow Homer
Bosch
THERE IT IS!
THE TEMPLE OF DENDUR. IT'S ACTUALLY A ROMAN TEMPLE, COMMISSIONED WHILE EGYPT WAS OCCUPIED BY ROMANS.
I DON'T SEE A PORTAL, THOUGH.
LET'S POKE AROUND INSIDE, SHALL WE?
WOOP!
SADIE! ARE YOU OKAY?
CARTER, IT'S AN AMBUSH!

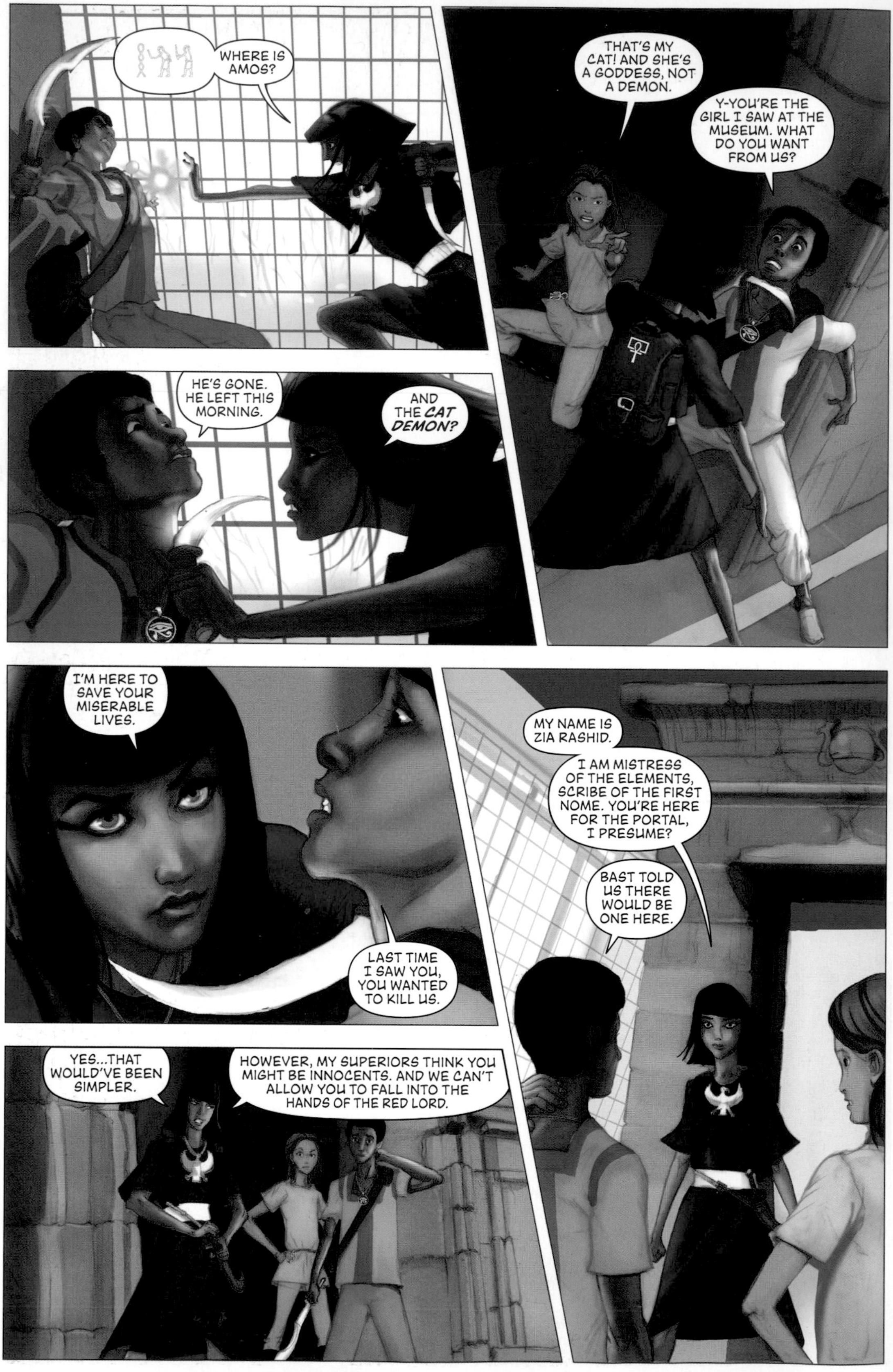

WHERE IS AMOS?
HE'S GONE. HE LEFT THIS MORNING.
AND THE *CAT DEMON?*
THAT'S MY CAT! AND SHE'S A GODDESS, NOT A DEMON.
Y-YOU'RE THE GIRL I SAW AT THE MUSEUM. WHAT DO YOU WANT FROM US?
I'M HERE TO SAVE YOUR MISERABLE LIVES.
LAST TIME I SAW YOU, YOU WANTED TO KILL US.
YES...THAT WOULD'VE BEEN SIMPLER.
HOWEVER, MY SUPERIORS THINK YOU MIGHT BE INNOCENTS. AND WE CAN'T ALLOW YOU TO FALL INTO THE HANDS OF THE RED LORD.
MY NAME IS ZIA RASHID.
I AM MISTRESS OF THE ELEMENTS, SCRIBE OF THE FIRST NOME. YOU'RE HERE FOR THE PORTAL, I PRESUME?
BAST TOLD US THERE WOULD BE ONE HERE.

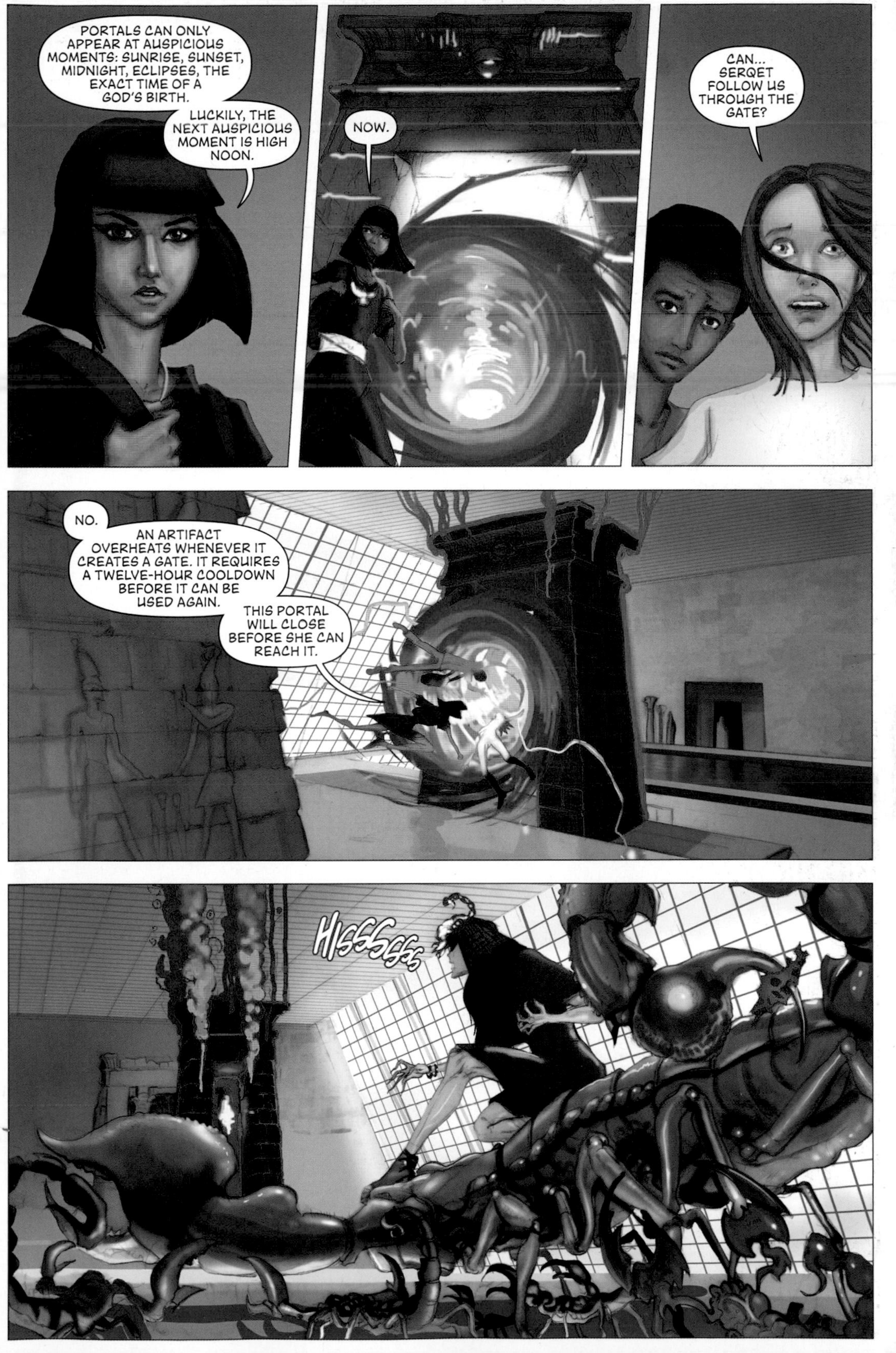
PORTALS CAN ONLY APPEAR AT AUSPICIOUS MOMENTS: SUNRISE, SUNSET, MIDNIGHT, ECLIPSES, THE EXACT TIME OF A GOD'S BIRTH.
LUCKILY, THE NEXT AUSPICIOUS MOMENT IS HIGH NOON.
NOW.
CAN... SERQET FOLLOW US THROUGH THE GATE?
NO.
AN ARTIFACT OVERHEATS WHENEVER IT CREATES A GATE. IT REQUIRES A TWELVE-HOUR COOLDOWN BEFORE IT CAN BE USED AGAIN.
THIS PORTAL WILL CLOSE BEFORE SHE CAN REACH IT.
HISSSsss

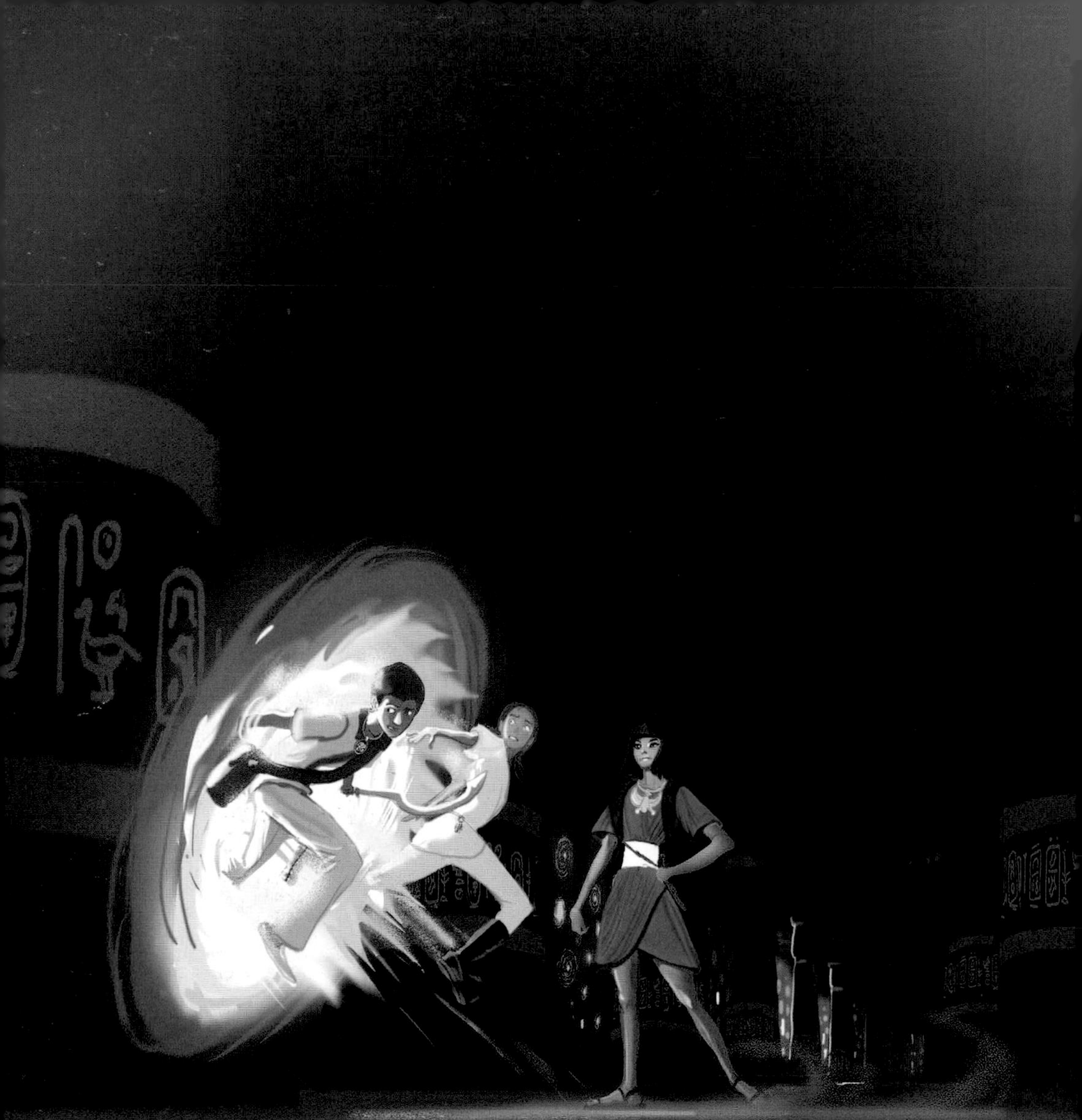

CHAPTER 3

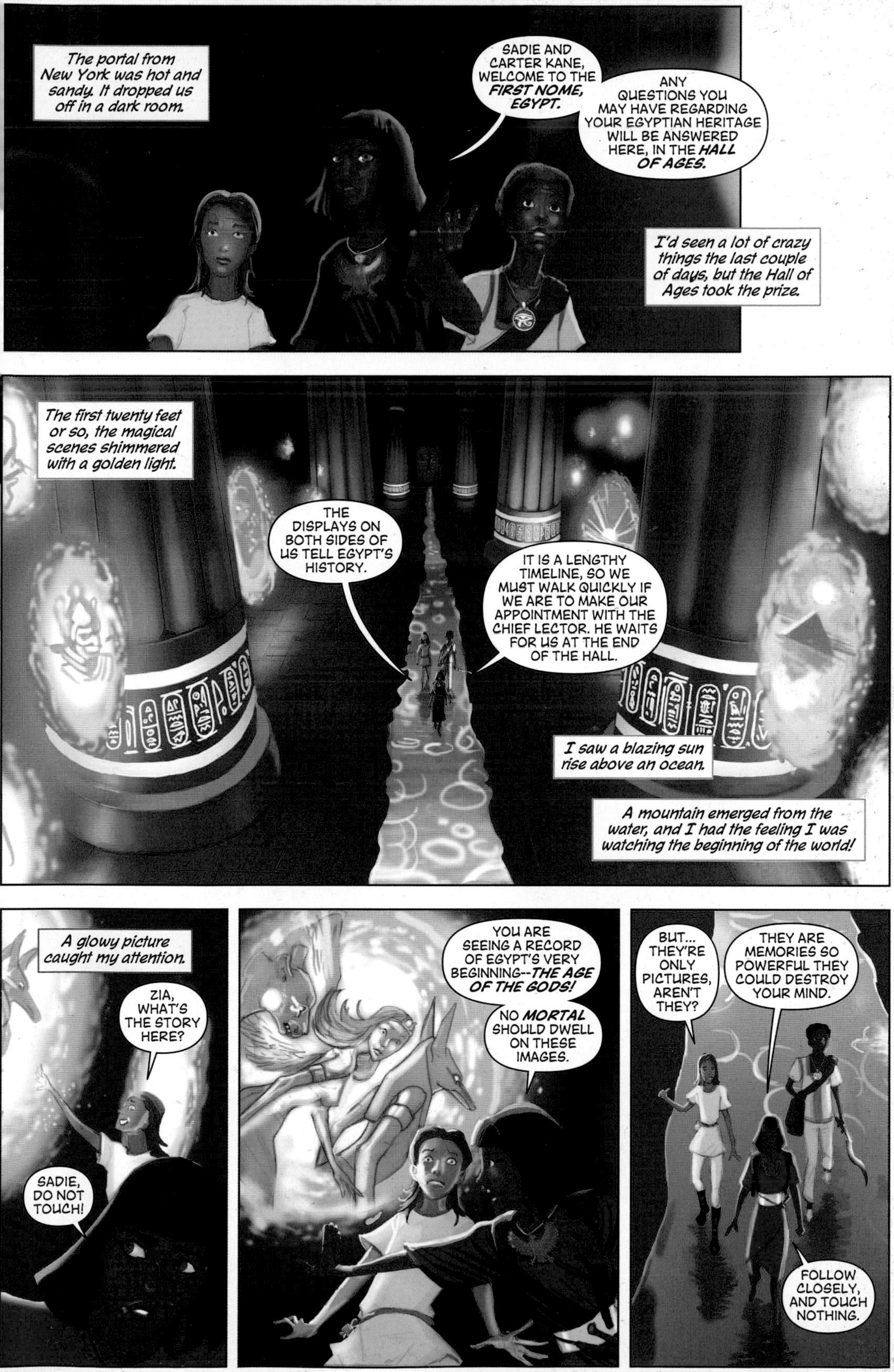

The portal from New York was hot and sandy. It dropped us off in a dark room.
SADIE AND CARTER KANE, WELCOME TO THE FIRST NOME, EGYPT.
ANY QUESTIONS YOU MAY HAVE REGARDING YOUR EGYPTIAN HERITAGE WILL BE ANSWERED HERE, IN THE HALL OF AGES.
I'd seen a lot of crazy things the last couple of days, but the Hall of Ages took the prize.
The first twenty feet or so, the magical scenes shimmered with a golden light.
THE DISPLAYS ON BOTH SIDES OF US TELL EGYPT'S HISTORY.
IT IS A LENGTHY TIMELINE, SO WE MUST WALK QUICKLY IF WE ARE TO MAKE OUR APPOINTMENT WITH THE CHIEF LECTOR. HE WAITS FOR US AT THE END OF THE HALL.
I saw a blazing sun rise above an ocean.
A mountain emerged from the water, and I had the feeling I was watching the beginning of the world!
A glowy picture caught my attention.
ZIA, WHAT'S THE STORY HERE?
SADIE, DO NOT TOUCH!
YOU ARE SEEING A RECORD OF EGYPT'S VERY BEGINNING--THE AGE OF THE GODS!
NO MORTAL SHOULD DWELL ON THESE IMAGES.
BUT... THEY'RE ONLY PICTURES, AREN'T THEY?
THEY ARE MEMORIES SO POWERFUL THEY COULD DESTROY YOUR MIND.
FOLLOW CLOSELY, AND TOUCH NOTHING.

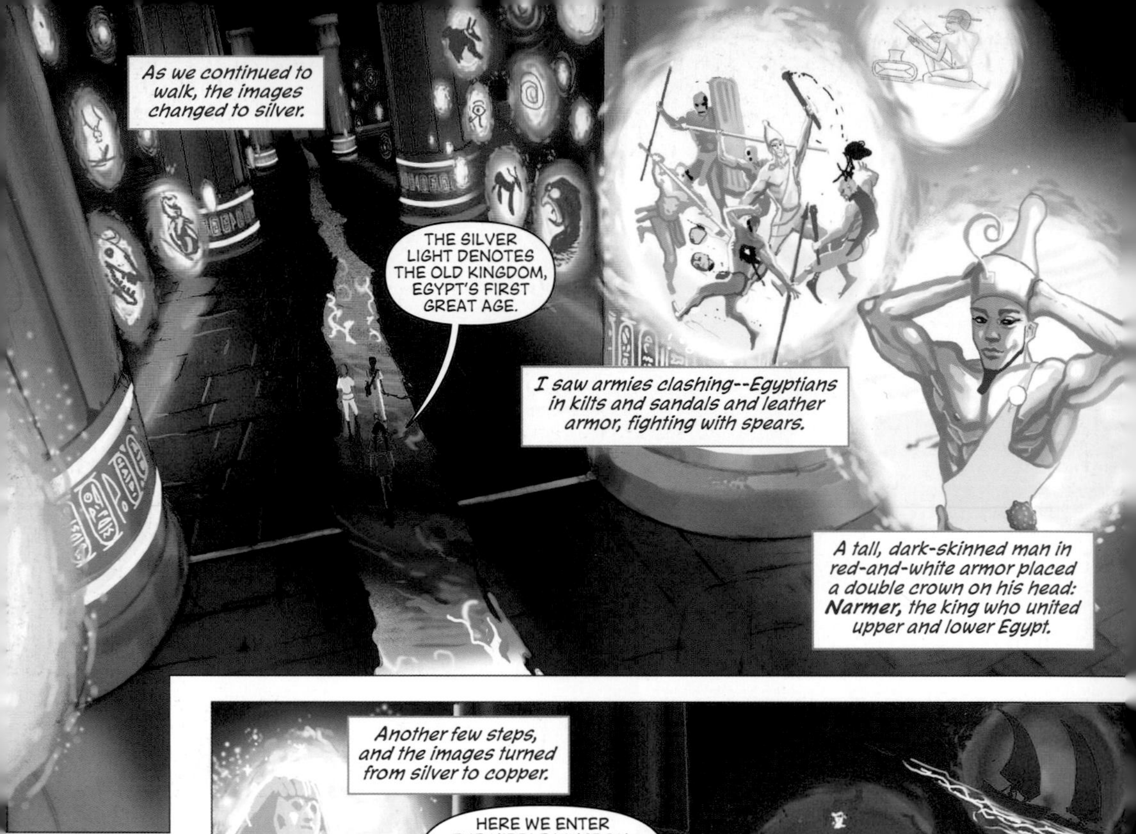
As we continued to walk, the images changed to silver.
THE SILVER LIGHT DENOTES THE OLD KINGDOM, EGYPT'S FIRST GREAT AGE.
I saw armies clashing--Egyptians in kilts and sandals and leather armor, fighting with spears.
A tall, dark-skinned man in red-and-white armor placed a double crown on his head: **Narmer,** the king who united upper and lower Egypt.

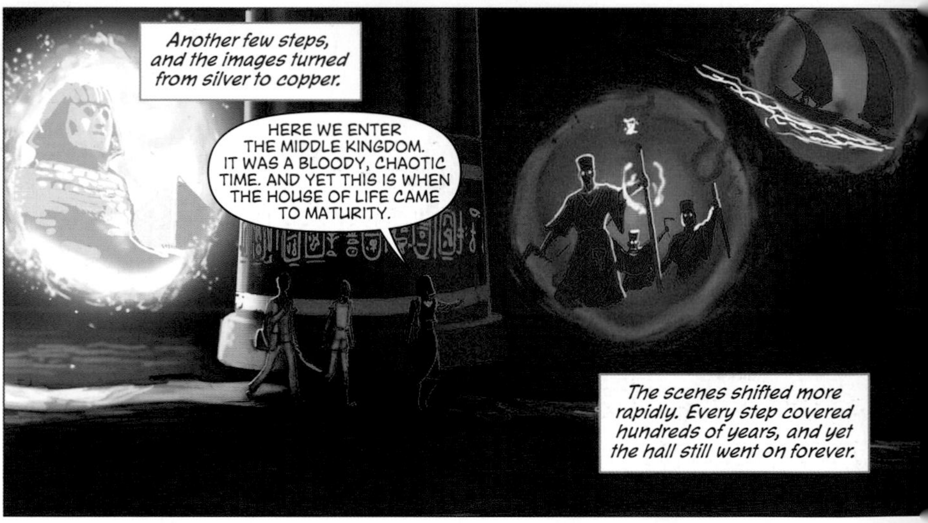
Another few steps, and the images turned from silver to copper.
HERE WE ENTER THE MIDDLE KINGDOM. IT WAS A BLOODY, CHAOTIC TIME. AND YET THIS IS WHEN THE HOUSE OF LIFE CAME TO MATURITY.
The scenes shifted more rapidly. Every step covered hundreds of years, and yet the hall still went on forever.

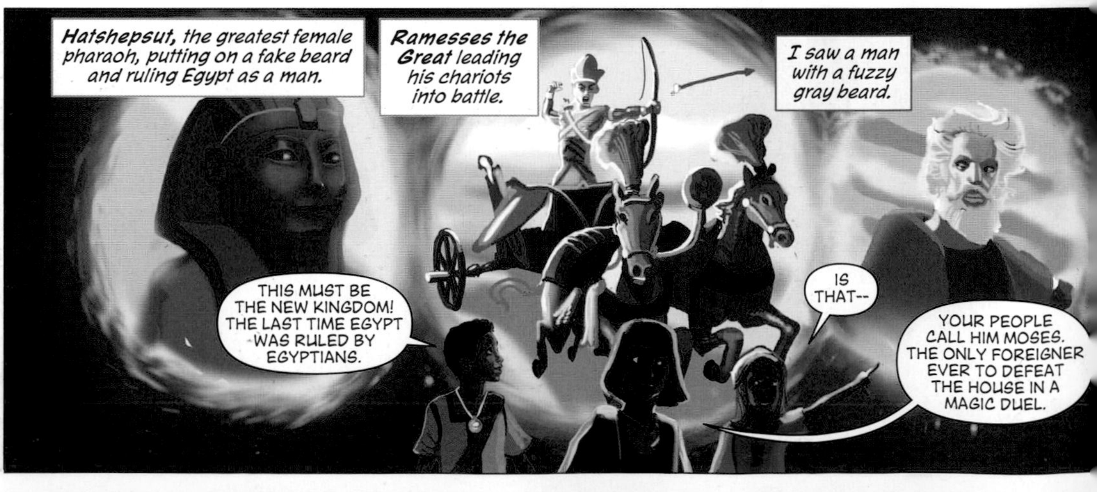
Hatshepsut, the greatest female pharaoh, putting on a fake beard and ruling Egypt as a man.
Ramesses the Great leading his chariots into battle.
I saw a man with a fuzzy gray beard.
THIS MUST BE THE NEW KINGDOM! THE LAST TIME EGYPT WAS RULED BY EGYPTIANS.
IS THAT--
YOUR PEOPLE CALL HIM MOSES. THE ONLY FOREIGNER EVER TO DEFEAT THE HOUSE IN A MAGIC DUEL.

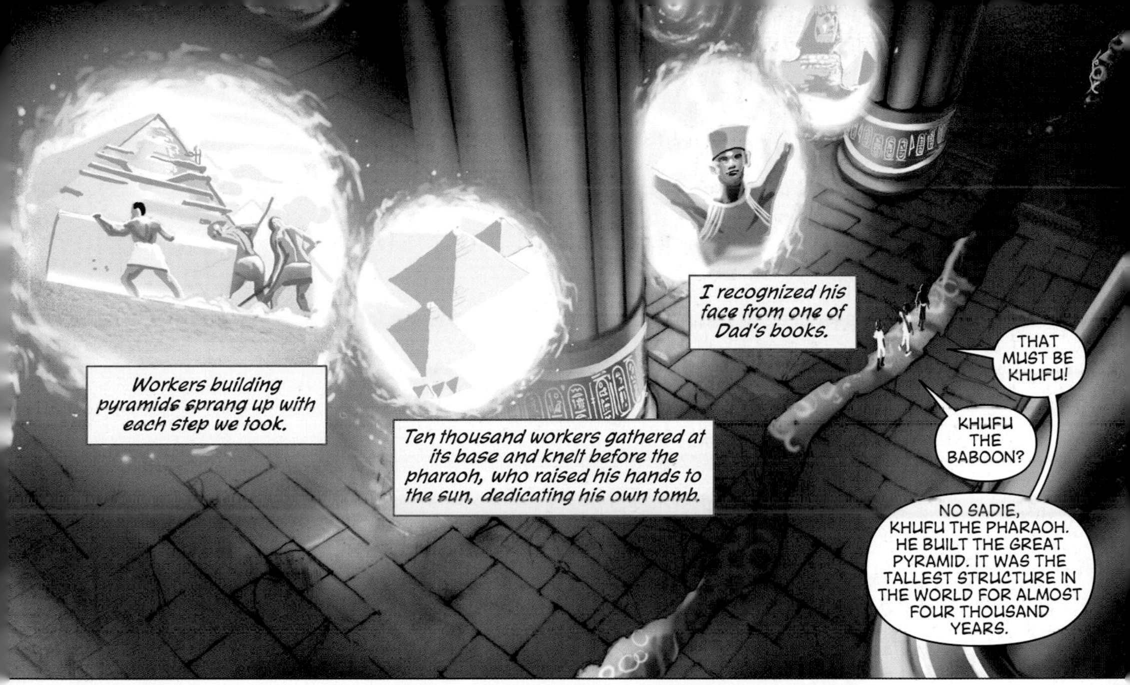
Workers building pyramids sprang up with each step we took.
Ten thousand workers gathered at its base and knelt before the pharaoh, who raised his hands to the sun, dedicating his own tomb.
I recognized his face from one of Dad's books.
THAT MUST BE KHUFU!
KHUFU THE BABOON?
NO SADIE, KHUFU THE PHARAOH. HE BUILT THE GREAT PYRAMID. IT WAS THE TALLEST STRUCTURE IN THE WORLD FOR ALMOST FOUR THOUSAND YEARS.

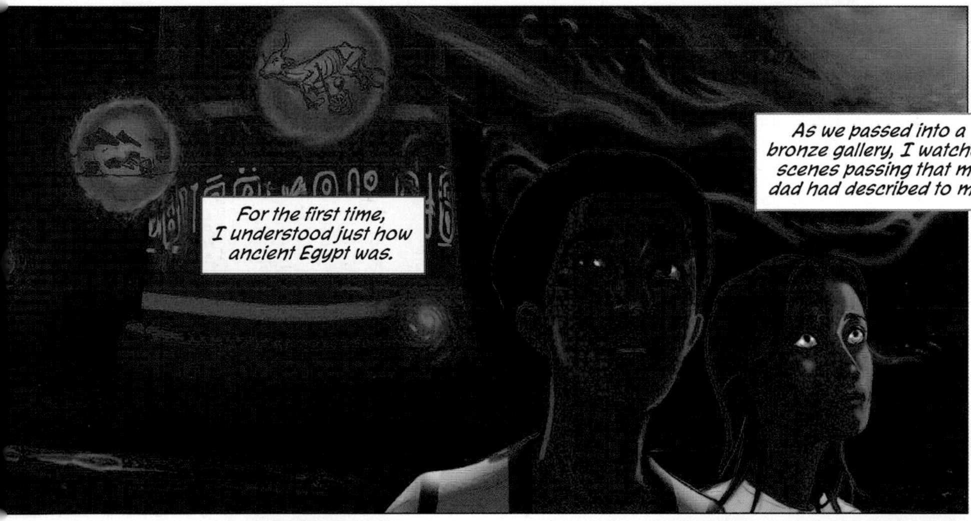
As we passed into a bronze gallery, I watched scenes passing that my dad had described to me.
For the first time, I understood just how ancient Egypt was.

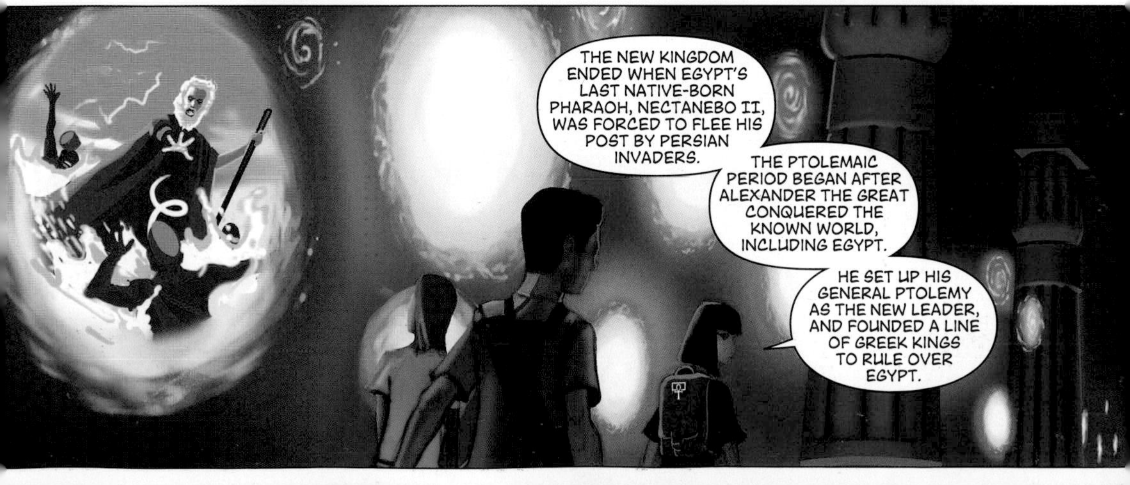
THE NEW KINGDOM ENDED WHEN EGYPT'S LAST NATIVE-BORN PHARAOH, NECTANEBO II, WAS FORCED TO FLEE HIS POST BY PERSIAN INVADERS.
THE PTOLEMAIC PERIOD BEGAN AFTER ALEXANDER THE GREAT CONQUERED THE KNOWN WORLD, INCLUDING EGYPT.
HE SET UP HIS GENERAL PTOLEMY AS THE NEW LEADER, AND FOUNDED A LINE OF GREEK KINGS TO RULE OVER EGYPT.

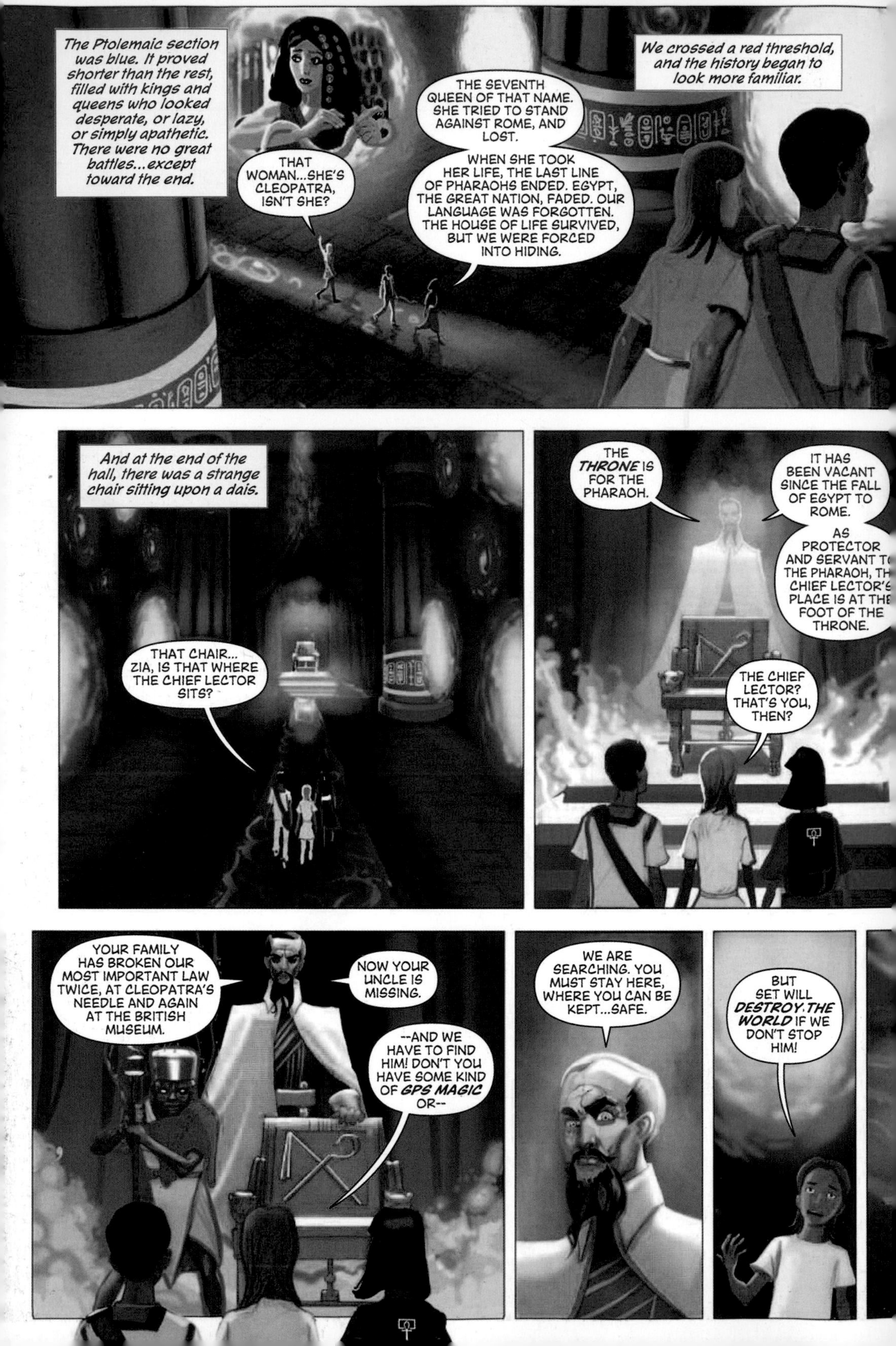
The Ptolemaic section was blue. It proved shorter than the rest, filled with kings and queens who looked desperate, or lazy, or simply apathetic. There were no great battles...except toward the end.
THAT WOMAN...SHE'S CLEOPATRA, ISN'T SHE?
THE SEVENTH QUEEN OF THAT NAME. SHE TRIED TO STAND AGAINST ROME, AND LOST.
WHEN SHE TOOK HER LIFE, THE LAST LINE OF PHARAOHS ENDED. EGYPT, THE GREAT NATION, FADED. OUR LANGUAGE WAS FORGOTTEN. THE HOUSE OF LIFE SURVIVED, BUT WE WERE FORCED INTO HIDING.
We crossed a red threshold, and the history began to look more familiar.
And at the end of the hall, there was a strange chair sitting upon a dais.
THAT CHAIR... ZIA, IS THAT WHERE THE CHIEF LECTOR SITS?
THE THRONE IS FOR THE PHARAOH.
IT HAS BEEN VACANT SINCE THE FALL OF EGYPT TO ROME.
AS PROTECTOR AND SERVANT TO THE PHARAOH, THE CHIEF LECTOR'S PLACE IS AT THE FOOT OF THE THRONE.
THE CHIEF LECTOR? THAT'S YOU, THEN?
YOUR FAMILY HAS BROKEN OUR MOST IMPORTANT LAW TWICE, AT CLEOPATRA'S NEEDLE AND AGAIN AT THE BRITISH MUSEUM.
NOW YOUR UNCLE IS MISSING.
--AND WE HAVE TO FIND HIM! DON'T YOU HAVE SOME KIND OF GPS MAGIC OR--
WE ARE SEARCHING. YOU MUST STAY HERE, WHERE YOU CAN BE KEPT...SAFE.
BUT SET WILL DESTROY THE WORLD IF WE DON'T STOP HIM!

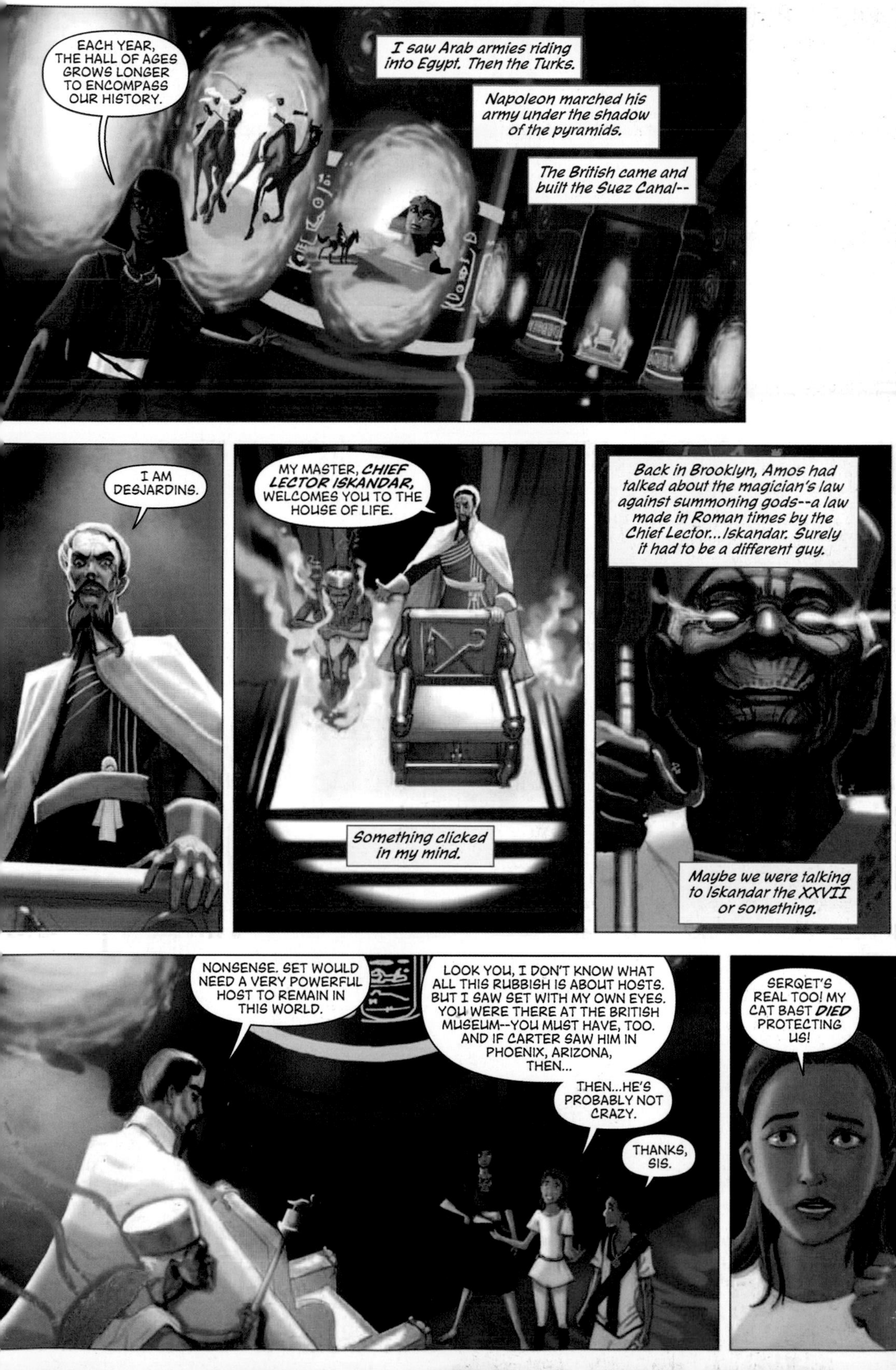
EACH YEAR, THE HALL OF AGES GROWS LONGER TO ENCOMPASS OUR HISTORY.
I saw Arab armies riding into Egypt. Then the Turks.
Napoleon marched his army under the shadow of the pyramids.
The British came and built the Suez Canal--
I AM DESJARDINS.
MY MASTER, CHIEF LECTOR ISKANDAR, WELCOMES YOU TO THE HOUSE OF LIFE.
Something clicked in my mind.
Back in Brooklyn, Amos had talked about the magician's law against summoning gods--a law made in Roman times by the Chief Lector... Iskandar. Surely it had to be a different guy.
Maybe we were talking to Iskandar the XXVII or something.
NONSENSE. SET WOULD NEED A VERY POWERFUL HOST TO REMAIN IN THIS WORLD.
LOOK YOU, I DON'T KNOW WHAT ALL THIS RUBBISH IS ABOUT HOSTS. BUT I SAW SET WITH MY OWN EYES. YOU WERE THERE AT THE BRITISH MUSEUM--YOU MUST HAVE, TOO. AND IF CARTER SAW HIM IN PHOENIX, ARIZONA, THEN...
THEN...HE'S PROBABLY NOT CRAZY.
THANKS, SIS.
SERQET'S REAL TOO! MY CAT BAST DIED PROTECTING US!

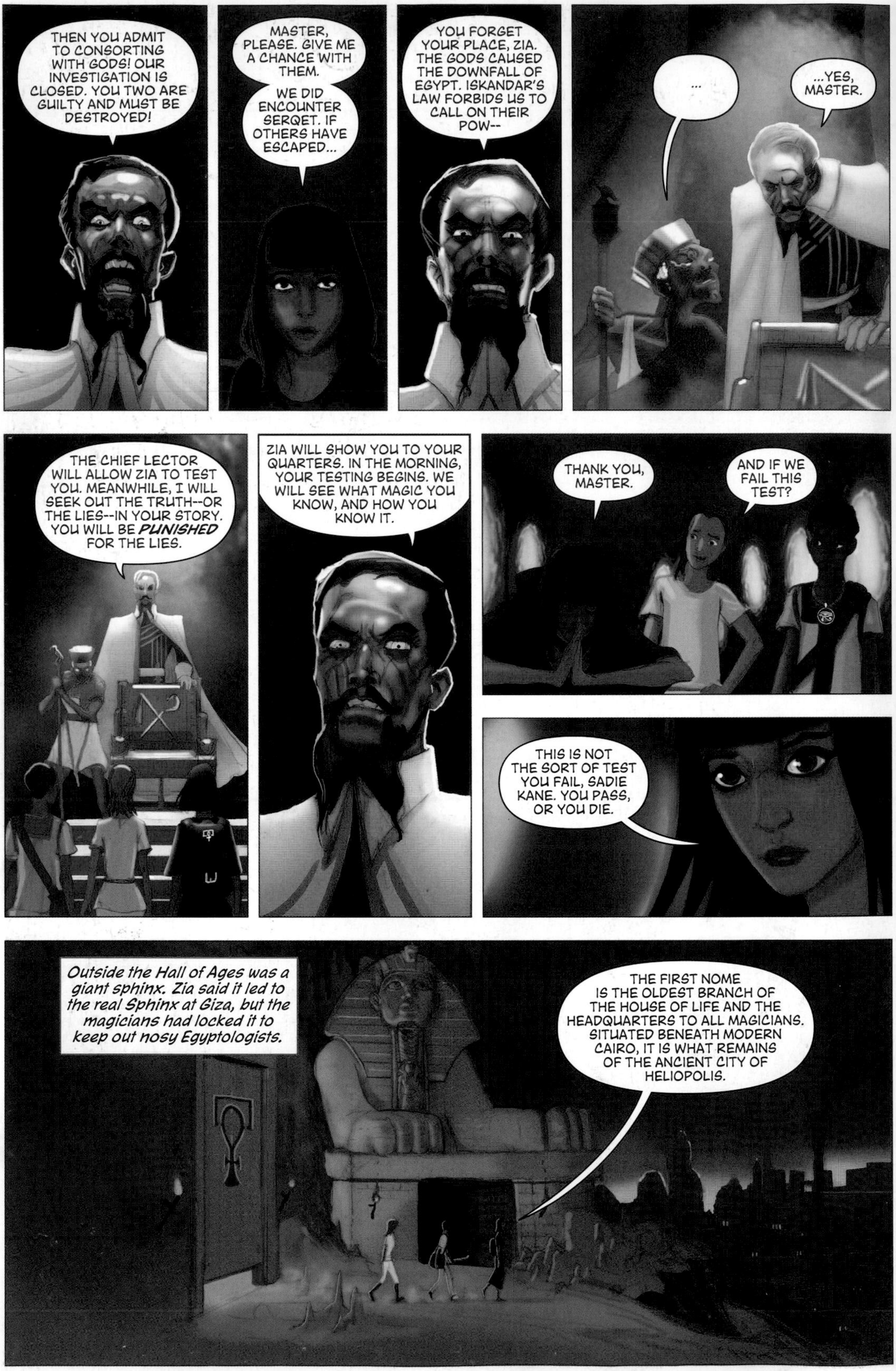
THEN YOU ADMIT TO CONSORTING WITH GODS! OUR INVESTIGATION IS CLOSED. YOU TWO ARE GUILTY AND MUST BE DESTROYED!
MASTER, PLEASE. GIVE ME A CHANCE WITH THEM.
WE DID ENCOUNTER SERQET. IF OTHERS HAVE ESCAPED...
YOU FORGET YOUR PLACE, ZIA. THE GODS CAUSED THE DOWNFALL OF EGYPT. ISKANDAR'S LAW FORBIDS US TO CALL ON THEIR POW--
...
...YES, MASTER.
THE CHIEF LECTOR WILL ALLOW ZIA TO TEST YOU. MEANWHILE, I WILL SEEK OUT THE TRUTH--OR THE LIES--IN YOUR STORY. YOU WILL BE ***PUNISHED*** FOR THE LIES.
ZIA WILL SHOW YOU TO YOUR QUARTERS. IN THE MORNING, YOUR TESTING BEGINS. WE WILL SEE WHAT MAGIC YOU KNOW, AND HOW YOU KNOW IT.
THANK YOU, MASTER.
AND IF WE FAIL THIS TEST?
THIS IS NOT THE SORT OF TEST YOU FAIL, SADIE KANE. YOU PASS, OR YOU DIE.
Outside the Hall of Ages was a giant sphinx. Zia said it led to the real Sphinx at Giza, but the magicians had locked it to keep out nosy Egyptologists.
THE FIRST NOME IS THE OLDEST BRANCH OF THE HOUSE OF LIFE AND THE HEADQUARTERS TO ALL MAGICIANS. SITUATED BENEATH MODERN CAIRO, IT IS WHAT REMAINS OF THE ANCIENT CITY OF HELIOPOLIS.

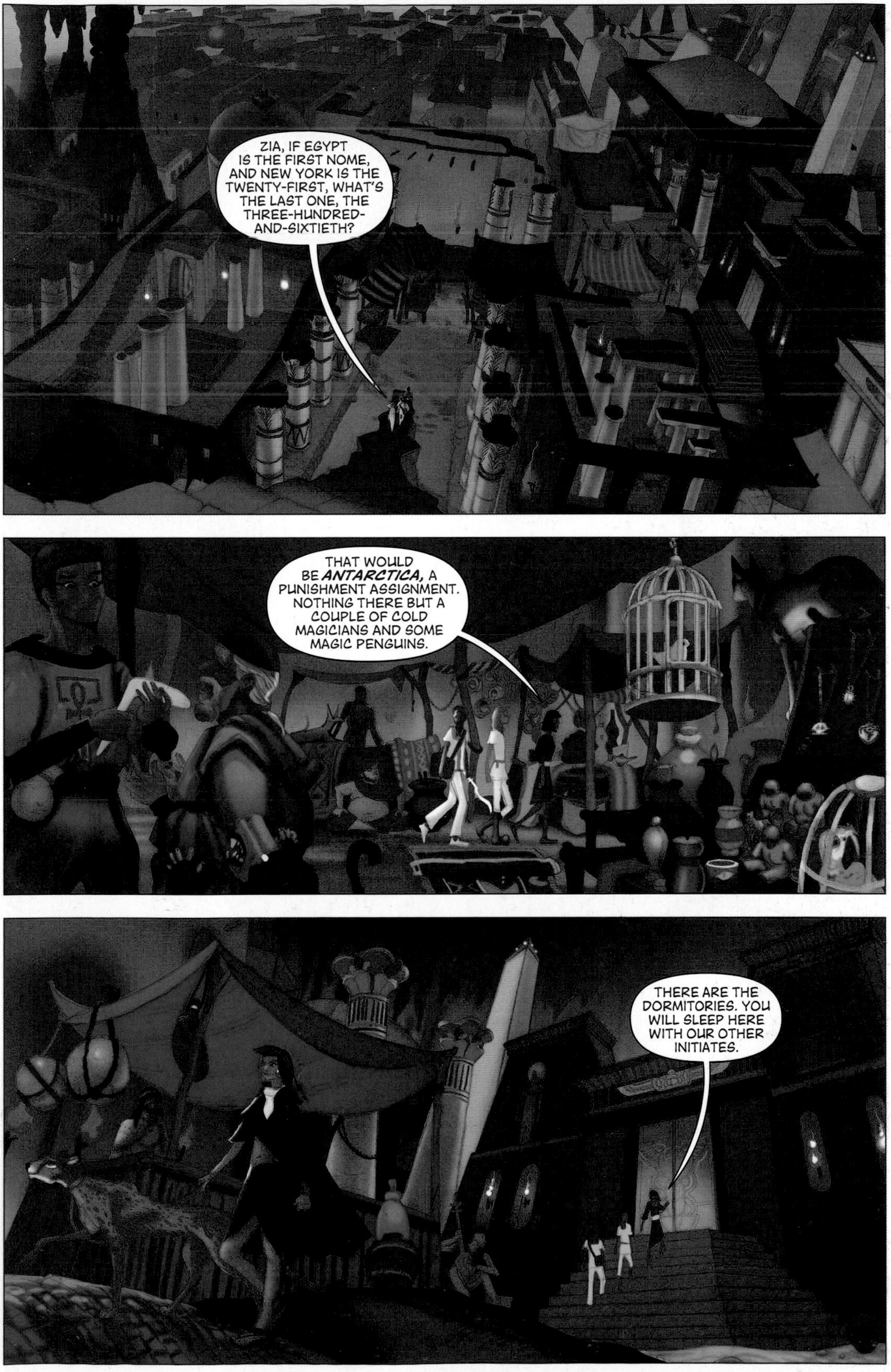
ZIA, IF EGYPT IS THE FIRST NOME, AND NEW YORK IS THE TWENTY-FIRST, WHAT'S THE LAST ONE, THE THREE-HUNDRED-AND-SIXTIETH?
THAT WOULD BE *ANTARCTICA,* A PUNISHMENT ASSIGNMENT. NOTHING THERE BUT A COUPLE OF COLD MAGICIANS AND SOME MAGIC PENGUINS.
THERE ARE THE DORMITORIES. YOU WILL SLEEP HERE WITH OUR OTHER INITIATES.

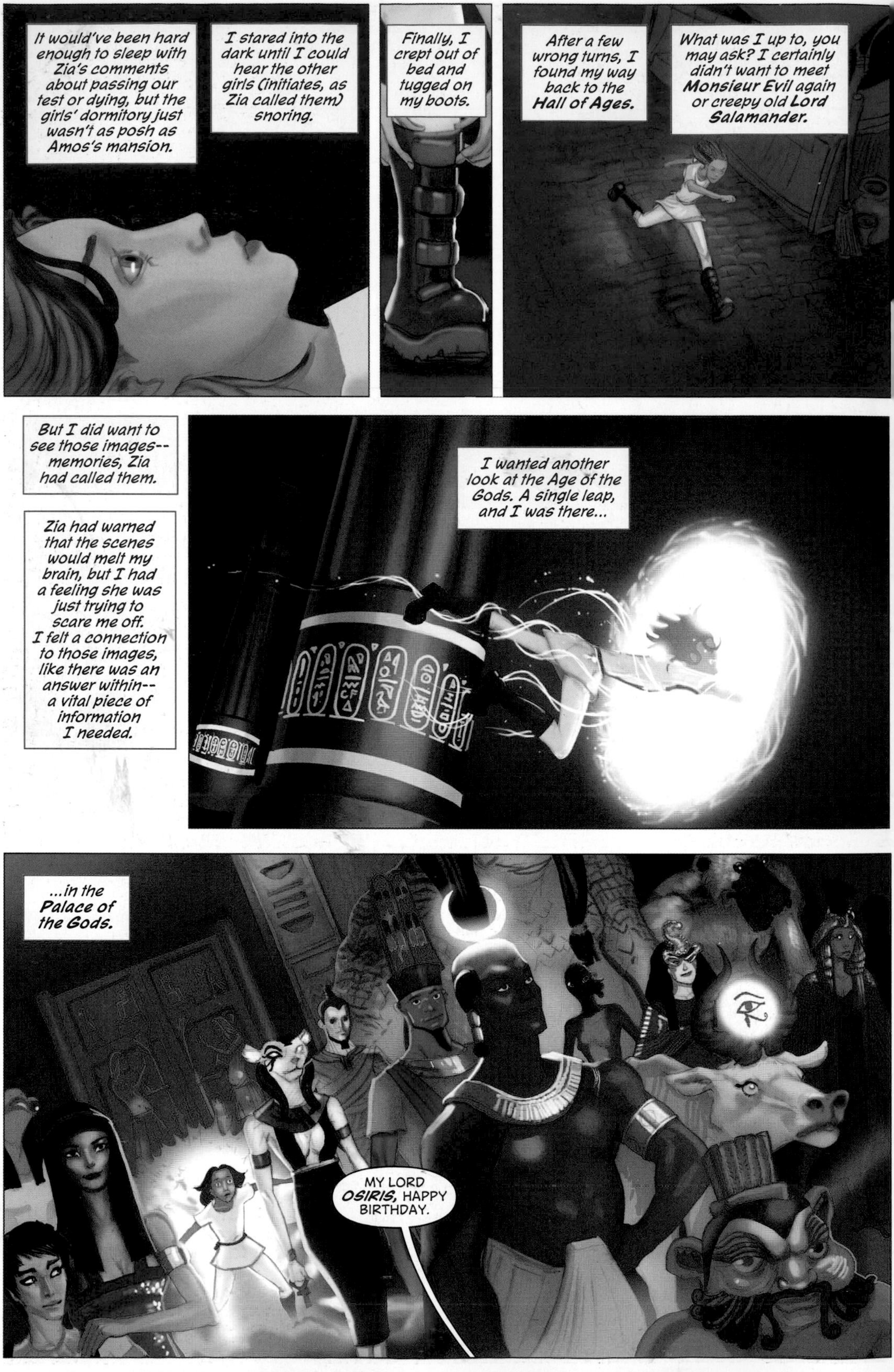
It would've been hard enough to sleep with Zia's comments about passing our test or dying, but the girls' dormitory just wasn't as posh as Amos's mansion.
I stared into the dark until I could hear the other girls (initiates, as Zia called them) snoring.
Finally, I crept out of bed and tugged on my boots.
After a few wrong turns, I found my way back to the Hall of Ages.
What was I up to, you may ask? I certainly didn't want to meet Monsieur Evil again or creepy old Lord Salamander.
But I did want to see those images--memories, Zia had called them.
Zia had warned that the scenes would melt my brain, but I had a feeling she was just trying to scare me off. I felt a connection to those images, like there was an answer within--a vital piece of information I needed.
I wanted another look at the Age of the Gods. A single leap, and I was there...
...in the Palace of the Gods.
MY LORD OSIRIS, HAPPY BIRTHDAY.

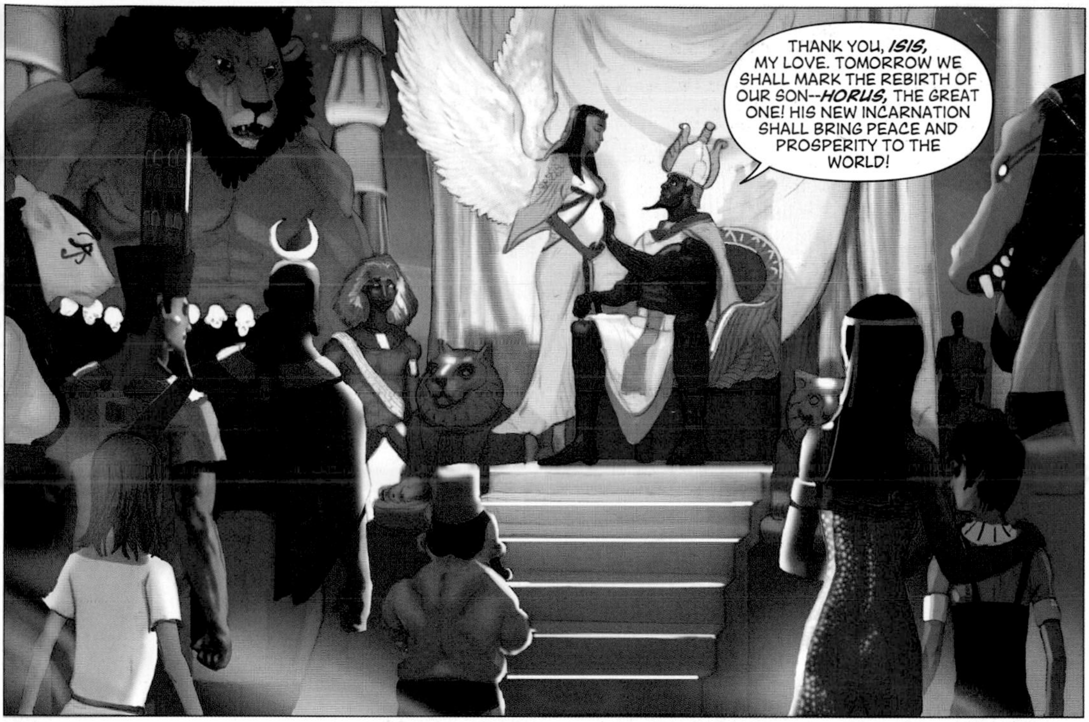
THANK YOU, *ISIS,* MY LOVE. TOMORROW WE SHALL MARK THE REBIRTH OF OUR SON--*HORUS,* THE GREAT ONE! HIS NEW INCARNATION SHALL BRING PEACE AND PROSPERITY TO THE WORLD!

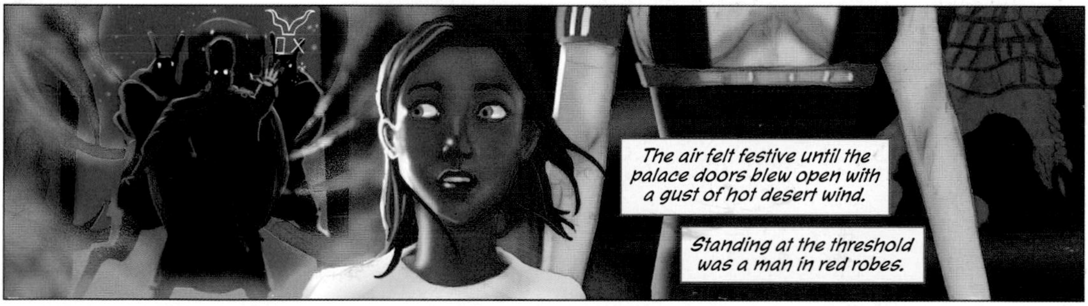
The air felt festive until the palace doors blew open with a gust of hot desert wind.
Standing at the threshold was a man in red robes.

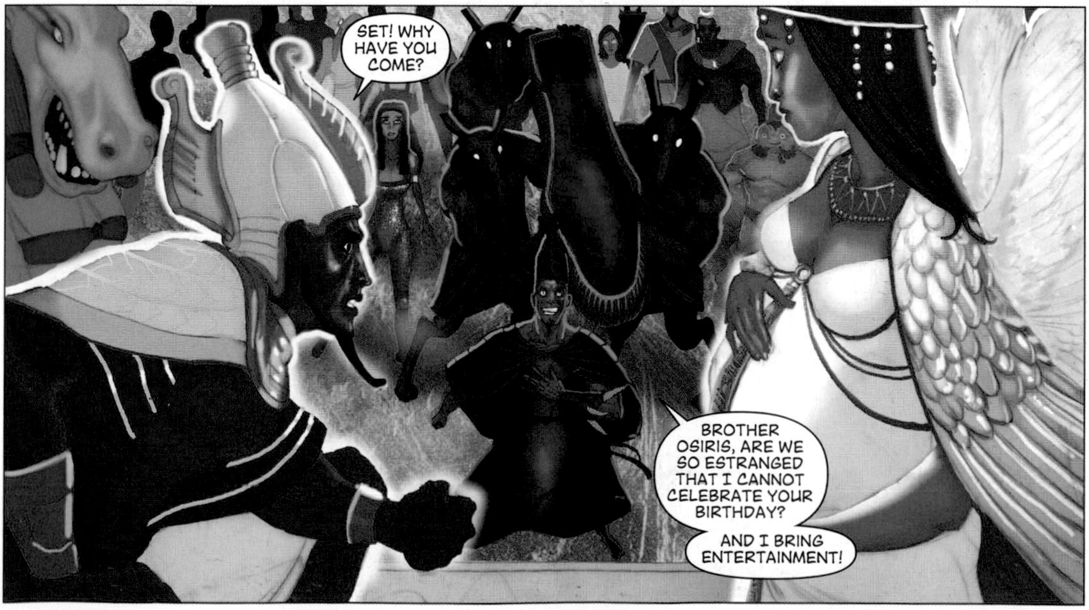
SET! WHY HAVE YOU COME?
BROTHER OSIRIS, ARE WE SO ESTRANGED THAT I CANNOT CELEBRATE YOUR BIRTHDAY?
AND I BRING ENTERTAINMENT!

THIS SLEEPING CASKET WAS MADE BY MY BEST CRAFTSMEN. THE GOD WHO LIES WITHIN, EVEN FOR A NIGHT, WILL SEE HIS POWERS INCREASE TENFOLD! IT IS A GIFT--

--FOR THE ONE AND ONLY GOD WHO FITS WITHIN IT PERFECTLY!

OSIRIS, MY BROTHER, WOULD YOU TO TRY IT FIRST?

MY LORD, DO NOT. SET DOES NOT BRING PRESENTS.

IT IS ONLY A GAME.

My heart began to race. It was the same box Set had used to imprison my dad at the British Museum.

No! I wanted to scream. Don't trust him!

VILLAIN!

TODAY, I AM *KING*, LOVELY ISIS!

But Osiris lay down, and the coffin fit him exactly. A cheer went up from the gods.

IT IS A PERFECT FIT!

ALL HAIL OSIRIS!

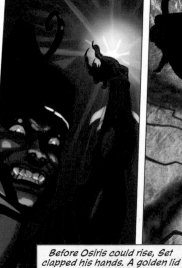

Before Osiris could rise, Set clapped his hands. A golden lid materialized above the box and slammed down on top of it.

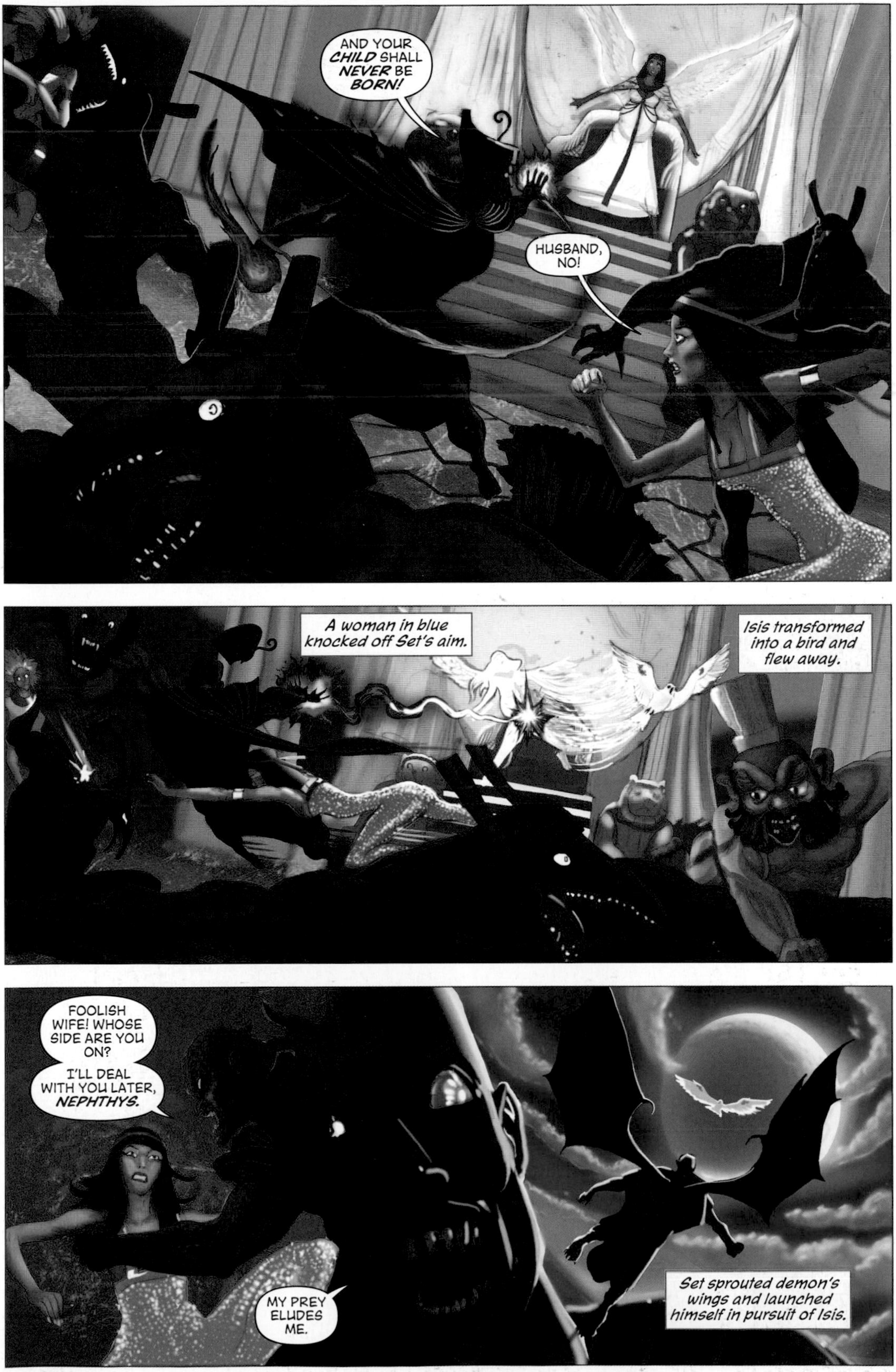
AND YOUR CHILD SHALL NEVER BE BORN!
HUSBAND, NO!
A woman in blue knocked off Set's aim.
Isis transformed into a bird and flew away.
FOOLISH WIFE! WHOSE SIDE ARE YOU ON?
I'LL DEAL WITH YOU LATER, NEPHTHYS.
MY PREY ELUDES ME.
Set sprouted demon's wings and launched himself in pursuit of Isis.

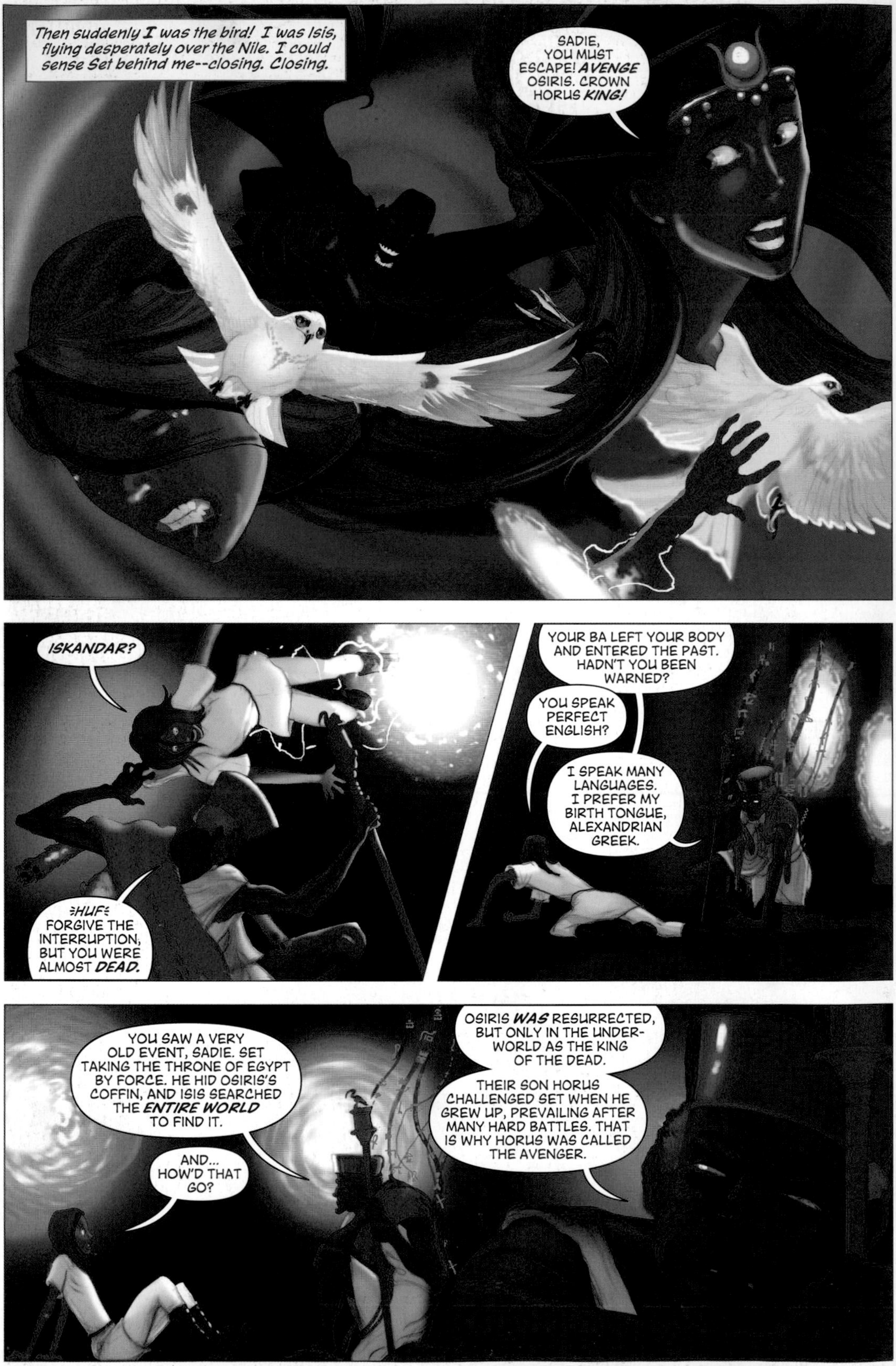
Then suddenly I was the bird! I was Isis, flying desperately over the Nile. I could sense Set behind me--closing. Closing.
SADIE, YOU MUST ESCAPE! AVENGE OSIRIS. CROWN HORUS KING!
ISKANDAR?
HUF FORGIVE THE INTERRUPTION, BUT YOU WERE ALMOST DEAD.
YOUR BA LEFT YOUR BODY AND ENTERED THE PAST. HADN'T YOU BEEN WARNED?
YOU SPEAK PERFECT ENGLISH?
I SPEAK MANY LANGUAGES. I PREFER MY BIRTH TONGUE, ALEXANDRIAN GREEK.
YOU SAW A VERY OLD EVENT, SADIE. SET TAKING THE THRONE OF EGYPT BY FORCE. HE HID OSIRIS'S COFFIN, AND ISIS SEARCHED THE ENTIRE WORLD TO FIND IT.
AND... HOW'D THAT GO?
OSIRIS WAS RESURRECTED, BUT ONLY IN THE UNDER-WORLD AS THE KING OF THE DEAD.
THEIR SON HORUS CHALLENGED SET WHEN HE GREW UP, PREVAILING AFTER MANY HARD BATTLES. THAT IS WHY HORUS WAS CALLED THE AVENGER.

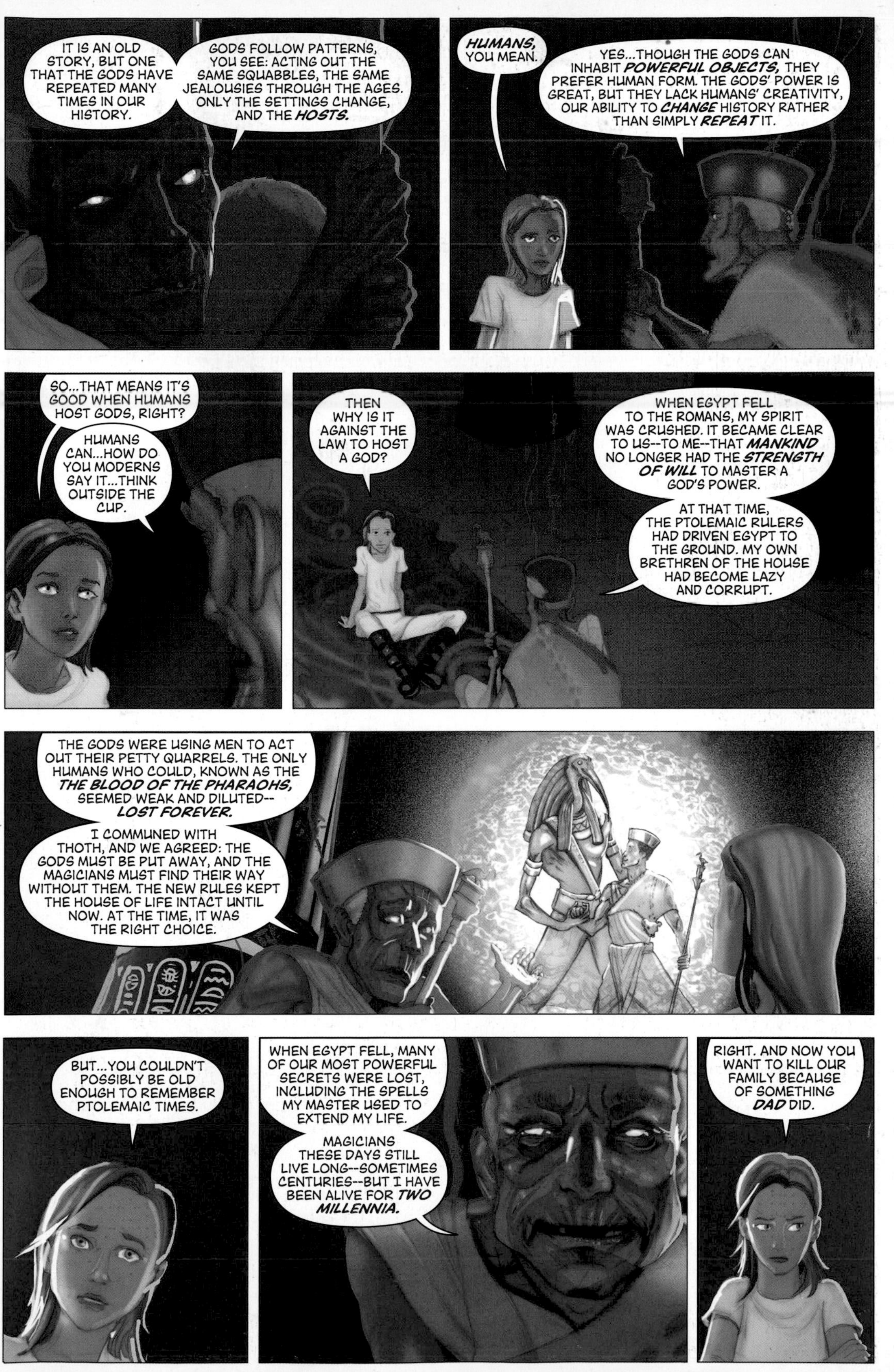
IT IS AN OLD STORY, BUT ONE THAT THE GODS HAVE REPEATED MANY TIMES IN OUR HISTORY.
GODS FOLLOW PATTERNS, YOU SEE: ACTING OUT THE SAME SQUABBLES, THE SAME JEALOUSIES THROUGH THE AGES. ONLY THE SETTINGS CHANGE, AND THE HOSTS.
HUMANS, YOU MEAN.
YES...THOUGH THE GODS CAN INHABIT POWERFUL OBJECTS, THEY PREFER HUMAN FORM. THE GODS' POWER IS GREAT, BUT THEY LACK HUMANS' CREATIVITY, OUR ABILITY TO CHANGE HISTORY RATHER THAN SIMPLY REPEAT IT.
SO...THAT MEANS IT'S GOOD WHEN HUMANS HOST GODS, RIGHT?
HUMANS CAN...HOW DO YOU MODERNS SAY IT...THINK OUTSIDE THE CUP.
THEN WHY IS IT AGAINST THE LAW TO HOST A GOD?
WHEN EGYPT FELL TO THE ROMANS, MY SPIRIT WAS CRUSHED. IT BECAME CLEAR TO US--TO ME--THAT MANKIND NO LONGER HAD THE STRENGTH OF WILL TO MASTER A GOD'S POWER.
AT THAT TIME, THE PTOLEMAIC RULERS HAD DRIVEN EGYPT TO THE GROUND. MY OWN BRETHREN OF THE HOUSE HAD BECOME LAZY AND CORRUPT.
THE GODS WERE USING MEN TO ACT OUT THEIR PETTY QUARRELS. THE ONLY HUMANS WHO COULD, KNOWN AS THE THE BLOOD OF THE PHARAOHS, SEEMED WEAK AND DILUTED-- LOST FOREVER.
I COMMUNED WITH THOTH, AND WE AGREED: THE GODS MUST BE PUT AWAY, AND THE MAGICIANS MUST FIND THEIR WAY WITHOUT THEM. THE NEW RULES KEPT THE HOUSE OF LIFE INTACT UNTIL NOW. AT THE TIME, IT WAS THE RIGHT CHOICE.
BUT...YOU COULDN'T POSSIBLY BE OLD ENOUGH TO REMEMBER PTOLEMAIC TIMES.
WHEN EGYPT FELL, MANY OF OUR MOST POWERFUL SECRETS WERE LOST, INCLUDING THE SPELLS MY MASTER USED TO EXTEND MY LIFE.
MAGICIANS THESE DAYS STILL LIVE LONG--SOMETIMES CENTURIES--BUT I HAVE BEEN ALIVE FOR TWO MILLENNIA.
RIGHT. AND NOW YOU WANT TO KILL OUR FAMILY BECAUSE OF SOMETHING DAD DID.

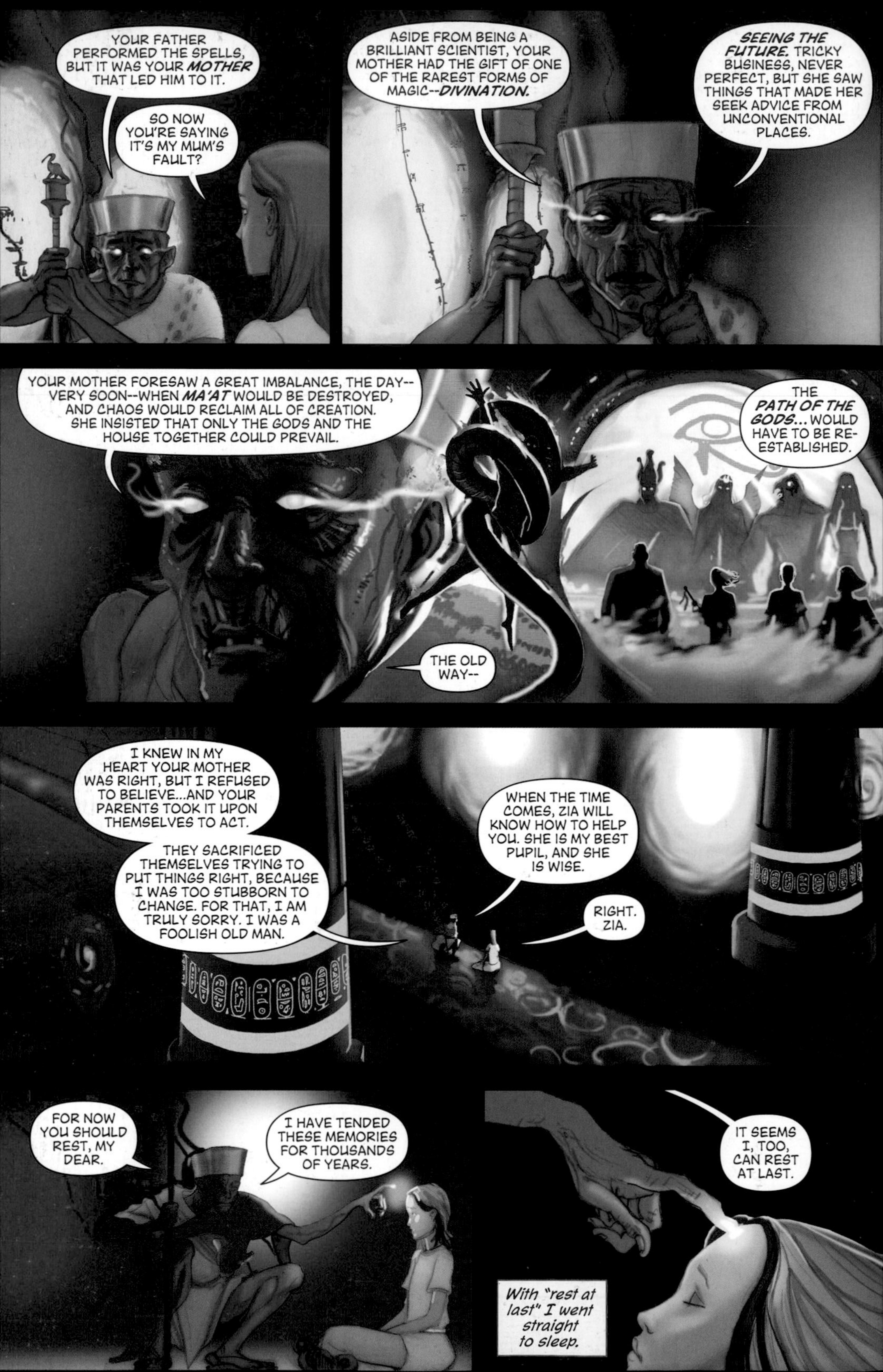
YOUR FATHER PERFORMED THE SPELLS, BUT IT WAS YOUR MOTHER THAT LED HIM TO IT.
SO NOW YOU'RE SAYING IT'S MY MUM'S FAULT?
ASIDE FROM BEING A BRILLIANT SCIENTIST, YOUR MOTHER HAD THE GIFT OF ONE OF THE RAREST FORMS OF MAGIC--DIVINATION.
SEEING THE FUTURE. TRICKY BUSINESS, NEVER PERFECT, BUT SHE SAW THINGS THAT MADE HER SEEK ADVICE FROM UNCONVENTIONAL PLACES.
YOUR MOTHER FORESAW A GREAT IMBALANCE, THE DAY--VERY SOON--WHEN MA'AT WOULD BE DESTROYED, AND CHAOS WOULD RECLAIM ALL OF CREATION. SHE INSISTED THAT ONLY THE GODS AND THE HOUSE TOGETHER COULD PREVAIL.
THE OLD WAY--
THE PATH OF THE GODS... WOULD HAVE TO BE RE-ESTABLISHED.
I KNEW IN MY HEART YOUR MOTHER WAS RIGHT, BUT I REFUSED TO BELIEVE...AND YOUR PARENTS TOOK IT UPON THEMSELVES TO ACT.
THEY SACRIFICED THEMSELVES TRYING TO PUT THINGS RIGHT, BECAUSE I WAS TOO STUBBORN TO CHANGE. FOR THAT, I AM TRULY SORRY. I WAS A FOOLISH OLD MAN.
WHEN THE TIME COMES, ZIA WILL KNOW HOW TO HELP YOU. SHE IS MY BEST PUPIL, AND SHE IS WISE.
RIGHT. ZIA.
FOR NOW YOU SHOULD REST, MY DEAR.
I HAVE TENDED THESE MEMORIES FOR THOUSANDS OF YEARS.
IT SEEMS I, TOO, CAN REST AT LAST.
With "rest at last" I went straight to sleep.

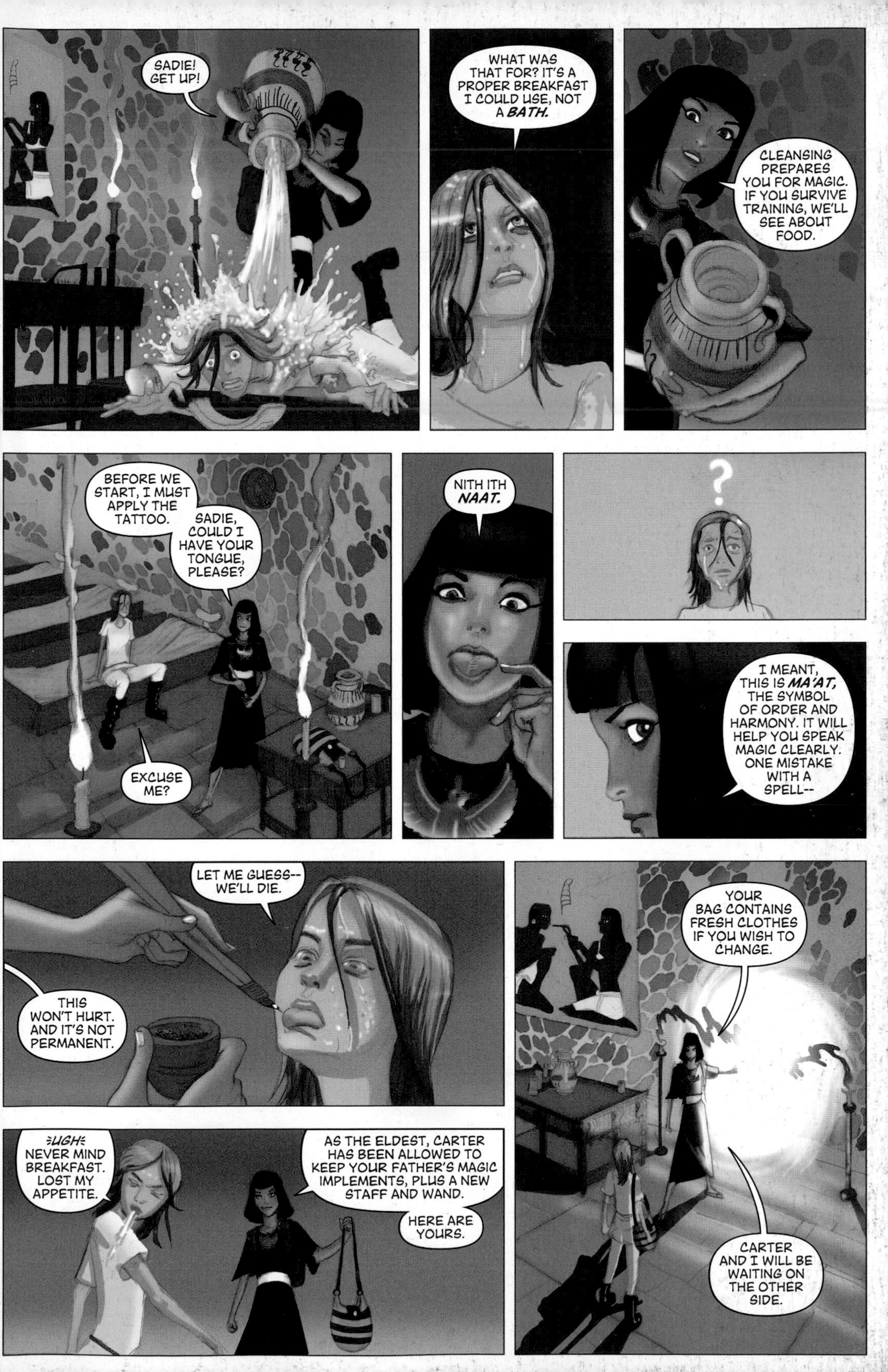
SADIE! GET UP!
WHAT WAS THAT FOR? IT'S A PROPER BREAKFAST I COULD USE, NOT A *BATH.*
CLEANSING PREPARES YOU FOR MAGIC. IF YOU SURVIVE TRAINING, WE'LL SEE ABOUT FOOD.
BEFORE WE START, I MUST APPLY THE TATTOO.
SADIE, COULD I HAVE YOUR TONGUE, PLEASE?
EXCUSE ME?
NITH ITH *NAAT.*
?
I MEANT, THIS IS *MA'AT,* THE SYMBOL OF ORDER AND HARMONY. IT WILL HELP YOU SPEAK MAGIC CLEARLY. ONE MISTAKE WITH A SPELL--
LET ME GUESS-- WE'LL DIE.
THIS WON'T HURT. AND IT'S NOT PERMANENT.
UGH
NEVER MIND BREAKFAST. LOST MY APPETITE.
AS THE ELDEST, CARTER HAS BEEN ALLOWED TO KEEP YOUR FATHER'S MAGIC IMPLEMENTS, PLUS A NEW STAFF AND WAND.
HERE ARE YOURS.
YOUR BAG CONTAINS FRESH CLOTHES IF YOU WISH TO CHANGE.
CARTER AND I WILL BE WAITING ON THE OTHER SIDE.

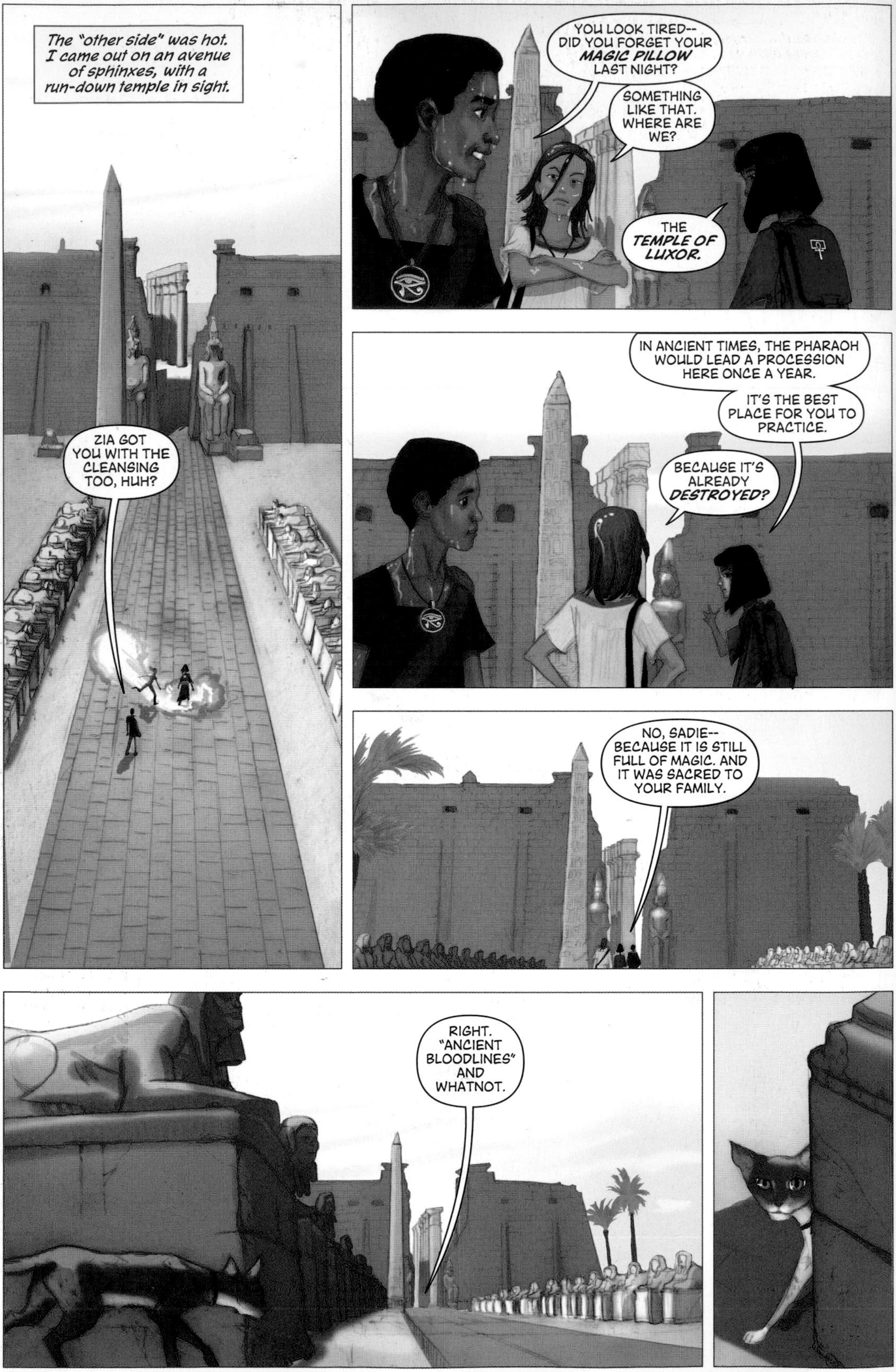

The "other side" was hot. I came out on an avenue of sphinxes, with a run-down temple in sight.
ZIA GOT YOU WITH THE CLEANSING TOO, HUH?
YOU LOOK TIRED-- DID YOU FORGET YOUR MAGIC PILLOW LAST NIGHT?
SOMETHING LIKE THAT. WHERE ARE WE?
THE TEMPLE OF LUXOR.
IN ANCIENT TIMES, THE PHARAOH WOULD LEAD A PROCESSION HERE ONCE A YEAR.
IT'S THE BEST PLACE FOR YOU TO PRACTICE.
BECAUSE IT'S ALREADY DESTROYED?
NO, SADIE-- BECAUSE IT IS STILL FULL OF MAGIC. AND IT WAS SACRED TO YOUR FAMILY.
RIGHT. "ANCIENT BLOODLINES" AND WHATNOT.

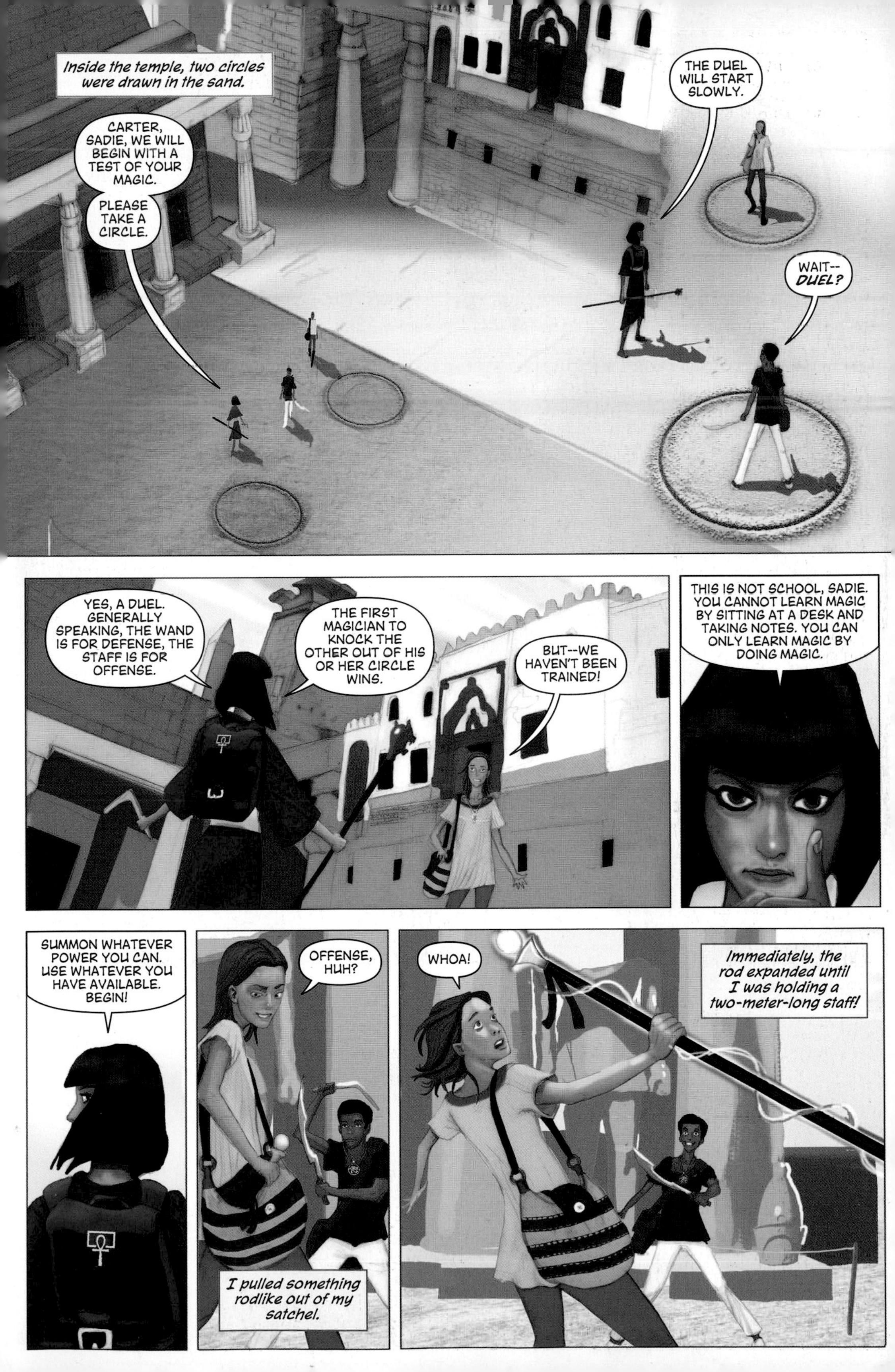
Inside the temple, two circles were drawn in the sand.
CARTER, SADIE, WE WILL BEGIN WITH A TEST OF YOUR MAGIC.
PLEASE TAKE A CIRCLE.
THE DUEL WILL START SLOWLY.
WAIT-- DUEL?
YES, A DUEL. GENERALLY SPEAKING, THE WAND IS FOR DEFENSE, THE STAFF IS FOR OFFENSE.
THE FIRST MAGICIAN TO KNOCK THE OTHER OUT OF HIS OR HER CIRCLE WINS.
BUT--WE HAVEN'T BEEN TRAINED!
THIS IS NOT SCHOOL, SADIE. YOU CANNOT LEARN MAGIC BY SITTING AT A DESK AND TAKING NOTES. YOU CAN ONLY LEARN MAGIC BY DOING MAGIC.
SUMMON WHATEVER POWER YOU CAN. USE WHATEVER YOU HAVE AVAILABLE. BEGIN!
OFFENSE, HUH?
I pulled something rodlike out of my satchel.
WHOA!
Immediately, the rod expanded until I was holding a two-meter-long staff!

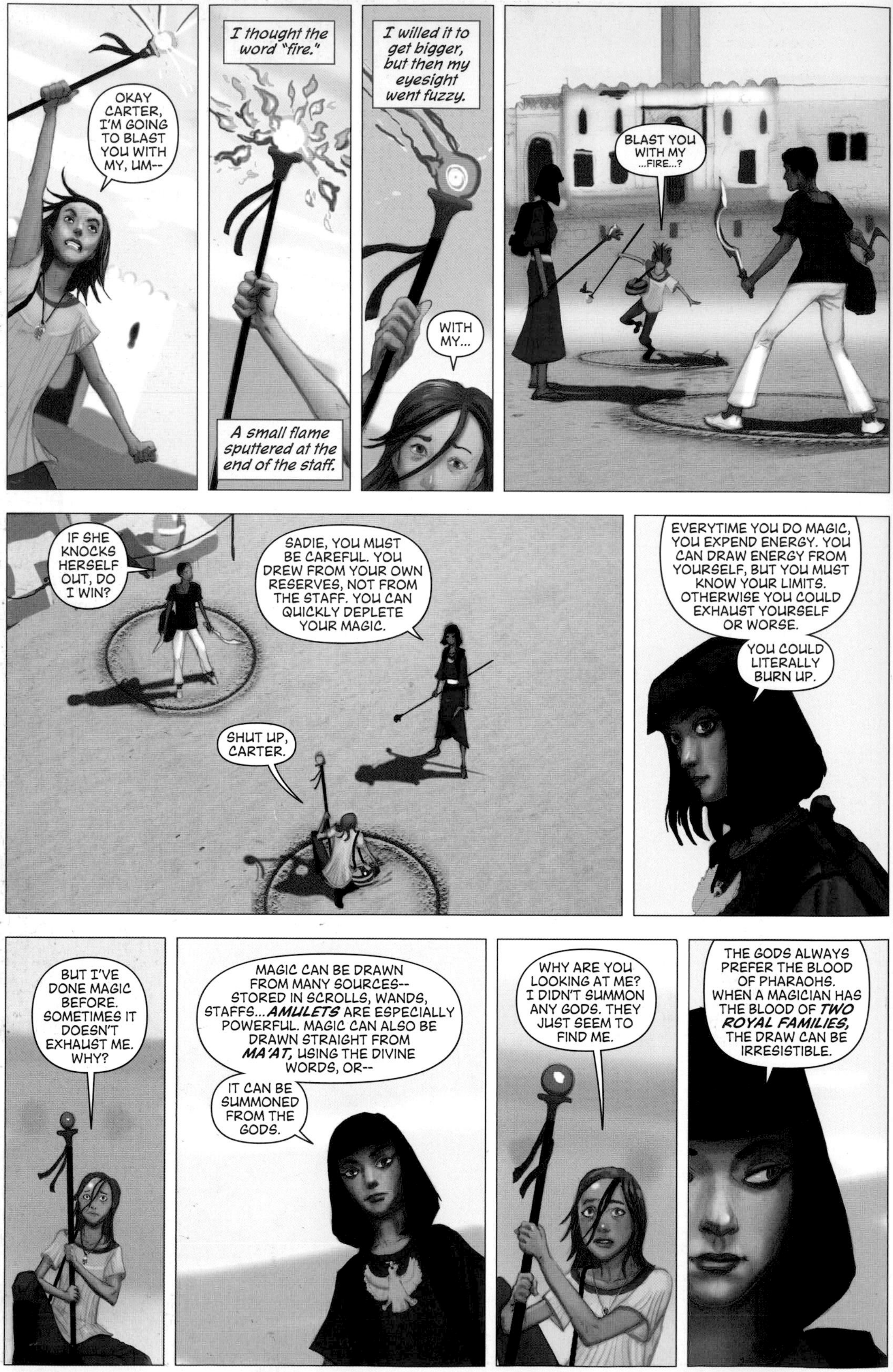
OKAY CARTER, I'M GOING TO BLAST YOU WITH MY, UM--
I thought the word "fire."
A small flame sputtered at the end of the staff.
I willed it to get bigger, but then my eyesight went fuzzy.
WITH MY...
BLAST YOU WITH MY ...FIRE...?
IF SHE KNOCKS HERSELF OUT, DO I WIN?
SADIE, YOU MUST BE CAREFUL. YOU DREW FROM YOUR OWN RESERVES, NOT FROM THE STAFF. YOU CAN QUICKLY DEPLETE YOUR MAGIC.
SHUT UP, CARTER.
EVERYTIME YOU DO MAGIC, YOU EXPEND ENERGY. YOU CAN DRAW ENERGY FROM YOURSELF, BUT YOU MUST KNOW YOUR LIMITS. OTHERWISE YOU COULD EXHAUST YOURSELF OR WORSE.
YOU COULD LITERALLY BURN UP.
BUT I'VE DONE MAGIC BEFORE. SOMETIMES IT DOESN'T EXHAUST ME. WHY?
MAGIC CAN BE DRAWN FROM MANY SOURCES-- STORED IN SCROLLS, WANDS, STAFFS...AMULETS ARE ESPECIALLY POWERFUL. MAGIC CAN ALSO BE DRAWN STRAIGHT FROM MA'AT, USING THE DIVINE WORDS, OR--
IT CAN BE SUMMONED FROM THE GODS.
WHY ARE YOU LOOKING AT ME? I DIDN'T SUMMON ANY GODS. THEY JUST SEEM TO FIND ME.
THE GODS ALWAYS PREFER THE BLOOD OF PHARAOHS. WHEN A MAGICIAN HAS THE BLOOD OF TWO ROYAL FAMILIES, THE DRAW CAN BE IRRESISTIBLE.

SO WHAT DOES THAT HAVE TO DO WITH US?

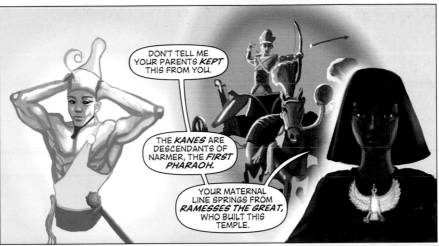

DON'T TELL ME YOUR PARENTS *KEPT* THIS FROM YOU.

THE *KANES* ARE DESCENDANTS OF NARMER, THE *FIRST PHARAOH.*

YOUR MATERNAL LINE SPRINGS FROM *RAMESSES THE GREAT,* WHO BUILT THIS TEMPLE.

Amos had said both sides of our family were very ancient. But the blood of pharaohs?

WHY DO YOU THINK YOU ARE SO *DANGEROUS* TO US?

YOU THINK WE'RE HOSTING GODS? THAT'S WHAT YOU'RE WORRIED ABOUT?

YOU DENY IT? THEN DUEL AND SHOW ME HOW WEAK YOUR MAGIC IS!

She wanted to see how dangerous we were? Well, fine.

UM, SADIE?

I focused on my staff. Maybe not fire. Cats have always liked me. Maybe...

I'd had the worst days ever. Lost my dad, lost pets, had gods trying to kill me--

Now this witch had the nerve to accuse me of breaking a law I didn't even know about two days ago! Something inside me snapped.

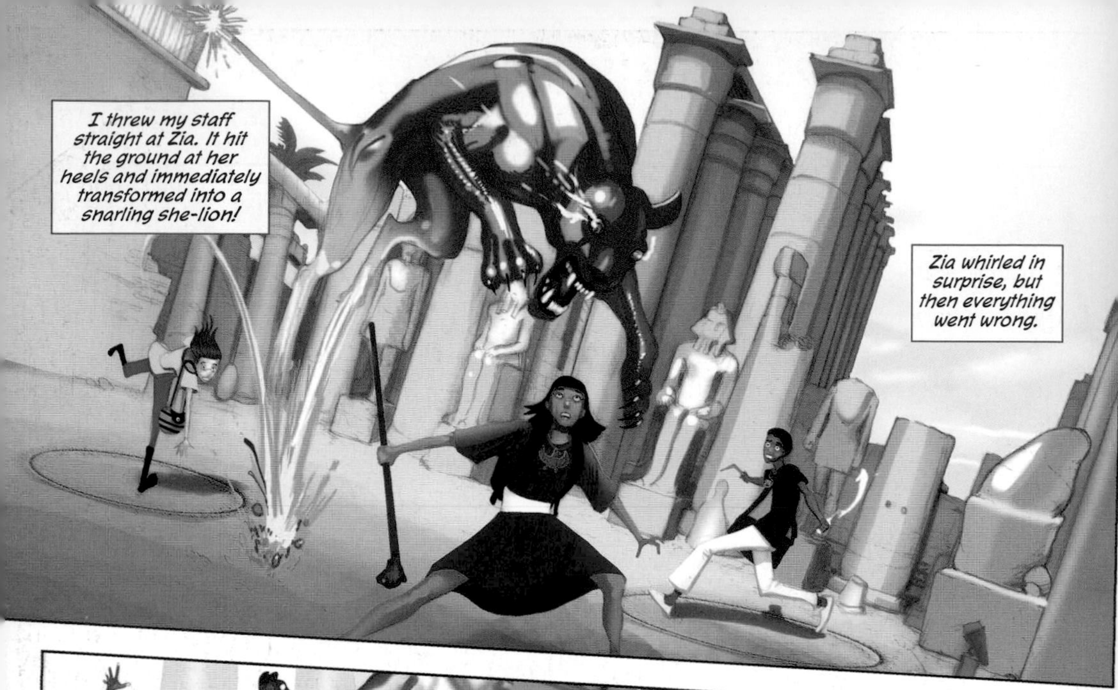
I threw my staff straight at Zia. It hit the ground at her heels and immediately transformed into a snarling she-lion!
Zia whirled in surprise, but then everything went wrong.

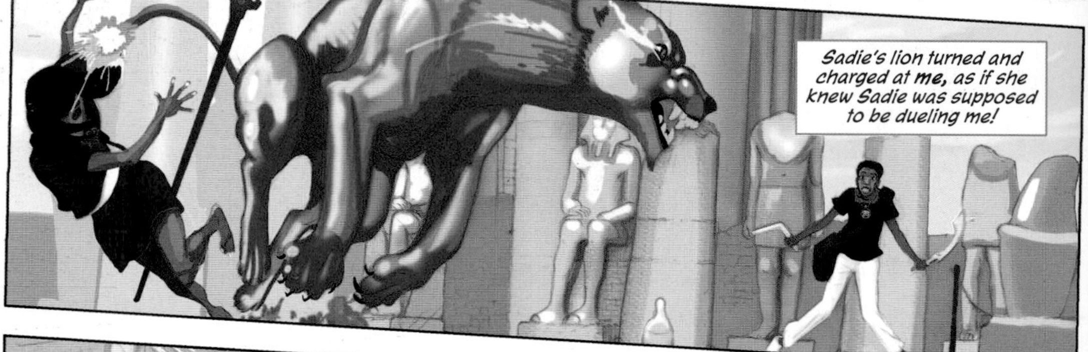
Sadie's lion turned and charged at **me,** as if she knew Sadie was supposed to be dueling me!

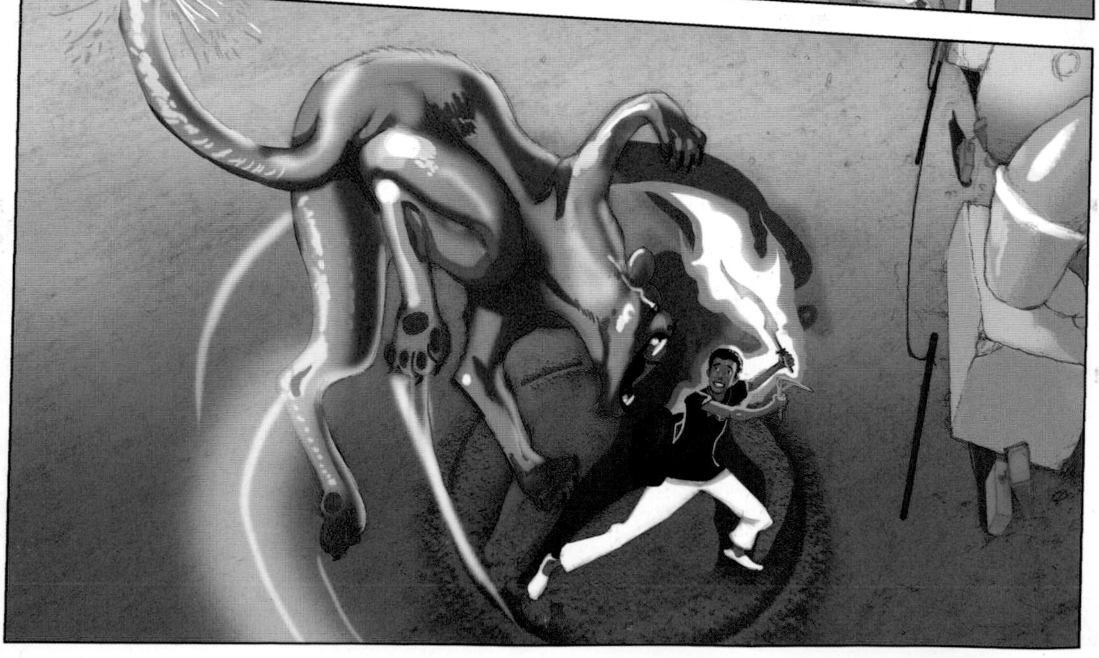

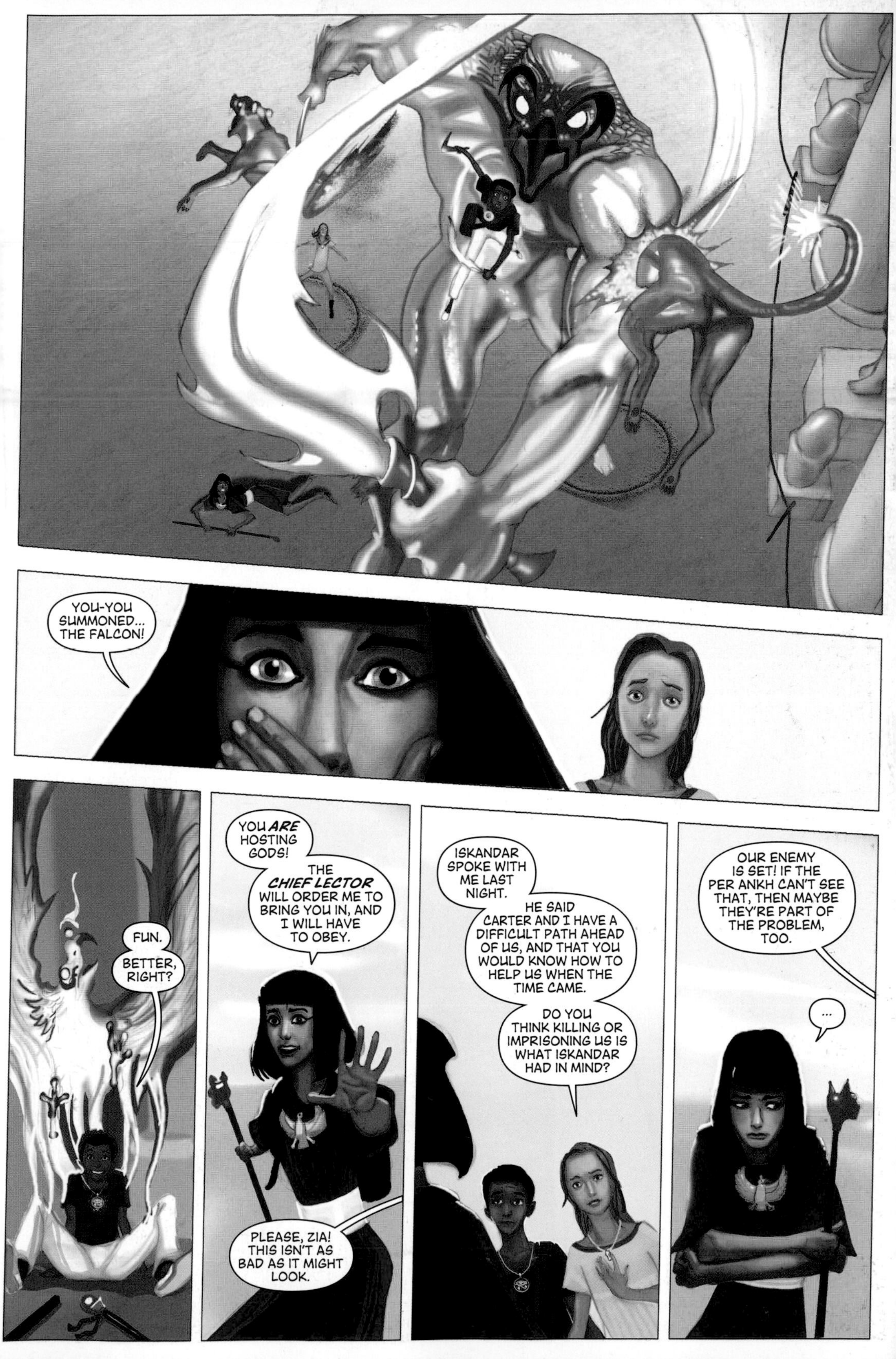
YOU-YOU SUMMONED... THE FALCON!
FUN.
BETTER, RIGHT?
YOU ARE HOSTING GODS!
THE CHIEF LECTOR WILL ORDER ME TO BRING YOU IN, AND I WILL HAVE TO OBEY.
PLEASE, ZIA! THIS ISN'T AS BAD AS IT MIGHT LOOK.
ISKANDAR SPOKE WITH ME LAST NIGHT.
HE SAID CARTER AND I HAVE A DIFFICULT PATH AHEAD OF US, AND THAT YOU WOULD KNOW HOW TO HELP US WHEN THE TIME CAME.
DO YOU THINK KILLING OR IMPRISONING US IS WHAT ISKANDAR HAD IN MIND?
OUR ENEMY IS SET! IF THE PER ANKH CAN'T SEE THAT, THEN MAYBE THEY'RE PART OF THE PROBLEM, TOO.
...

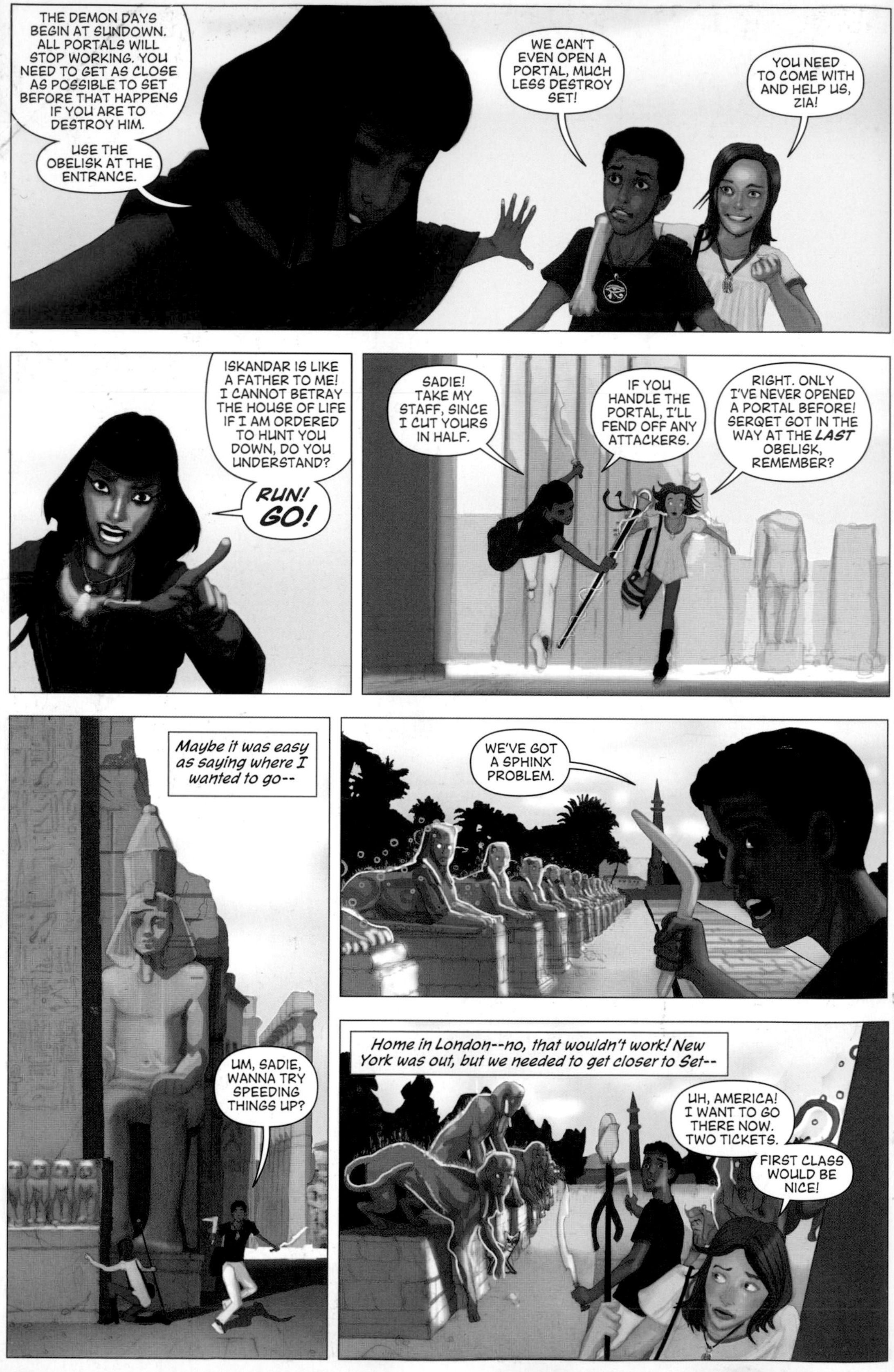
THE DEMON DAYS BEGIN AT SUNDOWN. ALL PORTALS WILL STOP WORKING. YOU NEED TO GET AS CLOSE AS POSSIBLE TO SET BEFORE THAT HAPPENS IF YOU ARE TO DESTROY HIM.
USE THE OBELISK AT THE ENTRANCE.
WE CAN'T EVEN OPEN A PORTAL, MUCH LESS DESTROY SET!
YOU NEED TO COME WITH AND HELP US, ZIA!
ISKANDAR IS LIKE A FATHER TO ME! I CANNOT BETRAY THE HOUSE OF LIFE IF I AM ORDERED TO HUNT YOU DOWN, DO YOU UNDERSTAND?
RUN! GO!
SADIE! TAKE MY STAFF, SINCE I CUT YOURS IN HALF.
IF YOU HANDLE THE PORTAL, I'LL FEND OFF ANY ATTACKERS.
RIGHT. ONLY I'VE NEVER OPENED A PORTAL BEFORE! SERQET GOT IN THE WAY AT THE LAST OBELISK, REMEMBER?
Maybe it was easy as saying where I wanted to go--
UM, SADIE, WANNA TRY SPEEDING THINGS UP?
WE'VE GOT A SPHINX PROBLEM.
Home in London--no, that wouldn't work! New York was out, but we needed to get closer to Set--
UH, AMERICA! I WANT TO GO THERE NOW. TWO TICKETS.
FIRST CLASS WOULD BE NICE!

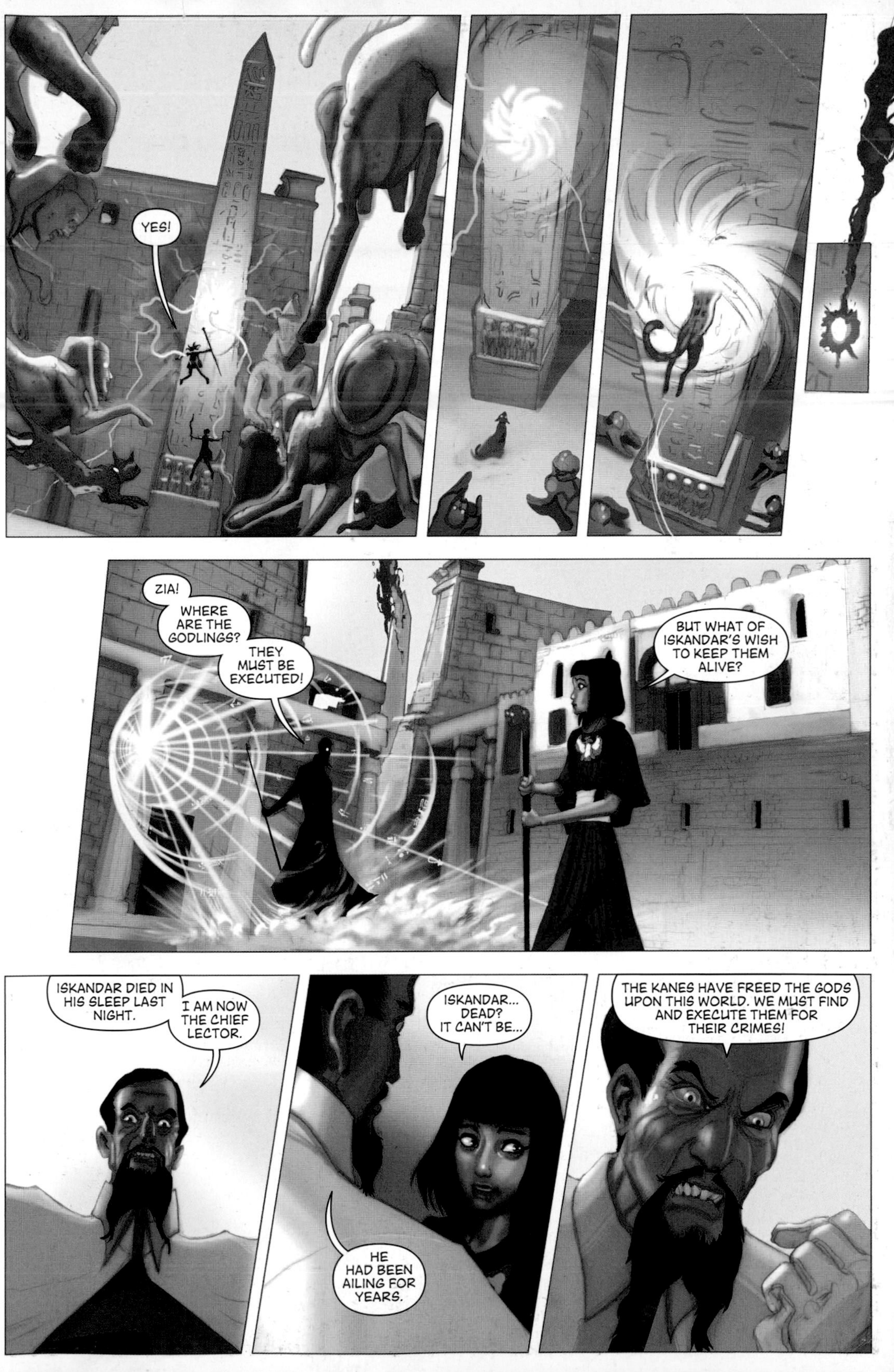
YES!
ZIA!
WHERE ARE THE GODLINGS?
THEY MUST BE EXECUTED!
BUT WHAT OF ISKANDAR'S WISH TO KEEP THEM ALIVE?
ISKANDAR DIED IN HIS SLEEP LAST NIGHT.
I AM NOW THE CHIEF LECTOR.
ISKANDAR... DEAD? IT CAN'T BE...
HE HAD BEEN AILING FOR YEARS.
THE KANES HAVE FREED THE GODS UPON THIS WORLD. WE MUST FIND AND EXECUTE THEM FOR THEIR CRIMES!

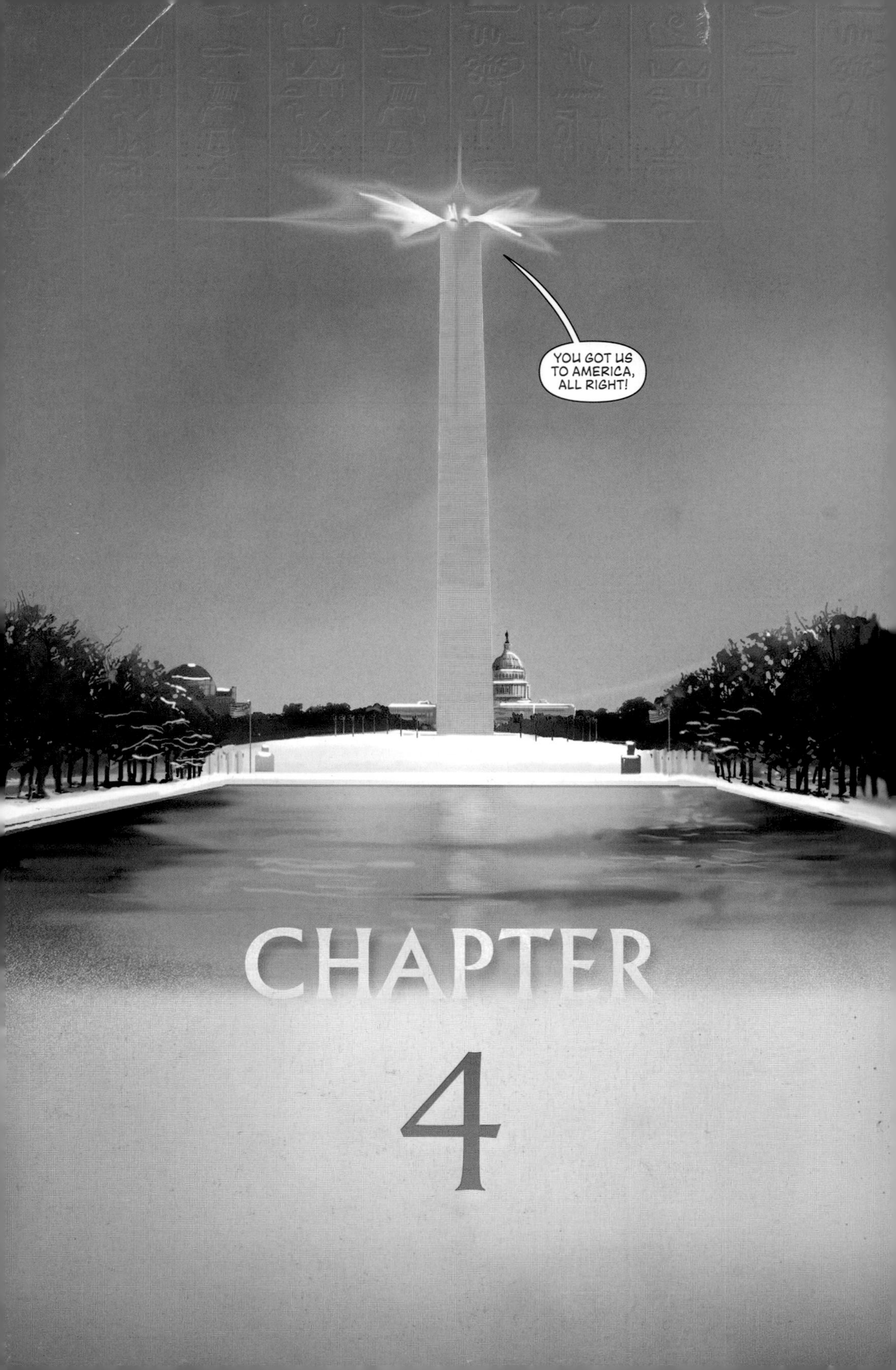
YOU GOT US TO AMERICA, ALL RIGHT!

CHAPTER 4

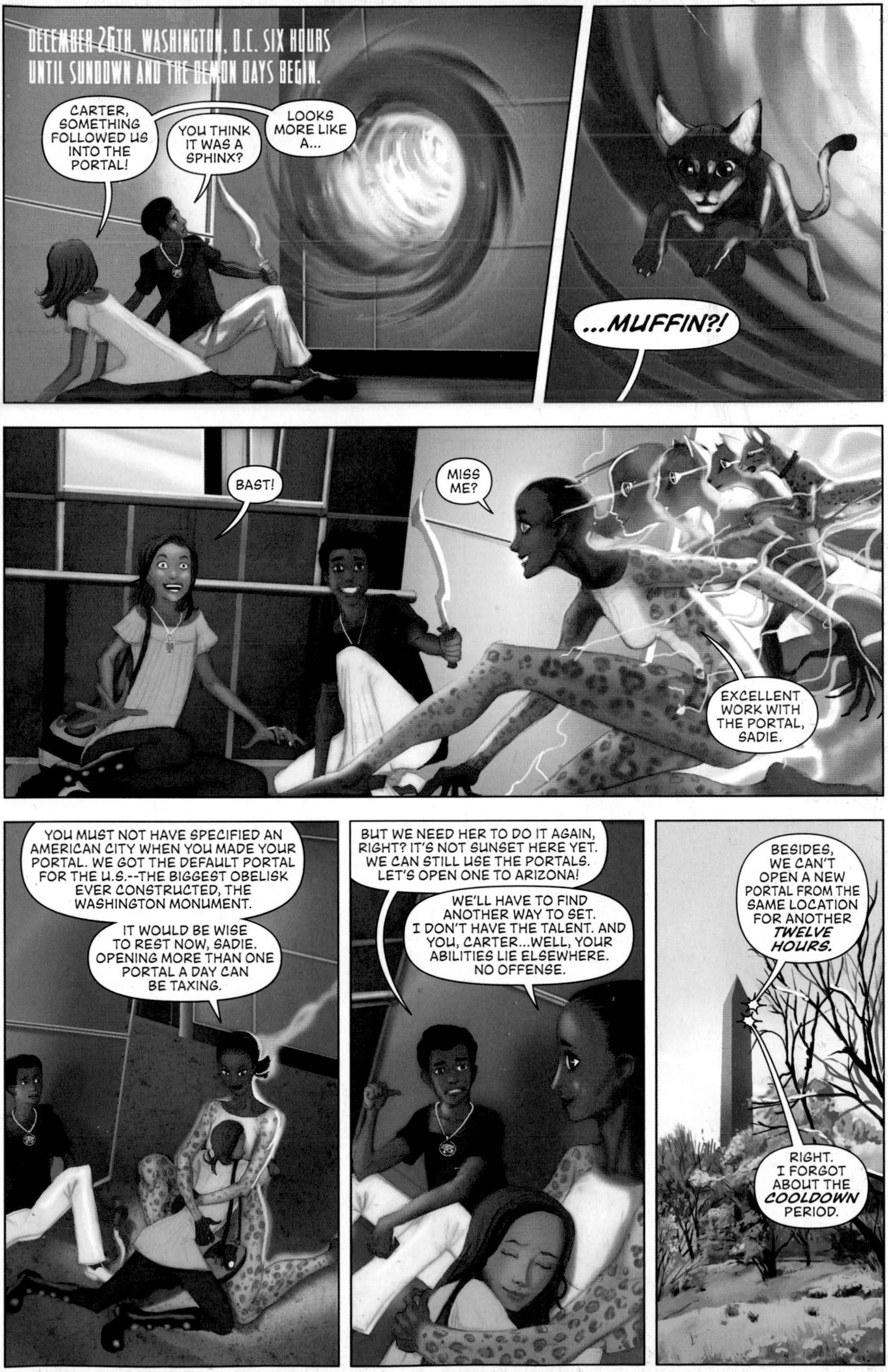
DECEMBER 26TH. WASHINGTON, D.C. SIX HOURS UNTIL SUNDOWN AND THE DEMON DAYS BEGIN.
CARTER, SOMETHING FOLLOWED US INTO THE PORTAL!
YOU THINK IT WAS A SPHINX?
LOOKS MORE LIKE A...
...MUFFIN?!
BAST!
MISS ME?
EXCELLENT WORK WITH THE PORTAL, SADIE.
YOU MUST NOT HAVE SPECIFIED AN AMERICAN CITY WHEN YOU MADE YOUR PORTAL. WE GOT THE DEFAULT PORTAL FOR THE U.S.--THE BIGGEST OBELISK EVER CONSTRUCTED, THE WASHINGTON MONUMENT.
IT WOULD BE WISE TO REST NOW, SADIE. OPENING MORE THAN ONE PORTAL A DAY CAN BE TAXING.
BUT WE NEED HER TO DO IT AGAIN, RIGHT? IT'S NOT SUNSET HERE YET. WE CAN STILL USE THE PORTALS. LET'S OPEN ONE TO ARIZONA!
WE'LL HAVE TO FIND ANOTHER WAY TO SET. I DON'T HAVE THE TALENT. AND YOU, CARTER...WELL, YOUR ABILITIES LIE ELSEWHERE. NO OFFENSE.
BESIDES, WE CAN'T OPEN A NEW PORTAL FROM THE SAME LOCATION FOR ANOTHER TWELVE HOURS.
RIGHT. I FORGOT ABOUT THE COOLDOWN PERIOD.

WE THOUGHT YOU WERE *DEAD!*

I HELD SERQET OFF AS LONG AS I COULD, SAVING JUST ENOUGH ENERGY TO REVERT TO MUFFIN'S FORM AND SLIP INTO THE DUAT.

BUT I THOUGHT YOU WEREN'T GOOD AT PORTALS.

I'M NOT, BUT AS A CREATURE OF THE DUAT, SLIPPING INTO ONE OF ITS SHALLOWEST LAYERS FOR A QUICK ESCAPE IS RELATIVELY EASY.

BY THE TIME I GOT TO THE MUSEUM, THE MAGICIANS HAD ALREADY CAPTURED YOU.

BAST, IT WAS TERRIBLE! THEY THINK WE'RE HOSTING GODS!

YES. YOU ARE *GODLINGS,* DEAR.

IT MUST HAVE HAPPENED AT THE MUSEUM. WEARING THEIR *SYMBOLS,* YOU PRACTICALLY INVITED THEIR POWER.

THEIR SYMBOLS?

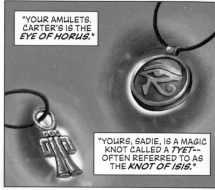

"YOUR AMULETS. CARTER'S IS THE *EYE OF HORUS.*"

"YOURS, SADIE, IS A MAGIC KNOT CALLED A *TYET*-- OFTEN REFERRED TO AS THE *KNOT OF ISIS.*"

IN THE HALL OF AGES, I SAW AN IMAGE OF ISIS, AND THEN I *WAS* ISIS, TRYING TO GET AWAY FROM SET, AND--OH, GOD. THAT'S IT, ISN'T IT? I'M HER!

I thought about the myths I knew--how Horus, the son of Osiris, had to avenge his father by defeating Set. And at Luxor I'd summoned an avatar with the head of a falcon, a symbol of Horus.

I was afraid to try it. But...

HELLO, CARTER.

...HORUS?

AH! I'VE BEEN POSSESSED!

PLEASE, CARTER, IT'S NOT POSSESSION. AS *HOSTS,* YOU ARE STILL QUITE HUMAN.

SO WHEN I ACTIVATED THE OBELISK AT LUXOR, WAS THAT ISIS OR ME?

BOTH, DEAR. AS BLOOD OF THE PHARAOHS, YOU AND CARTER HAVE GREAT ABILITIES ON YOUR OWN, BUT THE POWER OF THE GODS HAS GIVEN YOU AN EXTRA RESERVOIR TO DRAW ON.

IT HAS ALSO HASTENED YOUR DEVELOPMENT-- WHAT WOULD'VE TAKEN YOU YEARS TO LEARN, YOU'VE ACCOMPLISHED IN DAYS.

BUT IT'S ALSO WAY MORE DANGEROUS! THE MAGICIANS WANT TO KILL US NOW!

YES, AND IF YOU THINK YOU CAN SURVIVE WHAT'S COMING WITHOUT THE POWER OF THE GODS, THINK AGAIN. DON'T REPEAT YOUR MOTHER'S...

OUR MOTHER'S WHAT?

IT'S NOTHING.

TELL US, CAT!

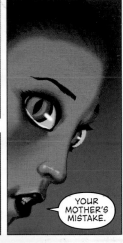
YOUR MOTHER'S MISTAKE.

IN FREEING ME FROM CLEOPATRA'S NEEDLE, YOUR FATHER UNLEASHED MORE ENERGY THAN EXPECTED.

THE BLAST WOULD'VE KILLED HIM HAD YOUR MOTHER NOT SHIELDED HIM. I OFFERED TO MERGE MY SPIRIT WITH HERS TO AID HER, BUT SHE WOULD NOT ALLOW IT.

I WASN'T ALONE IN THE OBELISK. I WAS TRAPPED THERE WITH A... CREATURE OF CHAOS.

YOUR MOTHER SACRIFICED HER LIFE--LITERALLY BURNED OUT--TO SEAL MY ENEMY INSIDE AND TO SAVE YOUR FATHER.

ALL RIGHT, SO TO STOP SET, WE CAN EITHER COMPLETELY GIVE OURSELVES OVER TO THE GODS OR BURN UP. GREAT.

REST, DEAR.

FOR NOW, WE'RE SAFE FROM THE HOUSE OF LIFE, AT LEAST.

I'M GOING TO SCOUT THE PERIMETER FOR THREATS. WE NEVER KNOW WHAT SET MIGHT SEND AFTER US.

WE NEED TO COME UP WITH A PLAN.

WHY DON'T YOU SLEEP ON IT? YOU USED A LOT OF ENERGY TODAY. I'LL KEEP WATCH UNTIL BAST GETS BACK.

I didn't want to miss anything. But I realized my eyelids *were* incredibly heavy.

ALL RIGHT THEN.

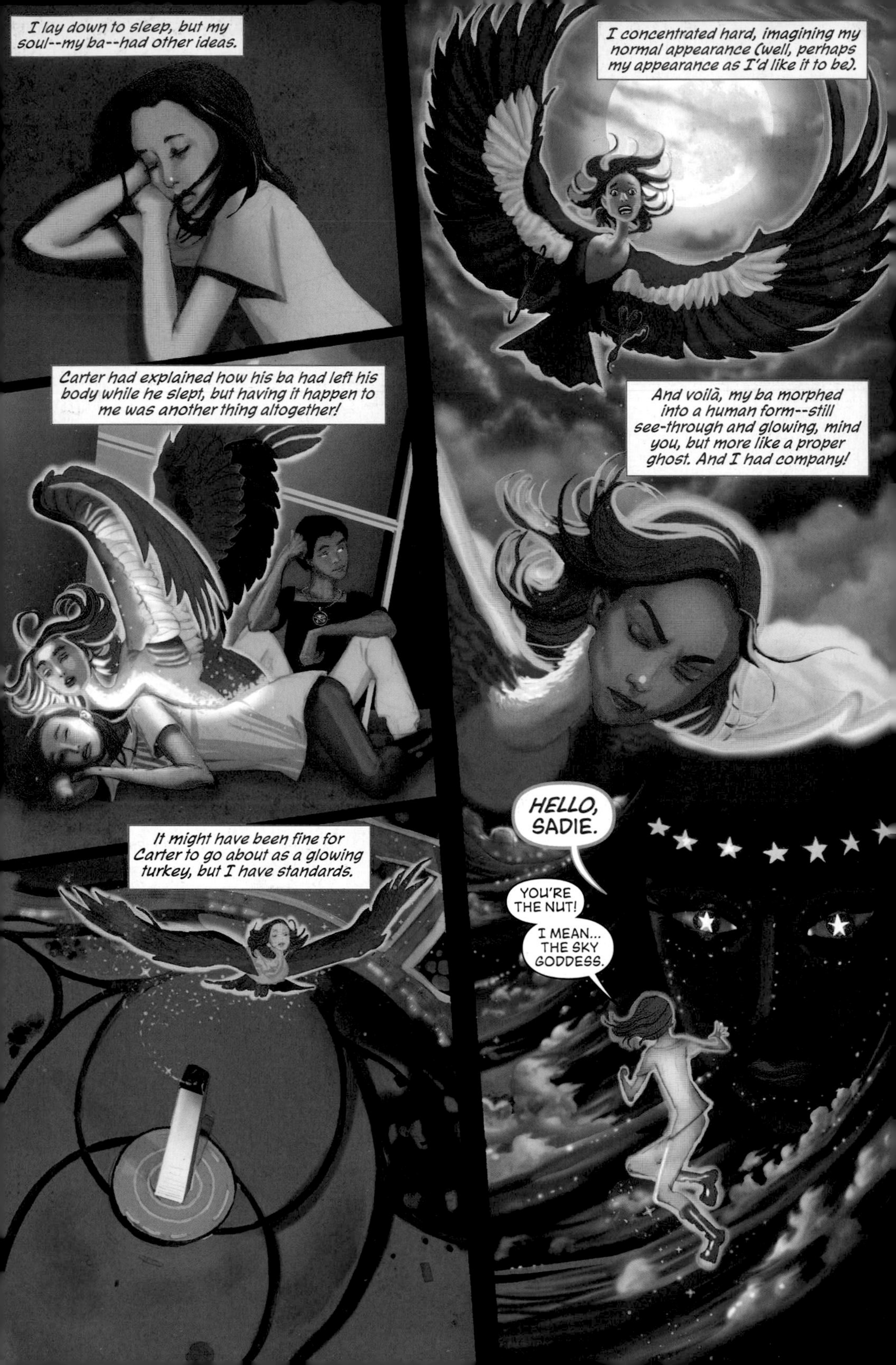
I lay down to sleep, but my soul--my ba--had other ideas.
Carter had explained how his ba had left his body while he slept, but having it happen to me was another thing altogether!
It might have been fine for Carter to go about as a glowing turkey, but I have standards.
I concentrated hard, imagining my normal appearance (well, perhaps my appearance as I'd like it to be).
And voilà, my ba morphed into a human form--still see-through and glowing, mind you, but more like a proper ghost. And I had company!
HELLO, SADIE.
YOU'RE THE NUT!
I MEAN... THE SKY GODDESS.

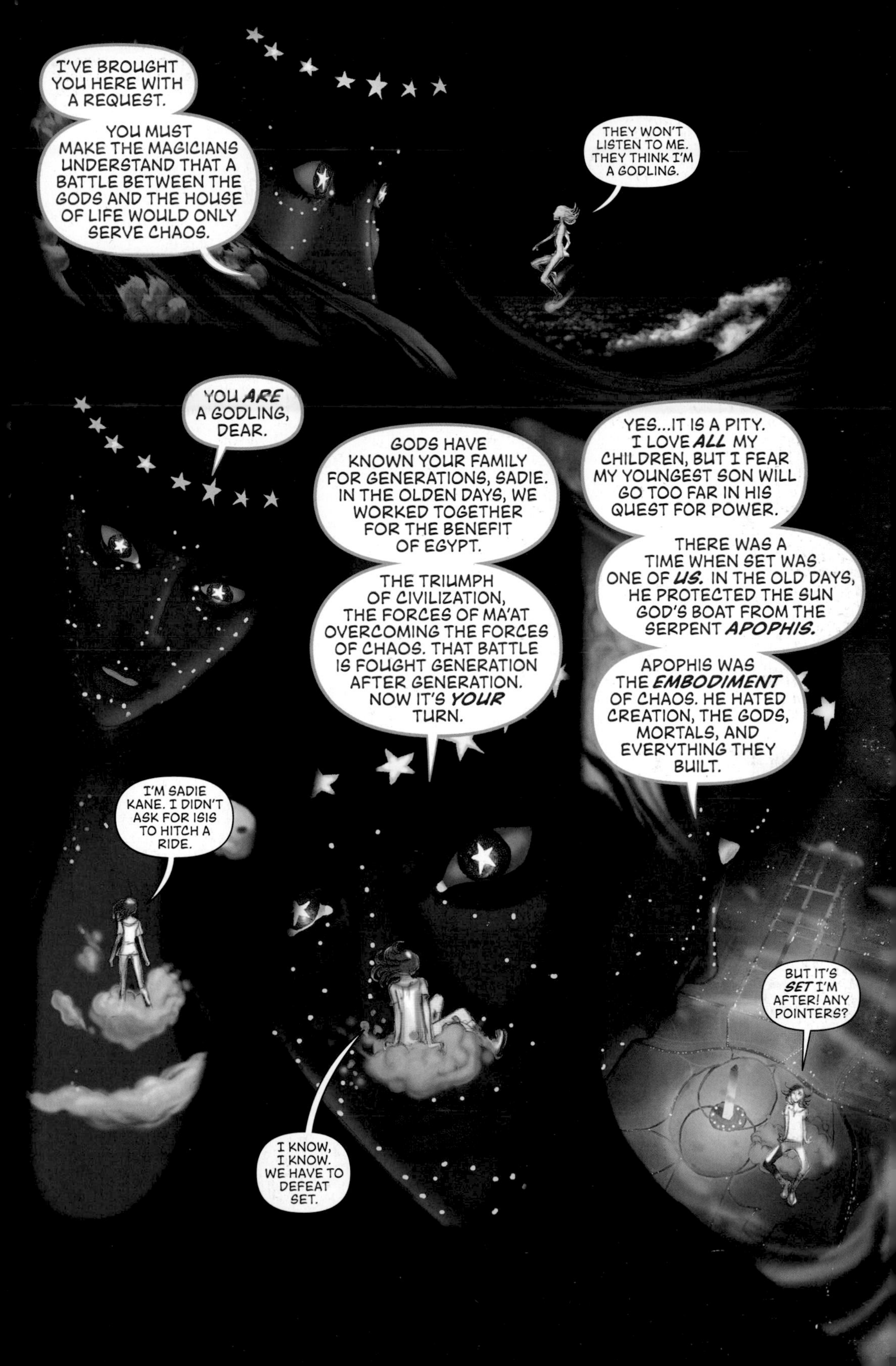
I'VE BROUGHT YOU HERE WITH A REQUEST.
YOU MUST MAKE THE MAGICIANS UNDERSTAND THAT A BATTLE BETWEEN THE GODS AND THE HOUSE OF LIFE WOULD ONLY SERVE CHAOS.
THEY WON'T LISTEN TO ME. THEY THINK I'M A GODLING.
YOU ARE A GODLING, DEAR.
I'M SADIE KANE. I DIDN'T ASK FOR ISIS TO HITCH A RIDE.
GODS HAVE KNOWN YOUR FAMILY FOR GENERATIONS, SADIE. IN THE OLDEN DAYS, WE WORKED TOGETHER FOR THE BENEFIT OF EGYPT.
THE TRIUMPH OF CIVILIZATION, THE FORCES OF MA'AT OVERCOMING THE FORCES OF CHAOS. THAT BATTLE IS FOUGHT GENERATION AFTER GENERATION. NOW IT'S YOUR TURN.
I KNOW, I KNOW. WE HAVE TO DEFEAT SET.
YES...IT IS A PITY. I LOVE ALL MY CHILDREN, BUT I FEAR MY YOUNGEST SON WILL GO TOO FAR IN HIS QUEST FOR POWER.
THERE WAS A TIME WHEN SET WAS ONE OF US. IN THE OLD DAYS, HE PROTECTED THE SUN GOD'S BOAT FROM THE SERPENT APOPHIS.
APOPHIS WAS THE EMBODIMENT OF CHAOS. HE HATED CREATION, THE GODS, MORTALS, AND EVERYTHING THEY BUILT.
BUT IT'S SET I'M AFTER! ANY POINTERS?

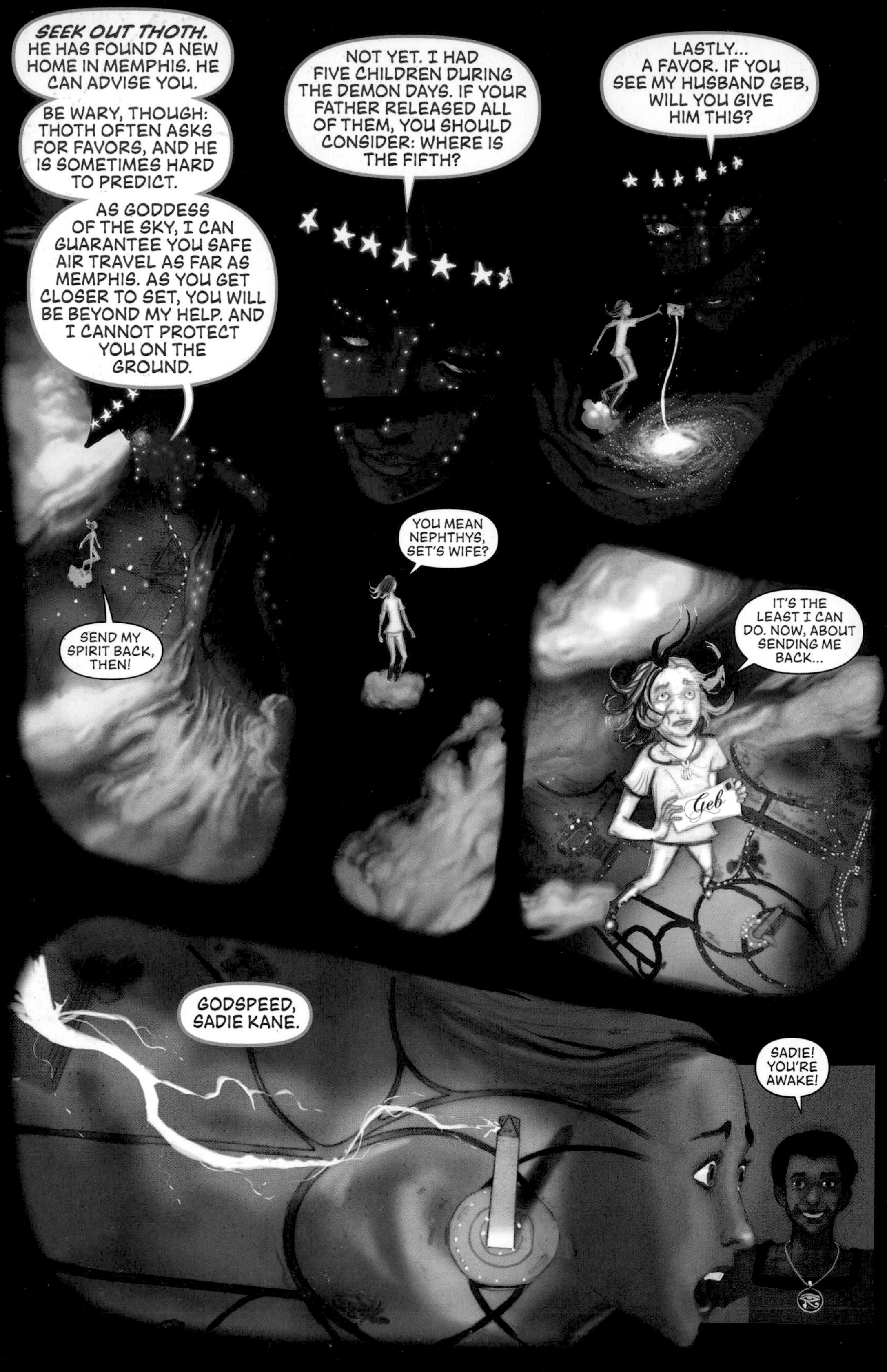
SEEK OUT THOTH. HE HAS FOUND A NEW HOME IN MEMPHIS. HE CAN ADVISE YOU.
BE WARY, THOUGH: THOTH OFTEN ASKS FOR FAVORS, AND HE IS SOMETIMES HARD TO PREDICT.
AS GODDESS OF THE SKY, I CAN GUARANTEE YOU SAFE AIR TRAVEL AS FAR AS MEMPHIS. AS YOU GET CLOSER TO SET, YOU WILL BE BEYOND MY HELP. AND I CANNOT PROTECT YOU ON THE GROUND.
SEND MY SPIRIT BACK, THEN!
NOT YET. I HAD FIVE CHILDREN DURING THE DEMON DAYS. IF YOUR FATHER RELEASED ALL OF THEM, YOU SHOULD CONSIDER: WHERE IS THE FIFTH?
YOU MEAN NEPHTHYS, SET'S WIFE?
LASTLY... A FAVOR. IF YOU SEE MY HUSBAND GEB, WILL YOU GIVE HIM THIS?
Geb
IT'S THE LEAST I CAN DO. NOW, ABOUT SENDING ME BACK...
GODSPEED, SADIE KANE.
SADIE! YOU'RE AWAKE!

HOW LONG WAS I OUT?

A LONG TIME. WE CAN'T OPEN PORTALS ANYMORE. IT'S OSIRIS'S BIRTHDAY.

I remembered my dream with Nut. To my own disbelief, I pulled a sealed envelope out of my pocket.

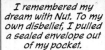

WHAT'S THAT?

BAST! YOU'RE BACK!

WITH BAD TIDINGS. SET'S MINION HAS TRACKED OUR SCENT. TAKE A LOOK OUT THE VIEWING WINDOW.

A GIFT FROM THE SKY GODDESS-- A LETTER TO GIVE TO GEB...AND THREE FIRST-CLASS PLANE TICKETS TO *MEMPHIS*!

GREAT. WE'RE GOING TO NEED THEM.

At the monument's base stood a weird creature.

WHAT *IS* IT? SOME KIND OF DOG?

THE *SET ANIMAL.*

IT DOESN'T HAVE A NAME?

IF IT DID, YOU WOULD NOT WANT TO SPEAK IT. IT SHARES SET'S STRENGTH, CUNNING...AND HIS EVIL NATURE.

HOW DO WE STOP IT?

THE SET ANIMAL IS THE PERFECT HUNTER. IF IT HAS OUR SCENT, THERE IS NO STOPPING IT.

THAT'S MESSED UP. EVASION TACTIC-- ELEVATOR OR STAIRS?

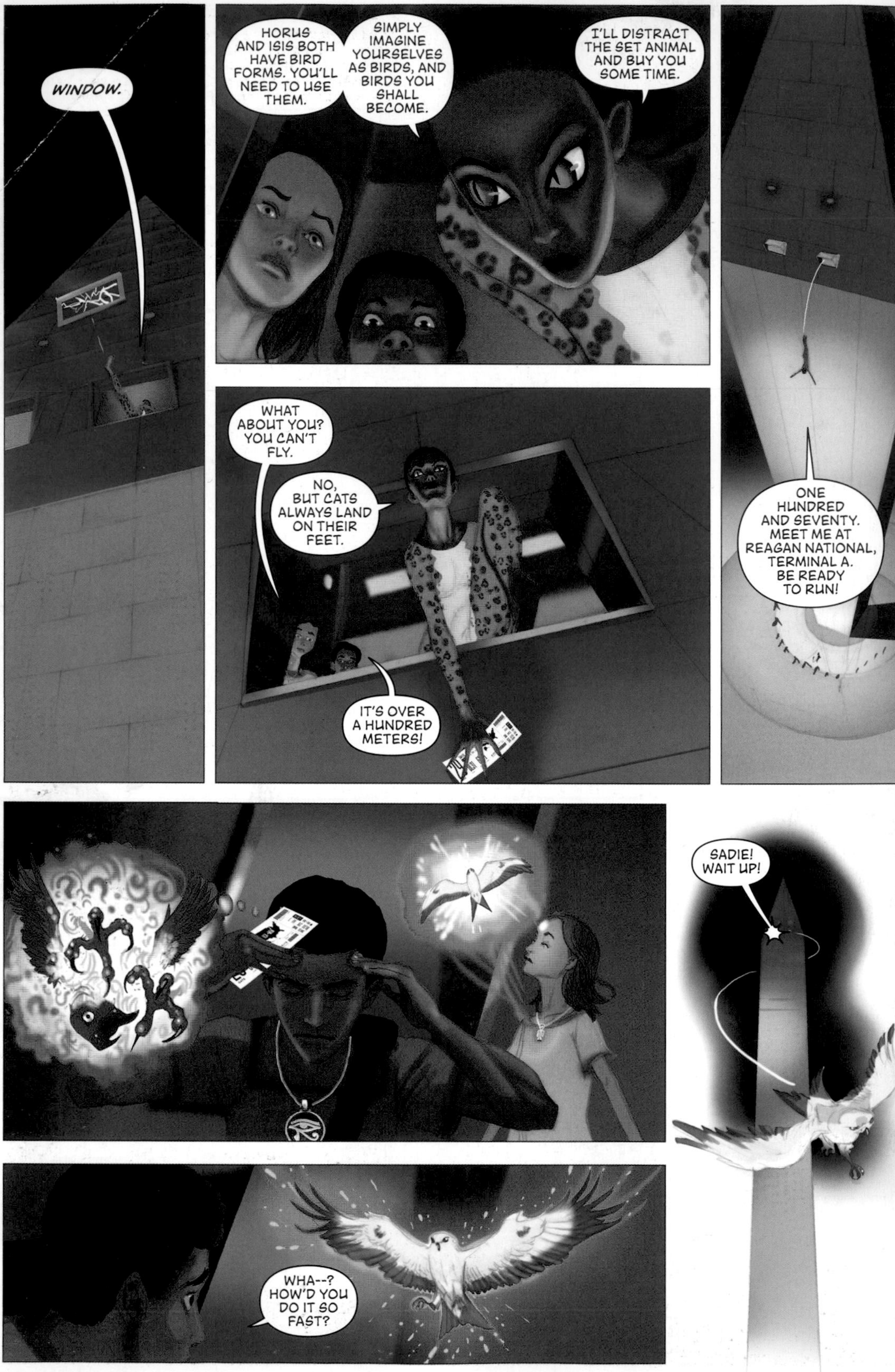
WINDOW.
HORUS AND ISIS BOTH HAVE BIRD FORMS. YOU'LL NEED TO USE THEM.
SIMPLY IMAGINE YOURSELVES AS BIRDS, AND BIRDS YOU SHALL BECOME.
I'LL DISTRACT THE SET ANIMAL AND BUY YOU SOME TIME.
WHAT ABOUT YOU? YOU CAN'T FLY.
NO, BUT CATS ALWAYS LAND ON THEIR FEET.
IT'S OVER A HUNDRED METERS!
ONE HUNDRED AND SEVENTY. MEET ME AT REAGAN NATIONAL, TERMINAL A. BE READY TO RUN!
SADIE! WAIT UP!
WHA--? HOW'D YOU DO IT SO FAST?

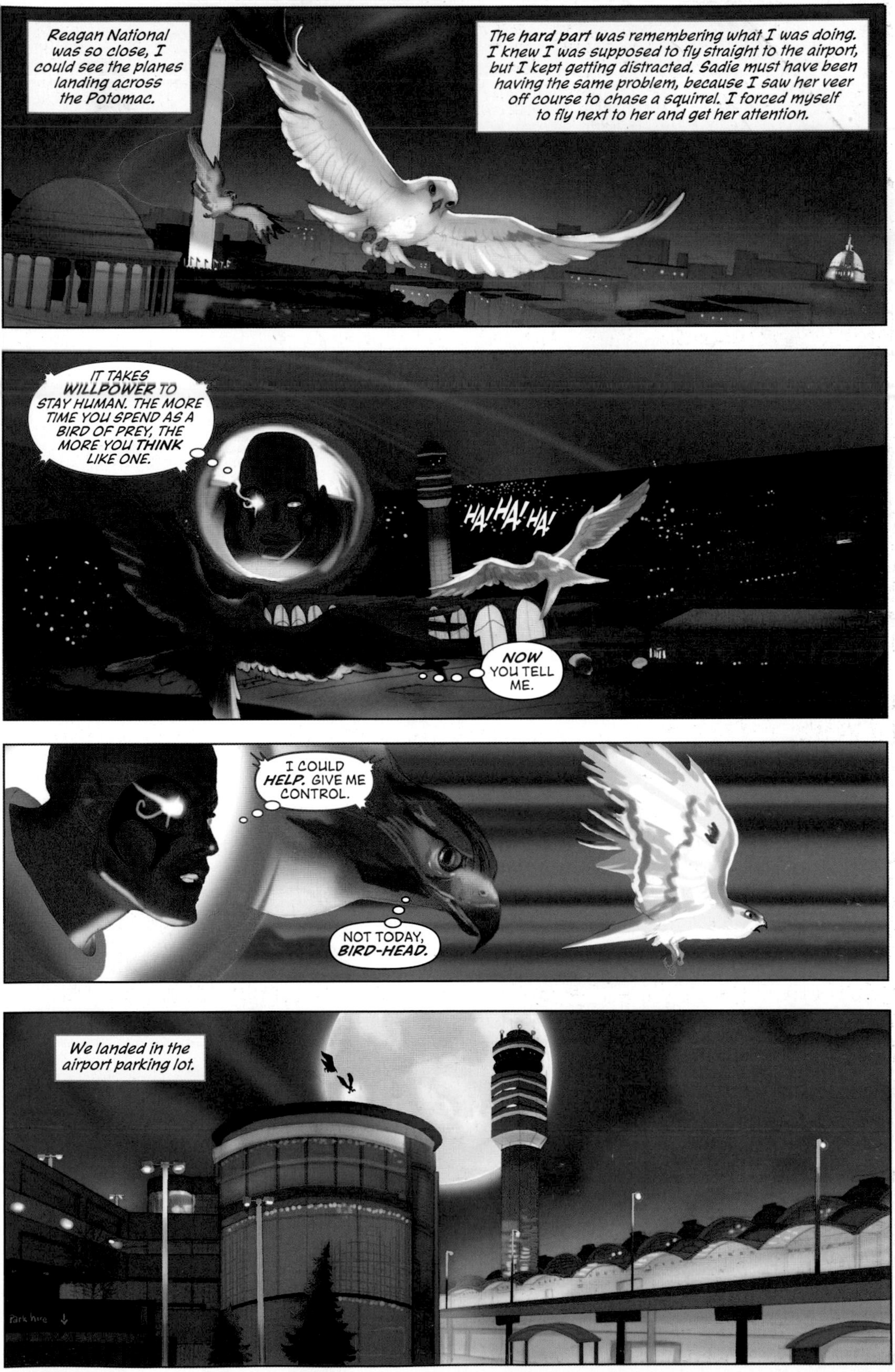

Reagan National was so close, I could see the planes landing across the Potomac.
The hard part was remembering what I was doing. I knew I was supposed to fly straight to the airport, but I kept getting distracted. Sadie must have been having the same problem, because I saw her veer off course to chase a squirrel. I forced myself to fly next to her and get her attention.
IT TAKES WILLPOWER TO STAY HUMAN. THE MORE TIME YOU SPEND AS A BIRD OF PREY, THE MORE YOU THINK LIKE ONE.
HA! HA! HA!
NOW YOU TELL ME.
I COULD HELP. GIVE ME CONTROL.
NOT TODAY, BIRD-HEAD.
We landed in the airport parking lot.

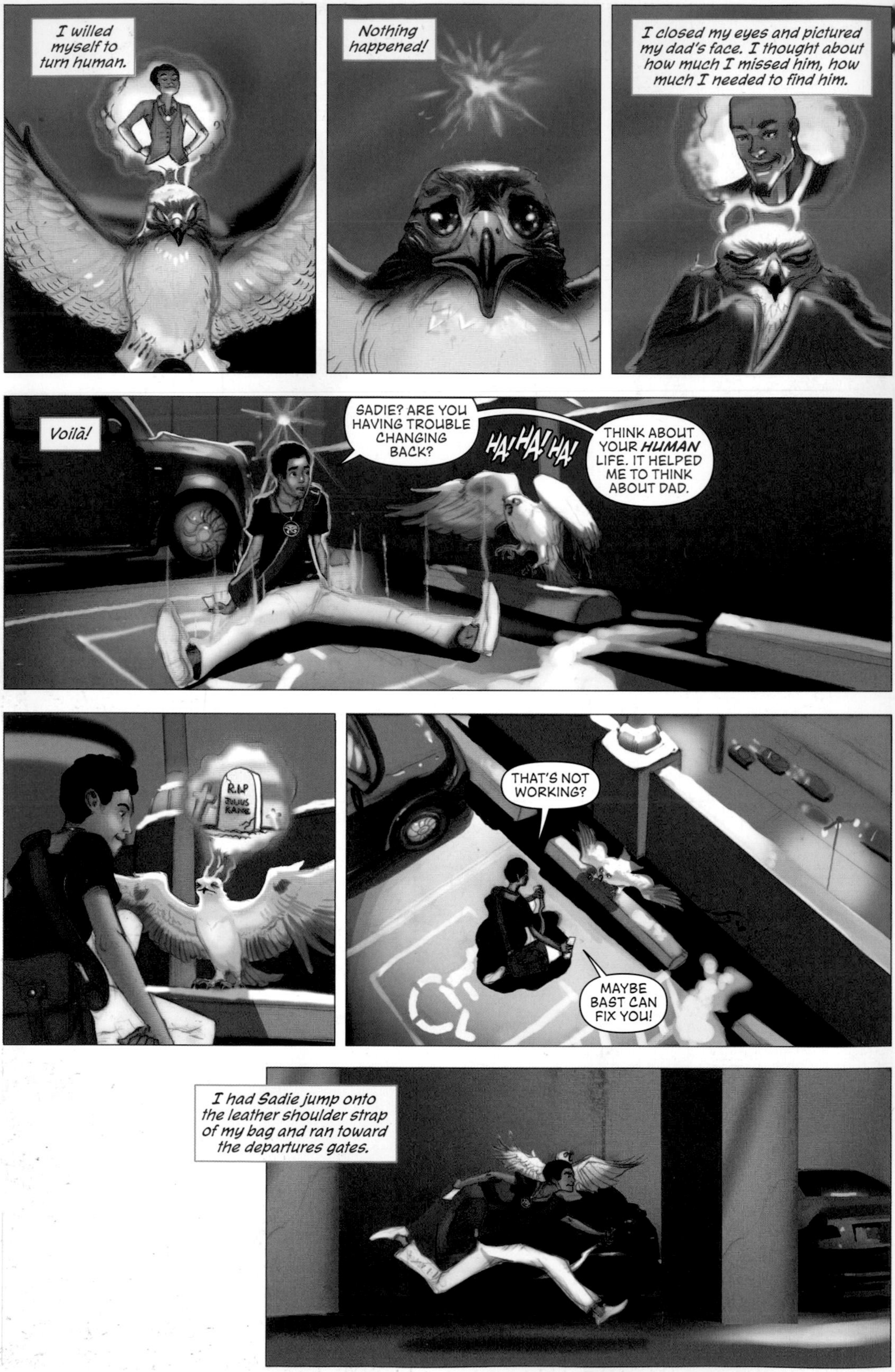
I willed myself to turn human.
Nothing happened!
I closed my eyes and pictured my dad's face. I thought about how much I missed him, how much I needed to find him.
Voilà!
SADIE? ARE YOU HAVING TROUBLE CHANGING BACK?
HA! HA! HA!
THINK ABOUT YOUR ***HUMAN*** LIFE. IT HELPED ME TO THINK ABOUT DAD.
THAT'S NOT WORKING?
MAYBE BAST CAN FIX YOU!
I had Sadie jump onto the leather shoulder strap of my bag and ran toward the departures gates.

Bast caught up with us near the departures entrance.

CARTER, HOW DO YOU EXPECT TO GET THROUGH AIRPORT SECURITY CARRYING A SWORD?

UM, I--

AND WHAT'S WRONG WITH SADIE?

SHE CAN'T CHANGE BACK.

HMM. SOMETHING WE'LL HAVE TO FIX LATER.

STOW YOUR THINGS IN THE DUAT BEFORE YOU DRAW ATTENTION TO YOURSELF.

UH...I DON'T KNOW HOW TO DO THAT. WHEN DID YOU HAVE TIME TO CHANGE YOUR CLOTHES?

BY MAGIC, CARTER.

TO OPEN THE DUAT, JUST IMAGINE A SPACE IN THE AIR, LIKE A SHELF OR A TREASURE CHEST--

A LOCKER? I'VE NEVER HAD A SCHOOL LOCKER.

FINE. GIVE IT A COMBINATION LOCK--ANYTHING YOU WANT.

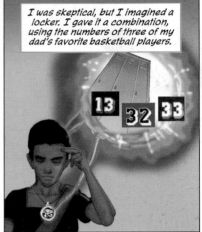

I was skeptical, but I imagined a locker. I gave it a combination, using the numbers of three of my dad's favorite basketball players.

13 32 33

IMAGINE OPENING THE LOCKER WITH YOUR COMBINATION. THEN HIDE YOUR THINGS INSIDE.

WHEN YOU NEED IT AGAIN, JUST CALL IT TO MIND, AND IT SHOULD APPEAR.

I held out my sword and bag and let them go, sure they would smash to the floor.

Instead, they disappeared!

COOL TRICK!

YES. NOW COME! WE HAVEN'T MUCH TIME!

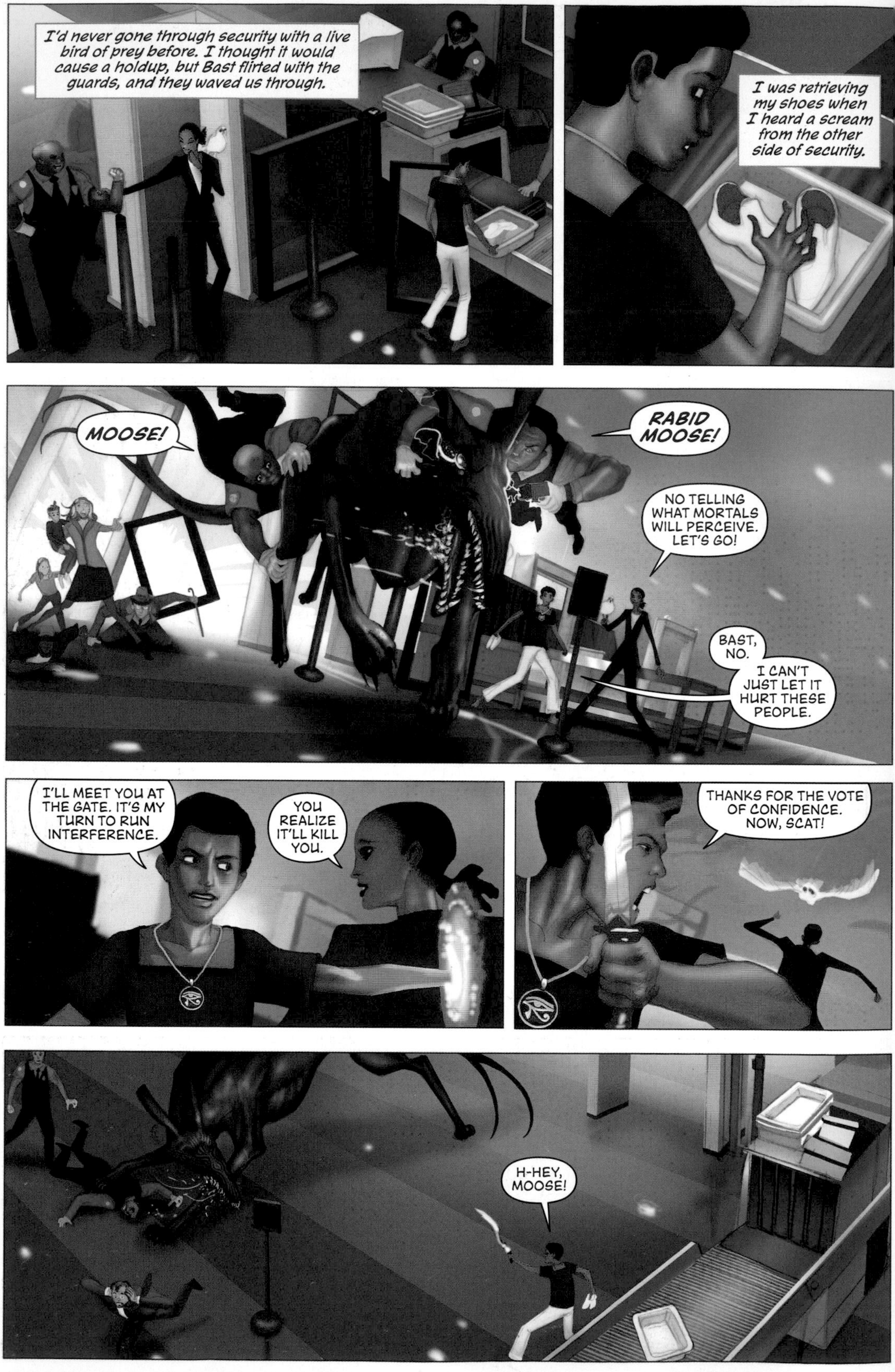

I'd never gone through security with a live bird of prey before. I thought it would cause a holdup, but Bast flirted with the guards, and they waved us through.
I was retrieving my shoes when I heard a scream from the other side of security.
MOOSE!
RABID MOOSE!
NO TELLING WHAT MORTALS WILL PERCEIVE. LET'S GO!
BAST, NO.
I CAN'T JUST LET IT HURT THESE PEOPLE.
I'LL MEET YOU AT THE GATE. IT'S MY TURN TO RUN INTERFERENCE.
YOU REALIZE IT'LL KILL YOU.
THANKS FOR THE VOTE OF CONFIDENCE. NOW, SCAT!
H-HEY, MOOSE!

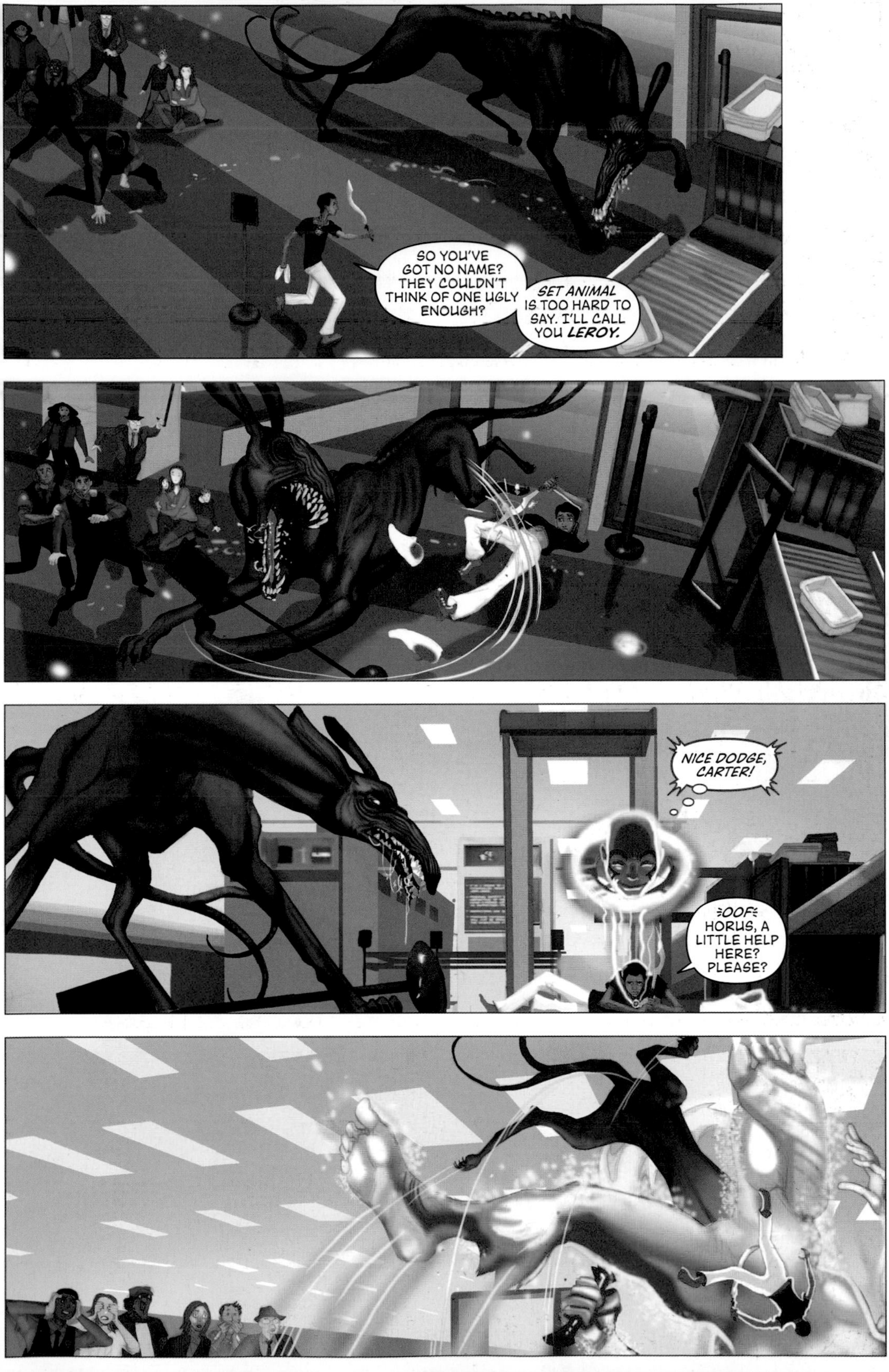
SO YOU'VE GOT NO NAME? THEY COULDN'T THINK OF ONE UGLY ENOUGH?
SET ANIMAL IS TOO HARD TO SAY. I'LL CALL YOU ***LEROY.***
NICE DODGE, CARTER!
OOF HORUS, A LITTLE HELP HERE? PLEASE?

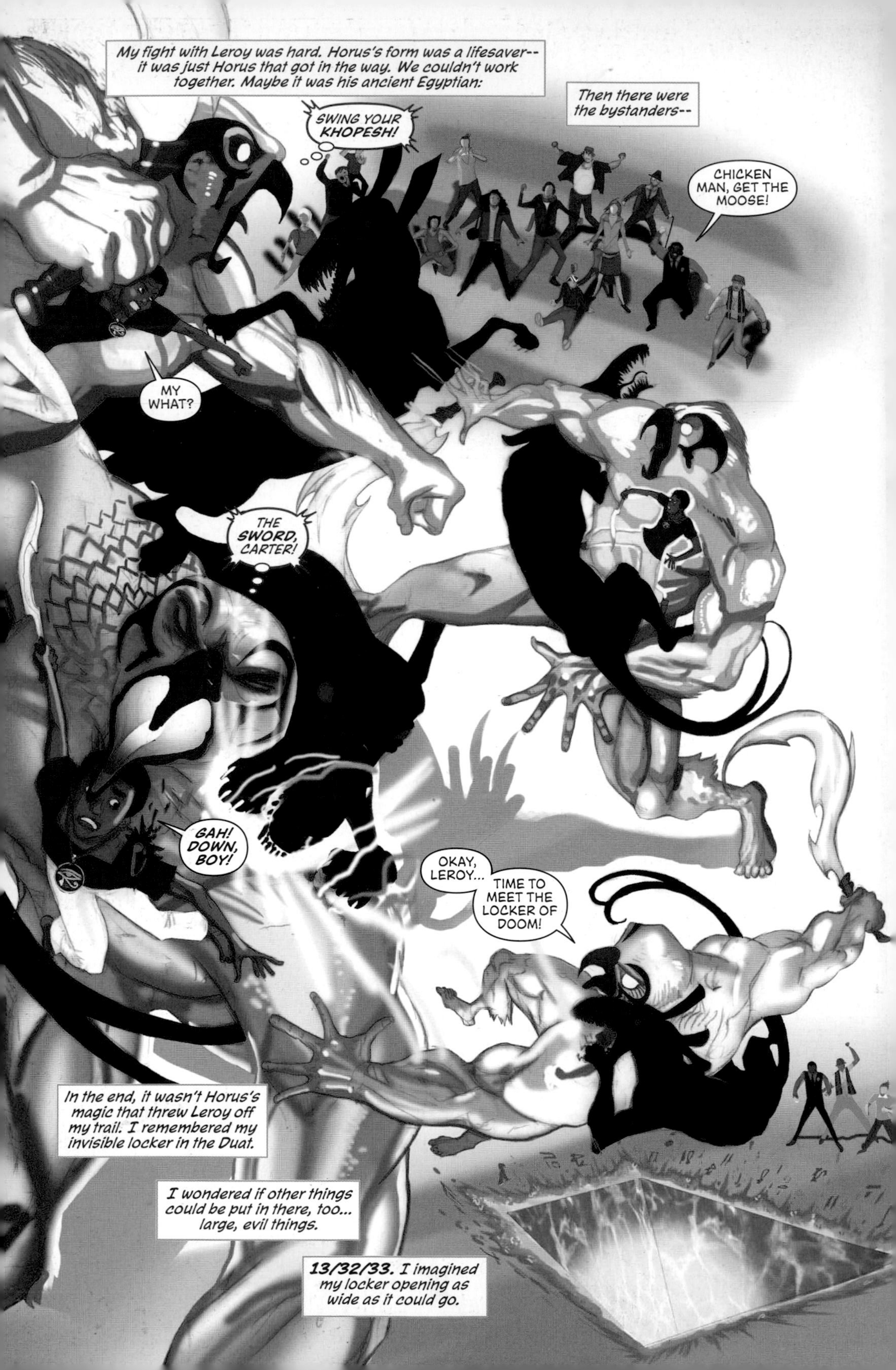
My fight with Leroy was hard. Horus's form was a lifesaver--it was just Horus that got in the way. We couldn't work together. Maybe it was his ancient Egyptian:
SWING YOUR KHOPESH!
MY WHAT?
Then there were the bystanders--
CHICKEN MAN, GET THE MOOSE!
THE SWORD, CARTER!
GAH! DOWN, BOY!
OKAY, LEROY...
TIME TO MEET THE LOCKER OF DOOM!
In the end, it wasn't Horus's magic that threw Leroy off my trail. I remembered my invisible locker in the Duat.
I wondered if other things could be put in there, too... large, evil things.
13/32/33. I imagined my locker opening as wide as it could go.

WHERE'D THE MOOSE GO?
HEY, KID! YOU OKAY?
I left my sword in the Duat and ran for the gate.
I reached our flight just as they were closing the door.
Apparently, word of the chicken man incident hadn't spread quite yet.
WHAT'S ALL THE NOISE UP THERE?
A MOOSE GOT THROUGH SECURITY. IT'S UNDER CONTROL NOW.
scan here

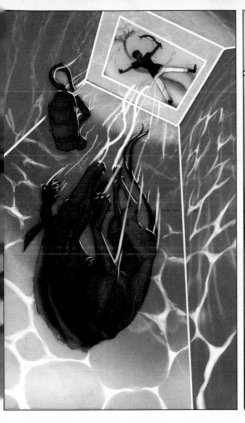

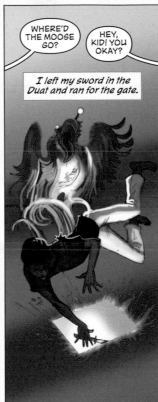

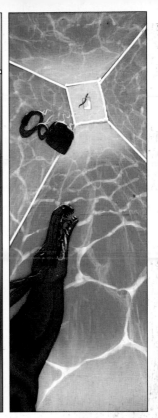

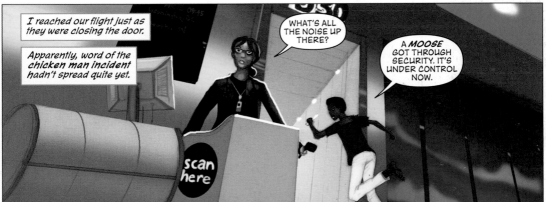

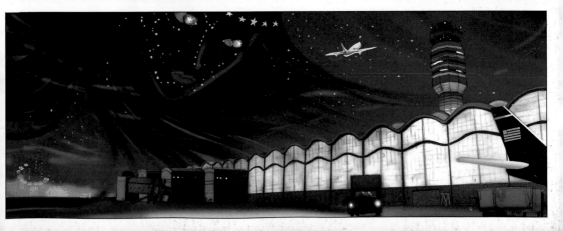

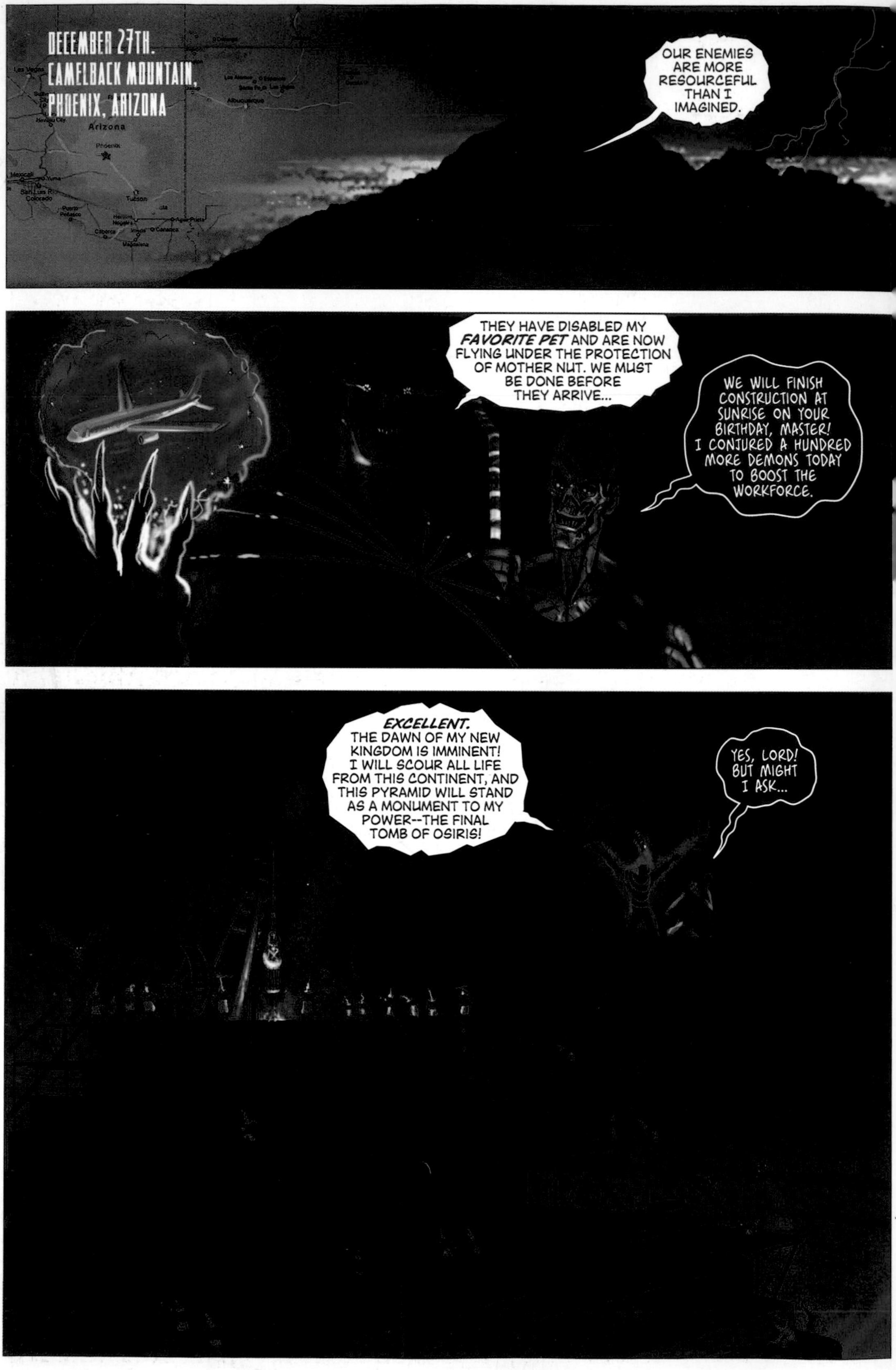
DECEMBER 27TH. CAMELBACK MOUNTAIN, PHOENIX, ARIZONA
OUR ENEMIES ARE MORE RESOURCEFUL THAN I IMAGINED.
THEY HAVE DISABLED MY *FAVORITE PET* AND ARE NOW FLYING UNDER THE PROTECTION OF MOTHER NUT. WE MUST BE DONE BEFORE THEY ARRIVE...
WE WILL FINISH CONSTRUCTION AT SUNRISE ON YOUR BIRTHDAY, MASTER! I CONJURED A HUNDRED MORE DEMONS TODAY TO BOOST THE WORKFORCE.
EXCELLENT. THE DAWN OF MY NEW KINGDOM IS IMMINENT! I WILL SCOUR ALL LIFE FROM THIS CONTINENT, AND THIS PYRAMID WILL STAND AS A MONUMENT TO MY POWER--THE FINAL TOMB OF OSIRIS!
YES, LORD! BUT MIGHT I ASK...

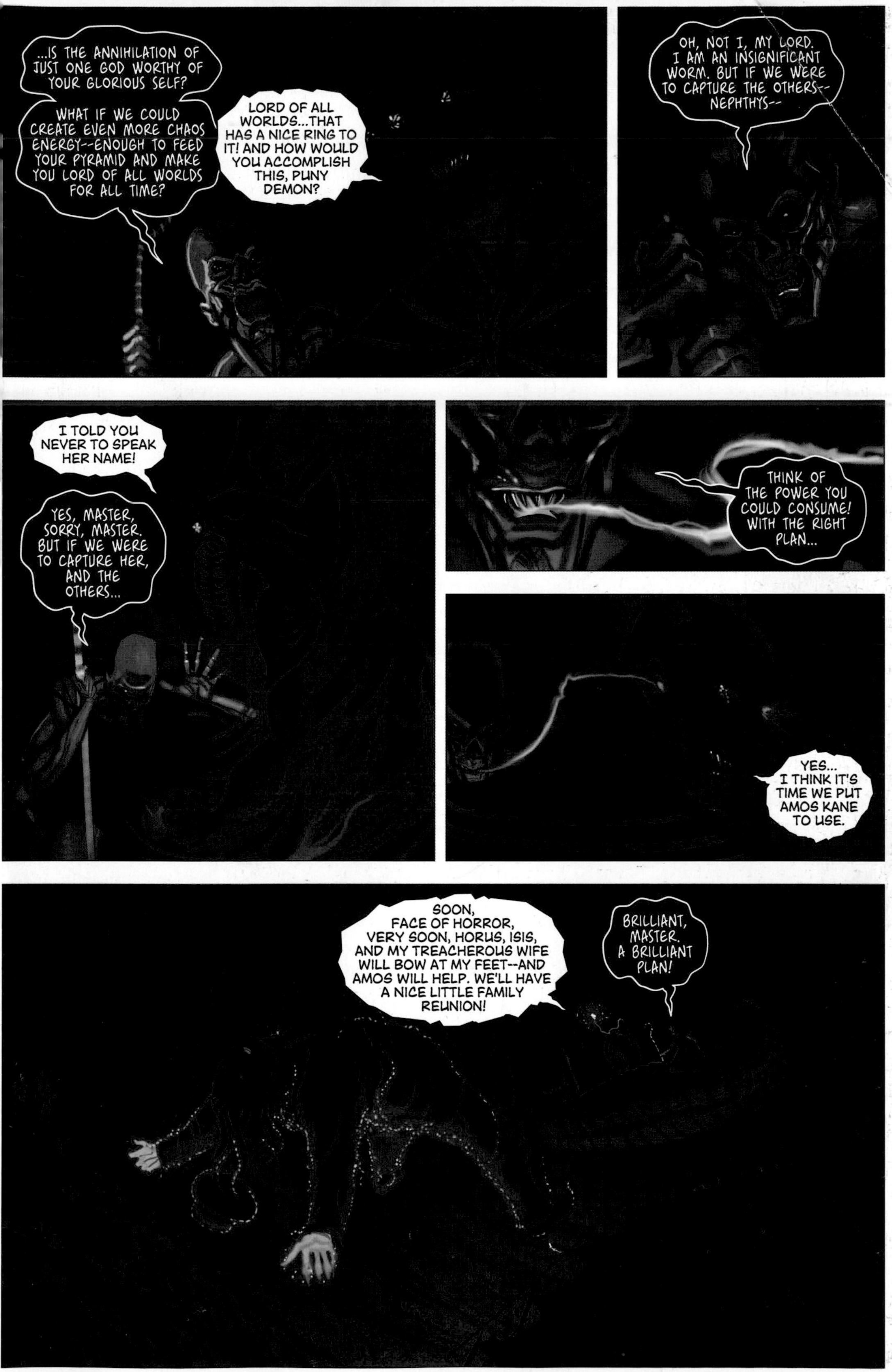
...IS THE ANNIHILATION OF JUST ONE GOD WORTHY OF YOUR GLORIOUS SELF?
WHAT IF WE COULD CREATE EVEN MORE CHAOS ENERGY--ENOUGH TO FEED YOUR PYRAMID AND MAKE YOU LORD OF ALL WORLDS FOR ALL TIME?
LORD OF ALL WORLDS...THAT HAS A NICE RING TO IT! AND HOW WOULD YOU ACCOMPLISH THIS, PUNY DEMON?
OH, NOT I, MY LORD. I AM AN INSIGNIFICANT WORM. BUT IF WE WERE TO CAPTURE THE OTHERS-- NEPHTHYS--
I TOLD YOU NEVER TO SPEAK HER NAME!
YES, MASTER, SORRY, MASTER. BUT IF WE WERE TO CAPTURE HER, AND THE OTHERS...
THINK OF THE POWER YOU COULD CONSUME! WITH THE RIGHT PLAN...
YES... I THINK IT'S TIME WE PUT AMOS KANE TO USE.
SOON, FACE OF HORROR, VERY SOON, HORUS, ISIS, AND MY TREACHEROUS WIFE WILL BOW AT MY FEET--AND AMOS WILL HELP. WE'LL HAVE A NICE LITTLE FAMILY REUNION!
BRILLIANT, MASTER. A BRILLIANT PLAN!

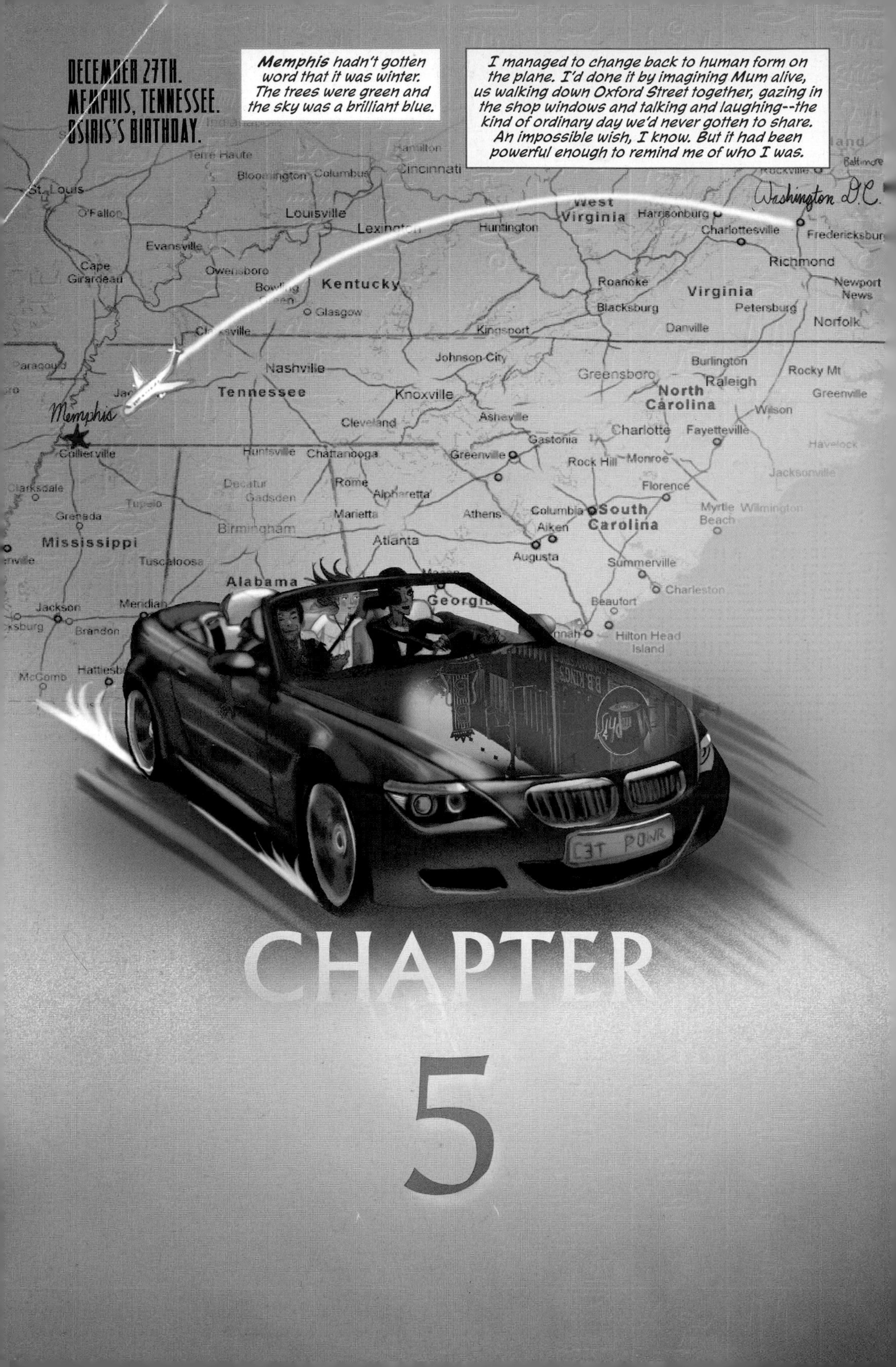
DECEMBER 27TH.
MEMPHIS, TENNESSEE.
OSIRIS'S BIRTHDAY.
Memphis hadn't gotten word that it was winter. The trees were green and the sky was a brilliant blue.
I managed to change back to human form on the plane. I'd done it by imagining Mum alive, us walking down Oxford Street together, gazing in the shop windows and talking and laughing--the kind of ordinary day we'd never gotten to share. An impossible wish, I know. But it had been powerful enough to remind me of who I was.
Washington D.C.
Memphis
St. Louis
Cincinnati
Louisville
Kentucky
West Virginia
Virginia
Richmond
Norfolk
Nashville
Tennessee
Knoxville
North Carolina
Raleigh
Charlotte
South Carolina
Mississippi
Alabama
Atlanta
Georgia
Charleston
C3T POWR

CHAPTER 5

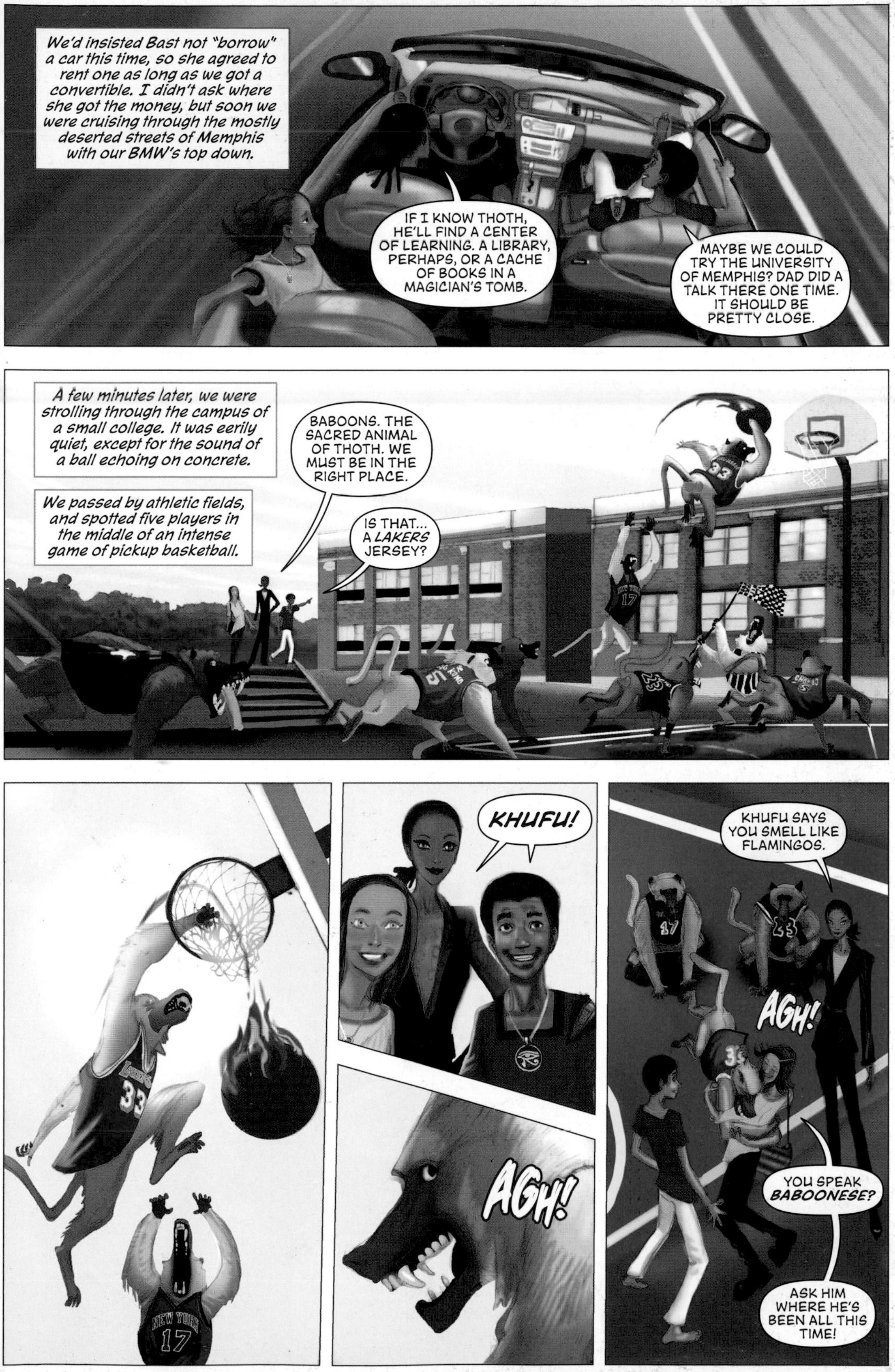
We'd insisted Bast not "borrow" a car this time, so she agreed to rent one as long as we got a convertible. I didn't ask where she got the money, but soon we were cruising through the mostly deserted streets of Memphis with our BMW's top down.
IF I KNOW THOTH, HE'LL FIND A CENTER OF LEARNING. A LIBRARY, PERHAPS, OR A CACHE OF BOOKS IN A MAGICIAN'S TOMB.
MAYBE WE COULD TRY THE UNIVERSITY OF MEMPHIS? DAD DID A TALK THERE ONE TIME. IT SHOULD BE PRETTY CLOSE.
A few minutes later, we were strolling through the campus of a small college. It was eerily quiet, except for the sound of a ball echoing on concrete.
We passed by athletic fields, and spotted five players in the middle of an intense game of pickup basketball.
BABOONS. THE SACRED ANIMAL OF THOTH. WE MUST BE IN THE RIGHT PLACE.
IS THAT... A LAKERS JERSEY?
KHUFU!
AGH!
KHUFU SAYS YOU SMELL LIKE FLAMINGOS.
AGH!
YOU SPEAK BABOONESE?
ASK HIM WHERE HE'S BEEN ALL THIS TIME!

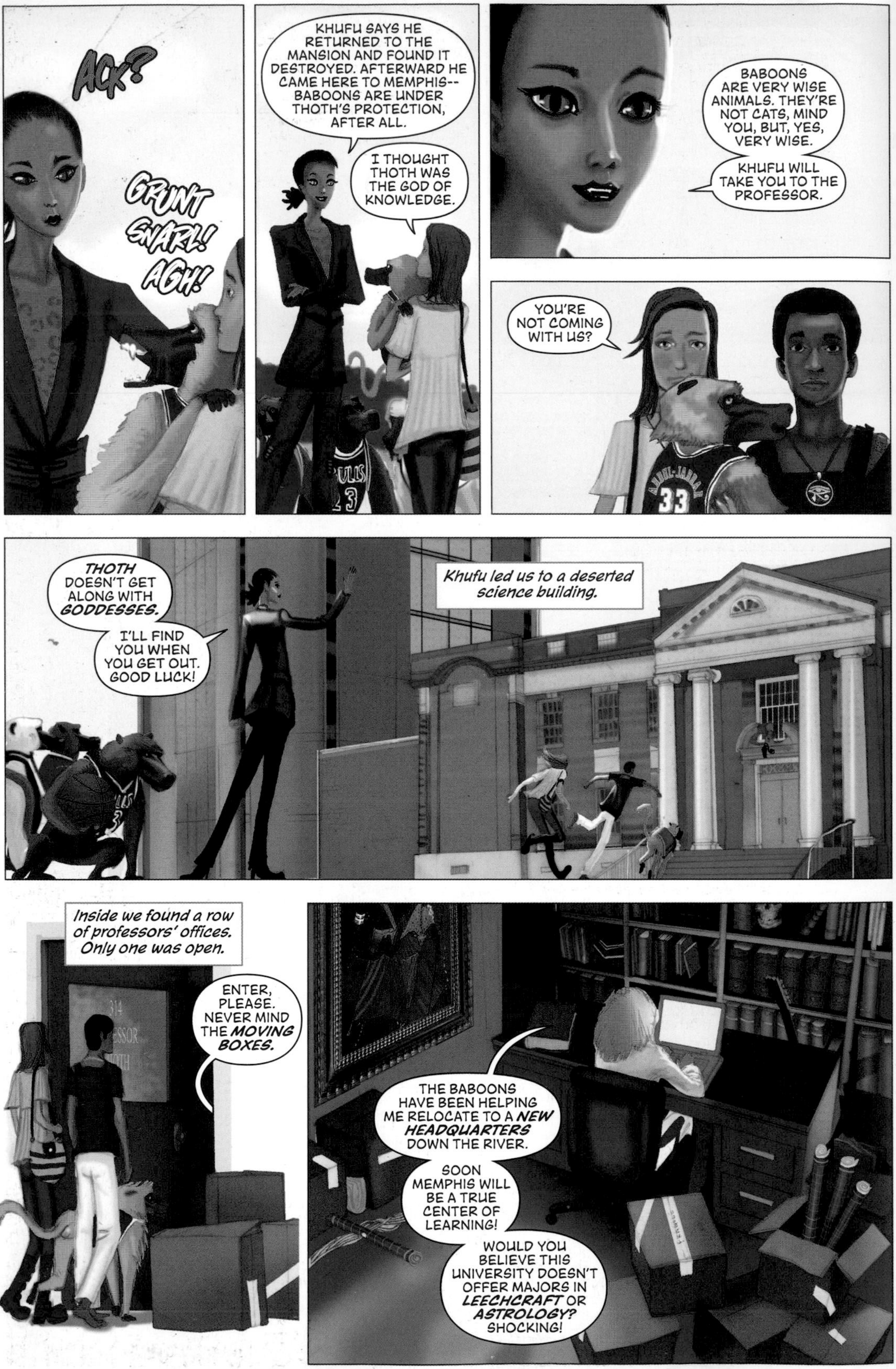
ACK?
GRUNT SNARL! AGH!
KHUFU SAYS HE RETURNED TO THE MANSION AND FOUND IT DESTROYED. AFTERWARD HE CAME HERE TO MEMPHIS-- BABOONS ARE UNDER THOTH'S PROTECTION, AFTER ALL.
I THOUGHT THOTH WAS THE GOD OF KNOWLEDGE.
BABOONS ARE VERY WISE ANIMALS. THEY'RE NOT CATS, MIND YOU, BUT, YES, VERY WISE.
KHUFU WILL TAKE YOU TO THE PROFESSOR.
YOU'RE NOT COMING WITH US?
THOTH DOESN'T GET ALONG WITH *GODDESSES.*
I'LL FIND YOU WHEN YOU GET OUT. GOOD LUCK!
Khufu led us to a deserted science building.
Inside we found a row of professors' offices. Only one was open.
ENTER, PLEASE. NEVER MIND THE *MOVING BOXES.*
THE BABOONS HAVE BEEN HELPING ME RELOCATE TO A *NEW HEADQUARTERS* DOWN THE RIVER.
SOON MEMPHIS WILL BE A TRUE CENTER OF LEARNING!
WOULD YOU BELIEVE THIS UNIVERSITY DOESN'T OFFER MAJORS IN *LEECHCRAFT* OR *ASTROLOGY?* SHOCKING!

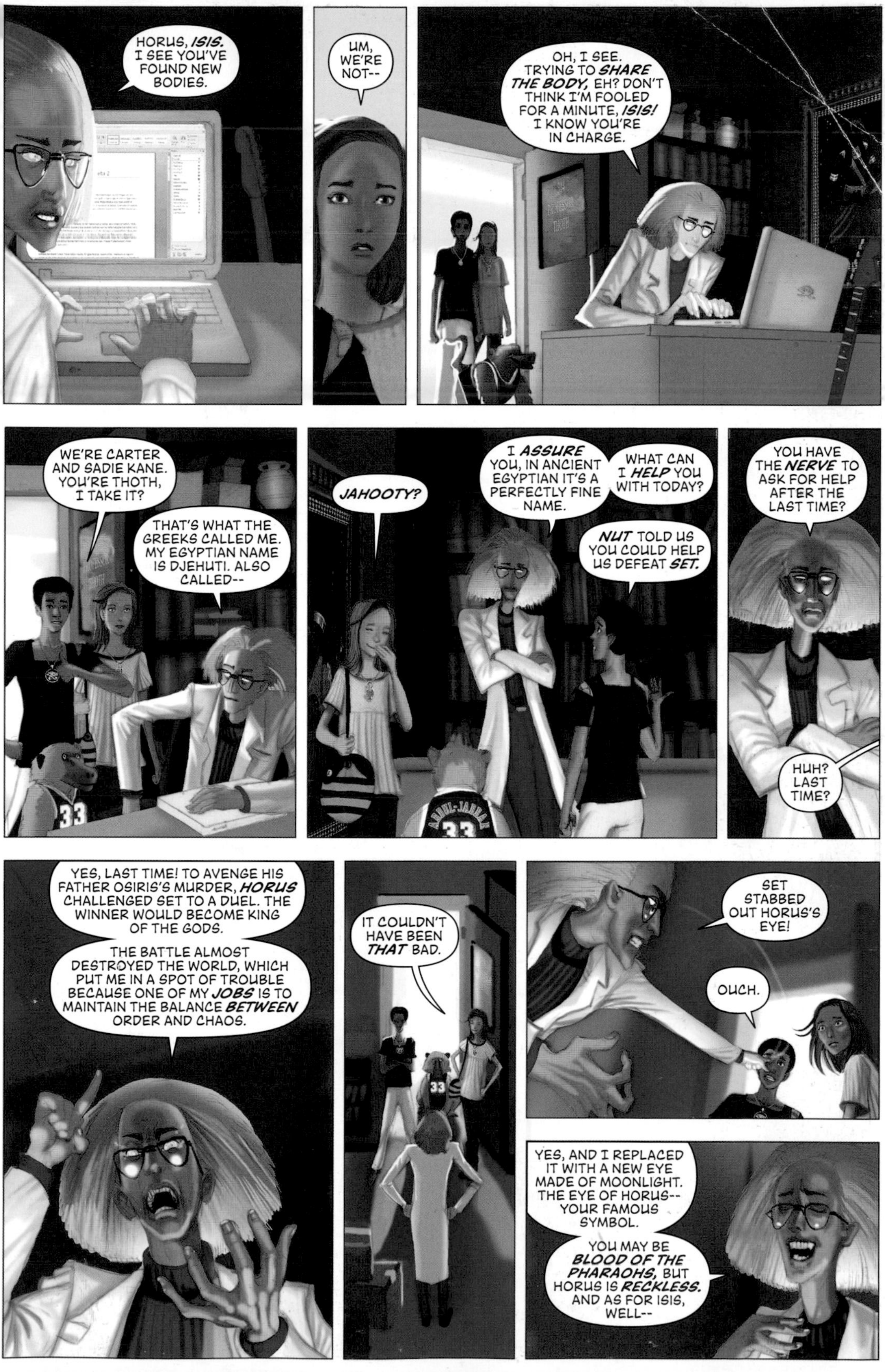
HORUS, ISIS. I SEE YOU'VE FOUND NEW BODIES.
UM, WE'RE NOT--
OH, I SEE. TRYING TO SHARE THE BODY, EH? DON'T THINK I'M FOOLED FOR A MINUTE, ISIS! I KNOW YOU'RE IN CHARGE.
WE'RE CARTER AND SADIE KANE. YOU'RE THOTH, I TAKE IT?
THAT'S WHAT THE GREEKS CALLED ME. MY EGYPTIAN NAME IS DJEHUTI. ALSO CALLED--
JAHOOTY?
I ASSURE YOU, IN ANCIENT EGYPTIAN IT'S A PERFECTLY FINE NAME.
WHAT CAN I HELP YOU WITH TODAY?
NUT TOLD US YOU COULD HELP US DEFEAT SET.
YOU HAVE THE NERVE TO ASK FOR HELP AFTER THE LAST TIME?
HUH? LAST TIME?
YES, LAST TIME! TO AVENGE HIS FATHER OSIRIS'S MURDER, HORUS CHALLENGED SET TO A DUEL. THE WINNER WOULD BECOME KING OF THE GODS.
THE BATTLE ALMOST DESTROYED THE WORLD, WHICH PUT ME IN A SPOT OF TROUBLE BECAUSE ONE OF MY JOBS IS TO MAINTAIN THE BALANCE BETWEEN ORDER AND CHAOS.
IT COULDN'T HAVE BEEN THAT BAD.
SET STABBED OUT HORUS'S EYE!
OUCH.
YES, AND I REPLACED IT WITH A NEW EYE MADE OF MOONLIGHT. THE EYE OF HORUS-- YOUR FAMOUS SYMBOL.
YOU MAY BE BLOOD OF THE PHARAOHS, BUT HORUS IS RECKLESS. AND AS FOR ISIS, WELL--

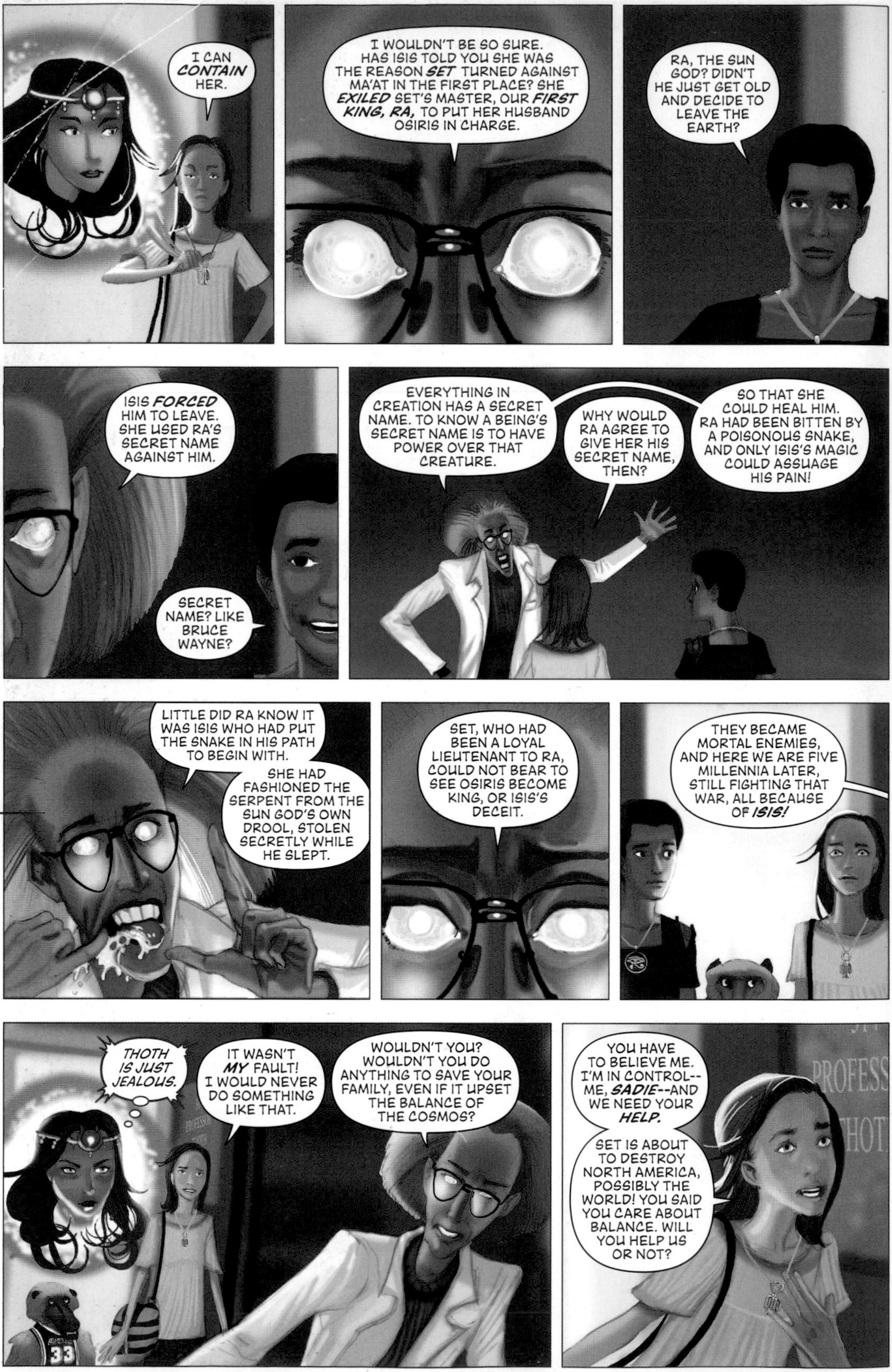
I CAN *CONTAIN* HER.
I WOULDN'T BE SO SURE. HAS ISIS TOLD YOU SHE WAS THE REASON *SET* TURNED AGAINST MA'AT IN THE FIRST PLACE? SHE *EXILED* SET'S MASTER, OUR *FIRST KING, RA,* TO PUT HER HUSBAND OSIRIS IN CHARGE.
RA, THE SUN GOD? DIDN'T HE JUST GET OLD AND DECIDE TO LEAVE THE EARTH?
ISIS *FORCED* HIM TO LEAVE. SHE USED RA'S SECRET NAME AGAINST HIM.
SECRET NAME? LIKE BRUCE WAYNE?
EVERYTHING IN CREATION HAS A SECRET NAME. TO KNOW A BEING'S SECRET NAME IS TO HAVE POWER OVER THAT CREATURE.
WHY WOULD RA AGREE TO GIVE HER HIS SECRET NAME, THEN?
SO THAT SHE COULD HEAL HIM. RA HAD BEEN BITTEN BY A POISONOUS SNAKE, AND ONLY ISIS'S MAGIC COULD ASSUAGE HIS PAIN!
LITTLE DID RA KNOW IT WAS ISIS WHO HAD PUT THE SNAKE IN HIS PATH TO BEGIN WITH.
SHE HAD FASHIONED THE SERPENT FROM THE SUN GOD'S OWN DROOL, STOLEN SECRETLY WHILE HE SLEPT.
SET, WHO HAD BEEN A LOYAL LIEUTENANT TO RA, COULD NOT BEAR TO SEE OSIRIS BECOME KING, OR ISIS'S DECEIT.
THEY BECAME MORTAL ENEMIES, AND HERE WE ARE FIVE MILLENNIA LATER, STILL FIGHTING THAT WAR, ALL BECAUSE OF *ISIS!*
THOTH IS JUST JEALOUS.
IT WASN'T *MY* FAULT! I WOULD NEVER DO SOMETHING LIKE THAT.
WOULDN'T YOU? WOULDN'T YOU DO ANYTHING TO SAVE YOUR FAMILY, EVEN IF IT UPSET THE BALANCE OF THE COSMOS?
YOU HAVE TO BELIEVE ME. I'M IN CONTROL-- ME, *SADIE*--AND WE NEED YOUR *HELP.*
SET IS ABOUT TO DESTROY NORTH AMERICA, POSSIBLY THE WORLD! YOU SAID YOU CARE ABOUT BALANCE. WILL YOU HELP US OR NOT?

YOU ARE IN TROUBLE. SO LET ME ASK, WHY DO YOU THINK YOUR FATHER PUT YOU IN THIS POSITION? WHY DID HE RELEASE THE GODS?

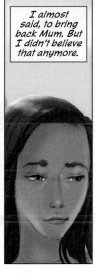

I almost said, to bring back Mum. But I didn't believe that anymore.

MY MUM SAW THE FUTURE. SOMETHING BAD WAS COMING. SHE AND DAD THOUGHT THE ONLY WAY TO STOP IT WAS TO RELEASE THE GODS.

EVEN THOUGH USING THE GODS IS AGAINST THE LAW OF THE HOUSE OF LIFE--A LAW THAT I CONVINCED ISKANDAR TO MAKE, BY THE WAY.

MY MUM CONVINCED ISKANDAR THAT THE *LAW* WAS WRONG. MAYBE HE COULDN'T ADMIT IT PUBLICLY, BUT WHATEVER IS COMING--IT'S SO BAD, GODS AND MORTALS ARE GOING TO NEED EACH OTHER.

HMM. VERY WELL. LET'S SEE IF YOU *ACT* AS WELL AS YOU *TALK.* IF YOU CAN PROVE TO ME THAT YOU TRULY HAVE CONTROL OF YOUR GODS, THAT YOU'RE NOT SIMPLY REPEATING THE SAME OLD PATTERNS, I WILL HELP YOU.

A *TEST?* WE ACCEPT.

Maybe being homeschooled, Carter didn't realize that a test is normally a bad thing.

WHAT SORT OF TEST?

THERE IS AN ITEM OF POWER I REQUIRE FROM A MAGICIAN'S TOMB IF I AM TO BE OF HELP.

BRING IT TO ME *WITHOUT USING GODLY MAGIC.* I WILL PROVIDE THE PORTAL.

BAST SAID WE CAN'T SUMMON PORTALS DURING THE DEMONS DAYS.

MORTALS CAN'T--

BUT A GOD OF MAGIC *CAN!*

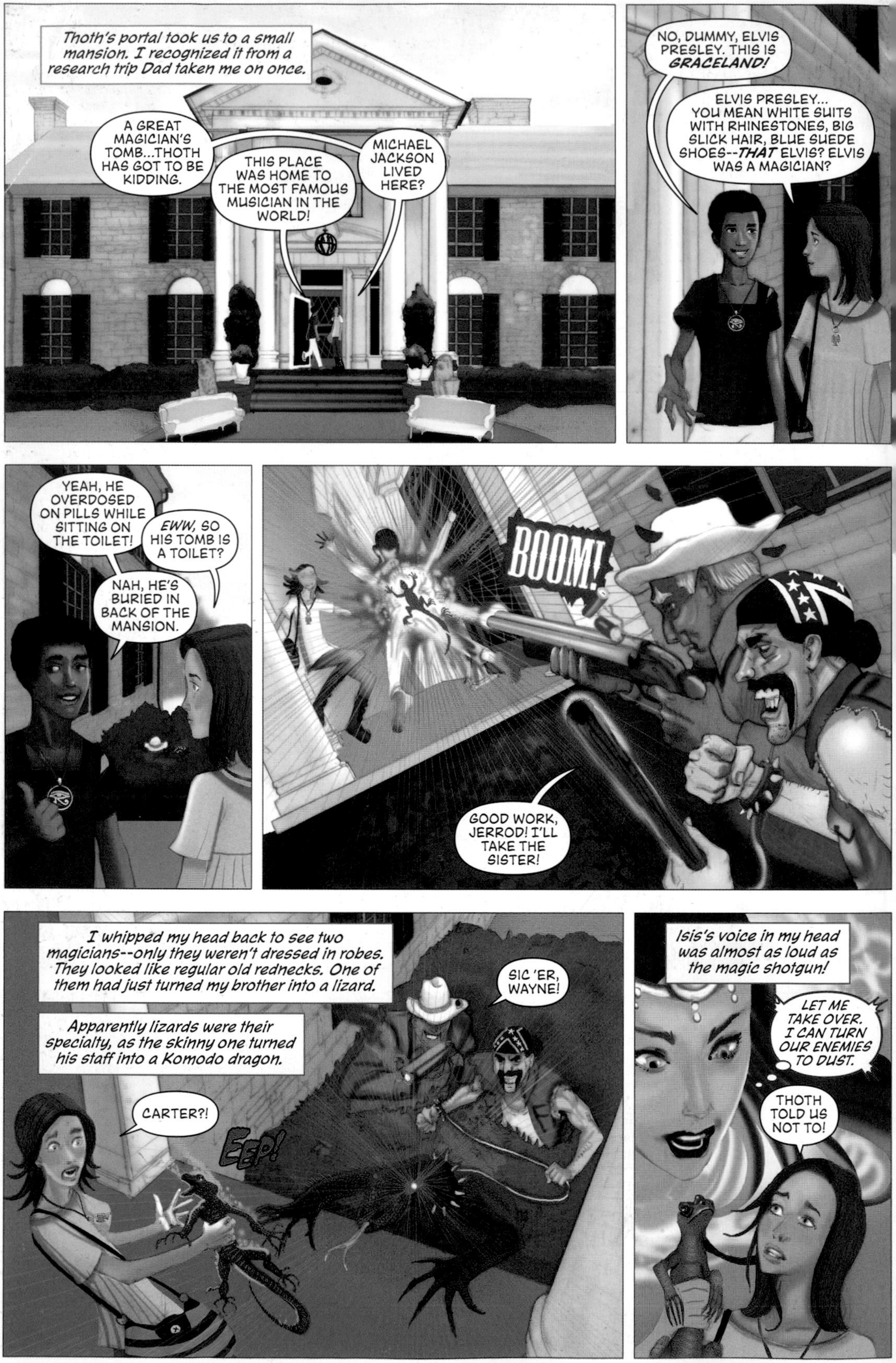
Thoth's portal took us to a small mansion. I recognized it from a research trip Dad taken me on once.
A GREAT MAGICIAN'S TOMB...THOTH HAS GOT TO BE KIDDING.
THIS PLACE WAS HOME TO THE MOST FAMOUS MUSICIAN IN THE WORLD!
MICHAEL JACKSON LIVED HERE?
NO, DUMMY, ELVIS PRESLEY. THIS IS GRACELAND!
ELVIS PRESLEY... YOU MEAN WHITE SUITS WITH RHINESTONES, BIG SLICK HAIR, BLUE SUEDE SHOES--THAT ELVIS? ELVIS WAS A MAGICIAN?
YEAH, HE OVERDOSED ON PILLS WHILE SITTING ON THE TOILET!
EWW, SO HIS TOMB IS A TOILET?
NAH, HE'S BURIED IN BACK OF THE MANSION.
BOOM!
GOOD WORK, JERROD! I'LL TAKE THE SISTER!
I whipped my head back to see two magicians--only they weren't dressed in robes. They looked like regular old rednecks. One of them had just turned my brother into a lizard.
Apparently lizards were their specialty, as the skinny one turned his staff into a Komodo dragon.
SIC 'ER, WAYNE!
CARTER?!
EEP!
Isis's voice in my head was almost as loud as the magic shotgun!
LET ME TAKE OVER. I CAN TURN OUR ENEMIES TO DUST.
THOTH TOLD US NOT TO!

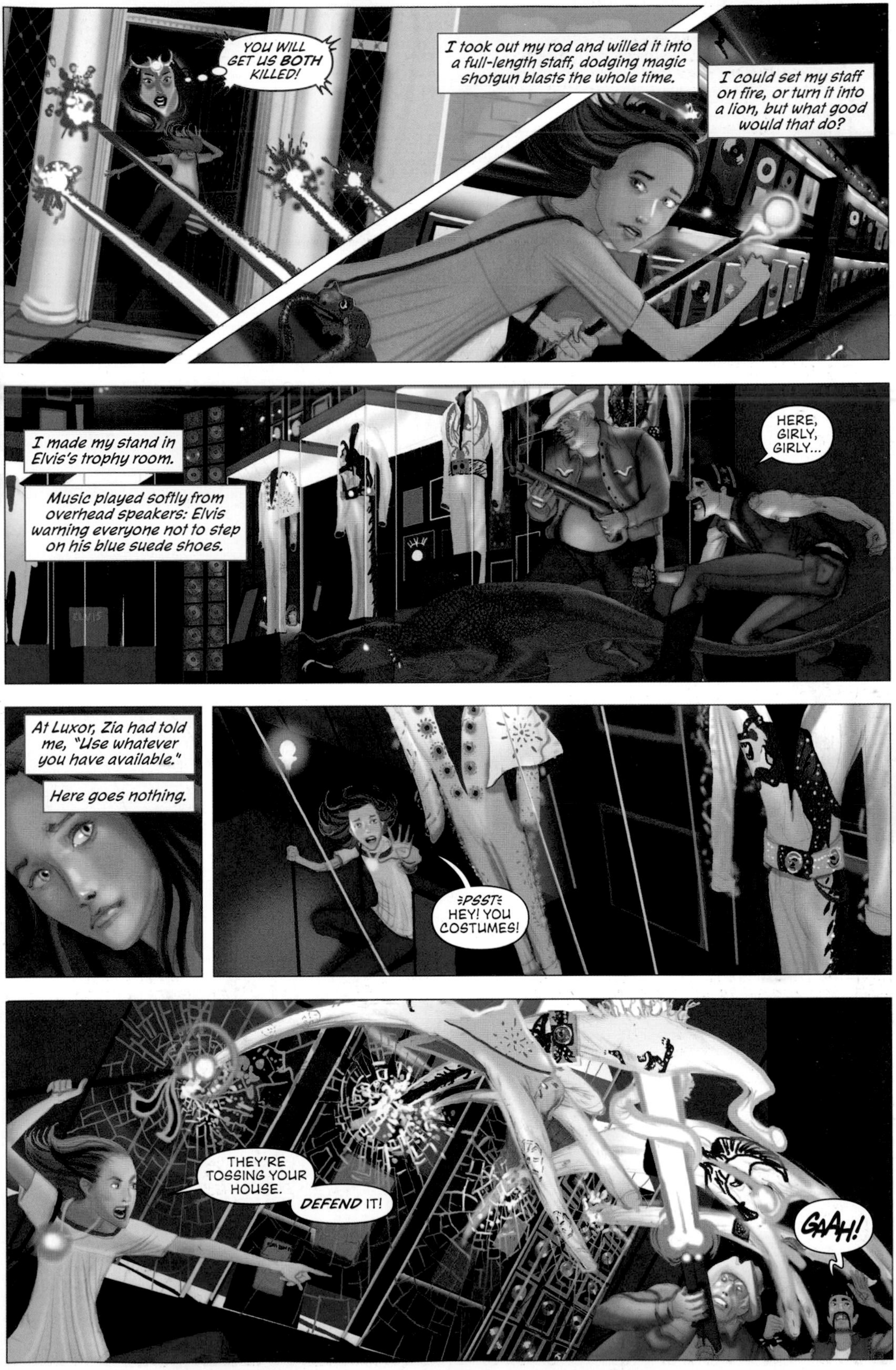
YOU WILL GET US BOTH KILLED!
I took out my rod and willed it into a full-length staff, dodging magic shotgun blasts the whole time.
I could set my staff on fire, or turn it into a lion, but what good would that do?
I made my stand in Elvis's trophy room.
Music played softly from overhead speakers: Elvis warning everyone not to step on his blue suede shoes.
HERE, GIRLY, GIRLY...
At Luxor, Zia had told me, "Use whatever you have available."
Here goes nothing.
PSST HEY! YOU COSTUMES!
THEY'RE TOSSING YOUR HOUSE. DEFEND IT!
GAAH!

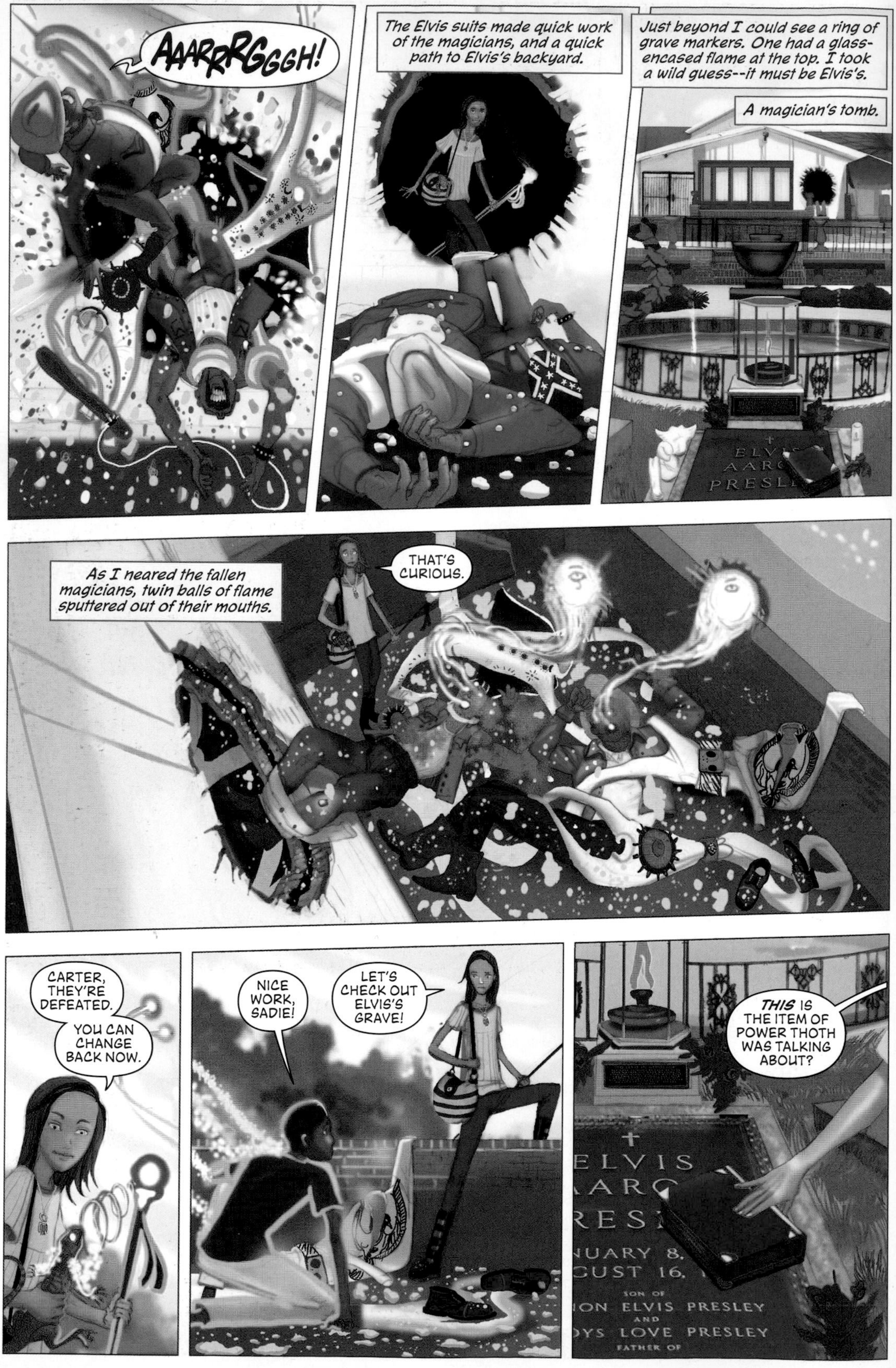
AAARRRGGGH!
The Elvis suits made quick work of the magicians, and a quick path to Elvis's backyard.
Just beyond I could see a ring of grave markers. One had a glass-encased flame at the top. I took a wild guess--it must be Elvis's.
A magician's tomb.
ELVIS
AARO
PRESL
As I neared the fallen magicians, twin balls of flame sputtered out of their mouths.
THAT'S CURIOUS.
CARTER, THEY'RE DEFEATED.
YOU CAN CHANGE BACK NOW.
NICE WORK, SADIE!
LET'S CHECK OUT ELVIS'S GRAVE!
THIS IS THE ITEM OF POWER THOTH WAS TALKING ABOUT?
ELVIS
AARO
RESL
NUARY 8,
GUST 16,
SON OF
ON ELVIS PRESLEY
AND
DYS LOVE PRESLEY
FATHER OF

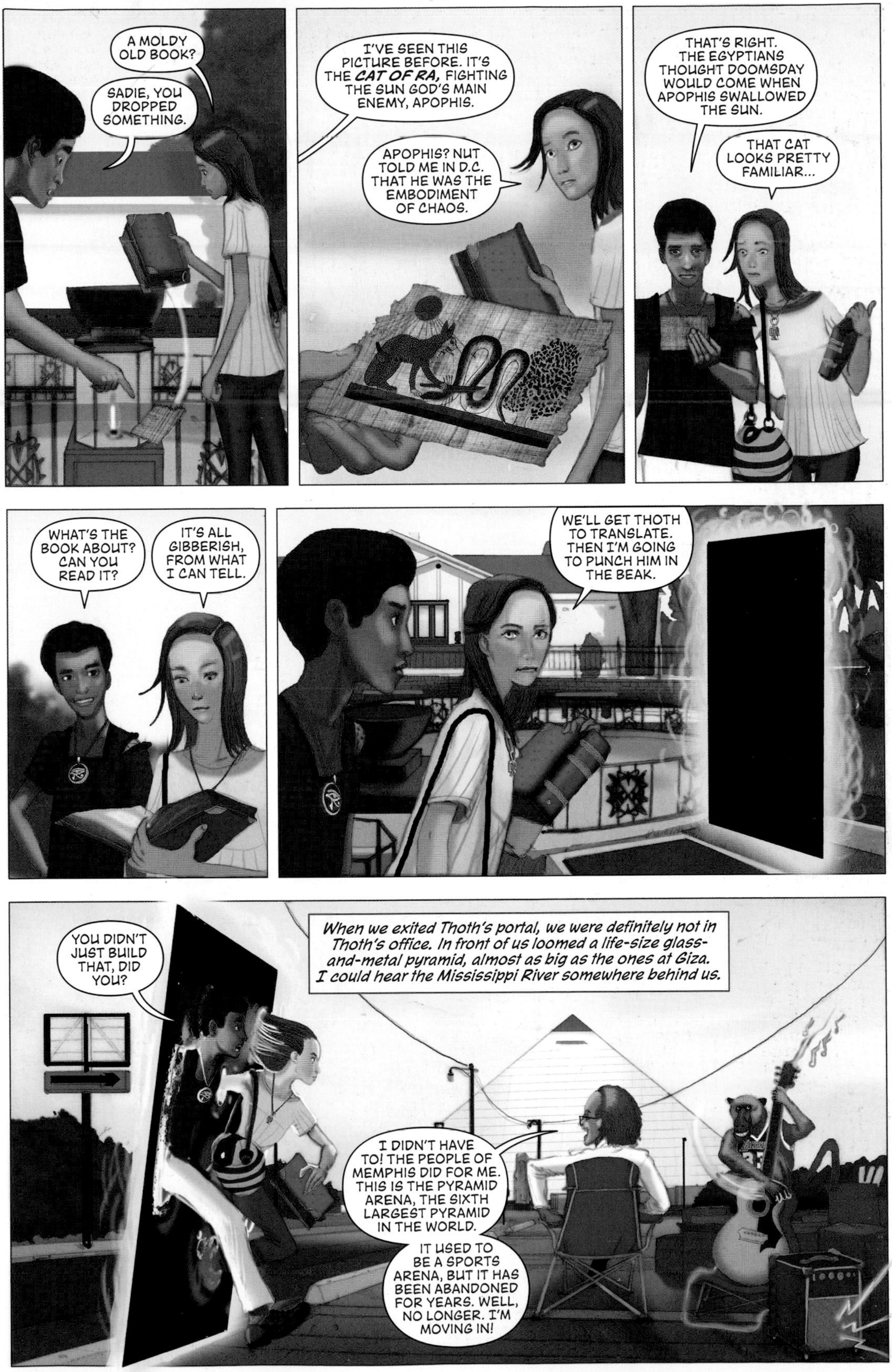
A MOLDY OLD BOOK?
SADIE, YOU DROPPED SOMETHING.
I'VE SEEN THIS PICTURE BEFORE. IT'S THE CAT OF RA, FIGHTING THE SUN GOD'S MAIN ENEMY, APOPHIS.
APOPHIS? NUT TOLD ME IN D.C. THAT HE WAS THE EMBODIMENT OF CHAOS.
THAT'S RIGHT. THE EGYPTIANS THOUGHT DOOMSDAY WOULD COME WHEN APOPHIS SWALLOWED THE SUN.
THAT CAT LOOKS PRETTY FAMILIAR...
WHAT'S THE BOOK ABOUT? CAN YOU READ IT?
IT'S ALL GIBBERISH, FROM WHAT I CAN TELL.
WE'LL GET THOTH TO TRANSLATE. THEN I'M GOING TO PUNCH HIM IN THE BEAK.
When we exited Thoth's portal, we were definitely not in Thoth's office. In front of us loomed a life-size glass-and-metal pyramid, almost as big as the ones at Giza. I could hear the Mississippi River somewhere behind us.
YOU DIDN'T JUST BUILD THAT, DID YOU?
I DIDN'T HAVE TO! THE PEOPLE OF MEMPHIS DID FOR ME. THIS IS THE PYRAMID ARENA, THE SIXTH LARGEST PYRAMID IN THE WORLD.
IT USED TO BE A SPORTS ARENA, BUT IT HAS BEEN ABANDONED FOR YEARS. WELL, NO LONGER. I'M MOVING IN!

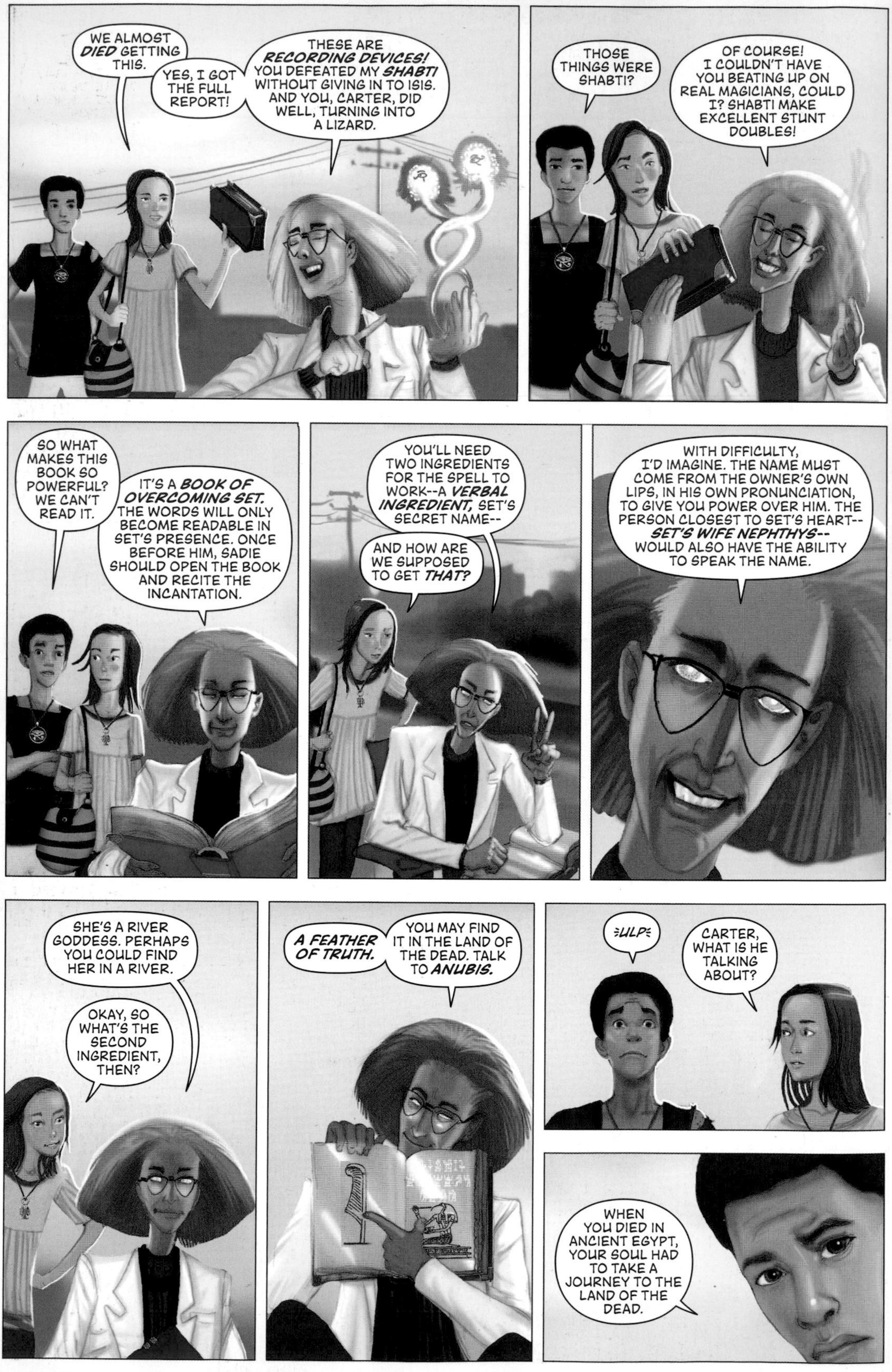
WE ALMOST DIED GETTING THIS.
YES, I GOT THE FULL REPORT!
THESE ARE RECORDING DEVICES! YOU DEFEATED MY SHABTI WITHOUT GIVING IN TO ISIS. AND YOU, CARTER, DID WELL, TURNING INTO A LIZARD.
THOSE THINGS WERE SHABTI?
OF COURSE! I COULDN'T HAVE YOU BEATING UP ON REAL MAGICIANS, COULD I? SHABTI MAKE EXCELLENT STUNT DOUBLES!
SO WHAT MAKES THIS BOOK SO POWERFUL? WE CAN'T READ IT.
IT'S A BOOK OF OVERCOMING SET. THE WORDS WILL ONLY BECOME READABLE IN SET'S PRESENCE. ONCE BEFORE HIM, SADIE SHOULD OPEN THE BOOK AND RECITE THE INCANTATION.
YOU'LL NEED TWO INGREDIENTS FOR THE SPELL TO WORK--A VERBAL INGREDIENT, SET'S SECRET NAME--
AND HOW ARE WE SUPPOSED TO GET THAT?
WITH DIFFICULTY, I'D IMAGINE. THE NAME MUST COME FROM THE OWNER'S OWN LIPS, IN HIS OWN PRONUNCIATION, TO GIVE YOU POWER OVER HIM. THE PERSON CLOSEST TO SET'S HEART--SET'S WIFE NEPHTHYS--WOULD ALSO HAVE THE ABILITY TO SPEAK THE NAME.
SHE'S A RIVER GODDESS. PERHAPS YOU COULD FIND HER IN A RIVER.
OKAY, SO WHAT'S THE SECOND INGREDIENT, THEN?
A FEATHER OF TRUTH.
YOU MAY FIND IT IN THE LAND OF THE DEAD. TALK TO ANUBIS.
ULP
CARTER, WHAT IS HE TALKING ABOUT?
WHEN YOU DIED IN ANCIENT EGYPT, YOUR SOUL HAD TO TAKE A JOURNEY TO THE LAND OF THE DEAD.

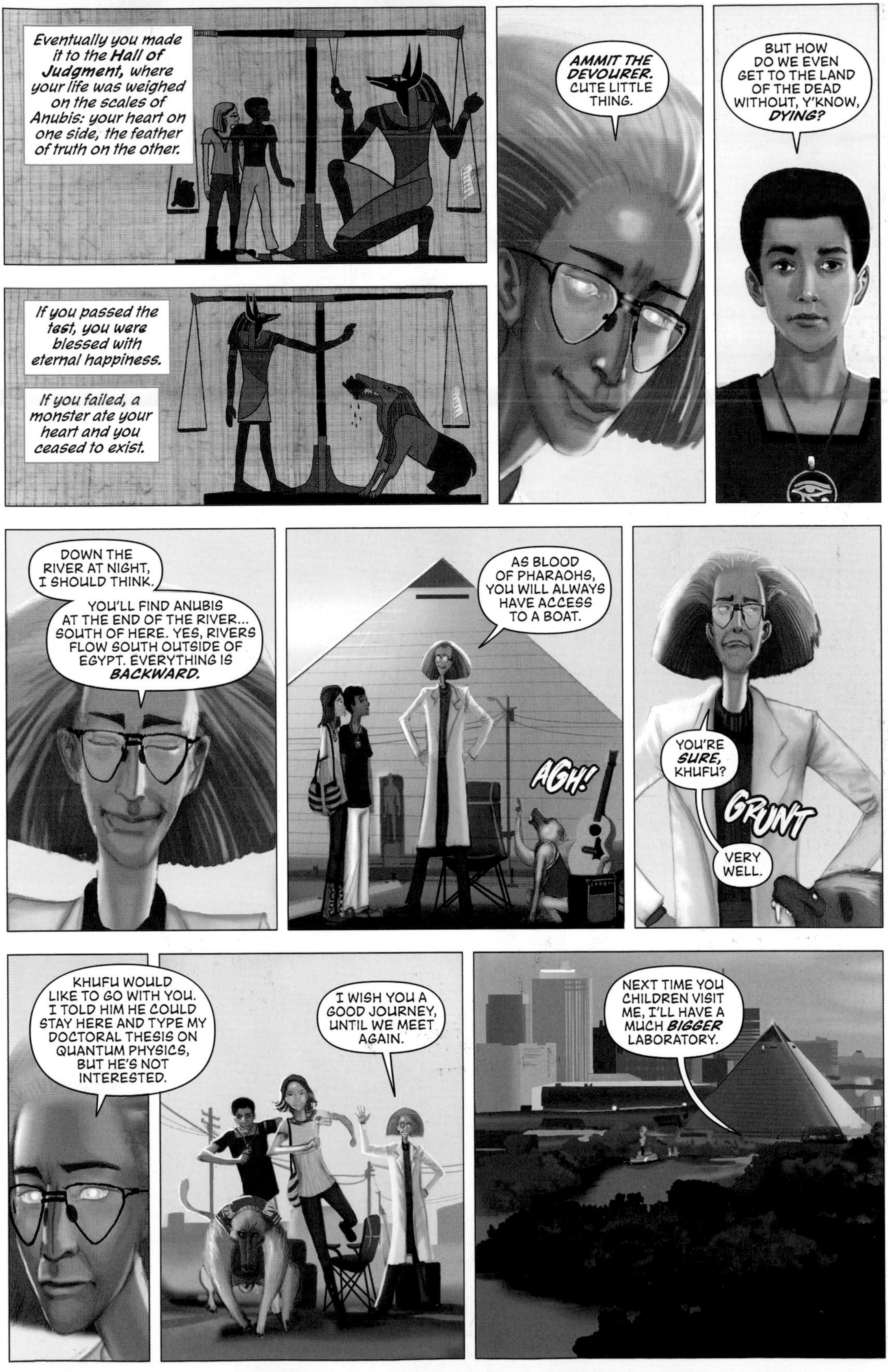
Eventually you made it to the Hall of Judgment, where your life was weighed on the scales of Anubis: your heart on one side, the feather of truth on the other.
AMMIT THE DEVOURER. CUTE LITTLE THING.
BUT HOW DO WE EVEN GET TO THE LAND OF THE DEAD WITHOUT, Y'KNOW, DYING?
If you passed the test, you were blessed with eternal happiness.
If you failed, a monster ate your heart and you ceased to exist.
DOWN THE RIVER AT NIGHT, I SHOULD THINK.
YOU'LL FIND ANUBIS AT THE END OF THE RIVER... SOUTH OF HERE. YES, RIVERS FLOW SOUTH OUTSIDE OF EGYPT. EVERYTHING IS BACKWARD.
AS BLOOD OF PHARAOHS, YOU WILL ALWAYS HAVE ACCESS TO A BOAT.
AGH!
YOU'RE SURE, KHUFU?
GRUNT
VERY WELL.
KHUFU WOULD LIKE TO GO WITH YOU. I TOLD HIM HE COULD STAY HERE AND TYPE MY DOCTORAL THESIS ON QUANTUM PHYSICS, BUT HE'S NOT INTERESTED.
I WISH YOU A GOOD JOURNEY, UNTIL WE MEET AGAIN.
NEXT TIME YOU CHILDREN VISIT ME, I'LL HAVE A MUCH BIGGER LABORATORY.

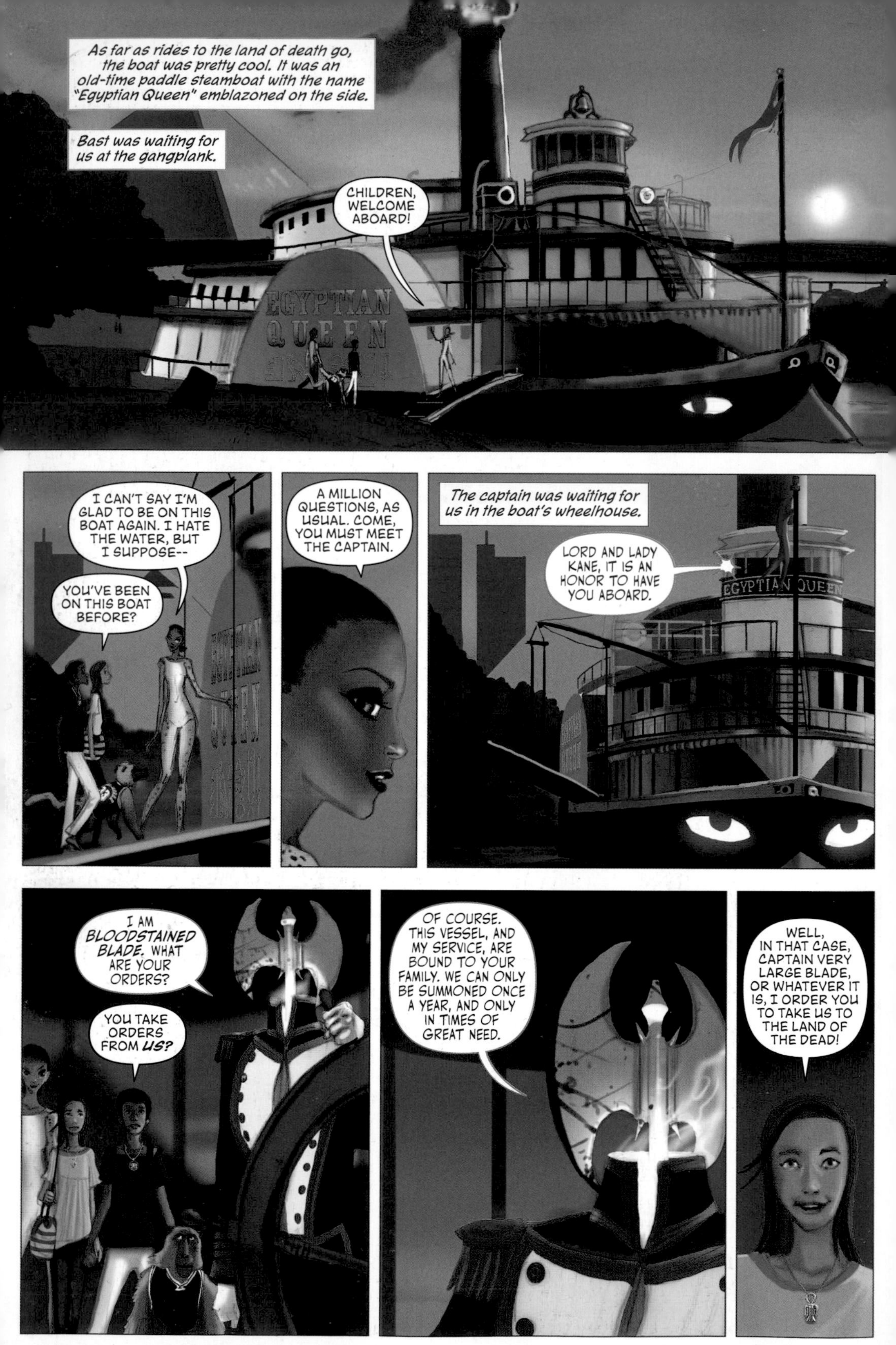

As far as rides to the land of death go, the boat was pretty cool. It was an old-time paddle steamboat with the name "Egyptian Queen" emblazoned on the side.
Bast was waiting for us at the gangplank.
CHILDREN, WELCOME ABOARD!
EGYPTIAN QUEEN
I CAN'T SAY I'M GLAD TO BE ON THIS BOAT AGAIN. I HATE THE WATER, BUT I SUPPOSE--
YOU'VE BEEN ON THIS BOAT BEFORE?
A MILLION QUESTIONS, AS USUAL. COME, YOU MUST MEET THE CAPTAIN.
The captain was waiting for us in the boat's wheelhouse.
LORD AND LADY KANE, IT IS AN HONOR TO HAVE YOU ABOARD.
EGYPTIAN QUEEN
I AM *BLOODSTAINED BLADE.* WHAT ARE YOUR ORDERS?
YOU TAKE ORDERS FROM *US?*
OF COURSE. THIS VESSEL, AND MY SERVICE, ARE BOUND TO YOUR FAMILY. WE CAN ONLY BE SUMMONED ONCE A YEAR, AND ONLY IN TIMES OF GREAT NEED.
WELL, IN THAT CASE, CAPTAIN VERY LARGE BLADE, OR WHATEVER IT IS, I ORDER YOU TO TAKE US TO THE LAND OF THE DEAD!

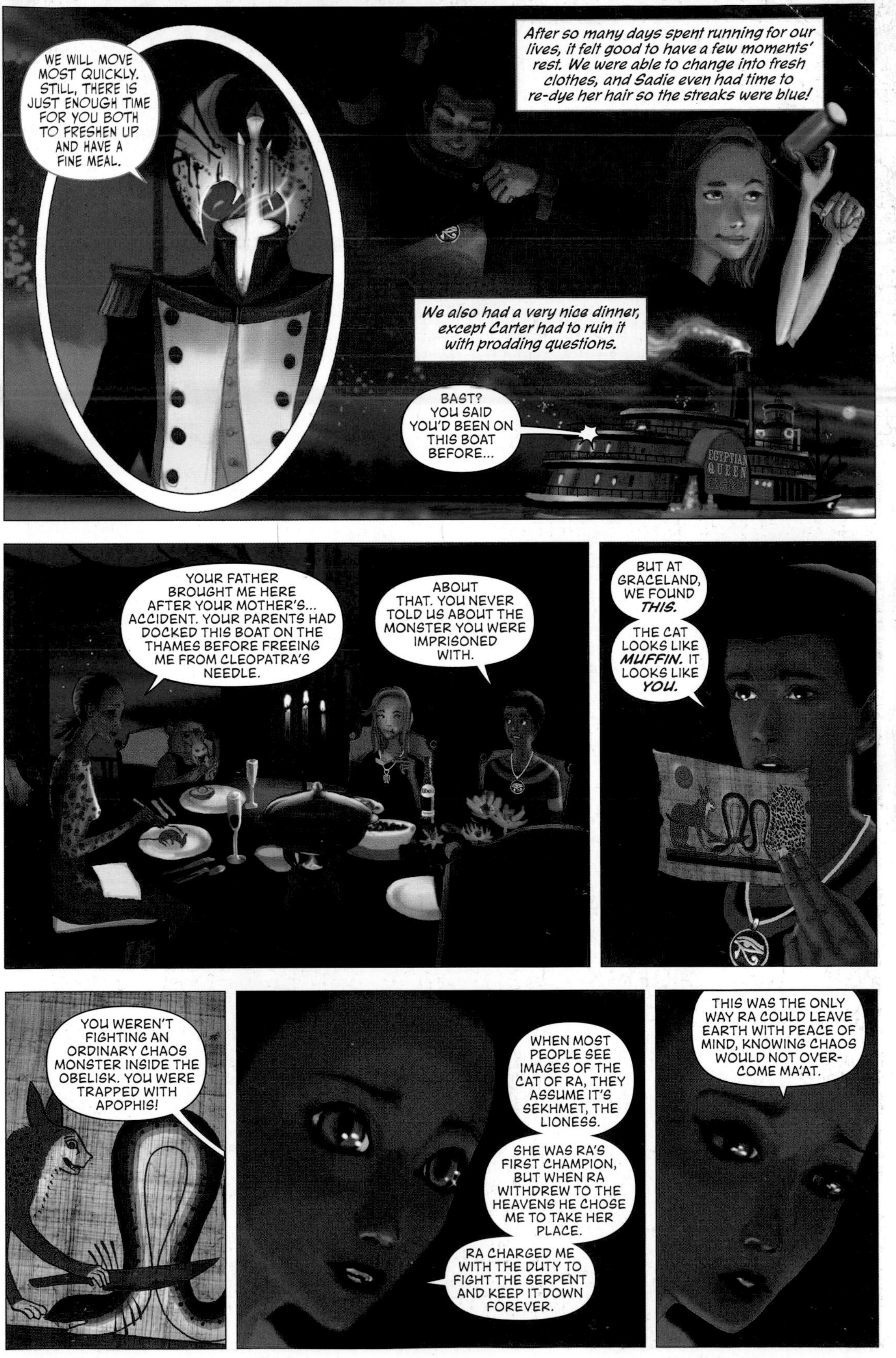

WE WILL MOVE MOST QUICKLY. STILL, THERE IS JUST ENOUGH TIME FOR YOU BOTH TO FRESHEN UP AND HAVE A FINE MEAL.
After so many days spent running for our lives, it felt good to have a few moments' rest. We were able to change into fresh clothes, and Sadie even had time to re-dye her hair so the streaks were blue!
We also had a very nice dinner, except Carter had to ruin it with prodding questions.
BAST? YOU SAID YOU'D BEEN ON THIS BOAT BEFORE...
EGYPTIAN QUEEN
YOUR FATHER BROUGHT ME HERE AFTER YOUR MOTHER'S... ACCIDENT. YOUR PARENTS HAD DOCKED THIS BOAT ON THE THAMES BEFORE FREEING ME FROM CLEOPATRA'S NEEDLE.
ABOUT THAT. YOU NEVER TOLD US ABOUT THE MONSTER YOU WERE IMPRISONED WITH.
BUT AT GRACELAND, WE FOUND *THIS.*
THE CAT LOOKS LIKE *MUFFIN.* IT LOOKS LIKE *YOU.*
YOU WEREN'T FIGHTING AN ORDINARY CHAOS MONSTER INSIDE THE OBELISK. YOU WERE TRAPPED WITH APOPHIS!
WHEN MOST PEOPLE SEE IMAGES OF THE CAT OF RA, THEY ASSUME IT'S SEKHMET, THE LIONESS.
SHE WAS RA'S FIRST CHAMPION, BUT WHEN RA WITHDREW TO THE HEAVENS HE CHOSE ME TO TAKE HER PLACE.
RA CHARGED ME WITH THE DUTY TO FIGHT THE SERPENT AND KEEP IT DOWN FOREVER.
THIS WAS THE ONLY WAY RA COULD LEAVE EARTH WITH PEACE OF MIND, KNOWING CHAOS WOULD NOT OVER-COME MA'AT.

"OVER THE EONS IT BECAME CLEAR TO ME THAT RA'S PLAN WAS FOR THE SERPENT AND ME TO RIP EACH OTHER TO NOTHINGNESS."

"IT WAS MY DUTY... AND YET, WHEN YOUR PARENTS CAME ALONG..."

THEY GAVE YOU AN ESCAPE ROUTE, AND YOU TOOK IT.

YOUR FATHER SAID IT WAS THE FIRST STEP IN RESTORING THE GODS. I WAS RELIEVED TO TAKE HIS OFFER, BUT IT DOES NOT CHANGE THE FACT THAT I WAS A COWARD. I FAILED IN MY DUTY.

I AM THE QUEEN OF CATS. I HAVE MANY STRENGTHS. BUT TO BE HONEST...CATS ARE NOT VERY BRAVE.

Bast's story made me feel a bit guilty. According to Thoth, Isis had caused Ra to retreat into the heavens.

So in a ridiculous, maddening way, Bast's imprisonment had been my fault. I wanted to punch myself to get even with Isis, but I suspected it would hurt.

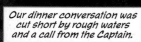

Our dinner conversation was cut short by rough waters and a call from the Captain.

ALL HANDS ON DECK!

Darkness swallowed the horizon, and along the riverbanks, the lights of towns changed to flickering fires, then winked out completely.

WE'RE COMING UPON THE *FIRST* CATARACT!

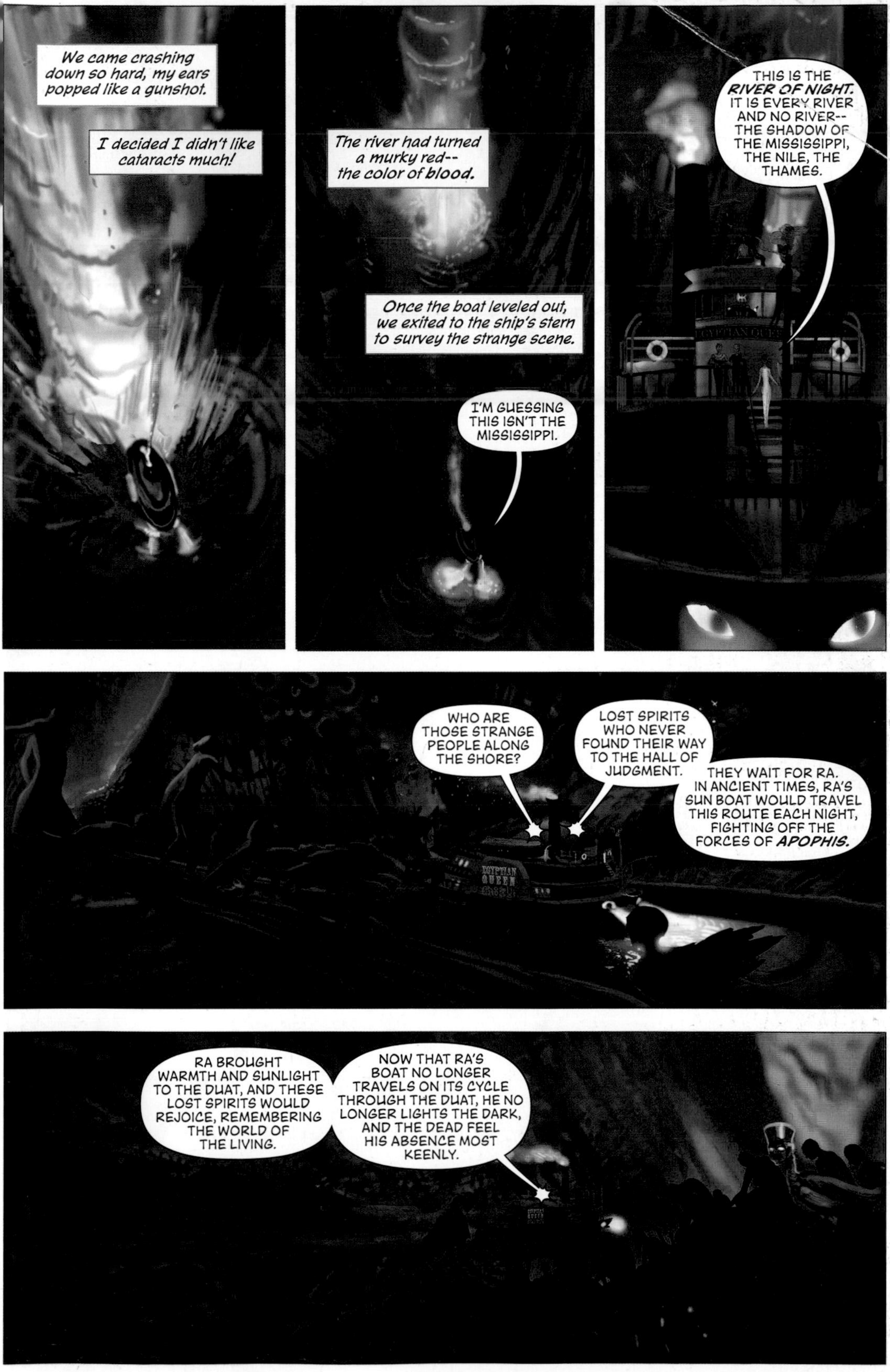
We came crashing down so hard, my ears popped like a gunshot.
I decided I didn't like cataracts much!
The river had turned a murky red-- the color of blood.
Once the boat leveled out, we exited to the ship's stern to survey the strange scene.
I'M GUESSING THIS ISN'T THE MISSISSIPPI.
THIS IS THE RIVER OF NIGHT. IT IS EVERY RIVER AND NO RIVER-- THE SHADOW OF THE MISSISSIPPI, THE NILE, THE THAMES.
WHO ARE THOSE STRANGE PEOPLE ALONG THE SHORE?
LOST SPIRITS WHO NEVER FOUND THEIR WAY TO THE HALL OF JUDGMENT.
THEY WAIT FOR RA. IN ANCIENT TIMES, RA'S SUN BOAT WOULD TRAVEL THIS ROUTE EACH NIGHT, FIGHTING OFF THE FORCES OF APOPHIS.
EGYPTIAN QUEEN
RA BROUGHT WARMTH AND SUNLIGHT TO THE DUAT, AND THESE LOST SPIRITS WOULD REJOICE, REMEMBERING THE WORLD OF THE LIVING.
NOW THAT RA'S BOAT NO LONGER TRAVELS ON ITS CYCLE THROUGH THE DUAT, HE NO LONGER LIGHTS THE DARK, AND THE DEAD FEEL HIS ABSENCE MOST KEENLY.

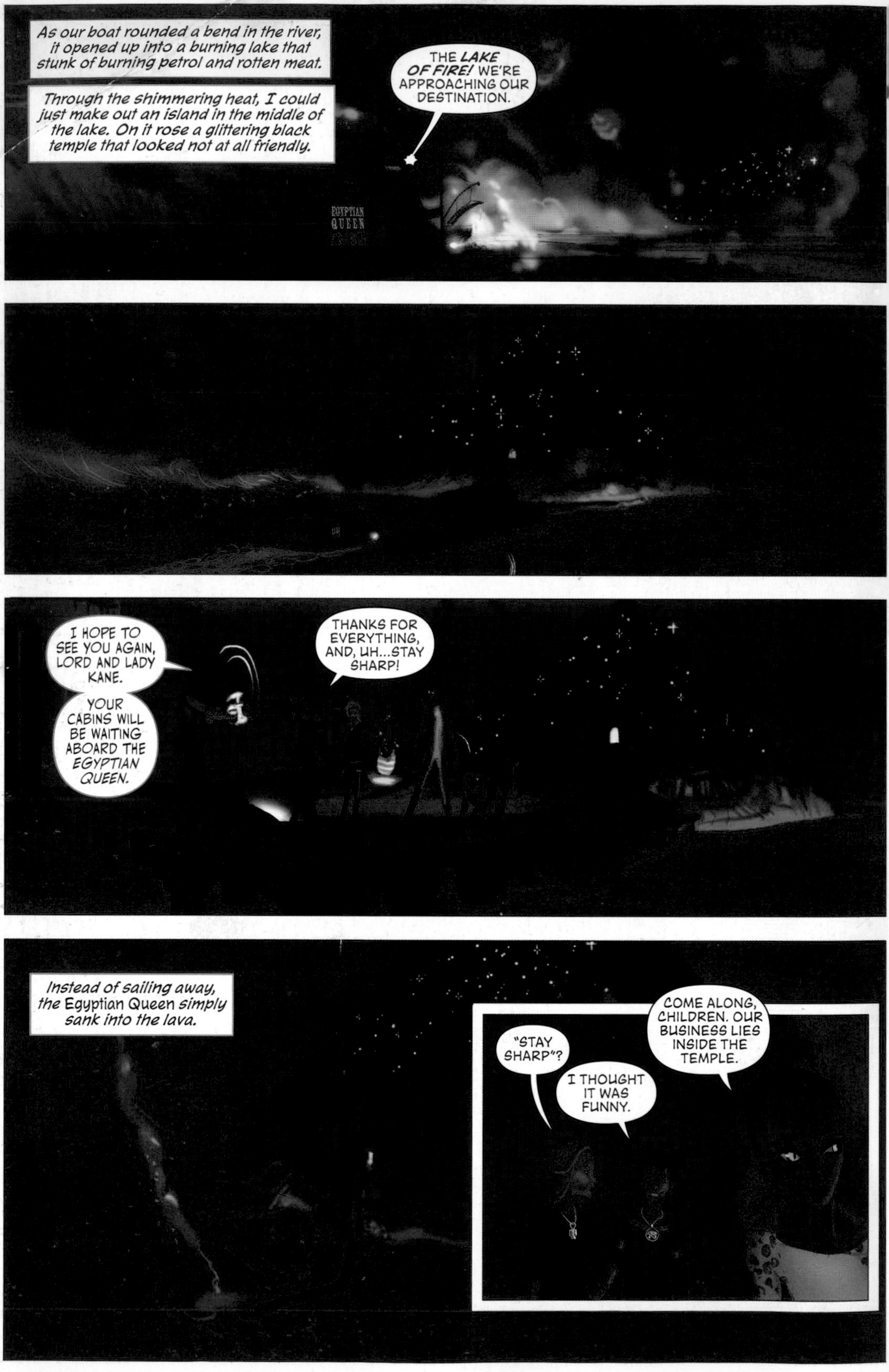
As our boat rounded a bend in the river, it opened up into a burning lake that stunk of burning petrol and rotten meat.
Through the shimmering heat, I could just make out an island in the middle of the lake. On it rose a glittering black temple that looked not at all friendly.
THE LAKE OF FIRE! WE'RE APPROACHING OUR DESTINATION.
EGYPTIAN QUEEN
I HOPE TO SEE YOU AGAIN, LORD AND LADY KANE.
YOUR CABINS WILL BE WAITING ABOARD THE EGYPTIAN QUEEN.
THANKS FOR EVERYTHING, AND, UH...STAY SHARP!
Instead of sailing away, the Egyptian Queen simply sank into the lava.
"STAY SHARP"?
I THOUGHT IT WAS FUNNY.
COME ALONG, CHILDREN. OUR BUSINESS LIES INSIDE THE TEMPLE.

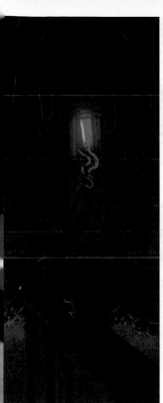

Sniff Sniff BE ALERT. HE'S CLOSE.

WHO?

THE DOG.

Deep in the temple we found a large circular chamber. The center of the room was dominated by a set of broken scales.

WELCOME TO THE LAST ROOM YOU WILL EVER SEE.

THE HALL OF JUDGMENT WAS ONCE A CENTER OF MA'AT, BUT WITHOUT OSIRIS SEATED AT HIS THRONE, IT IS FALLEN INTO RUINS.

I spotted a strange figure at the base of the scales.

IS THAT--

AMMIT THE DEVOURER. LOOK UPON HIM AND TREMBLE.

I ALWAYS IMAGINED HIM... BIGGER.

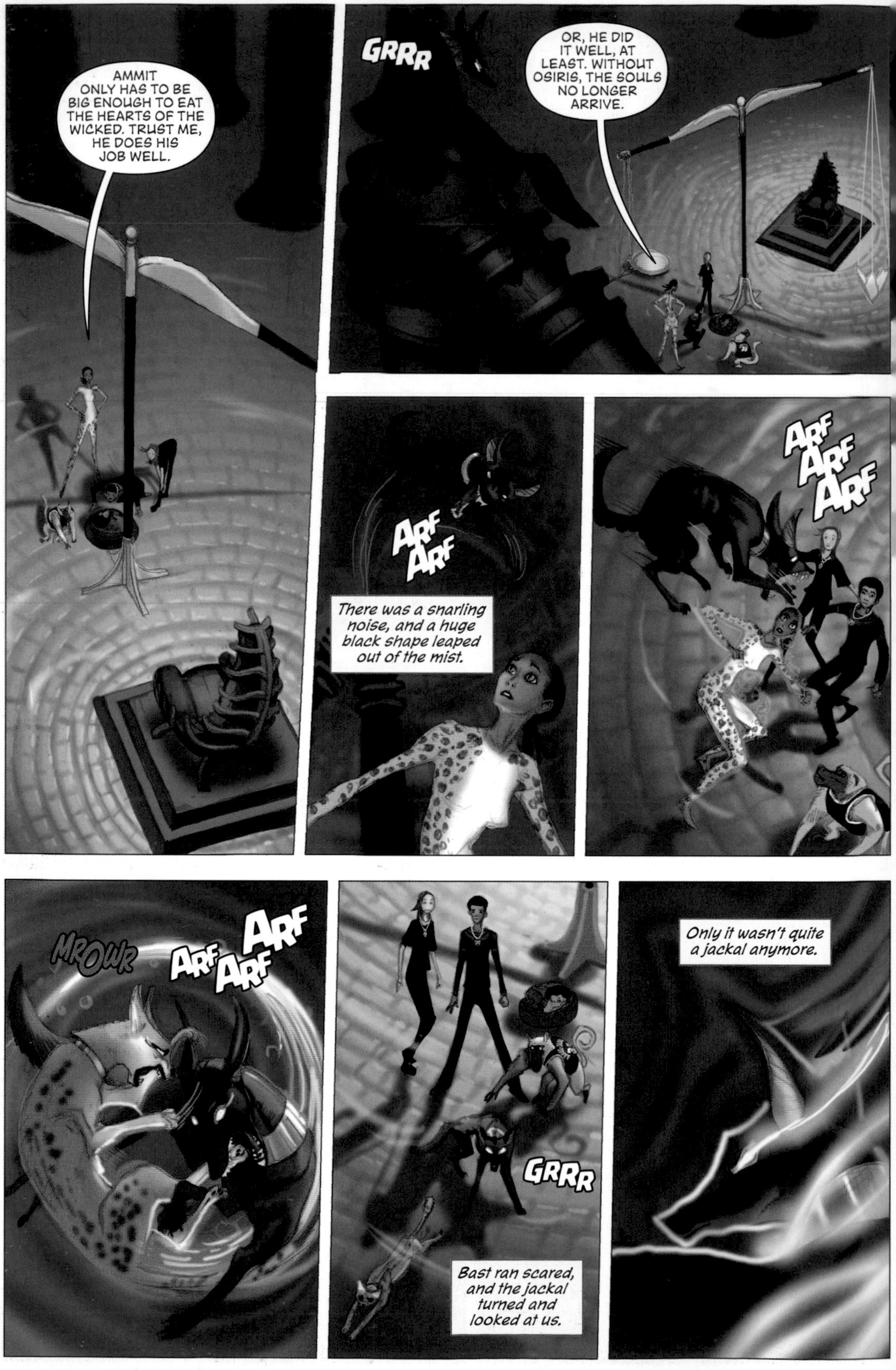
AMMIT ONLY HAS TO BE BIG ENOUGH TO EAT THE HEARTS OF THE WICKED. TRUST ME, HE DOES HIS JOB WELL.
GRRR
OR, HE DID IT WELL, AT LEAST. WITHOUT OSIRIS, THE SOULS NO LONGER ARRIVE.
ARF ARF
There was a snarling noise, and a huge black shape leaped out of the mist.
ARF ARF ARF
MROWR
ARF ARF ARF
GRRR
Bast ran scared, and the jackal turned and looked at us.
Only it wasn't quite a jackal anymore.

ǂHMMPHǂ I AM NOT A *DOG*.

The jackal morphed into a young man, and my heart almost stopped.

Anubis was drop-dead gorgeous.

AND YOU'RE NOT DEAD.

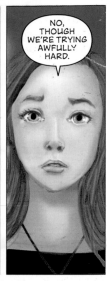

NO, THOUGH WE'RE TRYING AWFULLY HARD.

HMM, I SEE.

Khufu explained everything. Apparently baboon-speak was more efficient than human languages, because he told the whole story in a few barks.

SO YOU'RE *HORUS*.

WHICH MEANS YOU MUST BE...

I'M--I'M, UM--I. I'M *NOT* ISIS. I MEAN ISIS *IS* MILLING ABOUT INSIDE, BUT I'M NOT HER. SHE'S JUST... VISITING.

AND THE TWO OF YOU INTEND TO CHALLENGE SET?

THAT'S THE GENERAL IDEA. WILL YOU HELP?

IT DEPENDS. LET US TALK.

A fog rose from the floor.

Soon, I was lost in it!

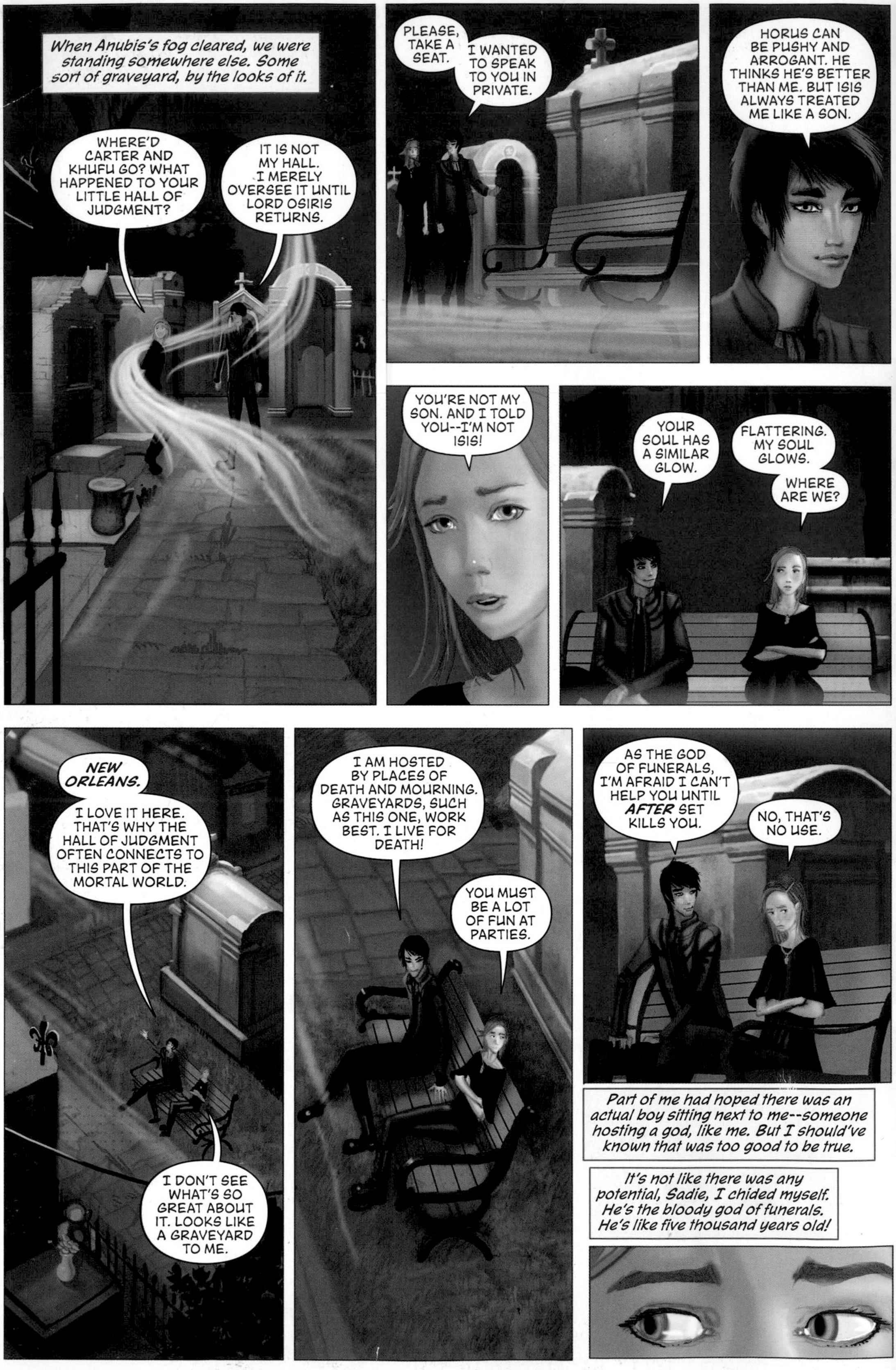
When Anubis's fog cleared, we were standing somewhere else. Some sort of graveyard, by the looks of it.
WHERE'D CARTER AND KHUFU GO? WHAT HAPPENED TO YOUR LITTLE HALL OF JUDGMENT?
IT IS NOT MY HALL. I MERELY OVERSEE IT UNTIL LORD OSIRIS RETURNS.
PLEASE, TAKE A SEAT.
I WANTED TO SPEAK TO YOU IN PRIVATE.
HORUS CAN BE PUSHY AND ARROGANT. HE THINKS HE'S BETTER THAN ME. BUT ISIS ALWAYS TREATED ME LIKE A SON.
YOU'RE NOT MY SON. AND I TOLD YOU--I'M NOT ISIS!
YOUR SOUL HAS A SIMILAR GLOW.
FLATTERING. MY SOUL GLOWS.
WHERE ARE WE?
NEW ORLEANS.
I LOVE IT HERE. THAT'S WHY THE HALL OF JUDGMENT OFTEN CONNECTS TO THIS PART OF THE MORTAL WORLD.
I DON'T SEE WHAT'S SO GREAT ABOUT IT. LOOKS LIKE A GRAVEYARD TO ME.
I AM HOSTED BY PLACES OF DEATH AND MOURNING. GRAVEYARDS, SUCH AS THIS ONE, WORK BEST. I LIVE FOR DEATH!
YOU MUST BE A LOT OF FUN AT PARTIES.
AS THE GOD OF FUNERALS, I'M AFRAID I CAN'T HELP YOU UNTIL AFTER SET KILLS YOU.
NO, THAT'S NO USE.
Part of me had hoped there was an actual boy sitting next to me--someone hosting a god, like me. But I should've known that was too good to be true.
It's not like there was any potential, Sadie, I chided myself. He's the bloody god of funerals. He's like five thousand years old!

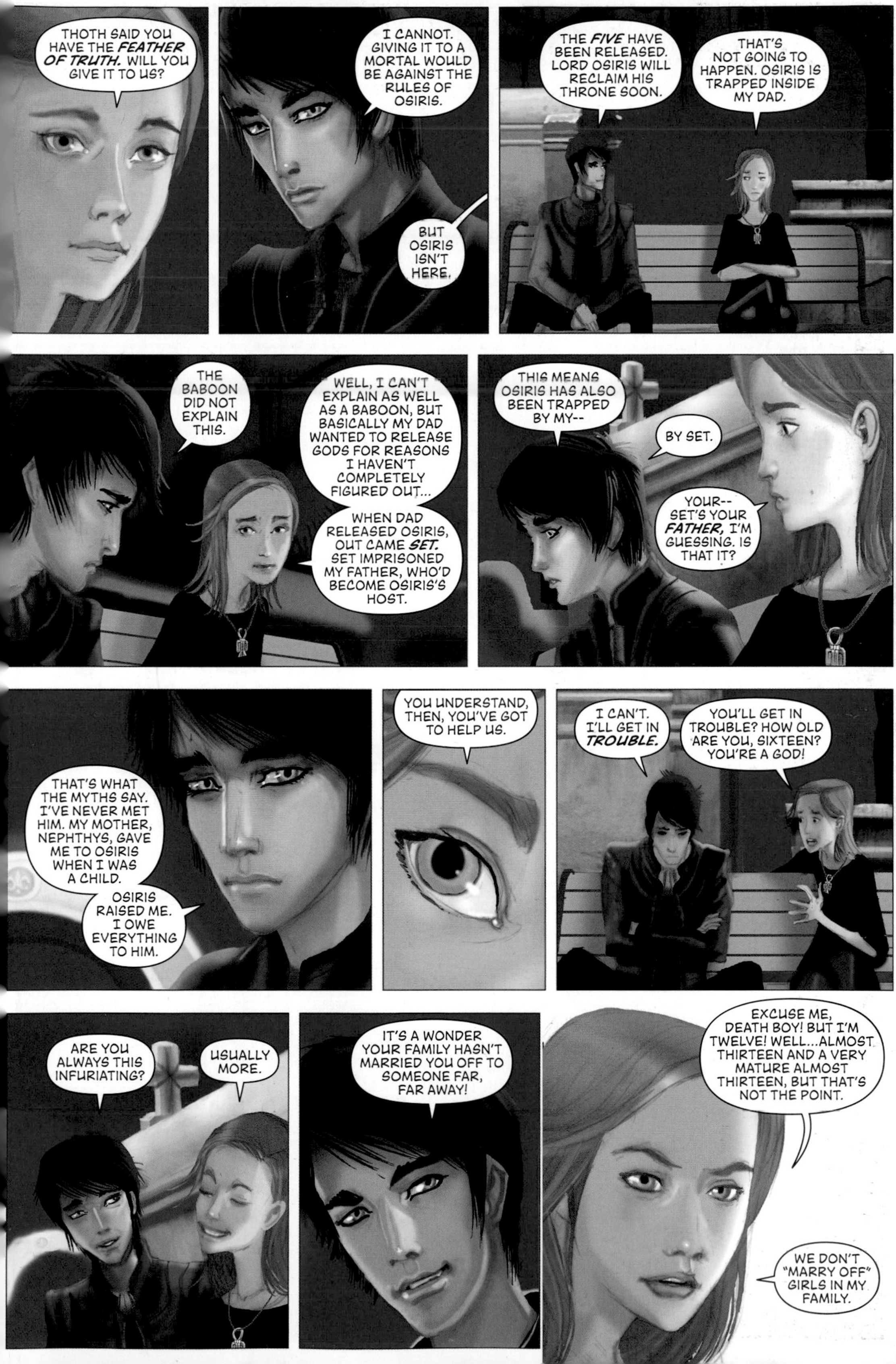
THOTH SAID YOU HAVE THE FEATHER OF TRUTH. WILL YOU GIVE IT TO US?
I CANNOT. GIVING IT TO A MORTAL WOULD BE AGAINST THE RULES OF OSIRIS.
BUT OSIRIS ISN'T HERE.
THE FIVE HAVE BEEN RELEASED. LORD OSIRIS WILL RECLAIM HIS THRONE SOON.
THAT'S NOT GOING TO HAPPEN. OSIRIS IS TRAPPED INSIDE MY DAD.
THE BABOON DID NOT EXPLAIN THIS.
WELL, I CAN'T EXPLAIN AS WELL AS A BABOON, BUT BASICALLY MY DAD WANTED TO RELEASE GODS FOR REASONS I HAVEN'T COMPLETELY FIGURED OUT...
WHEN DAD RELEASED OSIRIS, OUT CAME SET. SET IMPRISONED MY FATHER, WHO'D BECOME OSIRIS'S HOST.
THIS MEANS OSIRIS HAS ALSO BEEN TRAPPED BY MY--
BY SET.
YOUR-- SET'S YOUR FATHER, I'M GUESSING. IS THAT IT?
THAT'S WHAT THE MYTHS SAY. I'VE NEVER MET HIM. MY MOTHER, NEPHTHYS, GAVE ME TO OSIRIS WHEN I WAS A CHILD.
OSIRIS RAISED ME. I OWE EVERYTHING TO HIM.
YOU UNDERSTAND, THEN, YOU'VE GOT TO HELP US.
I CAN'T. I'LL GET IN TROUBLE.
YOU'LL GET IN TROUBLE? HOW OLD ARE YOU, SIXTEEN? YOU'RE A GOD!
ARE YOU ALWAYS THIS INFURIATING?
USUALLY MORE.
IT'S A WONDER YOUR FAMILY HASN'T MARRIED YOU OFF TO SOMEONE FAR, FAR AWAY!
EXCUSE ME, DEATH BOY! BUT I'M TWELVE! WELL...ALMOST THIRTEEN AND A VERY MATURE ALMOST THIRTEEN, BUT THAT'S NOT THE POINT.
WE DON'T "MARRY OFF" GIRLS IN MY FAMILY.

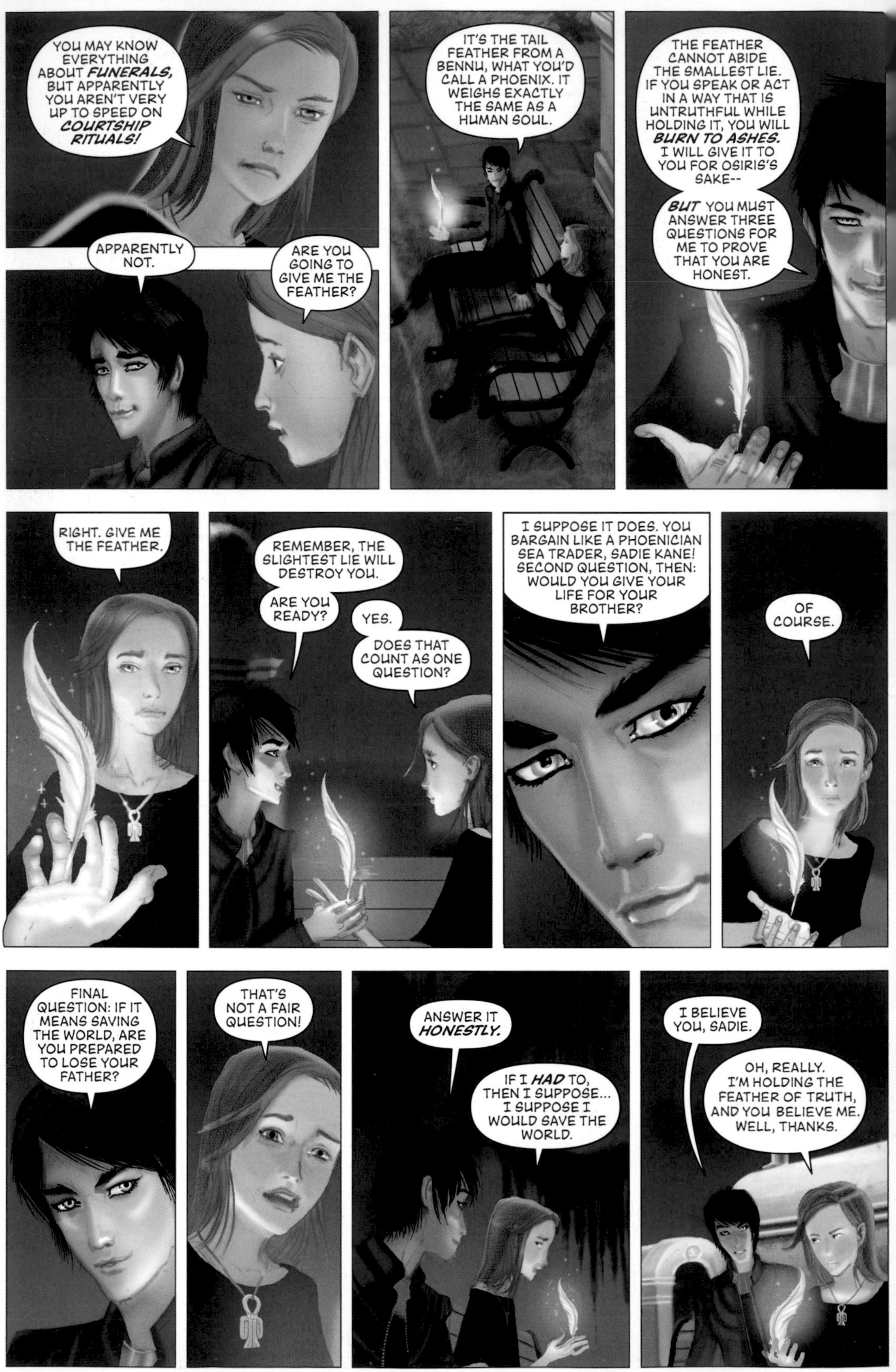
YOU MAY KNOW EVERYTHING ABOUT *FUNERALS,* BUT APPARENTLY YOU AREN'T VERY UP TO SPEED ON *COURTSHIP RITUALS!*
APPARENTLY NOT.
ARE YOU GOING TO GIVE ME THE FEATHER?
IT'S THE TAIL FEATHER FROM A BENNU, WHAT YOU'D CALL A PHOENIX. IT WEIGHS EXACTLY THE SAME AS A HUMAN SOUL.
THE FEATHER CANNOT ABIDE THE SMALLEST LIE. IF YOU SPEAK OR ACT IN A WAY THAT IS UNTRUTHFUL WHILE HOLDING IT, YOU WILL *BURN TO ASHES.* I WILL GIVE IT TO YOU FOR OSIRIS'S SAKE--
BUT YOU MUST ANSWER THREE QUESTIONS FOR ME TO PROVE THAT YOU ARE HONEST.
RIGHT. GIVE ME THE FEATHER.
REMEMBER, THE SLIGHTEST LIE WILL DESTROY YOU.
ARE YOU READY?
YES.
DOES THAT COUNT AS ONE QUESTION?
I SUPPOSE IT DOES. YOU BARGAIN LIKE A PHOENICIAN SEA TRADER, SADIE KANE! SECOND QUESTION, THEN: WOULD YOU GIVE YOUR LIFE FOR YOUR BROTHER?
OF COURSE.
FINAL QUESTION: IF IT MEANS SAVING THE WORLD, ARE YOU PREPARED TO LOSE YOUR FATHER?
THAT'S NOT A FAIR QUESTION!
ANSWER IT *HONESTLY.*
IF I *HAD* TO, THEN I SUPPOSE... I SUPPOSE I WOULD SAVE THE WORLD.
I BELIEVE YOU, SADIE.
OH, REALLY. I'M HOLDING THE FEATHER OF TRUTH, AND YOU BELIEVE ME. WELL, THANKS.

THE TRUTH IS HARSH. SPIRITS COME TO THE HALL OF JUDGMENT ALL THE TIME, AND THEY CANNOT LET GO OF THEIR FAULTS, TRUE FEELINGS, MISTAKES...

THEY DENY RIGHT UP UNTIL AMMIT DEVOURS THEIR SOULS FOR ETERNITY. IT TAKES *COURAGE* TO ADMIT THE TRUTH.

YEAH. I FEEL SO STRONG AND COURAGEOUS. THANKS.

YOU'VE GOT TWENTY-FOUR HOURS TO STOP SET--WHEN NEXT WE MEET--

YOU'LL BE JUST AS ANNOYING?

--OR PERHAPS YOU COULD BRING ME UP TO SPEED ON MODERN *COURTSHIP RITUALS.*

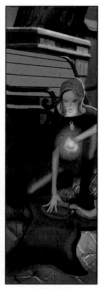

Seconds later, Carter, Bast, and Khufu materialized right behind me.

DID YOU GET THE FEATHER?

PLEASE, NO MORE QUESTIONS, THANK YOU VERY MUCH!

BECAUSE I AM IN NO MOOD TO TELL THE TRUTH.

LET'S GET OUT OF HERE. WE'VE GOT WORK TO DO!

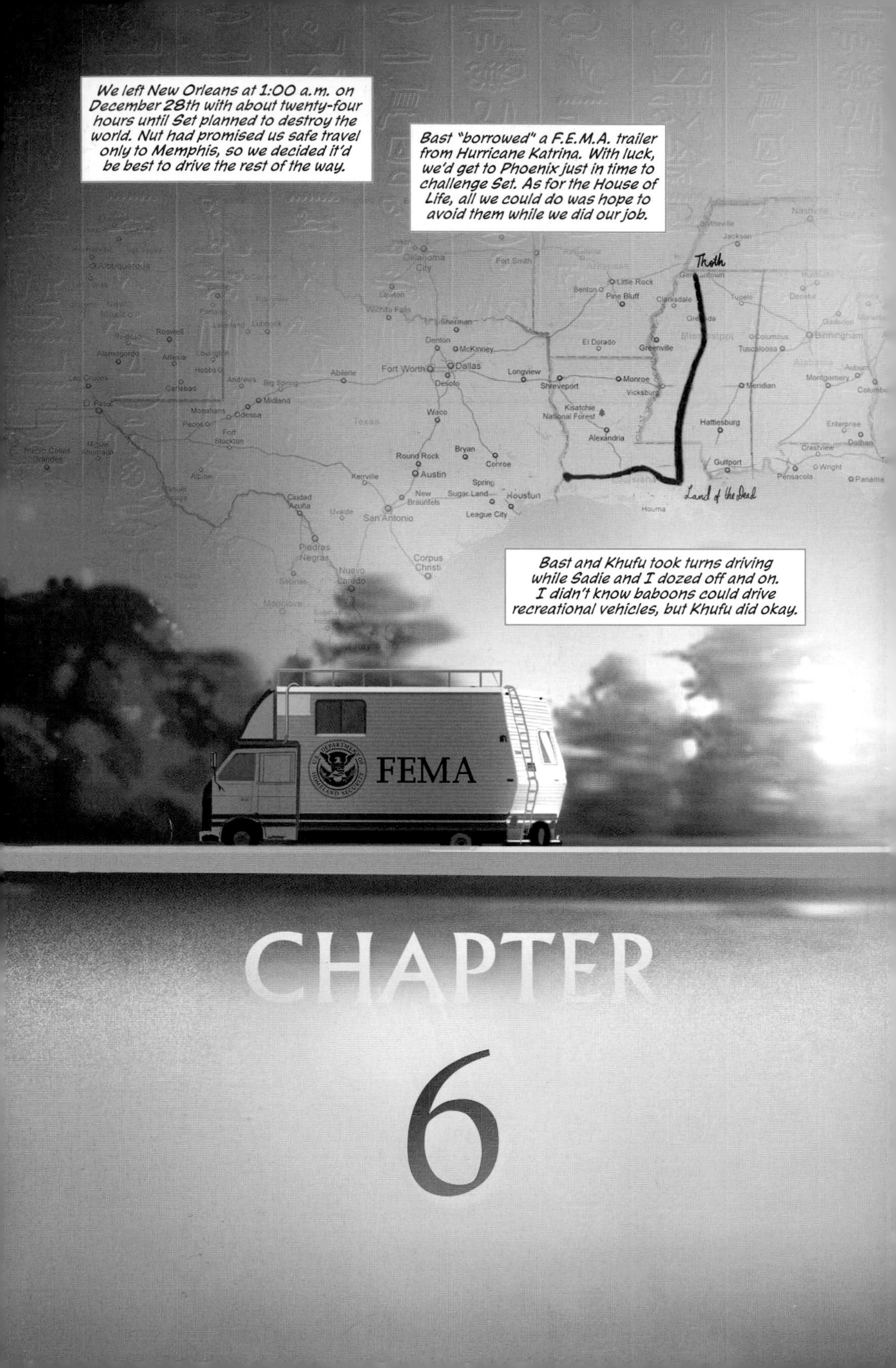
We left New Orleans at 1:00 a.m. on December 28th with about twenty-four hours until Set planned to destroy the world. Nut had promised us safe travel only to Memphis, so we decided it'd be best to drive the rest of the way.
Bast "borrowed" a F.E.M.A. trailer from Hurricane Katrina. With luck, we'd get to Phoenix just in time to challenge Set. As for the House of Life, all we could do was hope to avoid them while we did our job.
Thoth
Land of the Dead
Little Rock
Pine Bluff
Clarksdale
Greenville
Shreveport
Monroe
Vicksburg
Dallas
Fort Worth
Austin
Houston
San Antonio
Birmingham
Pensacola
Bast and Khufu took turns driving while Sadie and I dozed off and on. I didn't know baboons could drive recreational vehicles, but Khufu did okay.
FEMA

CHAPTER 6

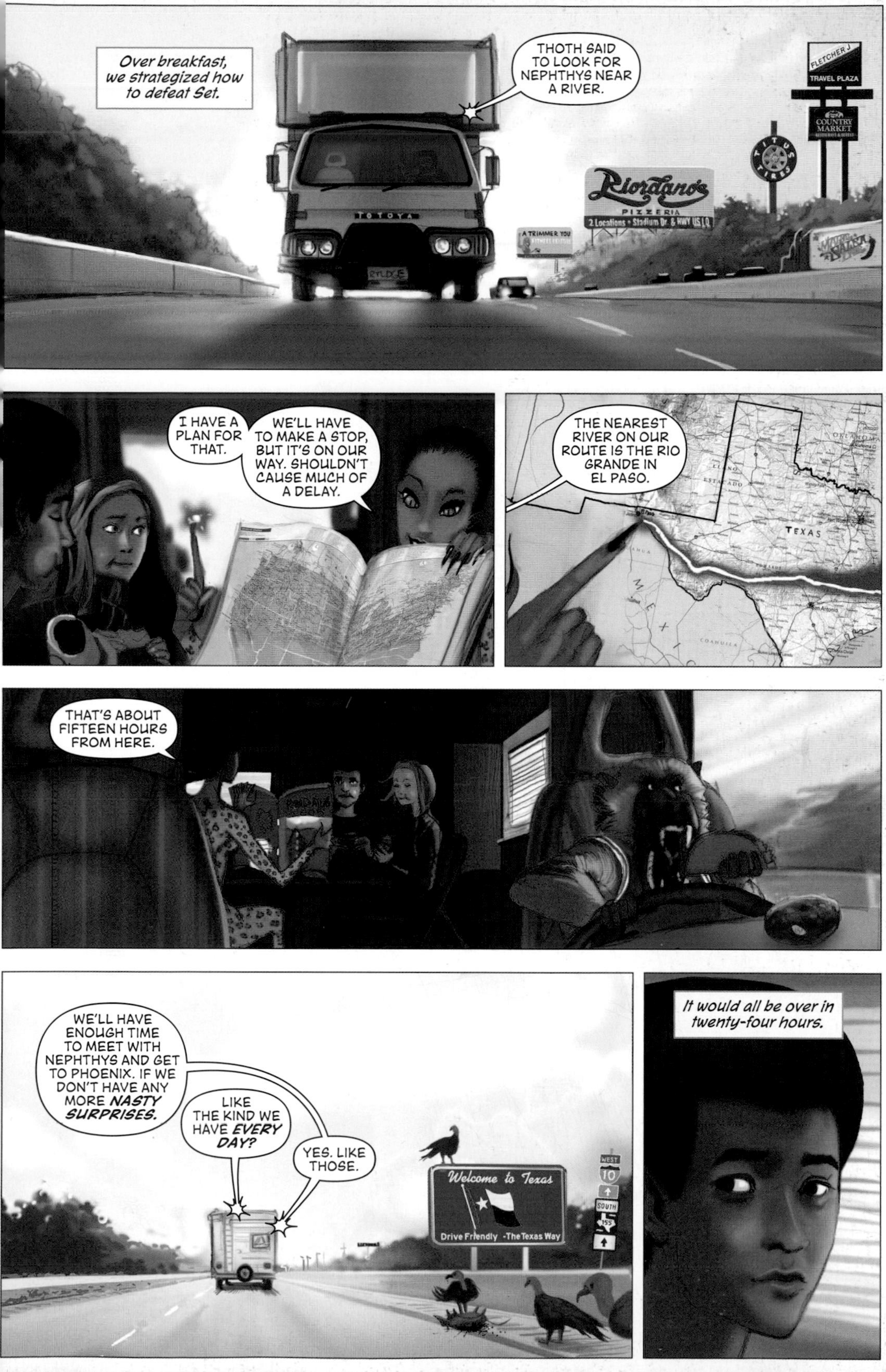

Over breakfast, we strategized how to defeat Set.
THOTH SAID TO LOOK FOR NEPHTHYS NEAR A RIVER.
FLETCHER J TRAVEL PLAZA
COUNTRY MARKET
TITUS TIRES
Riordano's PIZZERIA
A TRIMMER YOU
TOTOYA
I HAVE A PLAN FOR THAT.
WE'LL HAVE TO MAKE A STOP, BUT IT'S ON OUR WAY. SHOULDN'T CAUSE MUCH OF A DELAY.
THE NEAREST RIVER ON OUR ROUTE IS THE RIO GRANDE IN EL PASO.
TEXAS
THAT'S ABOUT FIFTEEN HOURS FROM HERE.
WE'LL HAVE ENOUGH TIME TO MEET WITH NEPHTHYS AND GET TO PHOENIX. IF WE DON'T HAVE ANY MORE ***NASTY SURPRISES.***
LIKE THE KIND WE HAVE ***EVERY DAY?***
YES. LIKE THOSE.
Welcome to Texas
Drive Friendly -The Texas Way
WEST
10
SOUTH
155
It would all be over in twenty-four hours.

Fourteen hours later, just before sunset, we reached the Rio Grande.

Bast led us down to the riverside.

AGH!

Khufu sniffed at the water...and snarled.

KHUFU SMELLS DANGER.

IT'S PROBABLY JUST ANCESTRAL MEMORY. THE RIVER WAS A DANGEROUS PLACE IN EGYPT.

SNAKES, HIPPOS, CROCODILES...ALL MANNER OF DEADLY CREATURES.

CROCODILES? DOES THE RIO GRANDE HAVE CROCODILES?

I VERY MUCH DOUBT IT. NOW, SADIE, IF YOU'D DO THE HONORS?

ME?

HOW?

JUST ASK FOR NEPHTHYS TO APPEAR. SHE WAS ISIS'S SISTER.

IF SHE'S ANYWHERE ON THIS SIDE OF THE DUAT, SHE SHOULD HEAR YOUR VOICE.

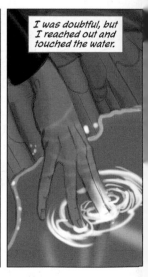

I was doubtful, but I reached out and touched the water.

HULLO, NEPHTHYS...?

ANYONE HOME?

CAN YOU HEAR HER?

JUST BARELY.

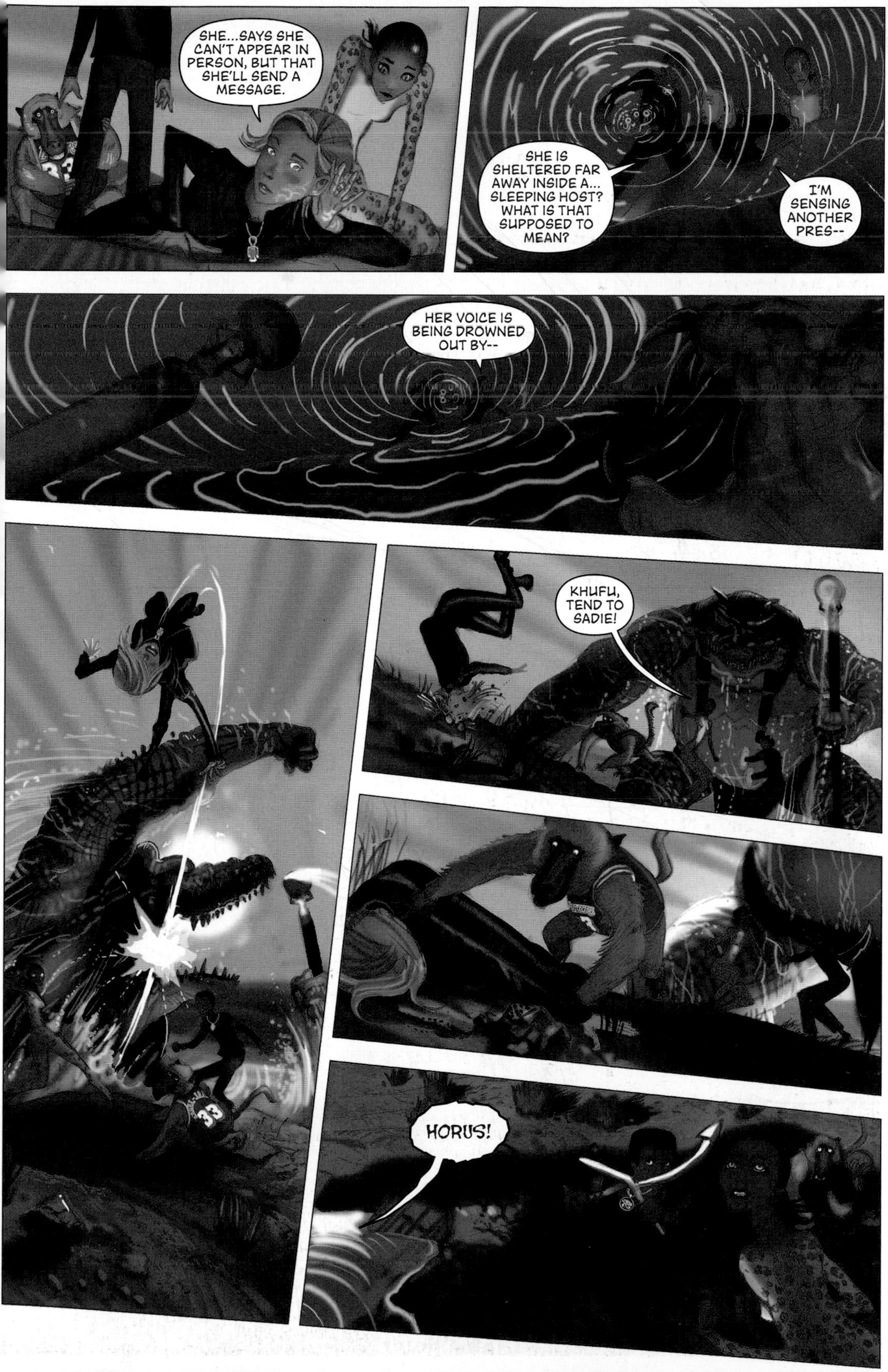
SHE...SAYS SHE CAN'T APPEAR IN PERSON, BUT THAT SHE'LL SEND A MESSAGE.
SHE IS SHELTERED FAR AWAY INSIDE A... SLEEPING HOST? WHAT IS THAT SUPPOSED TO MEAN?
I'M SENSING ANOTHER PRES--
HER VOICE IS BEING DROWNED OUT BY--
KHUFU, TEND TO SADIE!
HORUS!

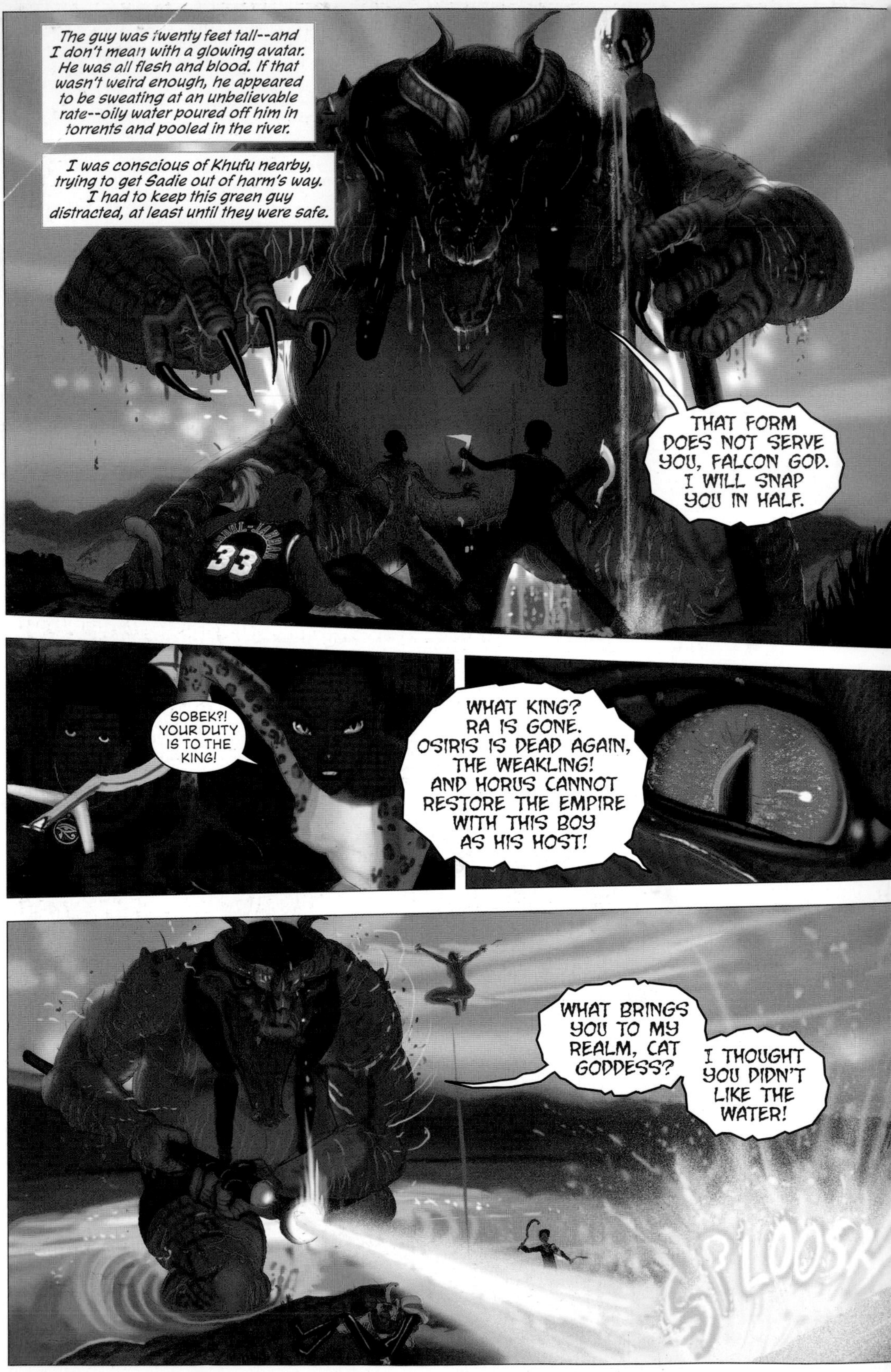

The guy was twenty feet tall--and I don't mean with a glowing avatar. He was all flesh and blood. If that wasn't weird enough, he appeared to be sweating at an unbelievable rate--oily water poured off him in torrents and pooled in the river.
I was conscious of Khufu nearby, trying to get Sadie out of harm's way. I had to keep this green guy distracted, at least until they were safe.
THAT FORM DOES NOT SERVE YOU, FALCON GOD. I WILL SNAP YOU IN HALF.
33
SOBEK?! YOUR DUTY IS TO THE KING!
WHAT KING? RA IS GONE. OSIRIS IS DEAD AGAIN, THE WEAKLING! AND HORUS CANNOT RESTORE THE EMPIRE WITH THIS BOY AS HIS HOST!
WHAT BRINGS YOU TO MY REALM, CAT GODDESS?
I THOUGHT YOU DIDN'T LIKE THE WATER!

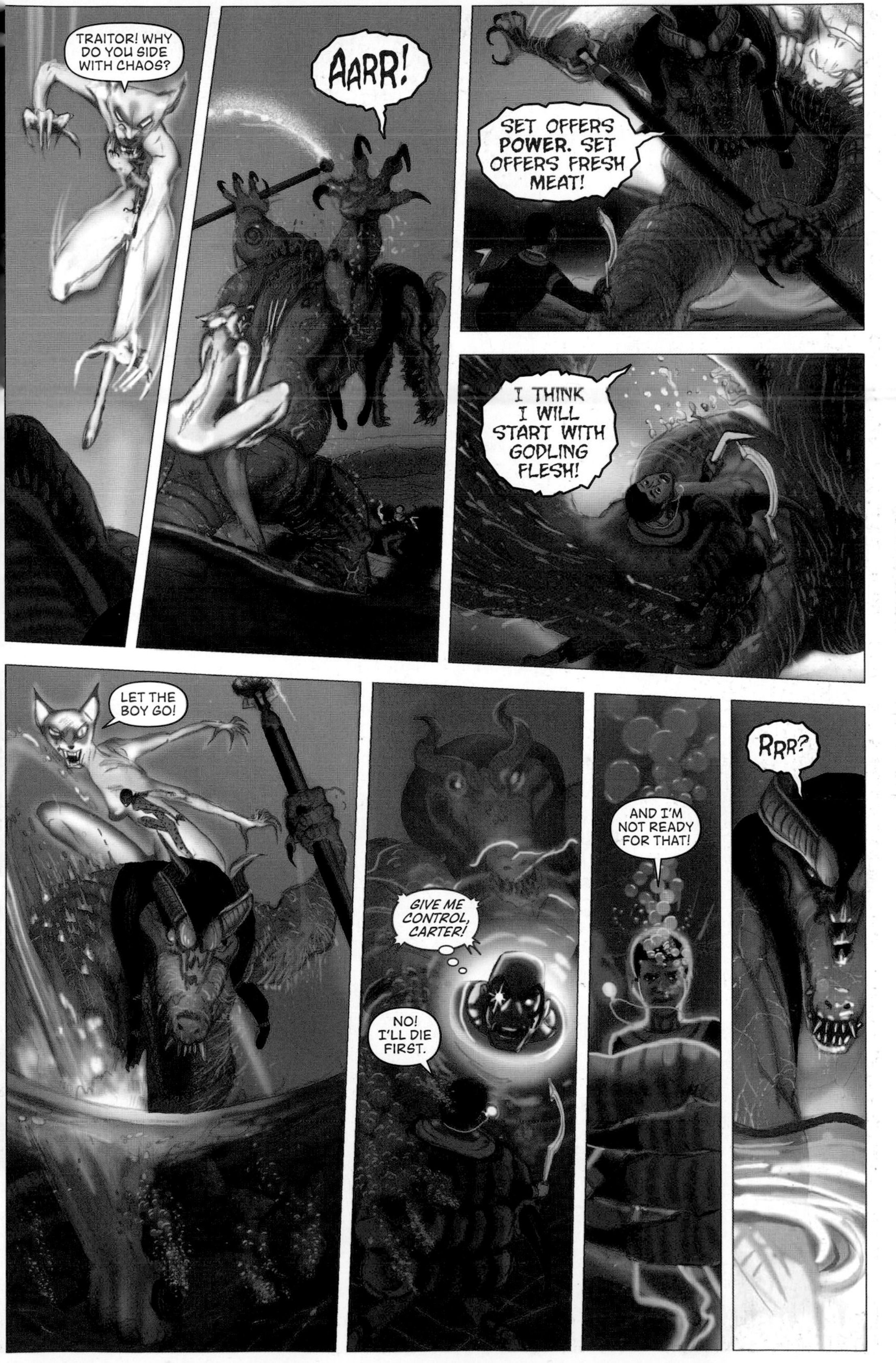
TRAITOR! WHY DO YOU SIDE WITH CHAOS?
AARR!
SET OFFERS POWER. SET OFFERS FRESH MEAT!
I THINK I WILL START WITH GODLING FLESH!
LET THE BOY GO!
GIVE ME CONTROL, CARTER!
NO! I'LL DIE FIRST.
AND I'M NOT READY FOR THAT!
RRR?

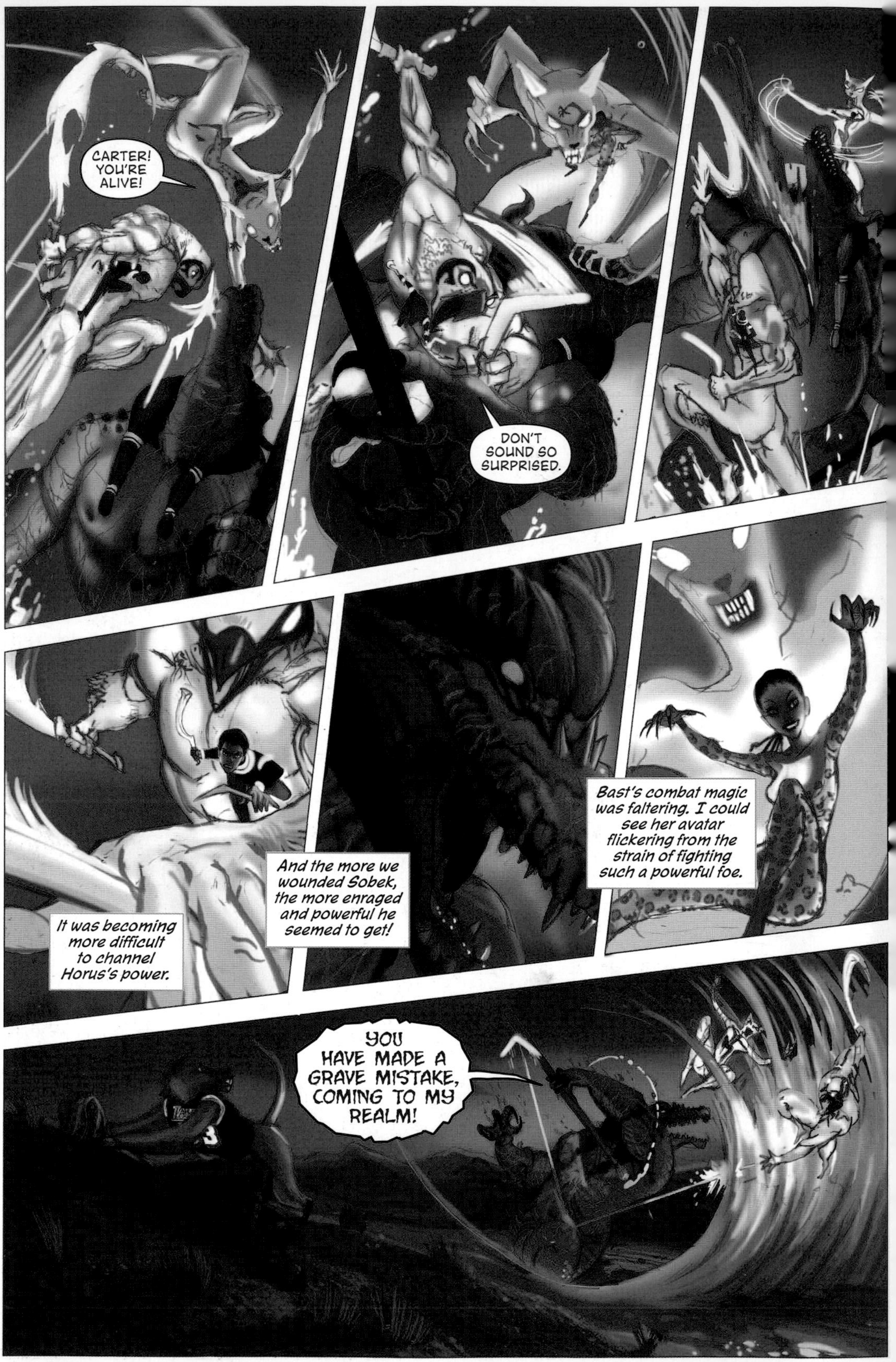
CARTER! YOU'RE ALIVE!
DON'T SOUND SO SURPRISED.
It was becoming more difficult to channel Horus's power.
And the more we wounded Sobek, the more enraged and powerful he seemed to get!
Bast's combat magic was faltering. I could see her avatar flickering from the strain of fighting such a powerful foe.
YOU HAVE MADE A GRAVE MISTAKE, COMING TO MY REALM!

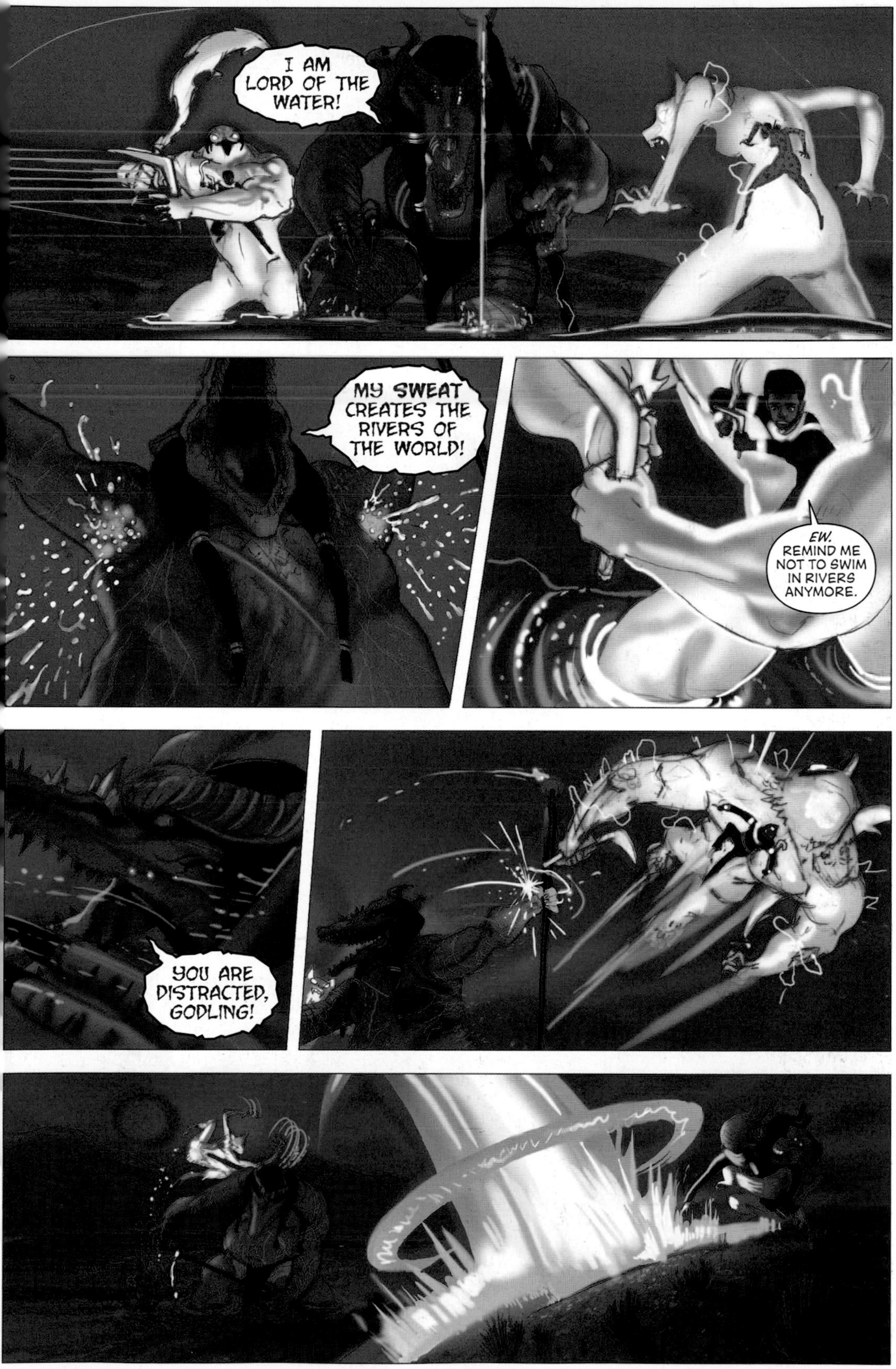
I AM LORD OF THE WATER!
MY SWEAT CREATES THE RIVERS OF THE WORLD!
EW. REMIND ME NOT TO SWIM IN RIVERS ANYMORE.
YOU ARE DISTRACTED, GODLING!

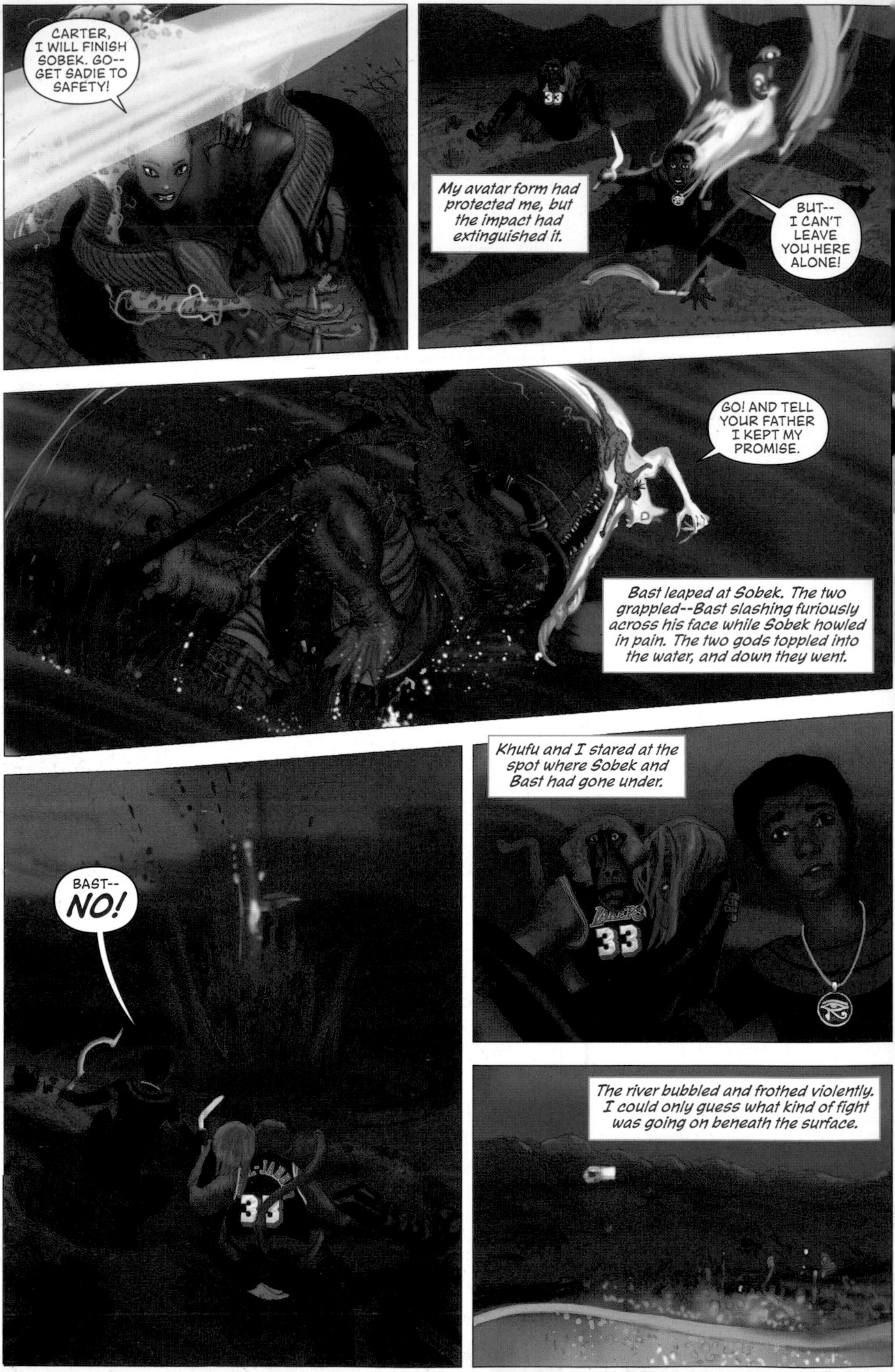
CARTER, I WILL FINISH SOBEK. GO-- GET SADIE TO SAFETY!
My avatar form had protected me, but the impact had extinguished it.
BUT-- I CAN'T LEAVE YOU HERE ALONE!
GO! AND TELL YOUR FATHER I KEPT MY PROMISE.
Bast leaped at Sobek. The two grappled--Bast slashing furiously across his face while Sobek howled in pain. The two gods toppled into the water, and down they went.
BAST-- NO!
Khufu and I stared at the spot where Sobek and Bast had gone under.
The river bubbled and frothed violently. I could only guess what kind of fight was going on beneath the surface.

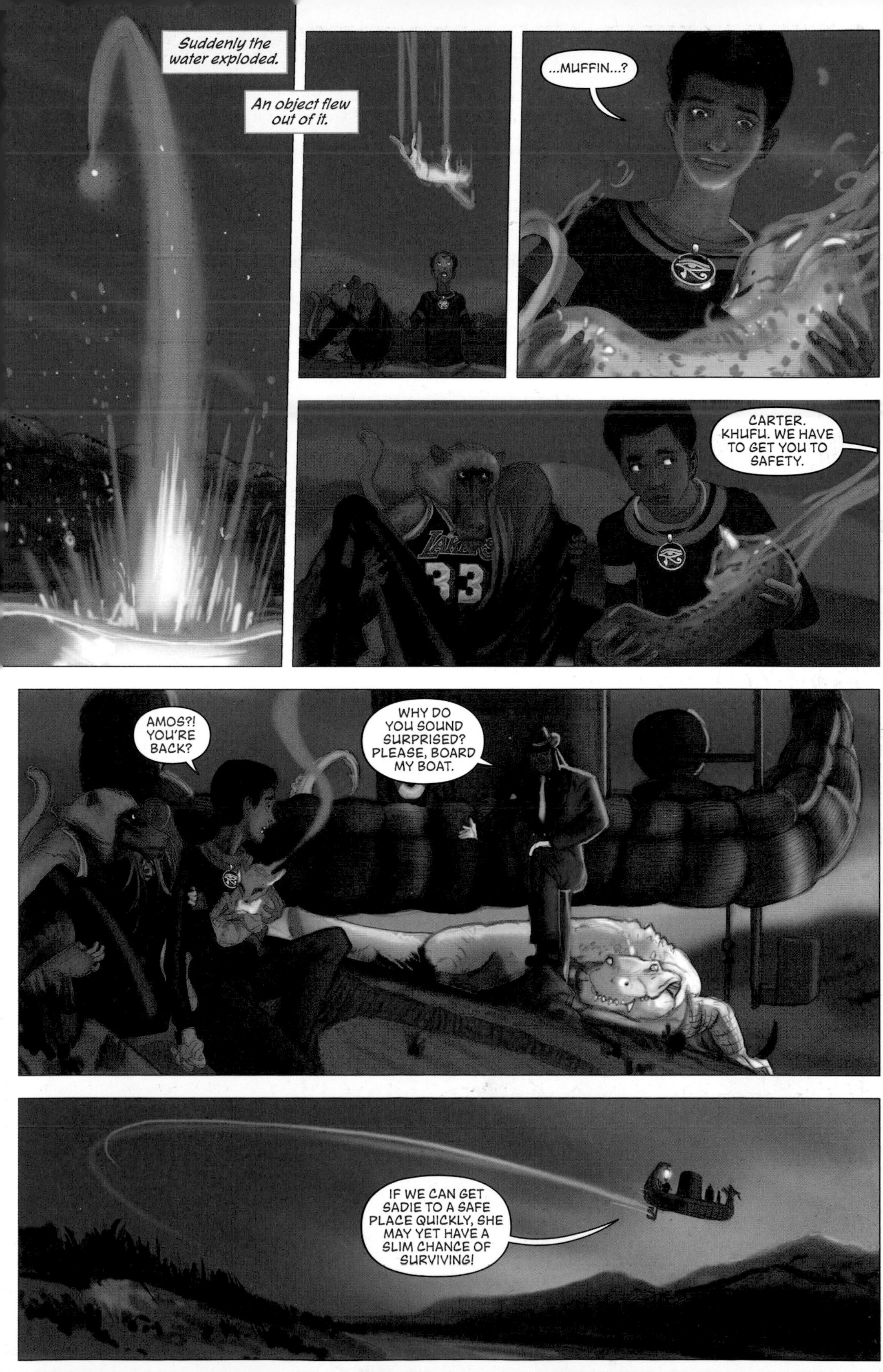
Suddenly the water exploded.
An object flew out of it.
...MUFFIN...?
CARTER. KHUFU. WE HAVE TO GET YOU TO SAFETY.
AMOS?! YOU'RE BACK?
WHY DO YOU SOUND SURPRISED? PLEASE, BOARD MY BOAT.
IF WE CAN GET SADIE TO A SAFE PLACE QUICKLY, SHE MAY YET HAVE A SLIM CHANCE OF SURVIVING!

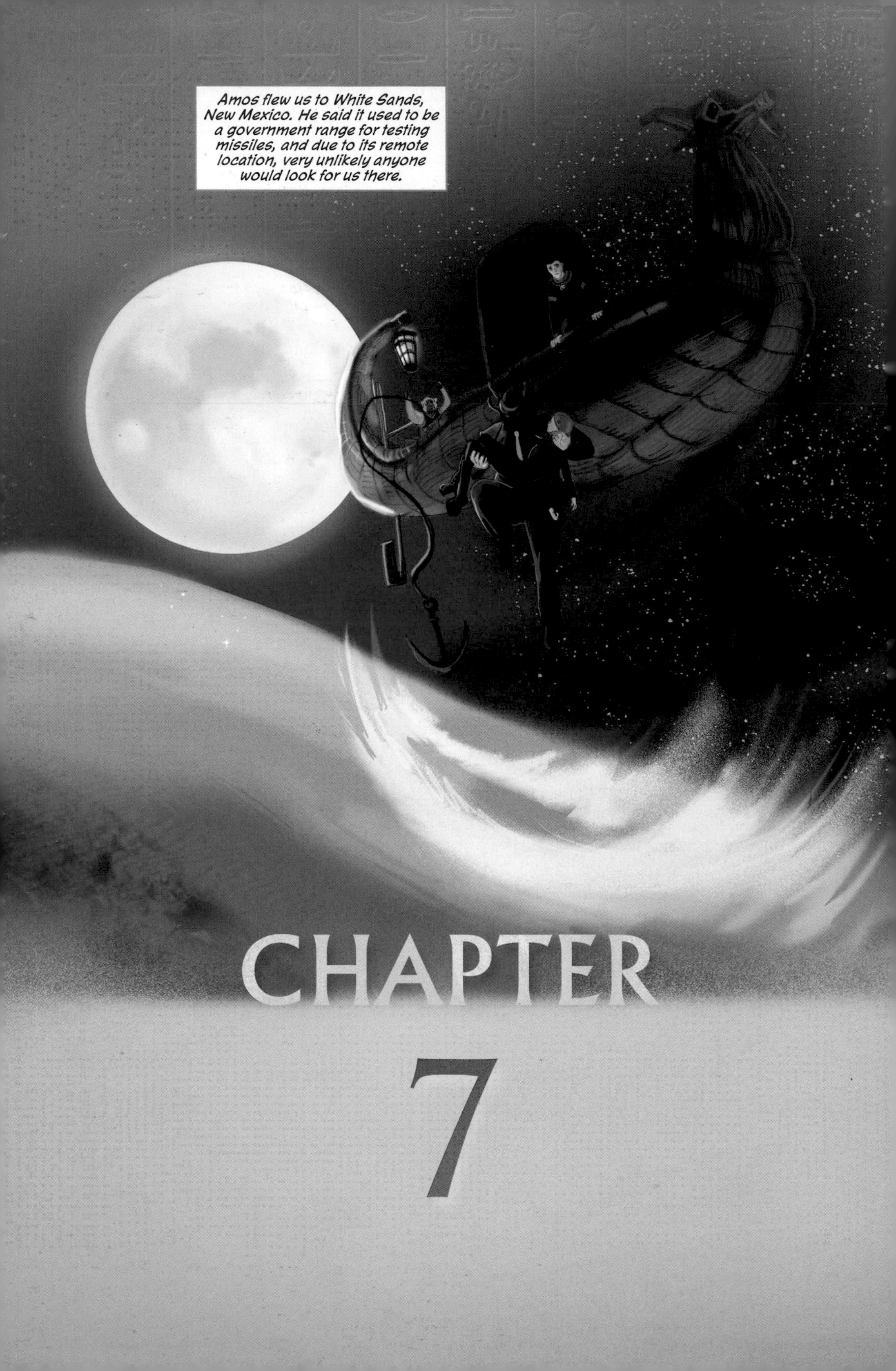
Amos flew us to White Sands, New Mexico. He said it used to be a government range for testing missiles, and due to its remote location, very unlikely anyone would look for us there.

CHAPTER 7

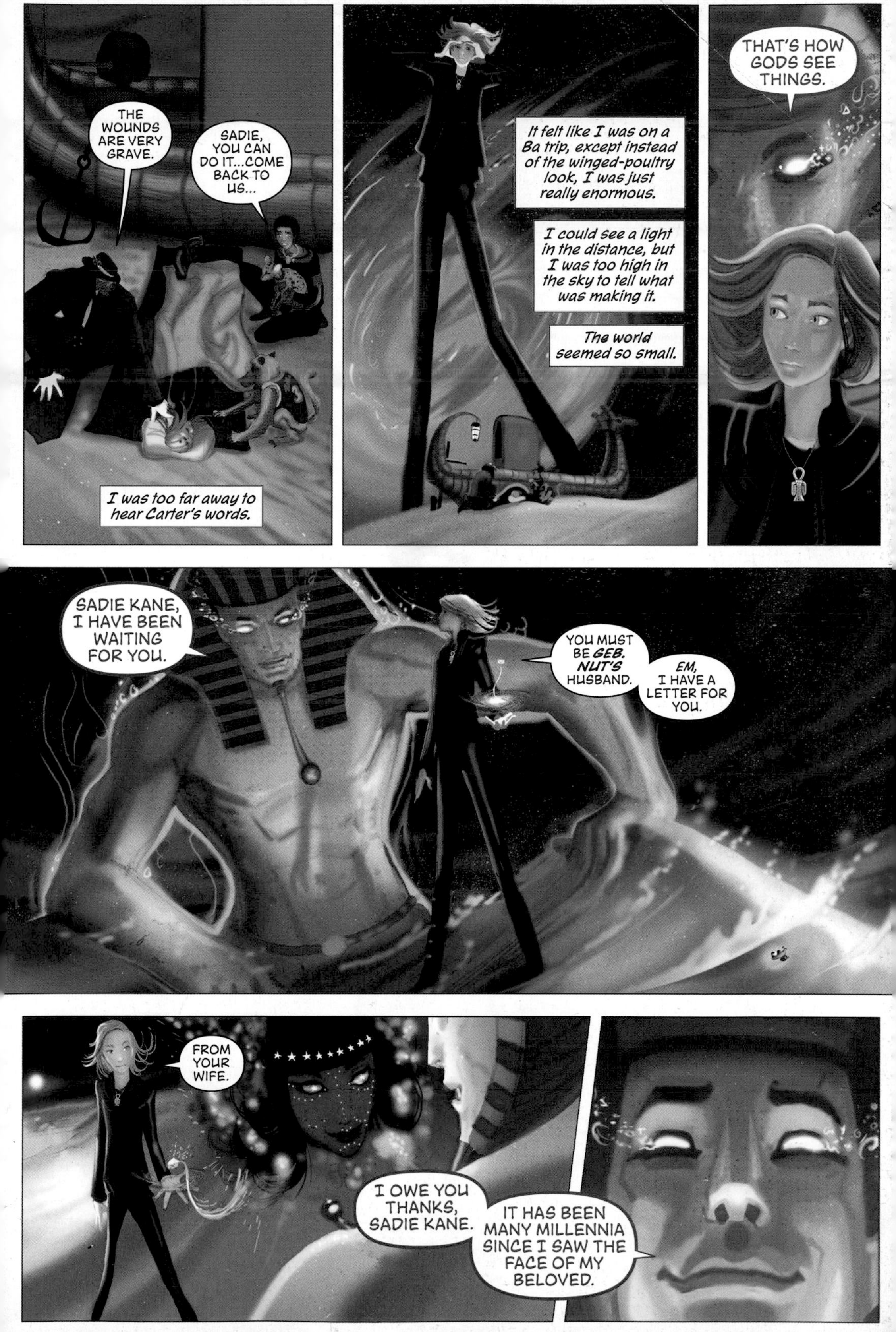
THE WOUNDS ARE VERY GRAVE.
SADIE, YOU CAN DO IT...COME BACK TO US...
I was too far away to hear Carter's words.
It felt like I was on a Ba trip, except instead of the winged-poultry look, I was just really enormous.
I could see a light in the distance, but I was too high in the sky to tell what was making it.
The world seemed so small.
THAT'S HOW GODS SEE THINGS.
SADIE KANE, I HAVE BEEN WAITING FOR YOU.
YOU MUST BE GEB. NUT'S HUSBAND.
EM, I HAVE A LETTER FOR YOU.
FROM YOUR WIFE.
I OWE YOU THANKS, SADIE KANE.
IT HAS BEEN MANY MILLENNIA SINCE I SAW THE FACE OF MY BELOVED.

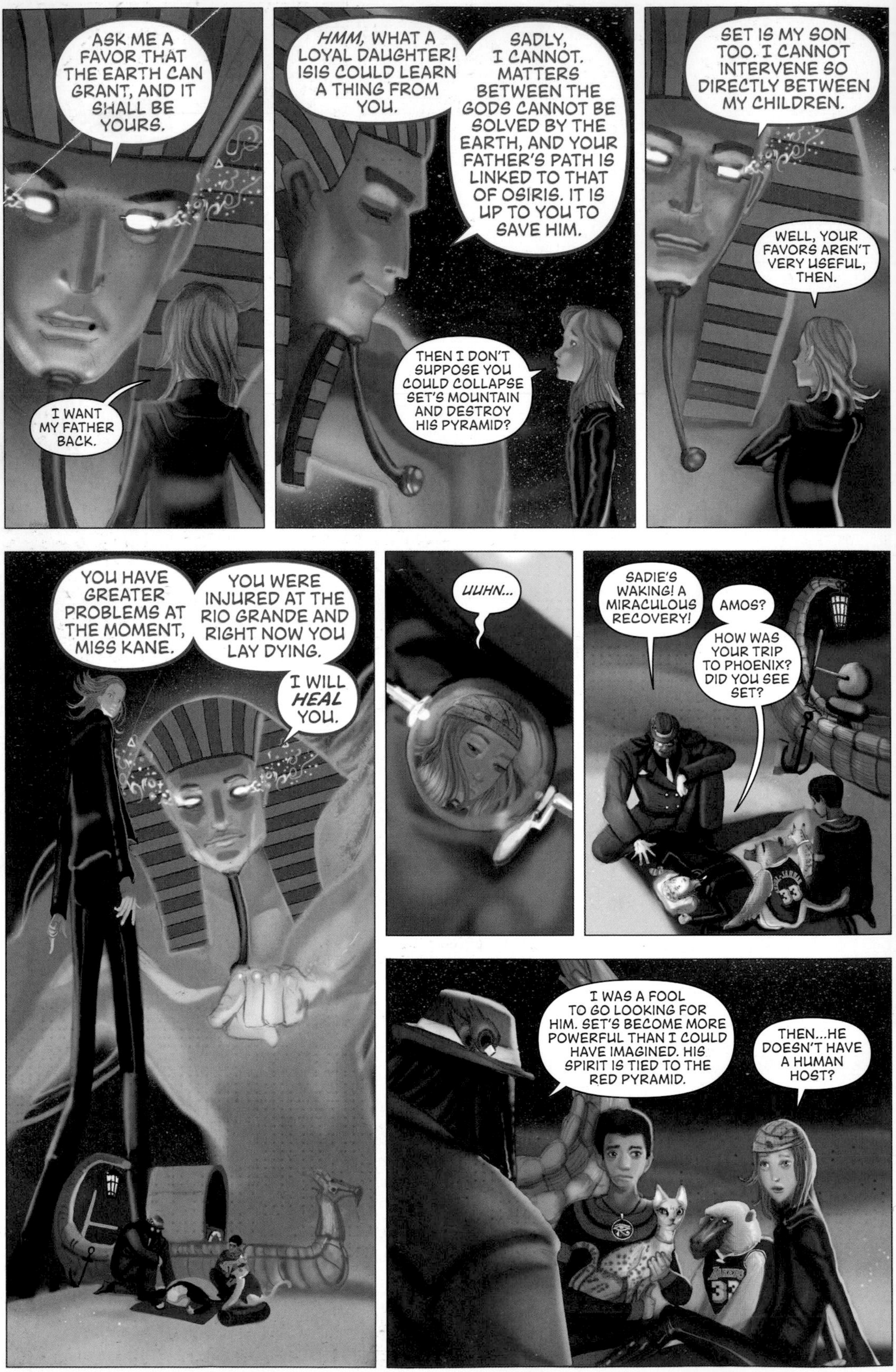

ASK ME A FAVOR THAT THE EARTH CAN GRANT, AND IT SHALL BE YOURS.
I WANT MY FATHER BACK.
HMM, WHAT A LOYAL DAUGHTER! ISIS COULD LEARN A THING FROM YOU.
SADLY, I CANNOT. MATTERS BETWEEN THE GODS CANNOT BE SOLVED BY THE EARTH, AND YOUR FATHER'S PATH IS LINKED TO THAT OF OSIRIS. IT IS UP TO YOU TO SAVE HIM.
THEN I DON'T SUPPOSE YOU COULD COLLAPSE SET'S MOUNTAIN AND DESTROY HIS PYRAMID?
SET IS MY SON TOO. I CANNOT INTERVENE SO DIRECTLY BETWEEN MY CHILDREN.
WELL, YOUR FAVORS AREN'T VERY USEFUL, THEN.
YOU HAVE GREATER PROBLEMS AT THE MOMENT, MISS KANE.
YOU WERE INJURED AT THE RIO GRANDE AND RIGHT NOW YOU LAY DYING.
I WILL ***HEAL*** YOU.
UUHN...
SADIE'S WAKING! A MIRACULOUS RECOVERY!
AMOS?
HOW WAS YOUR TRIP TO PHOENIX? DID YOU SEE SET?
I WAS A FOOL TO GO LOOKING FOR HIM. SET'S BECOME MORE POWERFUL THAN I COULD HAVE IMAGINED. HIS SPIRIT IS TIED TO THE RED PYRAMID.
THEN...HE DOESN'T HAVE A HUMAN HOST?

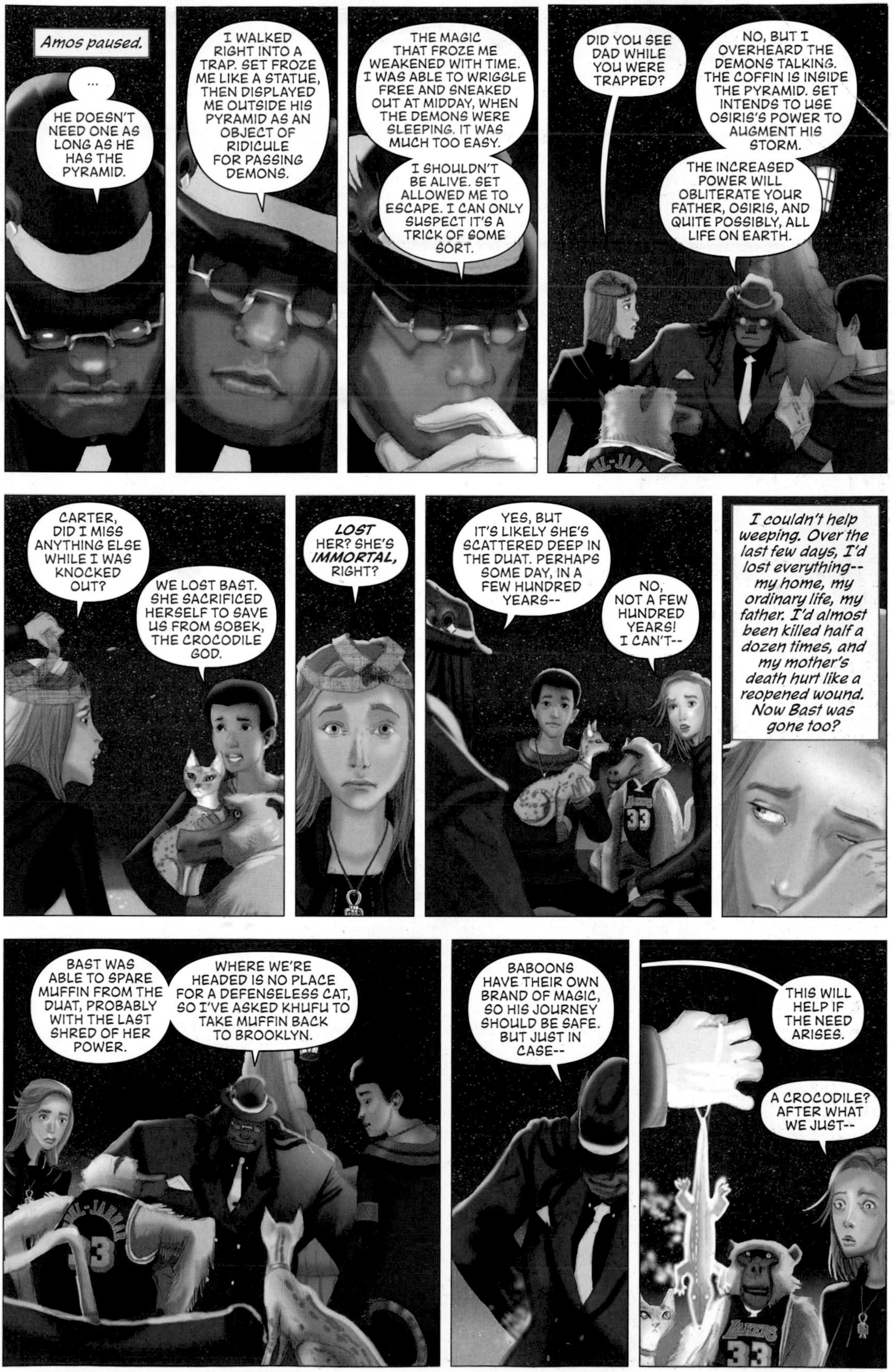
Amos paused.
...
HE DOESN'T NEED ONE AS LONG AS HE HAS THE PYRAMID.
I WALKED RIGHT INTO A TRAP. SET FROZE ME LIKE A STATUE, THEN DISPLAYED ME OUTSIDE HIS PYRAMID AS AN OBJECT OF RIDICULE FOR PASSING DEMONS.
THE MAGIC THAT FROZE ME WEAKENED WITH TIME. I WAS ABLE TO WRIGGLE FREE AND SNEAKED OUT AT MIDDAY, WHEN THE DEMONS WERE SLEEPING. IT WAS MUCH TOO EASY.
I SHOULDN'T BE ALIVE. SET ALLOWED ME TO ESCAPE. I CAN ONLY SUSPECT IT'S A TRICK OF SOME SORT.
DID YOU SEE DAD WHILE YOU WERE TRAPPED?
NO, BUT I OVERHEARD THE DEMONS TALKING. THE COFFIN IS INSIDE THE PYRAMID. SET INTENDS TO USE OSIRIS'S POWER TO AUGMENT HIS STORM.
THE INCREASED POWER WILL OBLITERATE YOUR FATHER, OSIRIS, AND QUITE POSSIBLY, ALL LIFE ON EARTH.
CARTER, DID I MISS ANYTHING ELSE WHILE I WAS KNOCKED OUT?
WE LOST BAST. SHE SACRIFICED HERSELF TO SAVE US FROM SOBEK, THE CROCODILE GOD.
LOST HER? SHE'S IMMORTAL, RIGHT?
YES, BUT IT'S LIKELY SHE'S SCATTERED DEEP IN THE DUAT. PERHAPS SOME DAY, IN A FEW HUNDRED YEARS--
NO, NOT A FEW HUNDRED YEARS! I CAN'T--
I couldn't help weeping. Over the last few days, I'd lost everything--my home, my ordinary life, my father. I'd almost been killed half a dozen times, and my mother's death hurt like a reopened wound. Now Bast was gone too?
BAST WAS ABLE TO SPARE MUFFIN FROM THE DUAT, PROBABLY WITH THE LAST SHRED OF HER POWER.
WHERE WE'RE HEADED IS NO PLACE FOR A DEFENSELESS CAT, SO I'VE ASKED KHUFU TO TAKE MUFFIN BACK TO BROOKLYN.
BABOONS HAVE THEIR OWN BRAND OF MAGIC, SO HIS JOURNEY SHOULD BE SAFE. BUT JUST IN CASE--
THIS WILL HELP IF THE NEED ARISES.
A CROCODILE? AFTER WHAT WE JUST--

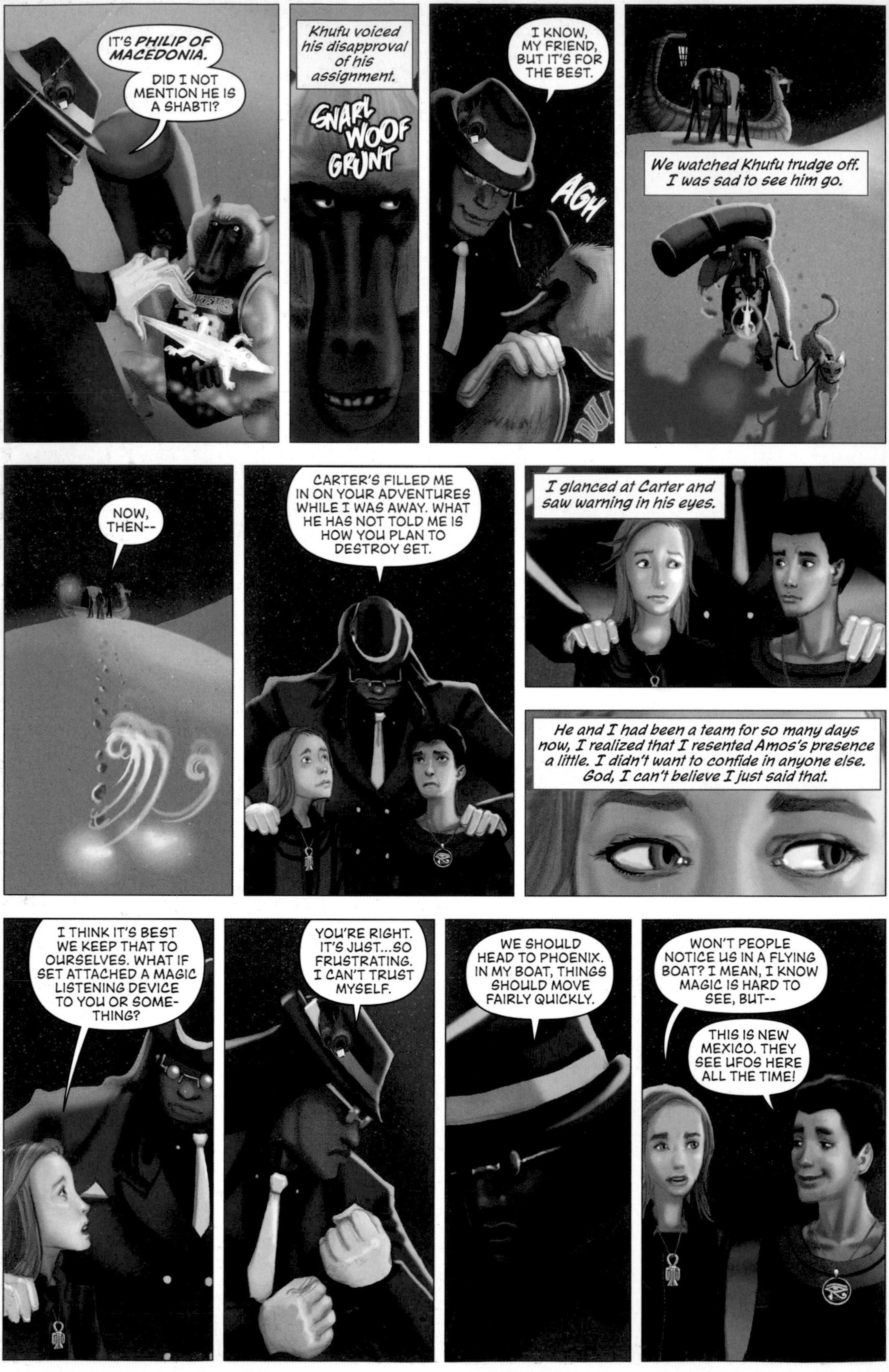

IT'S ***PHILIP OF MACEDONIA.***
DID I NOT MENTION HE IS A SHABTI?
Khufu voiced his disapproval of his assignment.
SNARL WOOF GRUNT
I KNOW, MY FRIEND, BUT IT'S FOR THE BEST.
AGH
We watched Khufu trudge off. I was sad to see him go.
NOW, THEN--
CARTER'S FILLED ME IN ON YOUR ADVENTURES WHILE I WAS AWAY. WHAT HE HAS NOT TOLD ME IS HOW YOU PLAN TO DESTROY SET.
I glanced at Carter and saw warning in his eyes.
He and I had been a team for so many days now, I realized that I resented Amos's presence a little. I didn't want to confide in anyone else. God, I can't believe I just said that.
I THINK IT'S BEST WE KEEP THAT TO OURSELVES. WHAT IF SET ATTACHED A MAGIC LISTENING DEVICE TO YOU OR SOME-THING?
YOU'RE RIGHT. IT'S JUST...SO FRUSTRATING. I CAN'T TRUST MYSELF.
WE SHOULD HEAD TO PHOENIX. IN MY BOAT, THINGS SHOULD MOVE FAIRLY QUICKLY.
WON'T PEOPLE NOTICE US IN A FLYING BOAT? I MEAN, I KNOW MAGIC IS HARD TO SEE, BUT--
THIS IS NEW MEXICO. THEY SEE UFOS HERE ALL THE TIME!

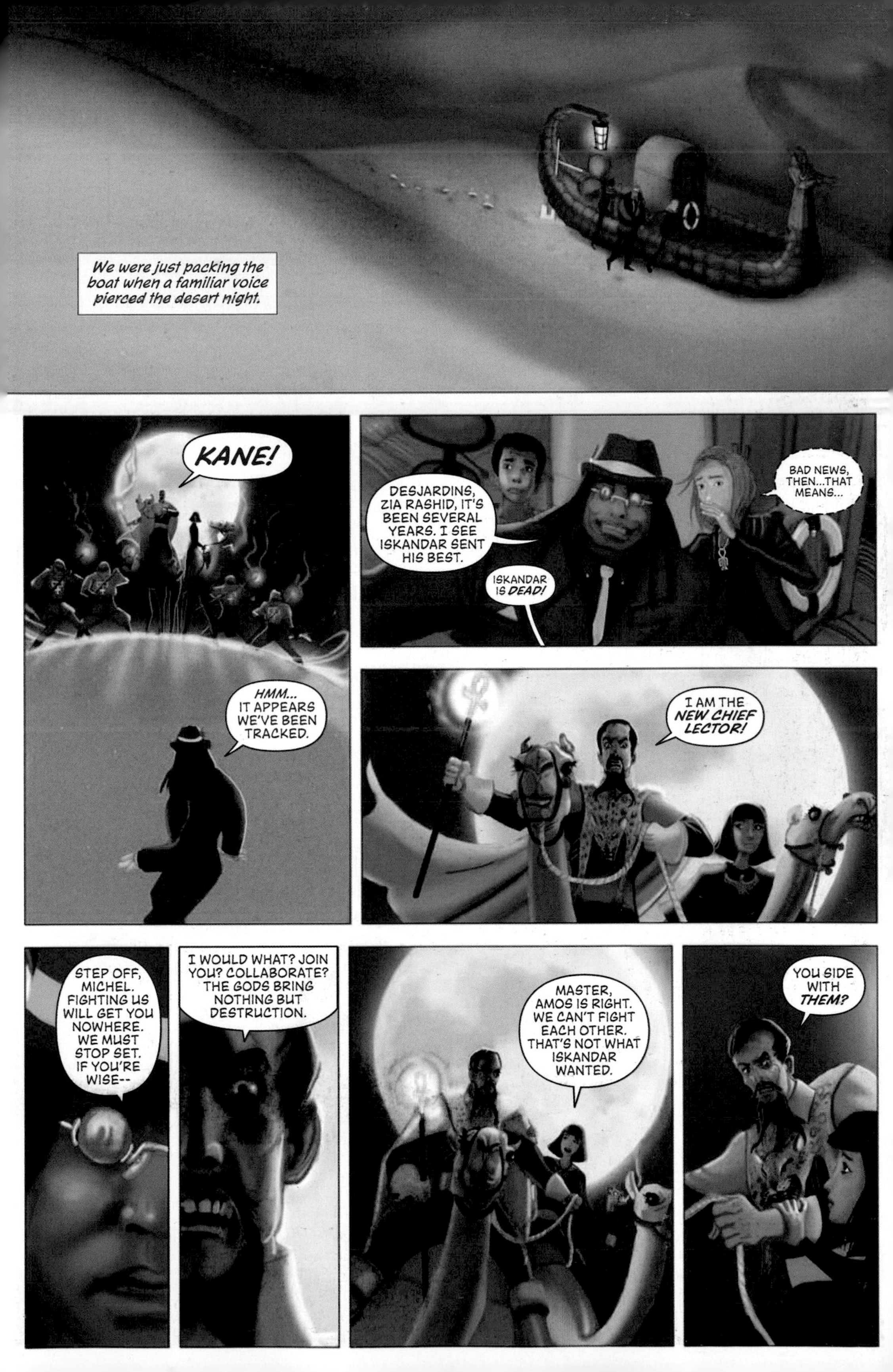
We were just packing the boat when a familiar voice pierced the desert night.
KANE!
HMM... IT APPEARS WE'VE BEEN TRACKED.
DESJARDINS, ZIA RASHID, IT'S BEEN SEVERAL YEARS. I SEE ISKANDAR SENT HIS BEST.
ISKANDAR IS *DEAD!*
BAD NEWS, THEN...THAT MEANS...
I AM THE *NEW CHIEF LECTOR!*
STEP OFF, MICHEL. FIGHTING US WILL GET YOU NOWHERE. WE MUST STOP SET. IF YOU'RE WISE--
I WOULD WHAT? JOIN YOU? COLLABORATE? THE GODS BRING NOTHING BUT DESTRUCTION.
MASTER, AMOS IS RIGHT. WE CAN'T FIGHT EACH OTHER. THAT'S NOT WHAT ISKANDAR WANTED.
YOU SIDE WITH *THEM?*

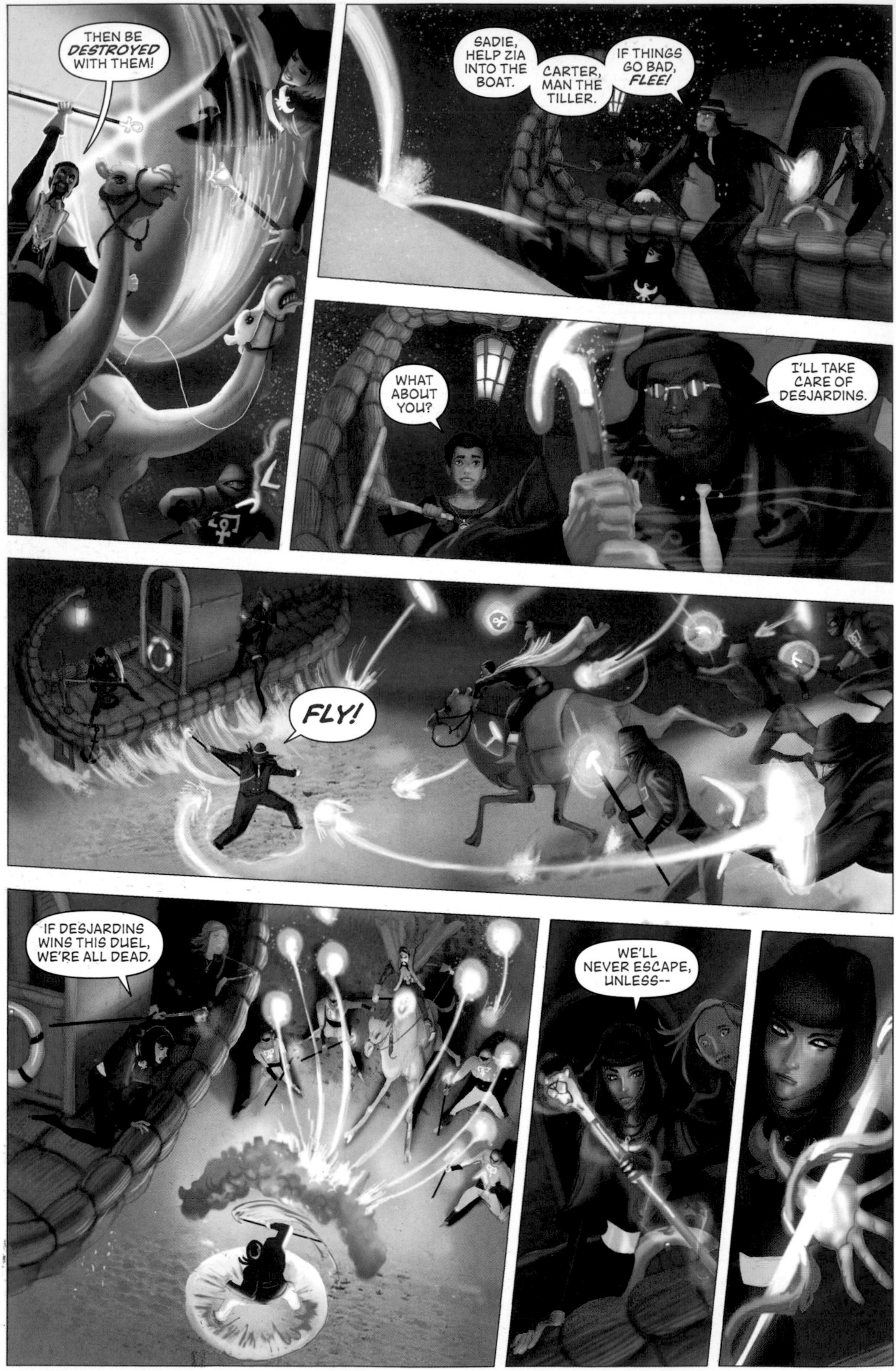
THEN BE *DESTROYED* WITH THEM!
SADIE, HELP ZIA INTO THE BOAT.
CARTER, MAN THE TILLER.
IF THINGS GO BAD, *FLEE!*
WHAT ABOUT YOU?
I'LL TAKE CARE OF DESJARDINS.
FLY!
IF DESJARDINS WINS THIS DUEL, WE'RE ALL DEAD.
WE'LL NEVER ESCAPE, UNLESS--

!?!...

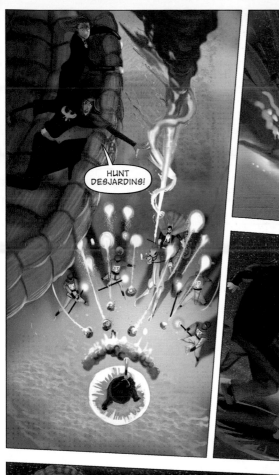

HUNT DESJARDINS!

ZIA! YOU *DARE* ATTACK *ME*?

ZIA-- WHAT DID YOU JUST DO?

A PILLAR OF FIRE--IT IS THE STRONGEST SPELL A *MASTER OF FIRE* CAN SUMMON. IT WILL CHASE DESJARDINS UNTIL IT DISSIPATES.

HOW LONG FOR *THAT*?

LONG ENOUGH TO GET AWAY...IT COMES AT THE EXPENSE OF MY MAGIC.

EXCELLENT WORK, ZIA!

I'LL TAKE CARE OF THE REMAINING MAGICIANS.

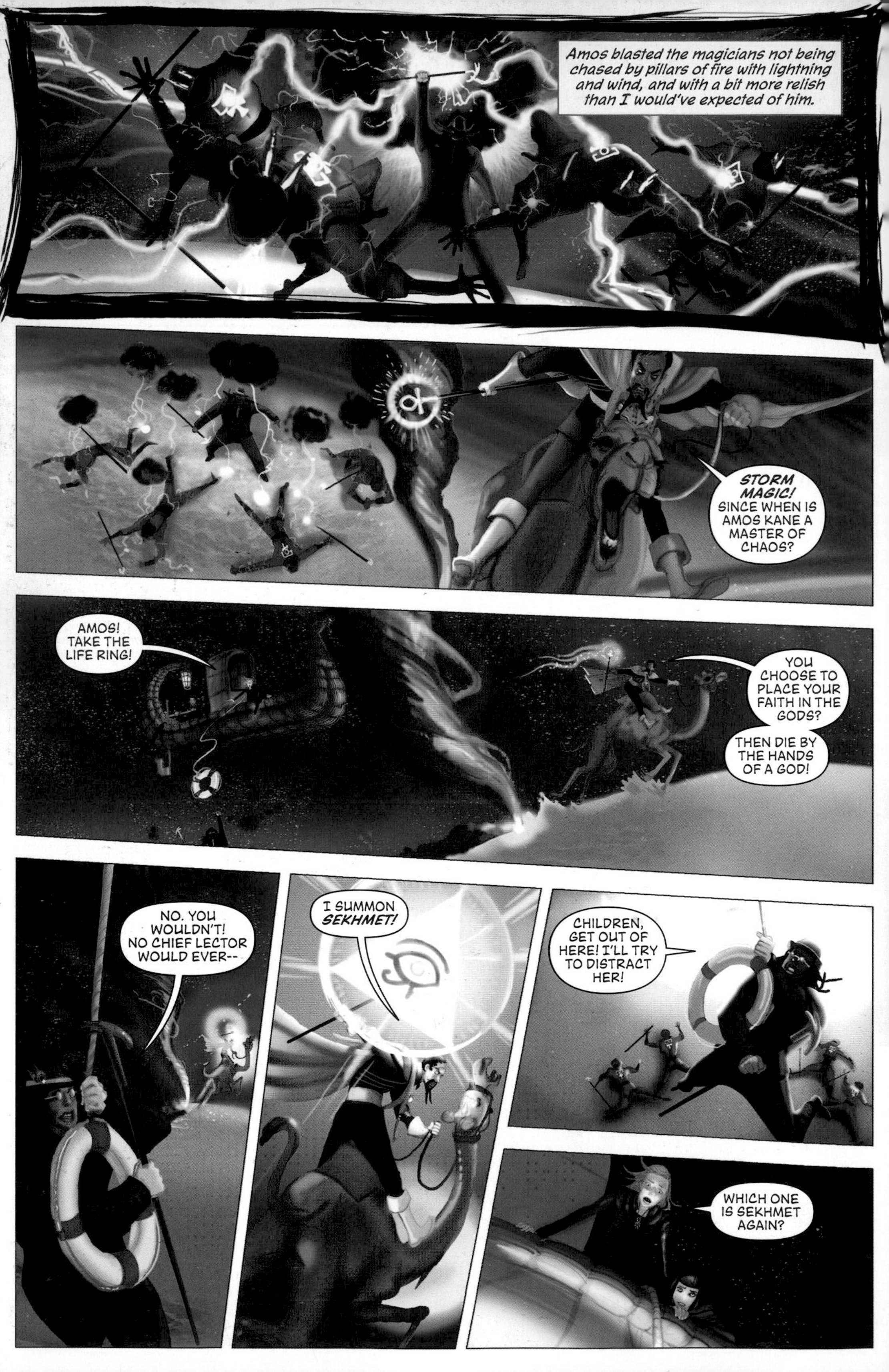
Amos blasted the magicians not being chased by pillars of fire with lightning and wind, and with a bit more relish than I would've expected of him.
STORM MAGIC! SINCE WHEN IS AMOS KANE A MASTER OF CHAOS?
AMOS! TAKE THE LIFE RING!
YOU CHOOSE TO PLACE YOUR FAITH IN THE GODS?
THEN DIE BY THE HANDS OF A GOD!
NO. YOU WOULDN'T! NO CHIEF LECTOR WOULD EVER--
I SUMMON SEKHMET!
CHILDREN, GET OUT OF HERE! I'LL TRY TO DISTRACT HER!
WHICH ONE IS SEKHMET AGAIN?

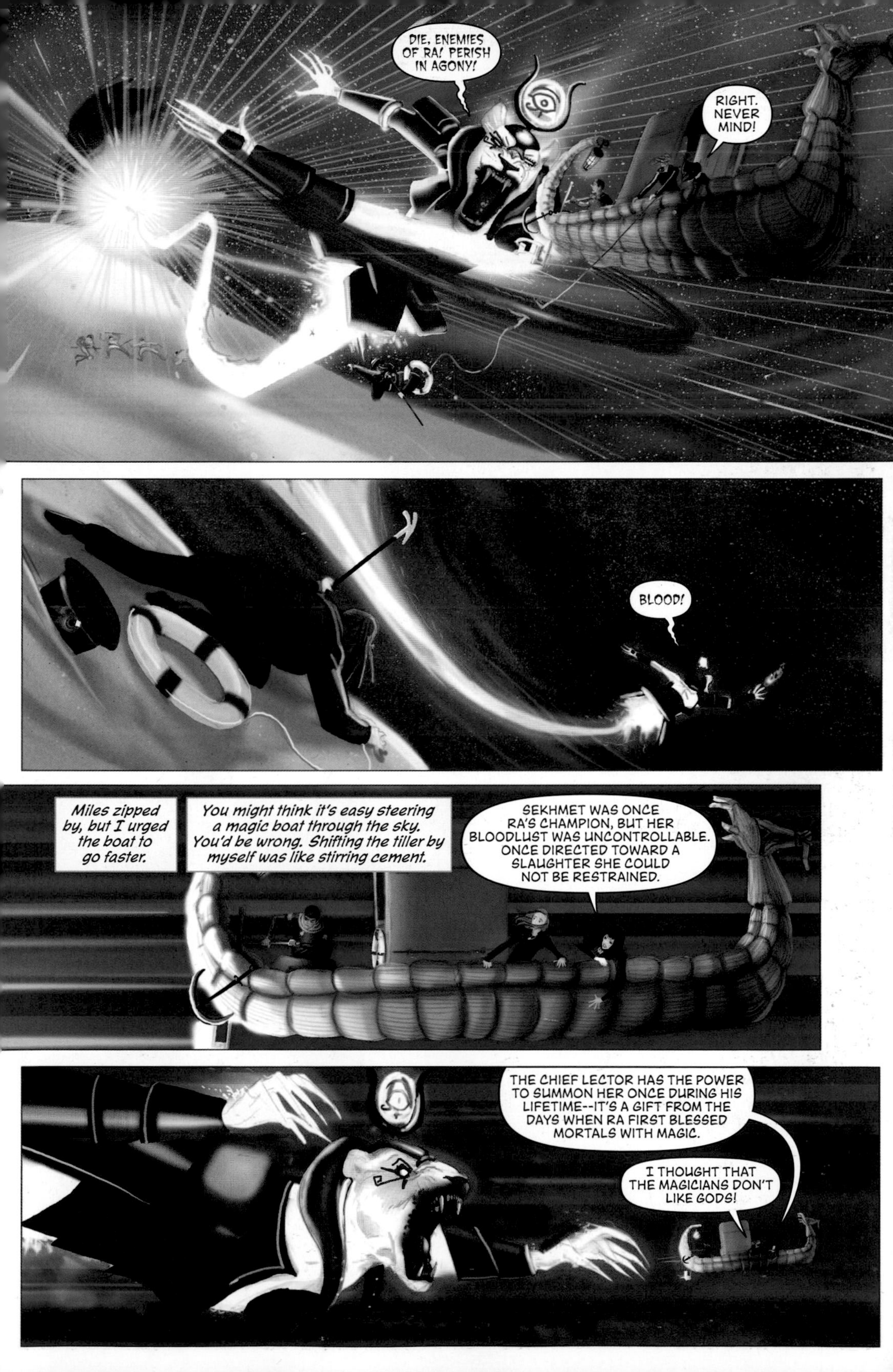

DIE, ENEMIES OF RA! PERISH IN AGONY!
RIGHT. NEVER MIND!
BLOOD!
Miles zipped by, but I urged the boat to go faster.
You might think it's easy steering a magic boat through the sky. You'd be wrong. Shifting the tiller by myself was like stirring cement.
SEKHMET WAS ONCE RA'S CHAMPION, BUT HER BLOODLUST WAS UNCONTROLLABLE. ONCE DIRECTED TOWARD A SLAUGHTER SHE COULD NOT BE RESTRAINED.
THE CHIEF LECTOR HAS THE POWER TO SUMMON HER ONCE DURING HIS LIFETIME--IT'S A GIFT FROM THE DAYS WHEN RA FIRST BLESSED MORTALS WITH MAGIC.
I THOUGHT THAT THE MAGICIANS DON'T LIKE GODS!

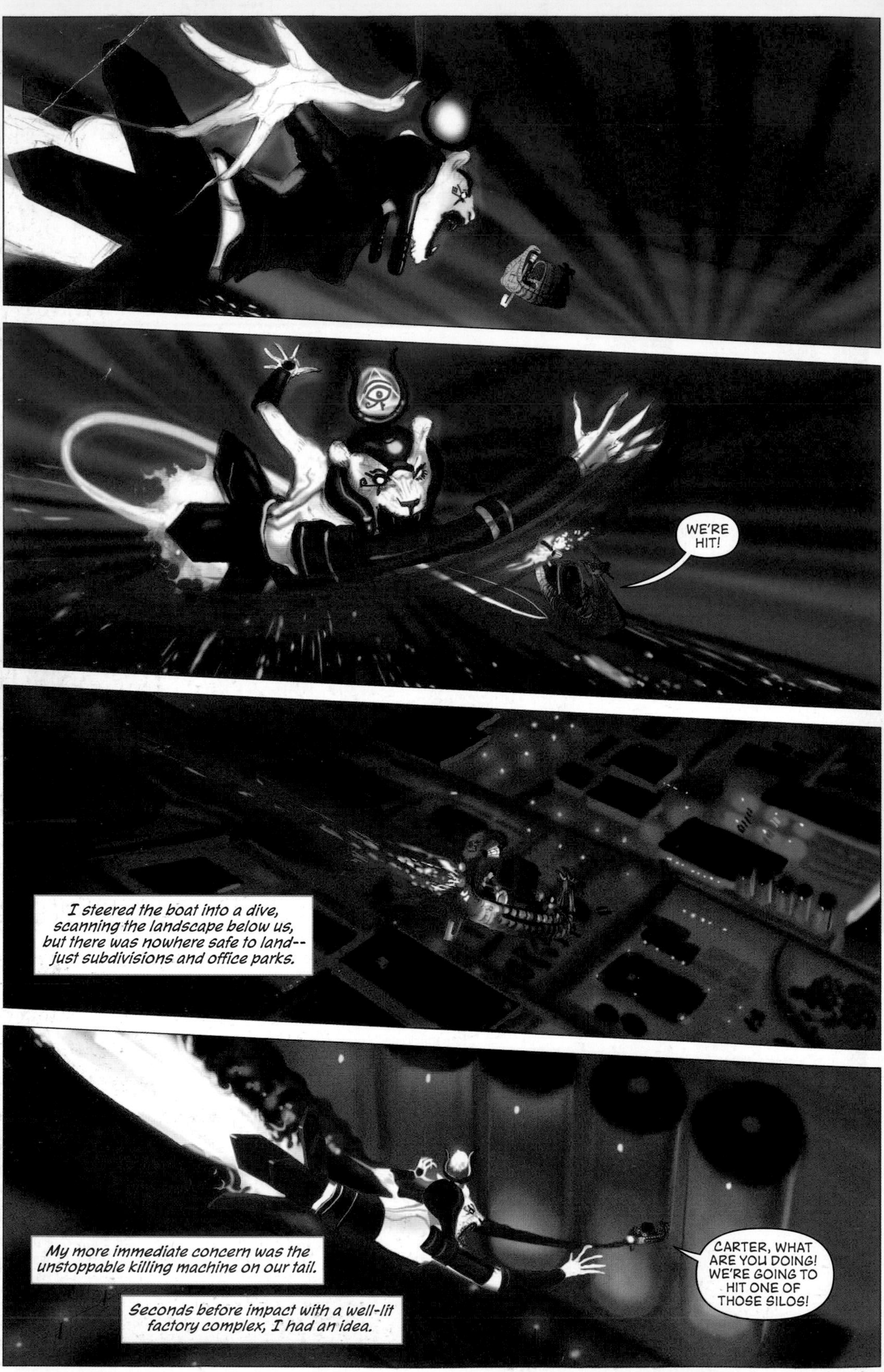
WE'RE HIT!
I steered the boat into a dive, scanning the landscape below us, but there was nowhere safe to land-- just subdivisions and office parks.
My more immediate concern was the unstoppable killing machine on our tail.
Seconds before impact with a well-lit factory complex, I had an idea.
CARTER, WHAT ARE YOU DOING! WE'RE GOING TO HIT ONE OF THOSE SILOS!

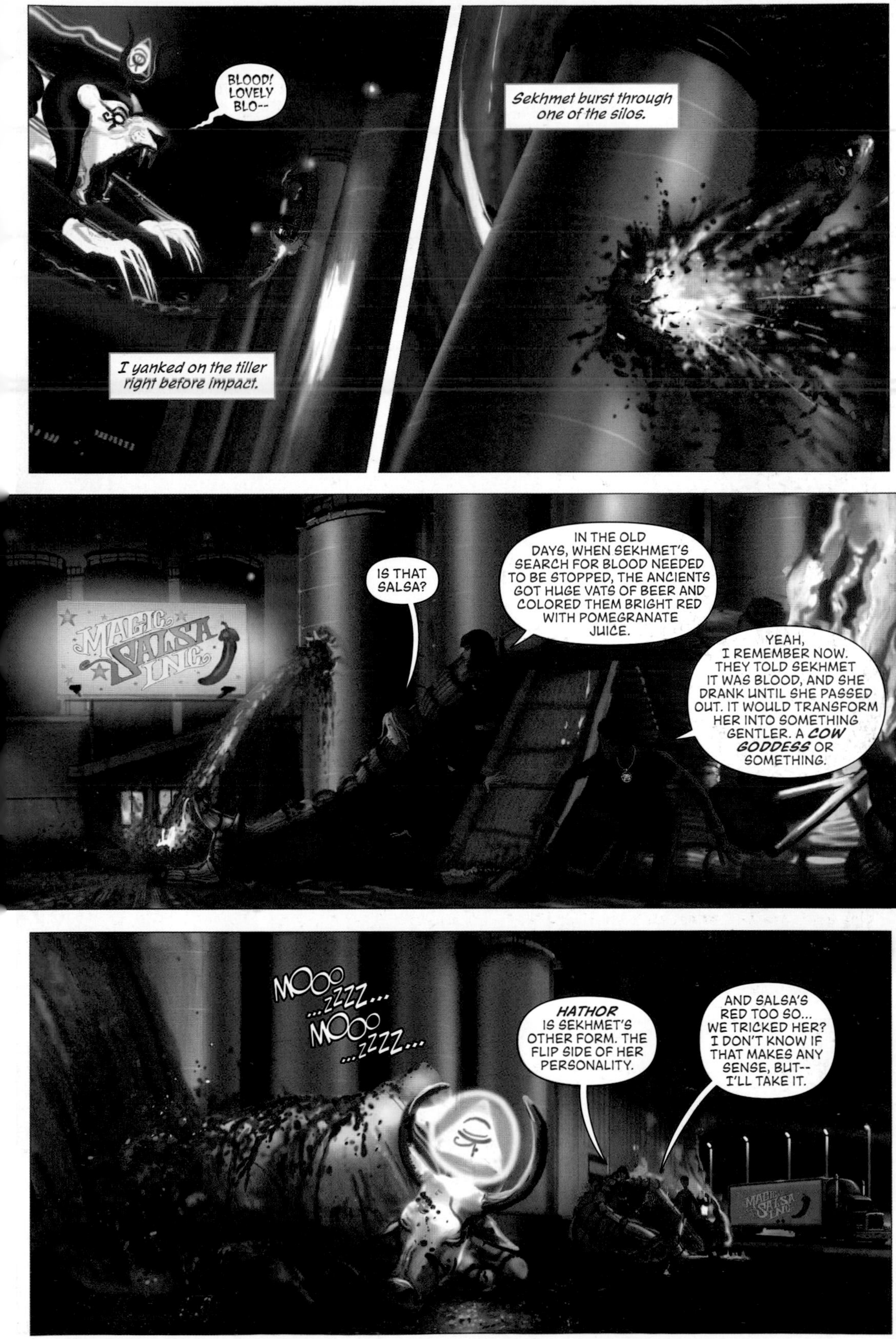
BLOOD! LOVELY BLO--
I yanked on the tiller right before impact.
Sekhmet burst through one of the silos.
MAGIC SALSA INC
IS THAT SALSA?
IN THE OLD DAYS, WHEN SEKHMET'S SEARCH FOR BLOOD NEEDED TO BE STOPPED, THE ANCIENTS GOT HUGE VATS OF BEER AND COLORED THEM BRIGHT RED WITH POMEGRANATE JUICE.
YEAH, I REMEMBER NOW. THEY TOLD SEKHMET IT WAS BLOOD, AND SHE DRANK UNTIL SHE PASSED OUT. IT WOULD TRANSFORM HER INTO SOMETHING GENTLER. A ***COW GODDESS*** OR SOMETHING.
MOOO ...ZZZZ... MOOO ...ZZZZ...
HATHOR IS SEKHMET'S OTHER FORM. THE FLIP SIDE OF HER PERSONALITY.
AND SALSA'S RED TOO SO... WE TRICKED HER? I DON'T KNOW IF THAT MAKES ANY SENSE, BUT-- I'LL TAKE IT.
MAGIC SALSA INC

IF WE HAVE ANY CHANCE OF STOPPING SET, WE MUST GET TO PHOENIX SOON.

"WE"? I DON'T RECALL INVITING *YOU.*

SURELY YOU DON'T THINK I HELPED DESJARDINS TRACK YOU DOWN?

I DON'T KNOW. *DID* YOU?

SADIE, LAY OFF.

ZIA SUMMONED THAT PILLAR-OF-FIRE THING. SHE SACRIFICED HER MAGIC TO SAVE US. WE *NEED* HER.

WELL, THE BOAT'S BURNED, SO HOW DO WE GET TO PHOENIX? WALK?

...

MAYBE WE CAN HITCH A RIDE!

MAGIC SALSA INC.

The cab was bigger than I'd thought. Behind the seat was a curtained area with a full-size bed, which Sadie claimed immediately.

DO YOU KNOW HOW TO DRIVE A LORRY?

I COULD PROBABLY DO IT IF MY LEGS WERE A LITTLE LONGER...

I HAVE AN IDEA!

DOUGHBOY! WE NEED TO TALK.

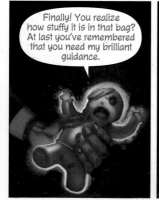

Finally! You realize how stuffy it is in that bag? At last you've remembered that you need my brilliant guidance.

WE'VE GOT GPS FOR GUIDANCE, DOUGHBOY. I JUST NEED YOU TO WORK THE PEDALS!

RIGHT. I'LL GET SOME SHUT-EYE AND LEAVE YOU TWO TOGETHER WITH YOUR DOUGHBOY.

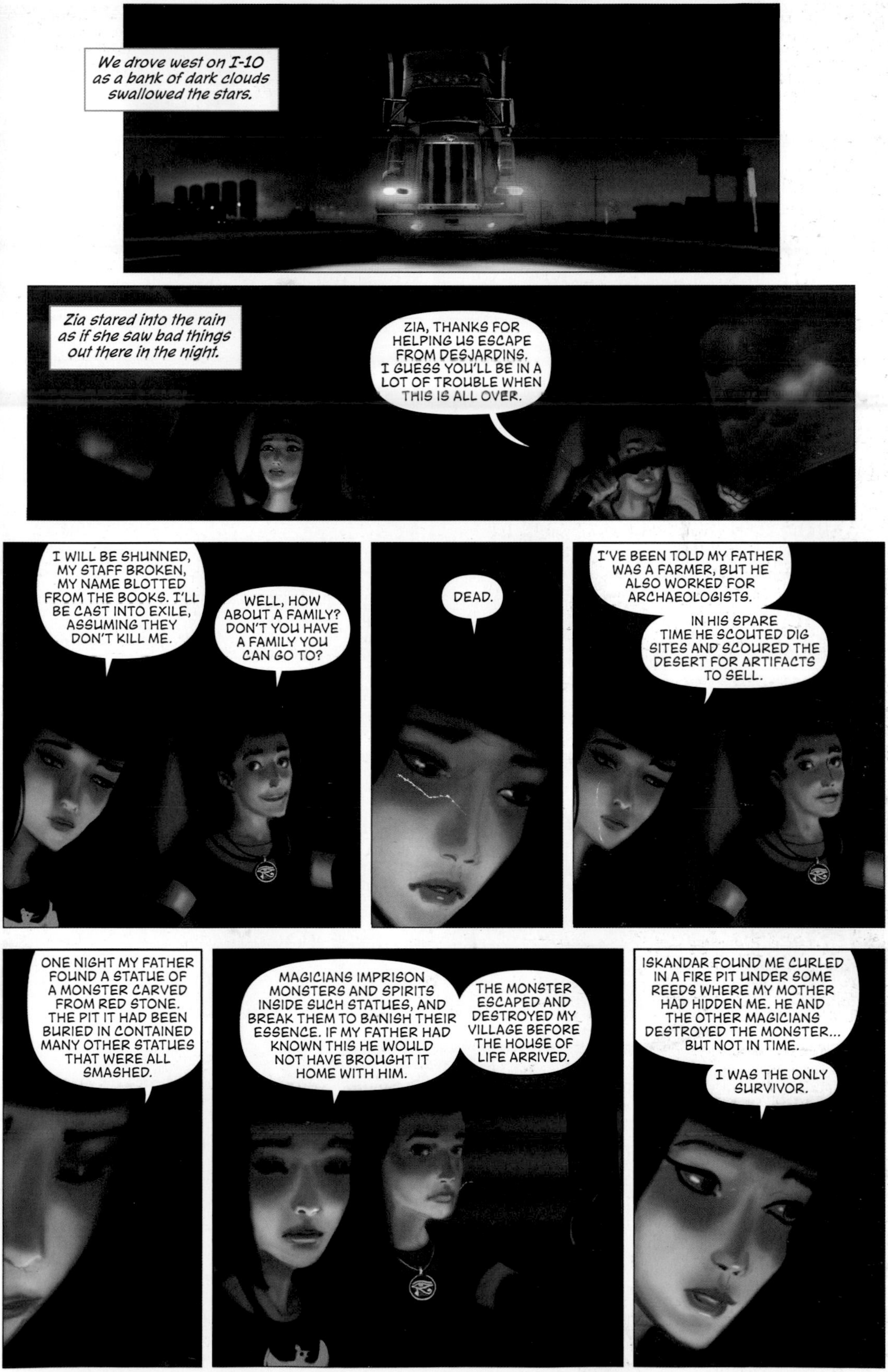
We drove west on I-10 as a bank of dark clouds swallowed the stars.
Zia stared into the rain as if she saw bad things out there in the night.
ZIA, THANKS FOR HELPING US ESCAPE FROM DESJARDINS. I GUESS YOU'LL BE IN A LOT OF TROUBLE WHEN THIS IS ALL OVER.
I WILL BE SHUNNED, MY STAFF BROKEN, MY NAME BLOTTED FROM THE BOOKS. I'LL BE CAST INTO EXILE, ASSUMING THEY DON'T KILL ME.
WELL, HOW ABOUT A FAMILY? DON'T YOU HAVE A FAMILY YOU CAN GO TO?
DEAD.
I'VE BEEN TOLD MY FATHER WAS A FARMER, BUT HE ALSO WORKED FOR ARCHAEOLOGISTS.
IN HIS SPARE TIME HE SCOUTED DIG SITES AND SCOURED THE DESERT FOR ARTIFACTS TO SELL.
ONE NIGHT MY FATHER FOUND A STATUE OF A MONSTER CARVED FROM RED STONE. THE PIT IT HAD BEEN BURIED IN CONTAINED MANY OTHER STATUES THAT WERE ALL SMASHED.
MAGICIANS IMPRISON MONSTERS AND SPIRITS INSIDE SUCH STATUES, AND BREAK THEM TO BANISH THEIR ESSENCE. IF MY FATHER HAD KNOWN THIS HE WOULD NOT HAVE BROUGHT IT HOME WITH HIM.
THE MONSTER ESCAPED AND DESTROYED MY VILLAGE BEFORE THE HOUSE OF LIFE ARRIVED.
ISKANDAR FOUND ME CURLED IN A FIRE PIT UNDER SOME REEDS WHERE MY MOTHER HAD HIDDEN ME. HE AND THE OTHER MAGICIANS DESTROYED THE MONSTER... BUT NOT IN TIME.
I WAS THE ONLY SURVIVOR.

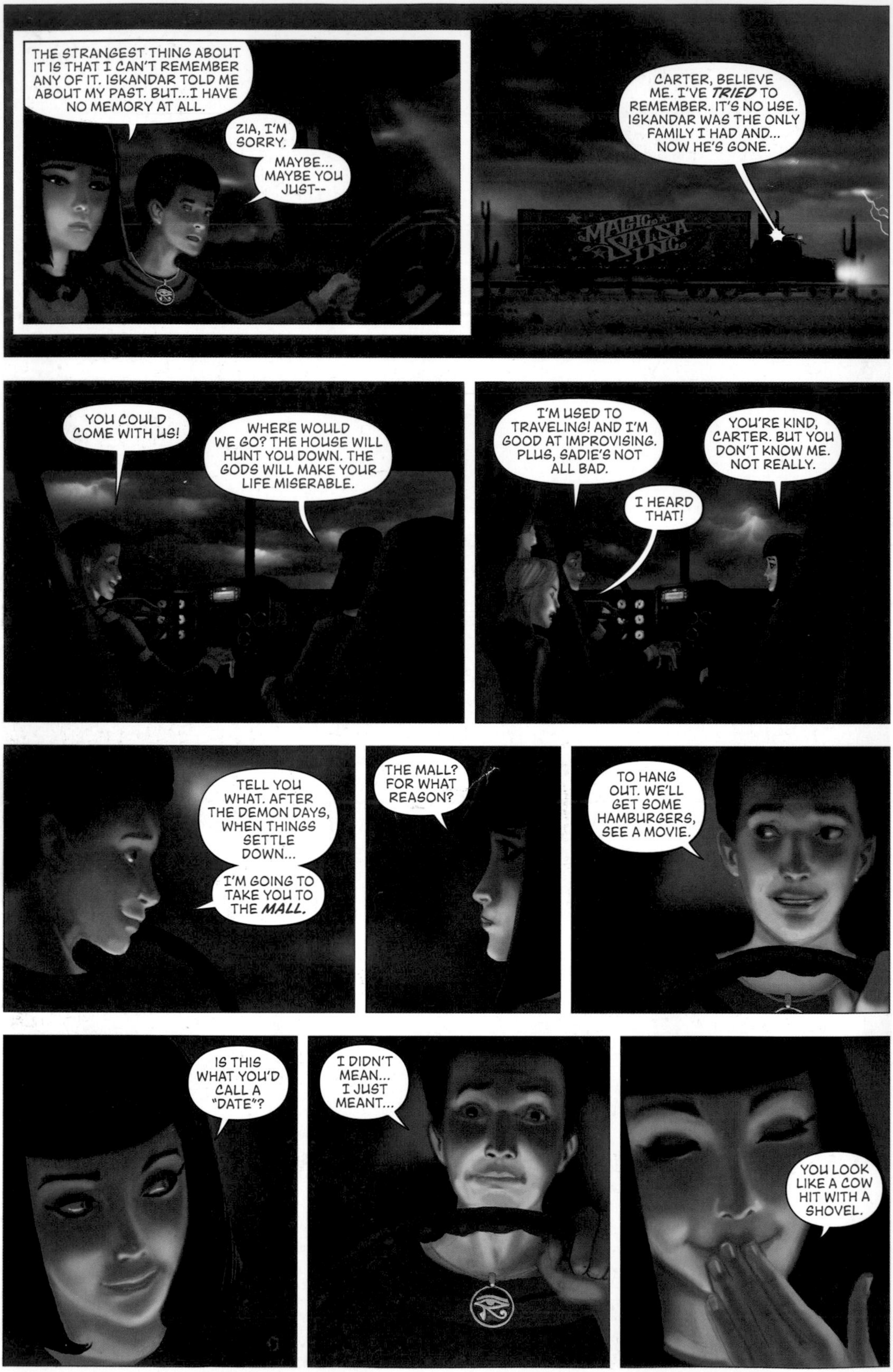
THE STRANGEST THING ABOUT IT IS THAT I CAN'T REMEMBER ANY OF IT. ISKANDAR TOLD ME ABOUT MY PAST. BUT...I HAVE NO MEMORY AT ALL.
ZIA, I'M SORRY.
MAYBE... MAYBE YOU JUST--
CARTER, BELIEVE ME. I'VE *TRIED* TO REMEMBER. IT'S NO USE. ISKANDAR WAS THE ONLY FAMILY I HAD AND... NOW HE'S GONE.
MAGIC SALSA INC
YOU COULD COME WITH US!
WHERE WOULD WE GO? THE HOUSE WILL HUNT YOU DOWN. THE GODS WILL MAKE YOUR LIFE MISERABLE.
I'M USED TO TRAVELING! AND I'M GOOD AT IMPROVISING. PLUS, SADIE'S NOT ALL BAD.
I HEARD THAT!
YOU'RE KIND, CARTER. BUT YOU DON'T KNOW ME. NOT REALLY.
TELL YOU WHAT. AFTER THE DEMON DAYS, WHEN THINGS SETTLE DOWN...
I'M GOING TO TAKE YOU TO THE *MALL.*
THE MALL? FOR WHAT REASON?
TO HANG OUT. WE'LL GET SOME HAMBURGERS, SEE A MOVIE.
IS THIS WHAT YOU'D CALL A "DATE"?
I DIDN'T MEAN... I JUST MEANT...
YOU LOOK LIKE A COW HIT WITH A SHOVEL.

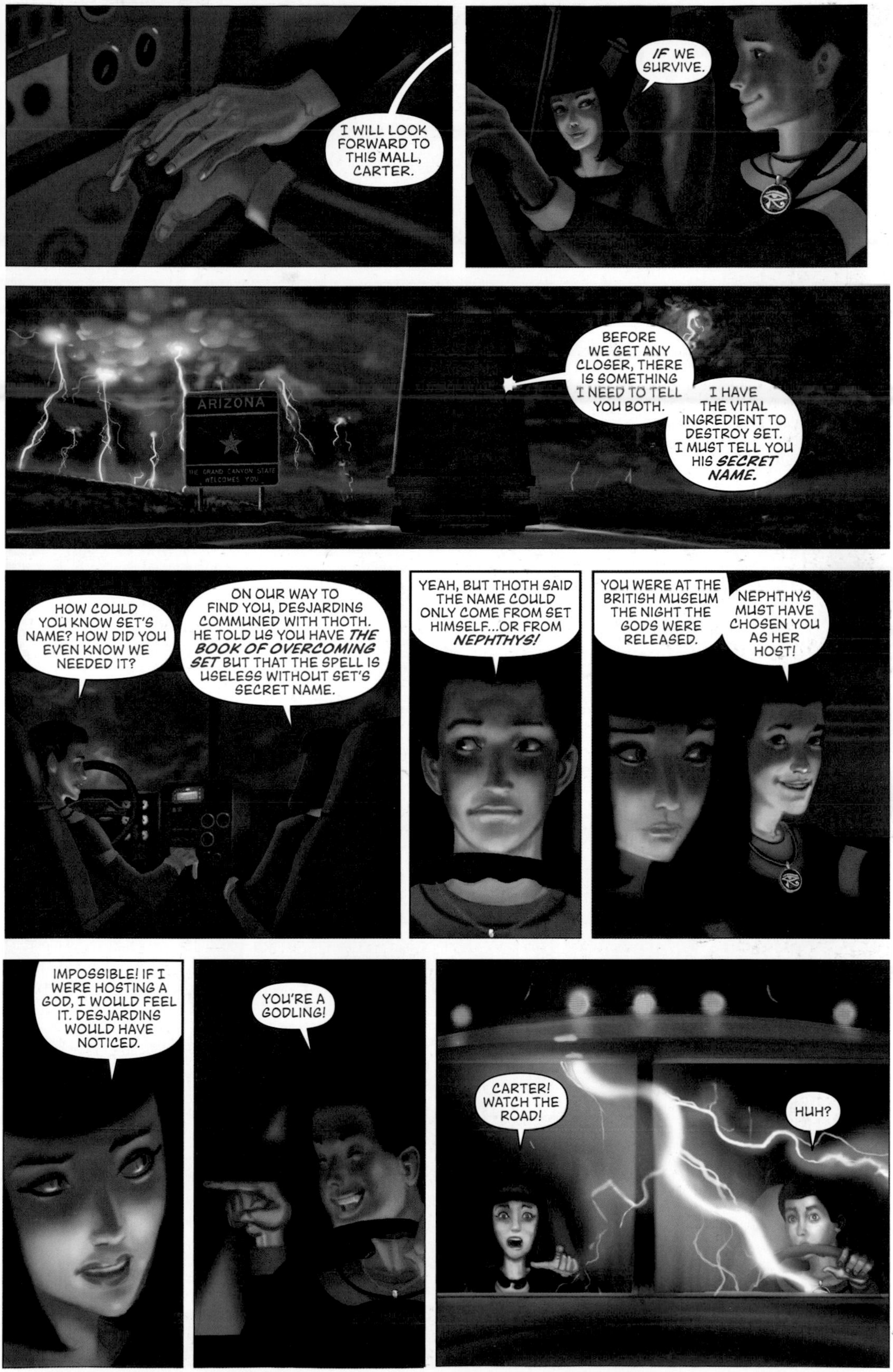
I WILL LOOK FORWARD TO THIS MALL, CARTER.
IF WE SURVIVE.
ARIZONA
THE GRAND CANYON STATE WELCOMES YOU
BEFORE WE GET ANY CLOSER, THERE IS SOMETHING I NEED TO TELL YOU BOTH.
I HAVE THE VITAL INGREDIENT TO DESTROY SET. I MUST TELL YOU HIS ***SECRET NAME.***
HOW COULD YOU KNOW SET'S NAME? HOW DID YOU EVEN KNOW WE NEEDED IT?
ON OUR WAY TO FIND YOU, DESJARDINS COMMUNED WITH THOTH. HE TOLD US YOU HAVE ***THE BOOK OF OVERCOMING SET*** BUT THAT THE SPELL IS USELESS WITHOUT SET'S SECRET NAME.
YEAH, BUT THOTH SAID THE NAME COULD ONLY COME FROM SET HIMSELF...OR FROM ***NEPHTHYS!***
YOU WERE AT THE BRITISH MUSEUM THE NIGHT THE GODS WERE RELEASED.
NEPHTHYS MUST HAVE CHOSEN YOU AS HER HOST!
IMPOSSIBLE! IF I WERE HOSTING A GOD, I WOULD FEEL IT. DESJARDINS WOULD HAVE NOTICED.
YOU'RE A GODLING!
CARTER! WATCH THE ROAD!
HUH?

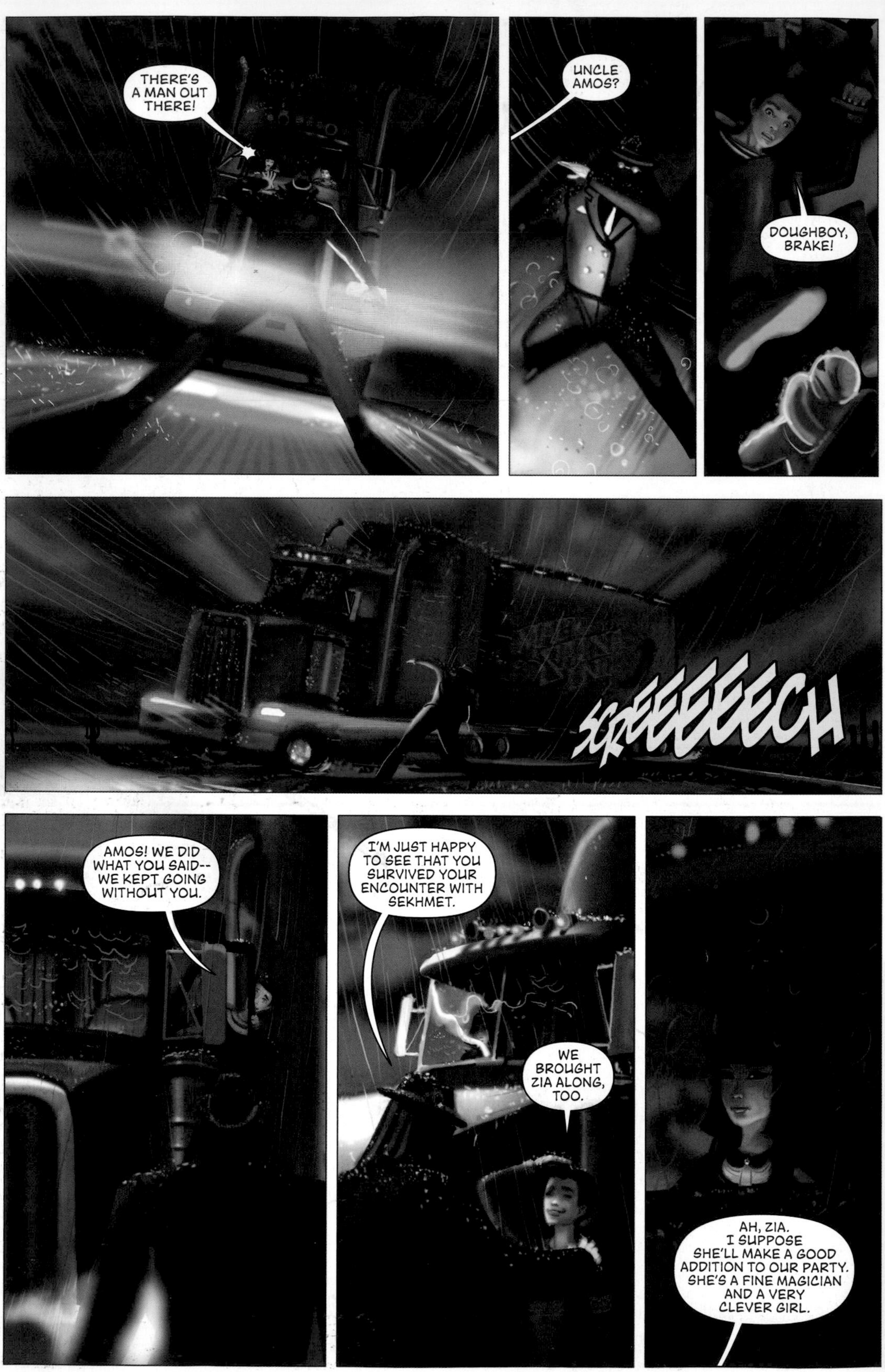
THERE'S A MAN OUT THERE!
UNCLE AMOS?
DOUGHBOY, BRAKE!
SCREEEEEECH
AMOS! WE DID WHAT YOU SAID-- WE KEPT GOING WITHOUT YOU.
I'M JUST HAPPY TO SEE THAT YOU SURVIVED YOUR ENCOUNTER WITH SEKHMET.
WE BROUGHT ZIA ALONG, TOO.
AH, ZIA. I SUPPOSE SHE'LL MAKE A GOOD ADDITION TO OUR PARTY. SHE'S A FINE MAGICIAN AND A VERY CLEVER GIRL.

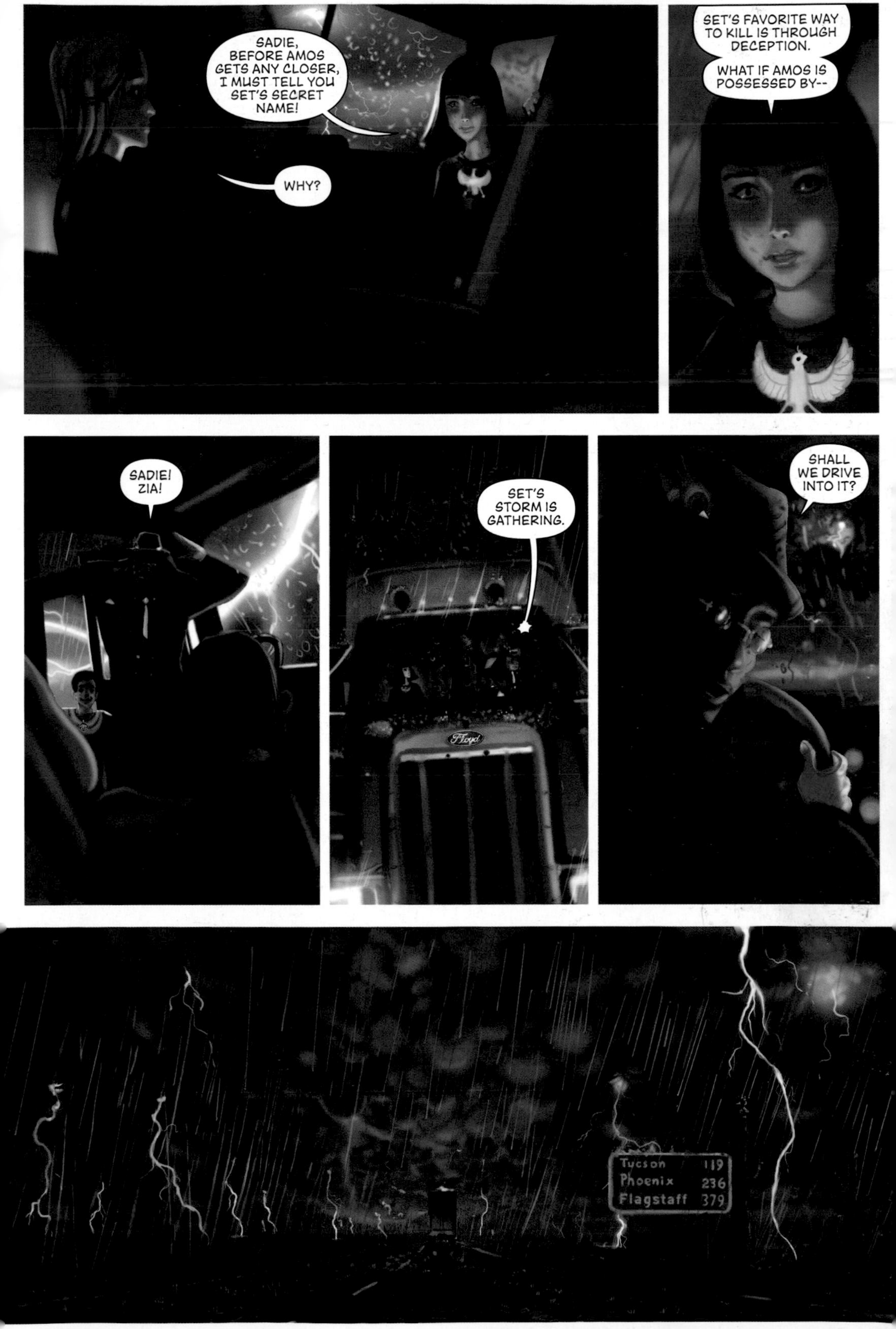
SADIE, BEFORE AMOS GETS ANY CLOSER, I MUST TELL YOU SET'S SECRET NAME!
WHY?
SET'S FAVORITE WAY TO KILL IS THROUGH DECEPTION.
WHAT IF AMOS IS POSSESSED BY--
SADIE! ZIA!
SET'S STORM IS GATHERING.
SHALL WE DRIVE INTO IT?
Tucson 119
Phoenix 236
Flagstaff 379

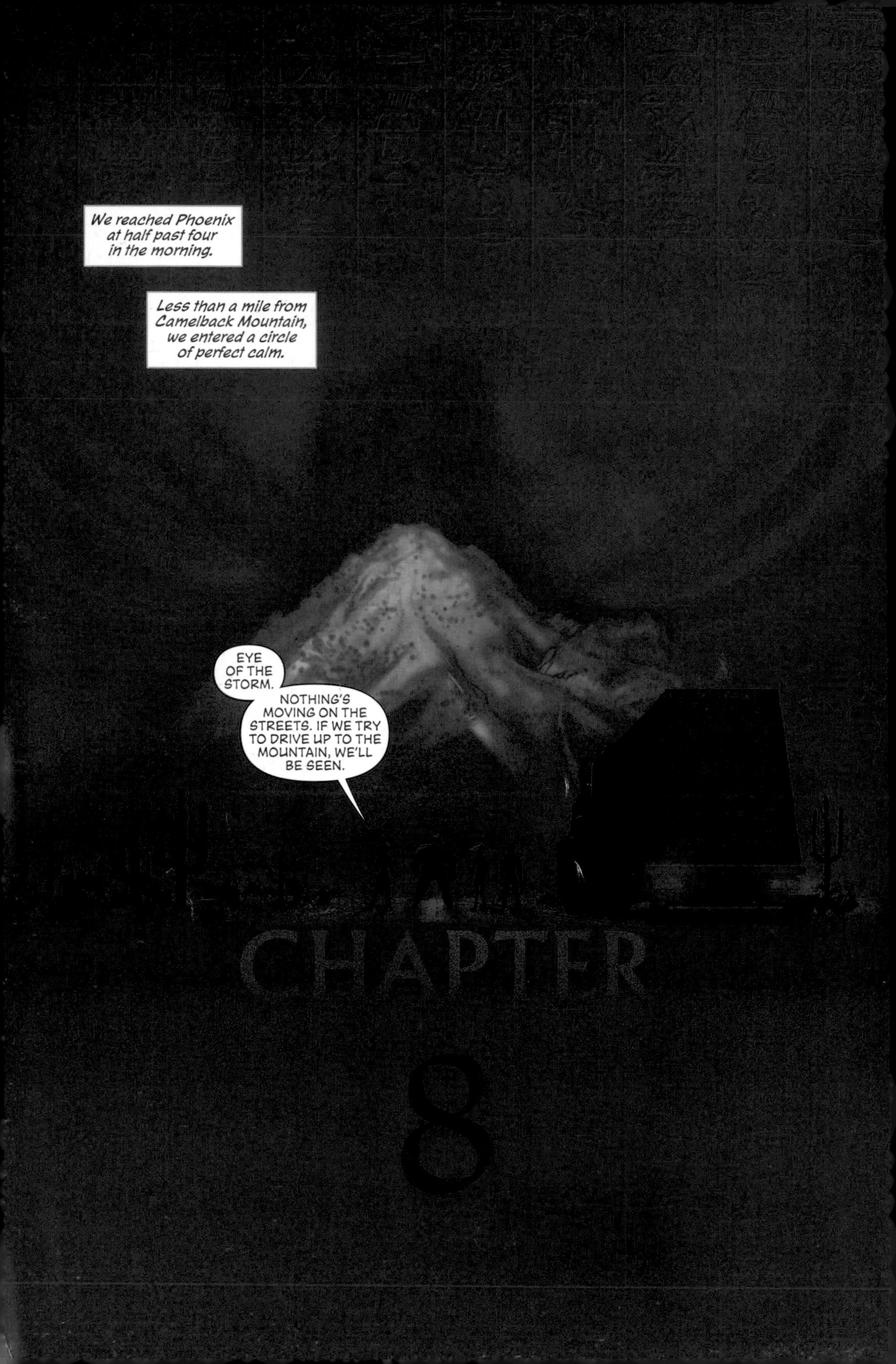
We reached Phoenix at half past four in the morning.
Less than a mile from Camelback Mountain, we entered a circle of perfect calm.
EYE OF THE STORM.
NOTHING'S MOVING ON THE STREETS. IF WE TRY TO DRIVE UP TO THE MOUNTAIN, WE'LL BE SEEN.
CHAPTER
8

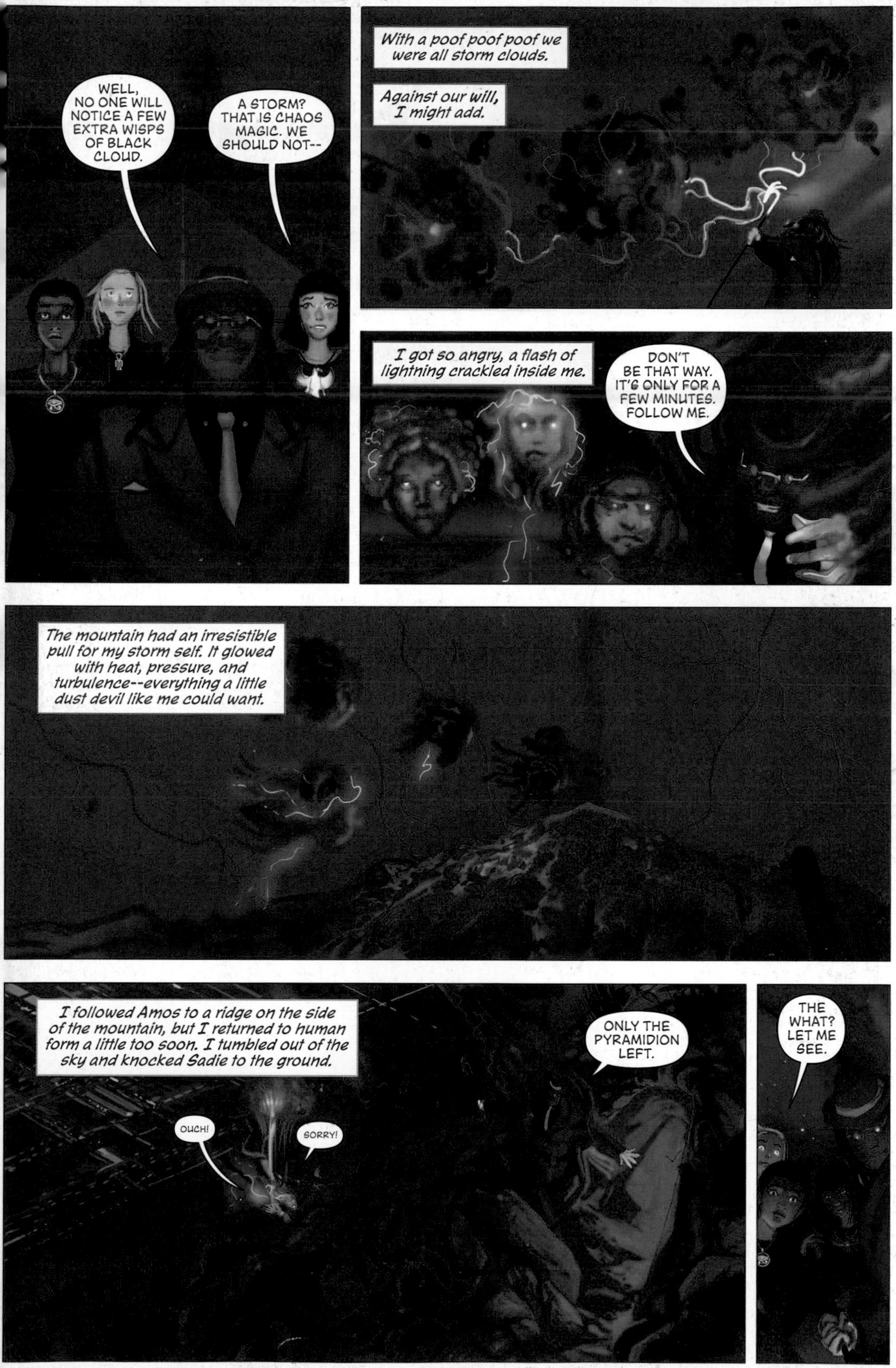
WELL, NO ONE WILL NOTICE A FEW EXTRA WISPS OF BLACK CLOUD.
A STORM? THAT IS CHAOS MAGIC. WE SHOULD NOT--
With a poof poof poof we were all storm clouds.
Against our will, I might add.
I got so angry, a flash of lightning crackled inside me.
DON'T BE THAT WAY. IT'S ONLY FOR A FEW MINUTES. FOLLOW ME.
The mountain had an irresistible pull for my storm self. It glowed with heat, pressure, and turbulence--everything a little dust devil like me could want.
I followed Amos to a ridge on the side of the mountain, but I returned to human form a little too soon. I tumbled out of the sky and knocked Sadie to the ground.
OUCH!
SORRY!
ONLY THE PYRAMIDION LEFT.
THE WHAT? LET ME SEE.

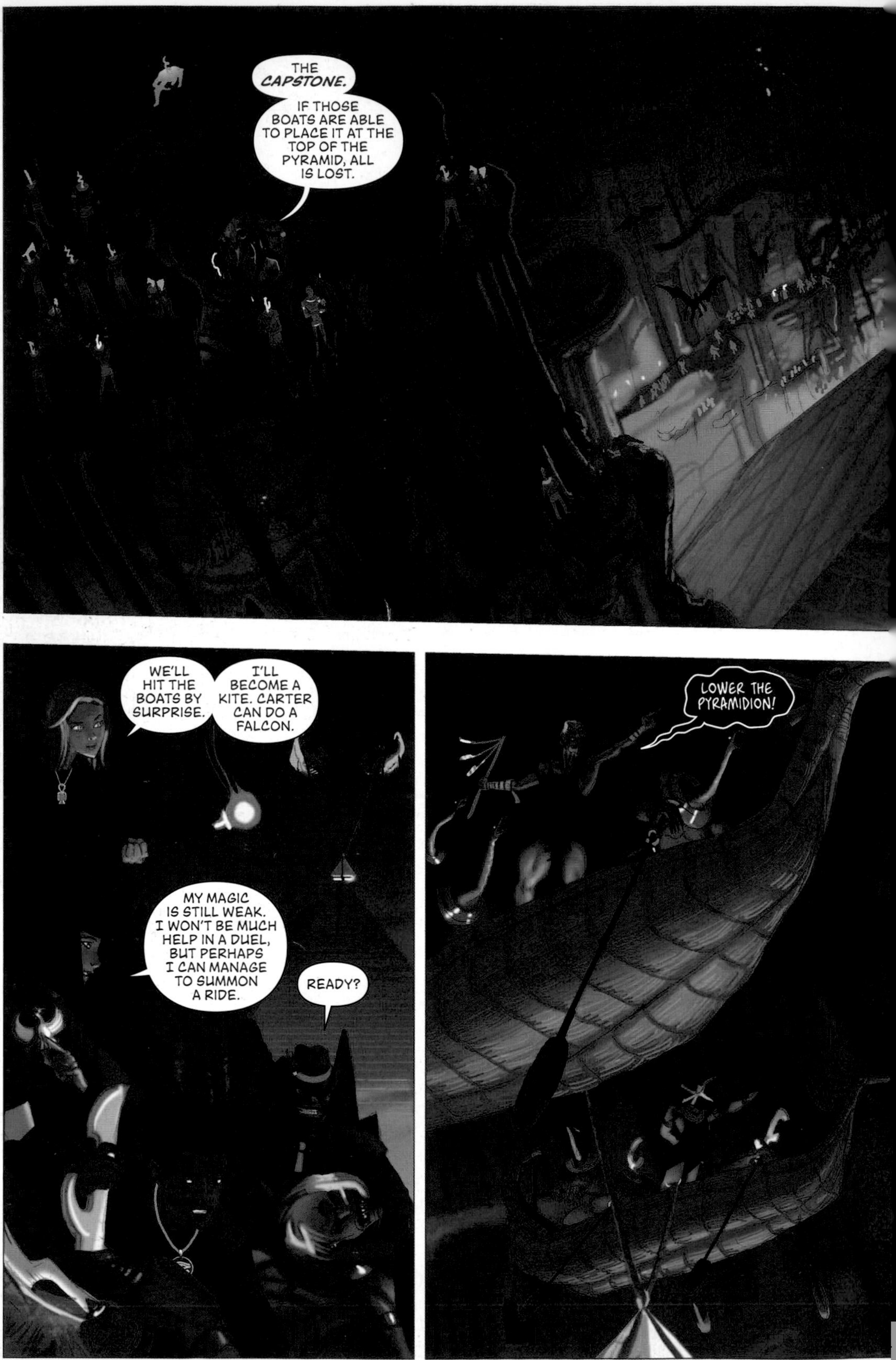
THE *CAPSTONE.*
IF THOSE BOATS ARE ABLE TO PLACE IT AT THE TOP OF THE PYRAMID, ALL IS LOST.
WE'LL HIT THE BOATS BY SURPRISE.
I'LL BECOME A KITE. CARTER CAN DO A FALCON.
MY MAGIC IS STILL WEAK. I WON'T BE MUCH HELP IN A DUEL, BUT PERHAPS I CAN MANAGE TO SUMMON A RIDE.
READY?
LOWER THE PYRAMIDION!

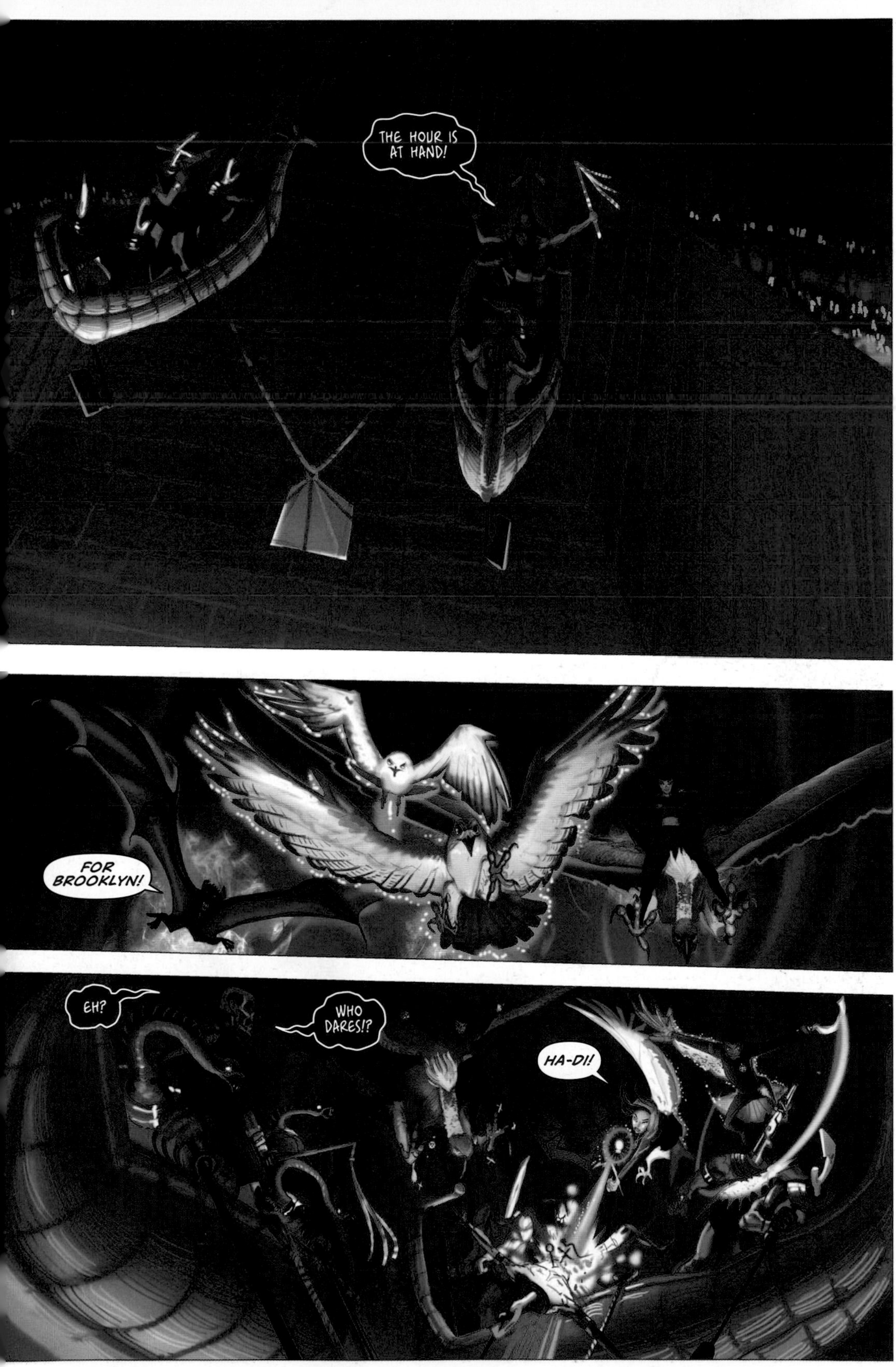
THE HOUR IS AT HAND!
FOR BROOKLYN!
EH?
WHO DARES!?
HA-DI!

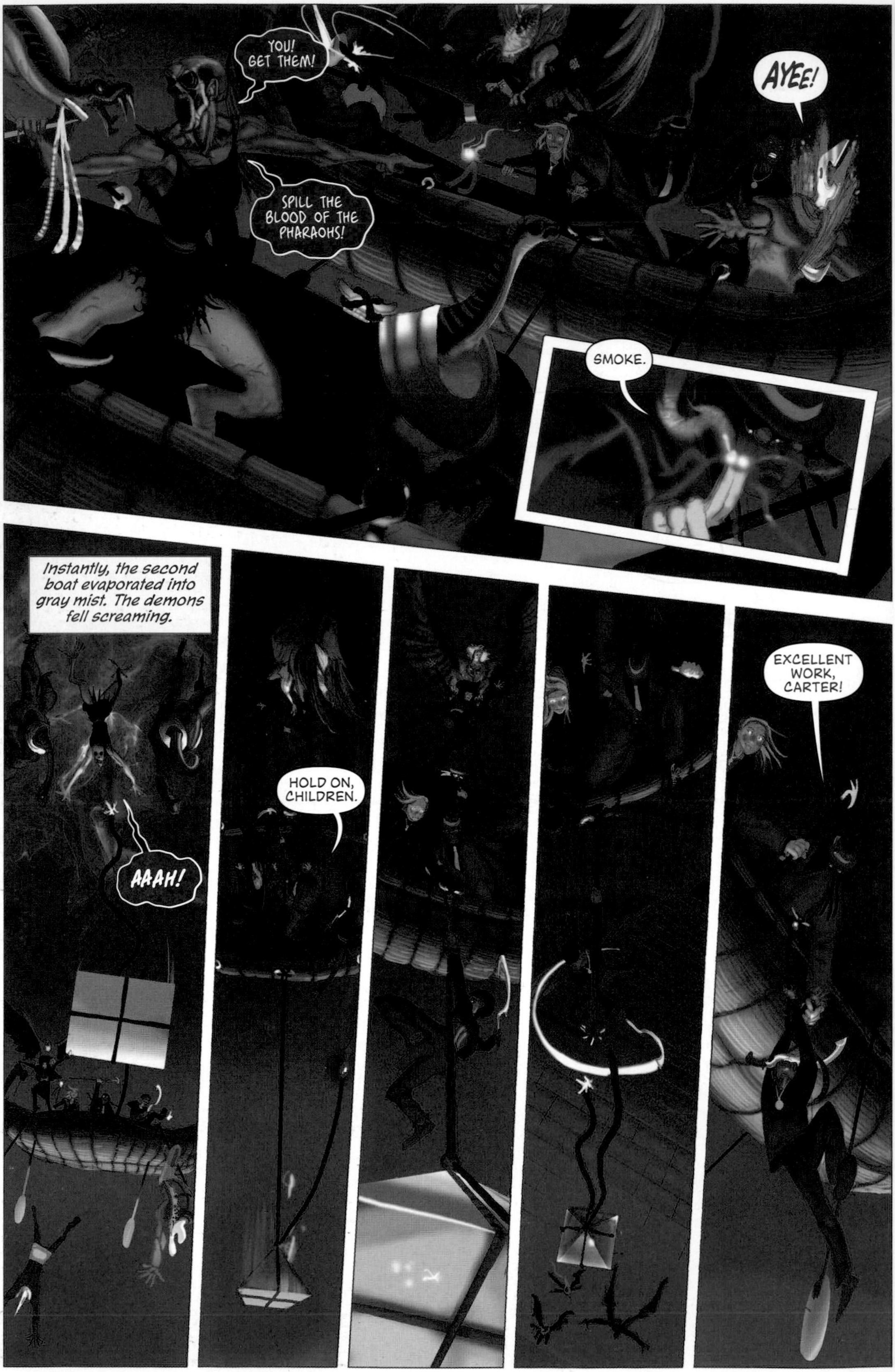
YOU! GET THEM!
AYEE!
SPILL THE BLOOD OF THE PHARAOHS!
SMOKE.
Instantly, the second boat evaporated into gray mist. The demons fell screaming.
AAAH!
HOLD ON, CHILDREN.
EXCELLENT WORK, CARTER!

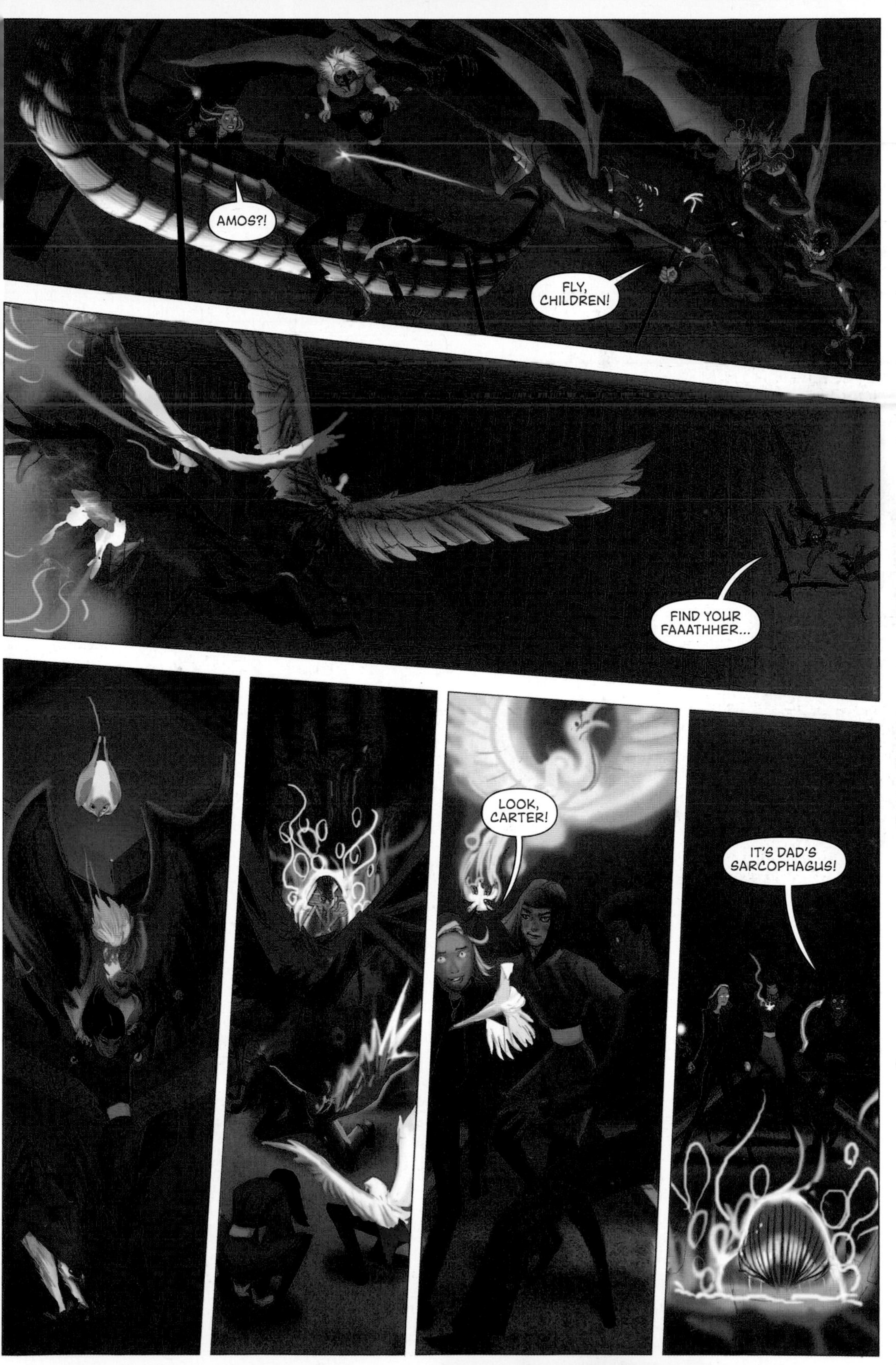
AMOS?!
FLY, CHILDREN!
FIND YOUR FAAATHHER...
LOOK, CARTER!
IT'S DAD'S SARCOPHAGUS!

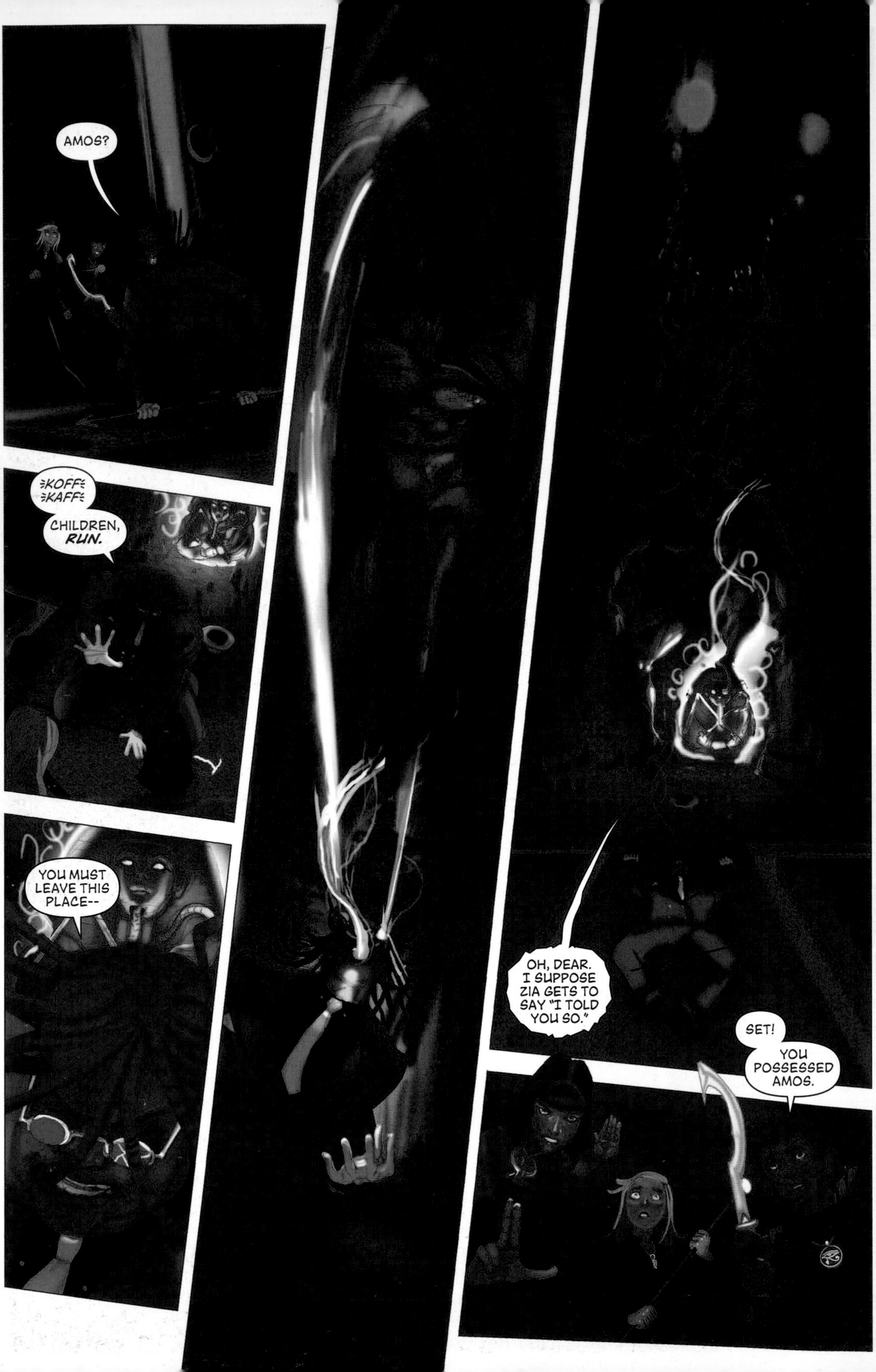
AMOS?
KOFF
KAFF
CHILDREN, **RUN.**
YOU MUST LEAVE THIS PLACE--
OH, DEAR. I SUPPOSE ZIA GETS TO SAY "I TOLD YOU SO."
SET!
YOU POSSESSED AMOS.

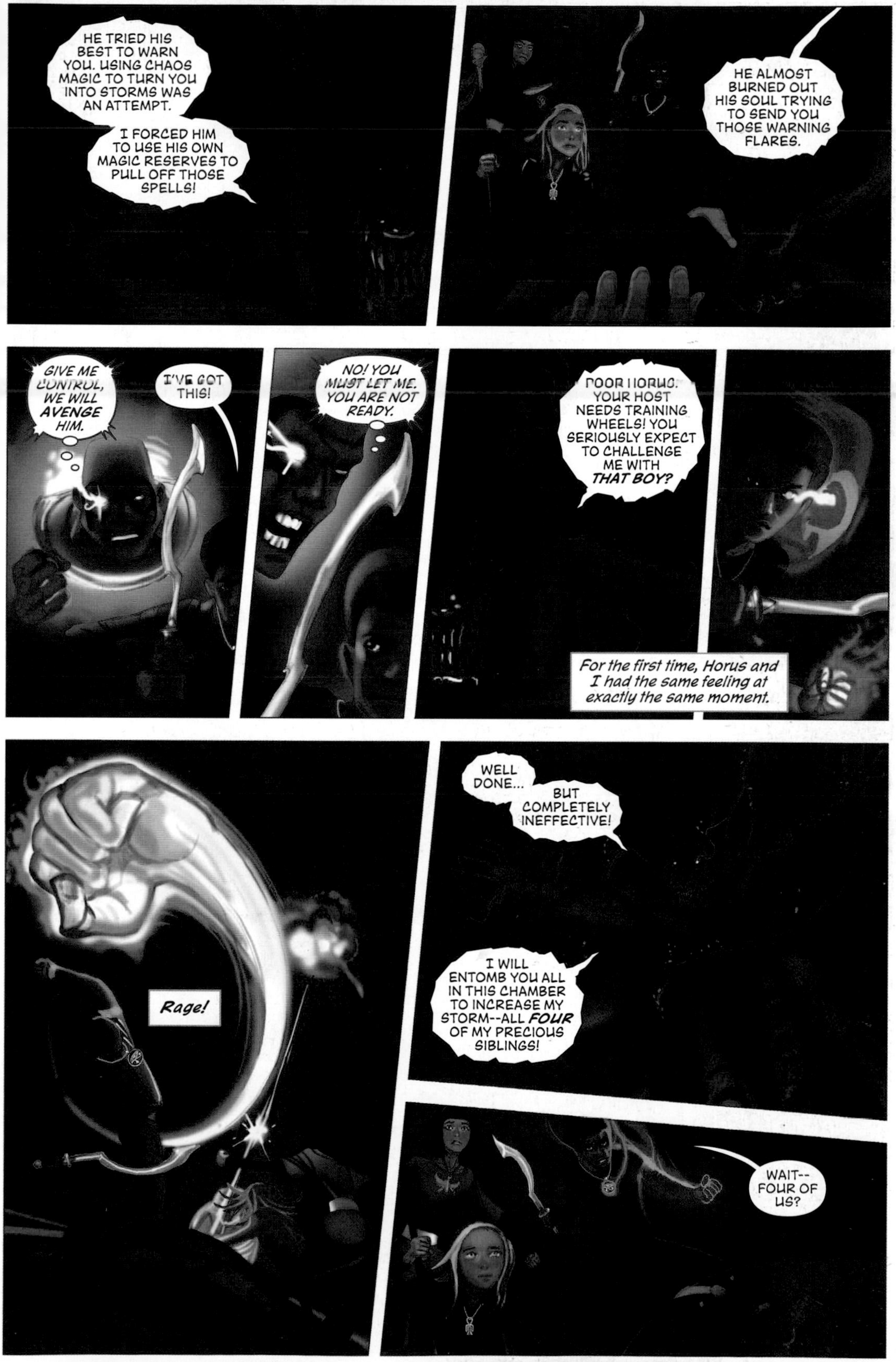
HE TRIED HIS BEST TO WARN YOU. USING CHAOS MAGIC TO TURN YOU INTO STORMS WAS AN ATTEMPT.
I FORCED HIM TO USE HIS OWN MAGIC RESERVES TO PULL OFF THOSE SPELLS!
HE ALMOST BURNED OUT HIS SOUL TRYING TO SEND YOU THOSE WARNING FLARES.
GIVE ME CONTROL, WE WILL ***AVENGE*** *HIM.*
I'VE GOT THIS!
NO! YOU MUST LET ME. YOU ARE NOT READY.
POOR HORUS. YOUR HOST NEEDS TRAINING WHEELS! YOU SERIOUSLY EXPECT TO CHALLENGE ME WITH ***THAT BOY?***
For the first time, Horus and I had the same feeling at exactly the same moment.
Rage!
WELL DONE...
BUT COMPLETELY INEFFECTIVE!
I WILL ENTOMB YOU ALL IN THIS CHAMBER TO INCREASE MY STORM--ALL ***FOUR*** OF MY PRECIOUS SIBLINGS!
WAIT-- FOUR OF US?

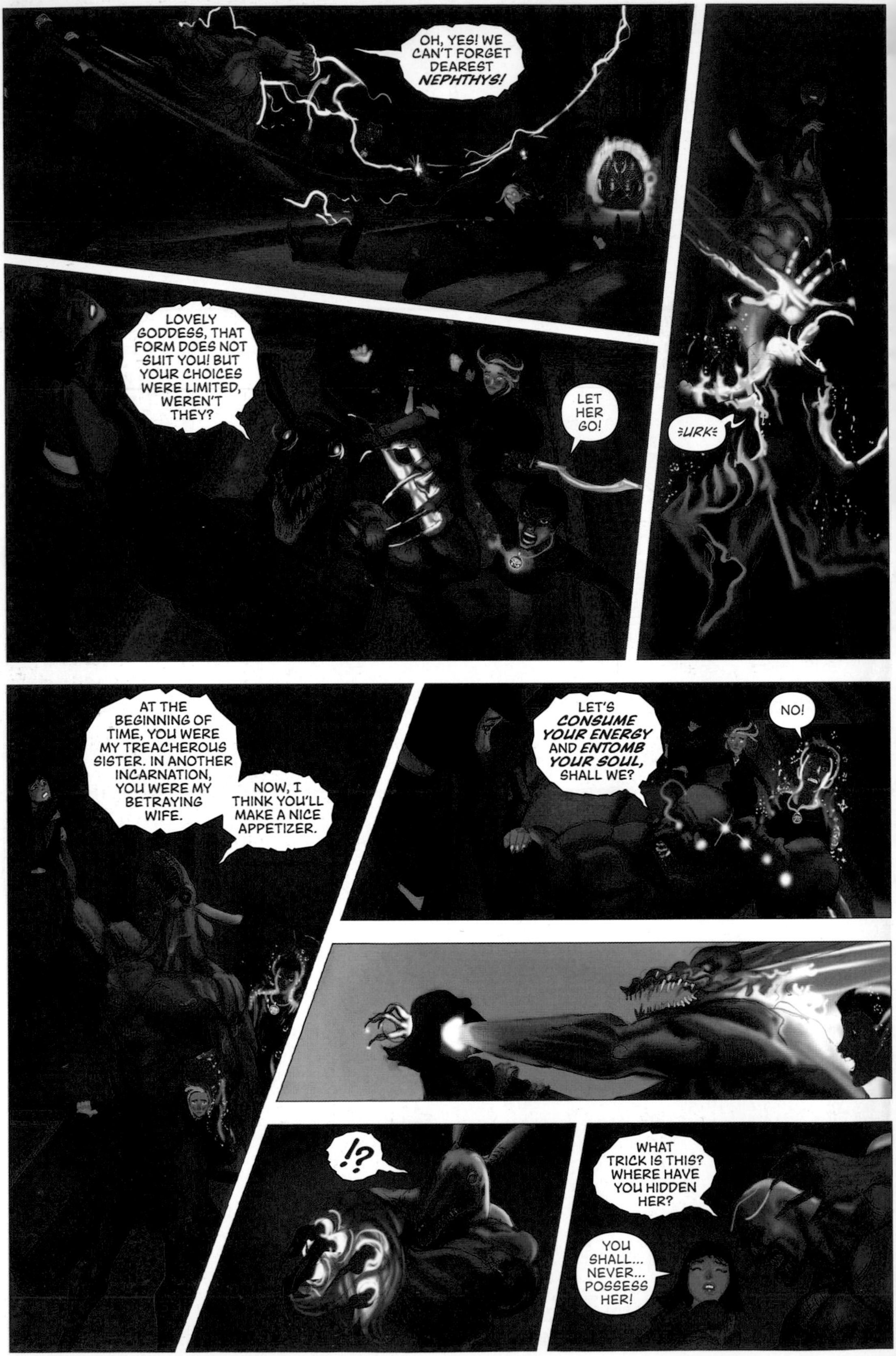
OH, YES! WE CAN'T FORGET DEAREST *NEPHTHYS!*
LOVELY GODDESS, THAT FORM DOES NOT SUIT YOU! BUT YOUR CHOICES WERE LIMITED, WEREN'T THEY?
LET HER GO!
URK
AT THE BEGINNING OF TIME, YOU WERE MY TREACHEROUS SISTER. IN ANOTHER INCARNATION, YOU WERE MY BETRAYING WIFE.
NOW, I THINK YOU'LL MAKE A NICE APPETIZER.
LET'S *CONSUME YOUR ENERGY* AND *ENTOMB YOUR SOUL,* SHALL WE?
NO!
!?
WHAT TRICK IS THIS? WHERE HAVE YOU HIDDEN HER?
YOU SHALL... NEVER... POSSESS HER!

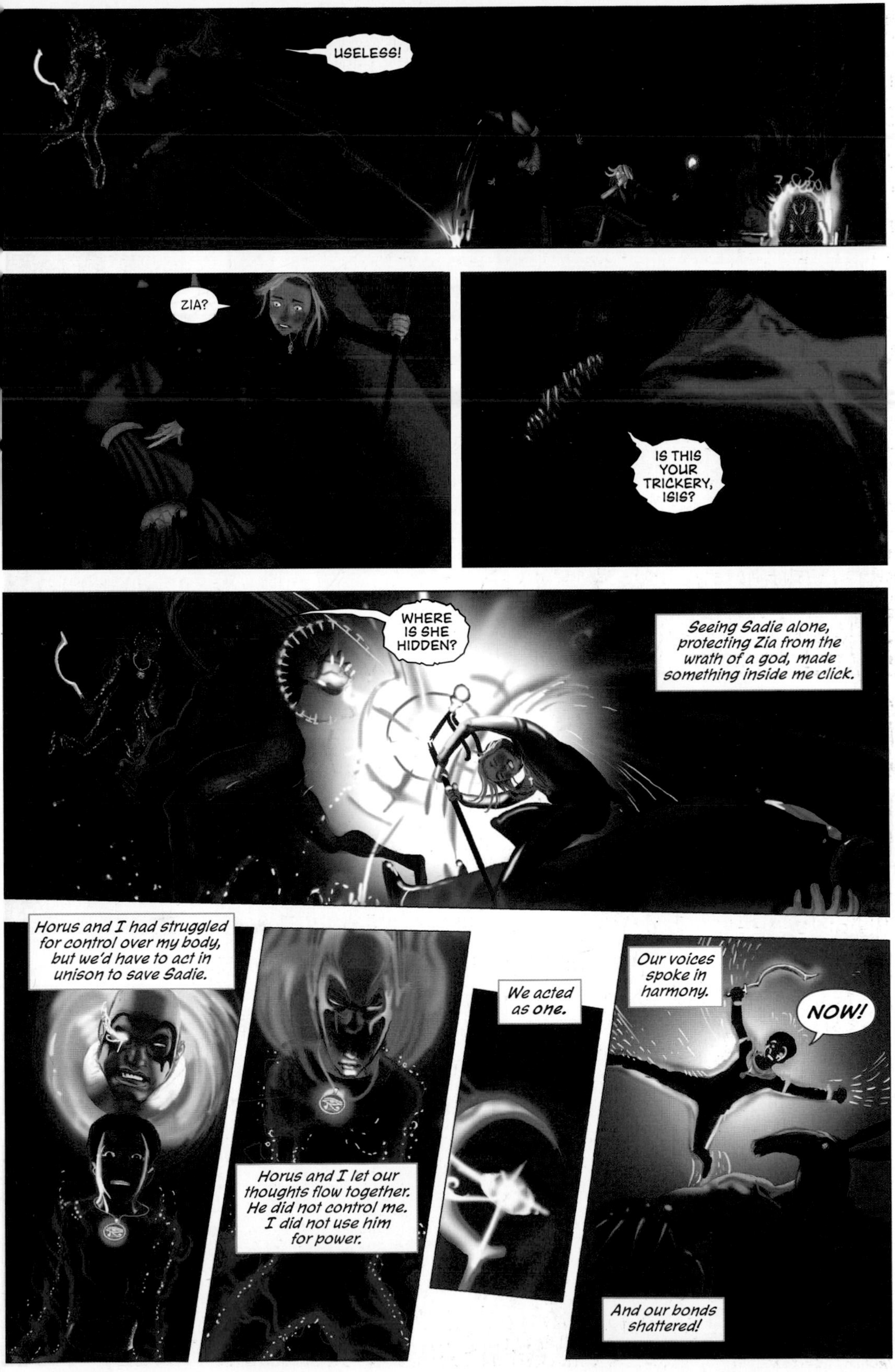
USELESS!
ZIA?
IS THIS YOUR TRICKERY, ISIS?
WHERE IS SHE HIDDEN?
Seeing Sadie alone, protecting Zia from the wrath of a god, made something inside me click.
Horus and I had struggled for control over my body, but we'd have to act in unison to save Sadie.
Horus and I let our thoughts flow together. He did not control me. I did not use him for power.
We acted as one.
Our voices spoke in harmony.
NOW!
And our bonds shattered!

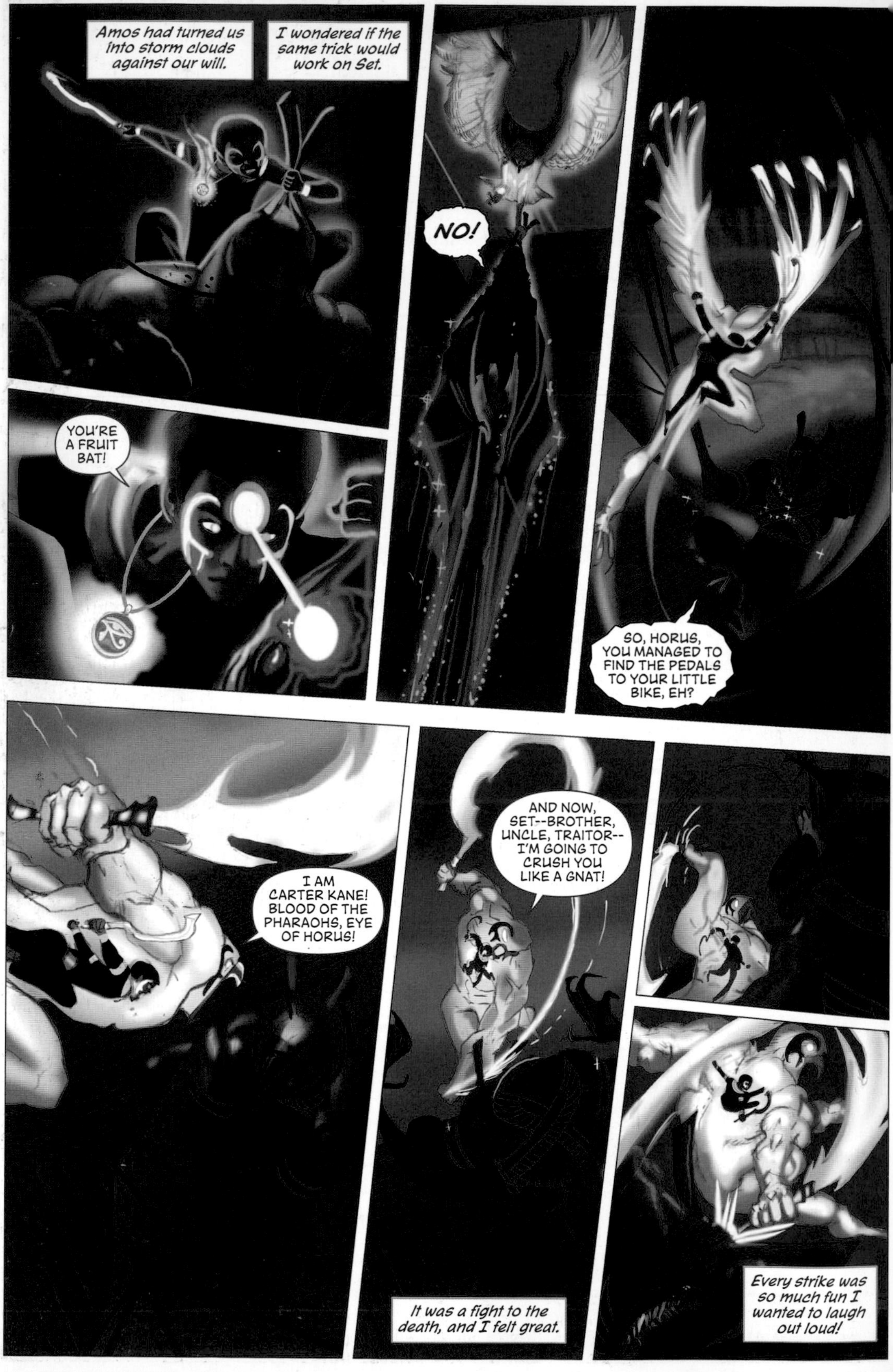
Amos had turned us into storm clouds against our will.
I wondered if the same trick would work on Set.
YOU'RE A FRUIT BAT!
NO!
SO, HORUS, YOU MANAGED TO FIND THE PEDALS TO YOUR LITTLE BIKE, EH?
I AM CARTER KANE! BLOOD OF THE PHARAOHS, EYE OF HORUS!
AND NOW, SET--BROTHER, UNCLE, TRAITOR--I'M GOING TO CRUSH YOU LIKE A GNAT!
It was a fight to the death, and I felt great.
Every strike was so much fun I wanted to laugh out loud!

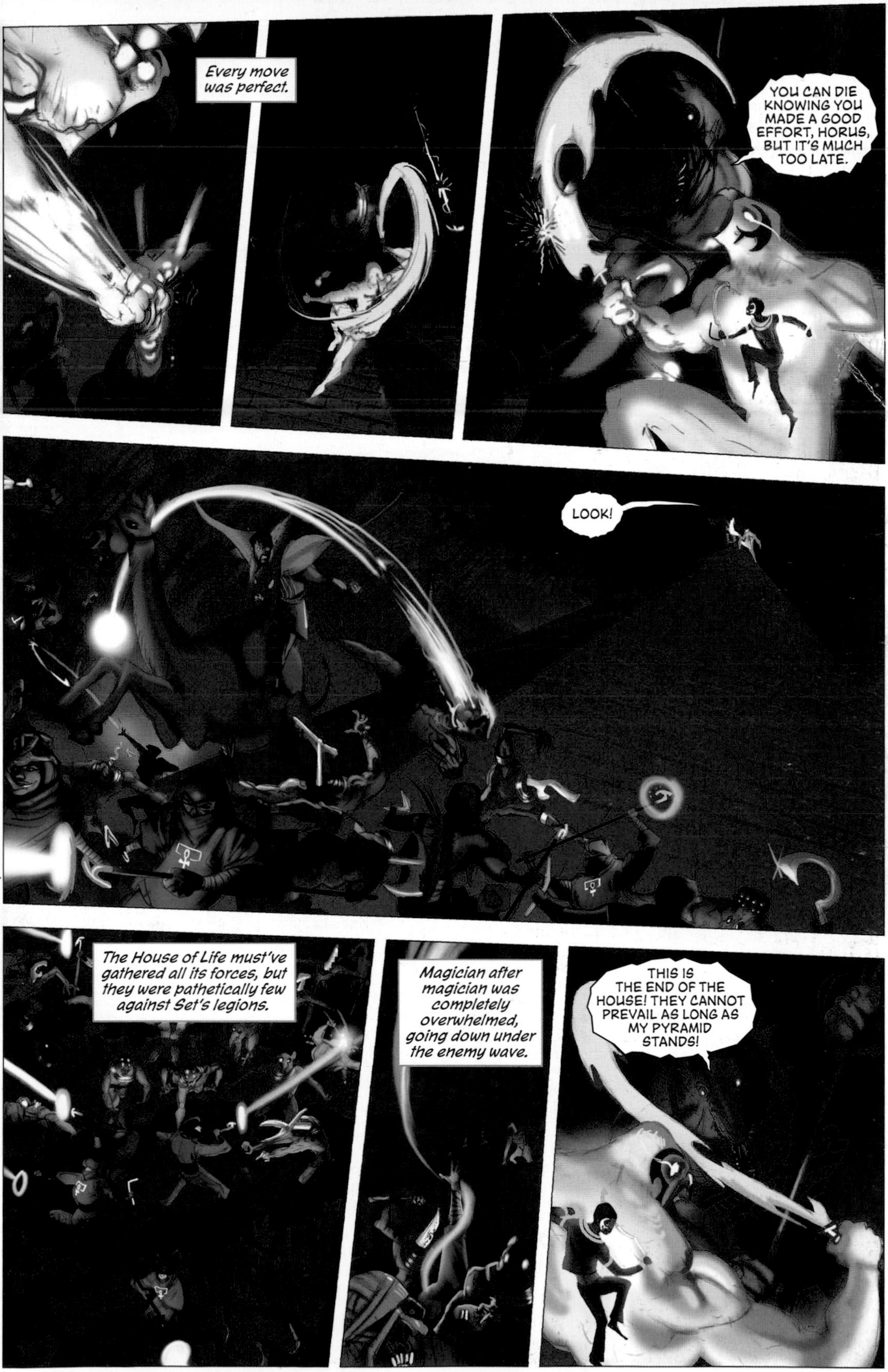
Every move was perfect.
YOU CAN DIE KNOWING YOU MADE A GOOD EFFORT, HORUS, BUT IT'S MUCH TOO LATE.
LOOK!
The House of Life must've gathered all its forces, but they were pathetically few against Set's legions.
Magician after magician was completely overwhelmed, going down under the enemy wave.
THIS IS THE END OF THE HOUSE! THEY CANNOT PREVAIL AS LONG AS MY PYRAMID STANDS!

When my brother the *chicken man* went off to play with his new friend the *fruit bat*, he left me to nurse two very wounded people.

Poor Amos's wounds seemed more magical than physical, but Zia's were another story.

HOLD STILL. MAYBE THERE'S SOME HEALING MAGIC OR--

SADIE. NO TIME. LISTEN.

SET'S NAME...IS *EVIL DAY.* HE WAS BORN, AND IT WAS AN *EVIL DAY.*

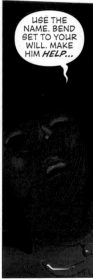

USE THE NAME. BEND SET TO YOUR WILL. MAKE HIM *HELP*...

HELP? HE JUST TRIED TO *KILL* YOU, ZIA. HE'S NOT THE HELPING TYPE.

GO... DESTROY THE PYRAMID...

I looked up to the ceiling. I didn't want to turn into a kite.

Then my eyes fixed on Dad's coffin, buried in the red throne.

SADIE, NO!

SET MUST BE DEALT WITH FIRST!

BUT IF I CAN FREE DAD...

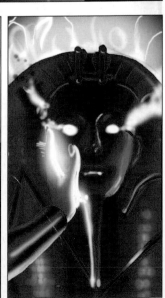

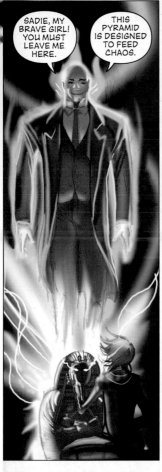

SADIE, MY BRAVE GIRL! YOU MUST LEAVE ME HERE.

THIS PYRAMID IS DESIGNED TO FEED CHAOS.

IF YOU FREE ME, OSIRIS'S POWER WILL BE RELEASED AND ABSORBED BY SET'S PYRAMID, AUGMENTING HIS STORM.

BUT-- I'M HERE TO *SAVE* YOU!

THE PYRAMID MUST BE DESTROYED, AND YOU KNOW HOW THAT MUST BE DONE.

MAY MA'AT GUIDE YOU, SADIE. I LOVE YOU.

MY GREATEST DUTY AS A FATHER WAS TO REALIZE THAT MY OWN DREAMS, MY OWN GOALS AND WISHES, EVEN MY LIFE IS SECONDARY TO MY CHILDREN'S.

THROUGH OUR SACRIFICES, YOUR MOTHER AND I HAVE SET THE STAGE. BUT IT IS *YOUR* STAGE.

I'M SORRY, SADIE.

WE'LL TALK ABOUT THAT LATER. RIGHT NOW, WE HAVE A GOD TO DEFEAT.

I pictured myself merging with Isis' soul.

I'd shared power with Isis before, but this was different.

My resolve, my anger, even my grief gave me confidence.

We understood each other.

We were one.

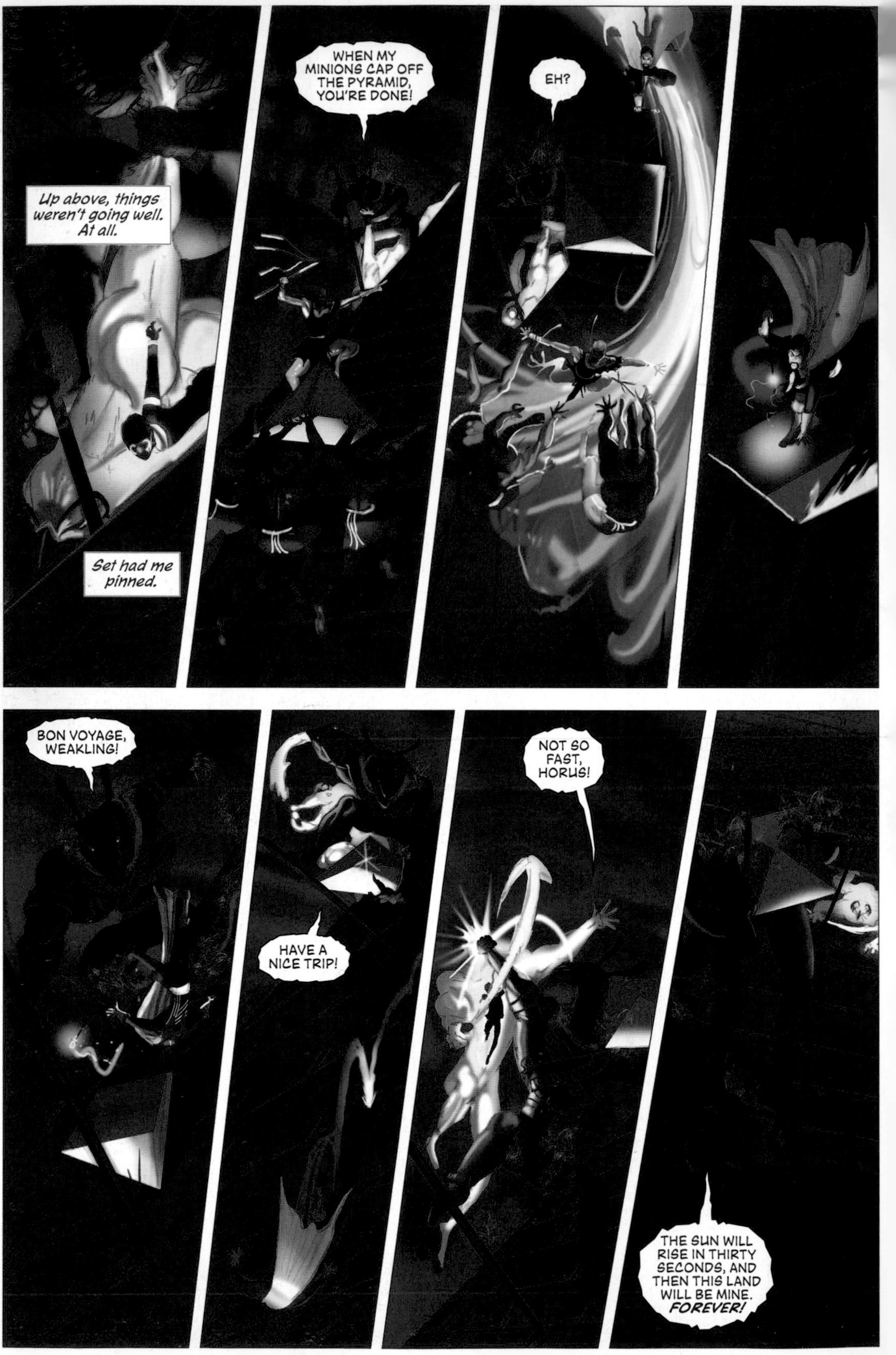
Up above, things weren't going well. At all.
Set had me pinned.
WHEN MY MINIONS CAP OFF THE PYRAMID, YOU'RE DONE!
EH?
BON VOYAGE, WEAKLING!
HAVE A NICE TRIP!
NOT SO FAST, HORUS!
THE SUN WILL RISE IN THIRTY SECONDS, AND THEN THIS LAND WILL BE MINE. FOREVER!

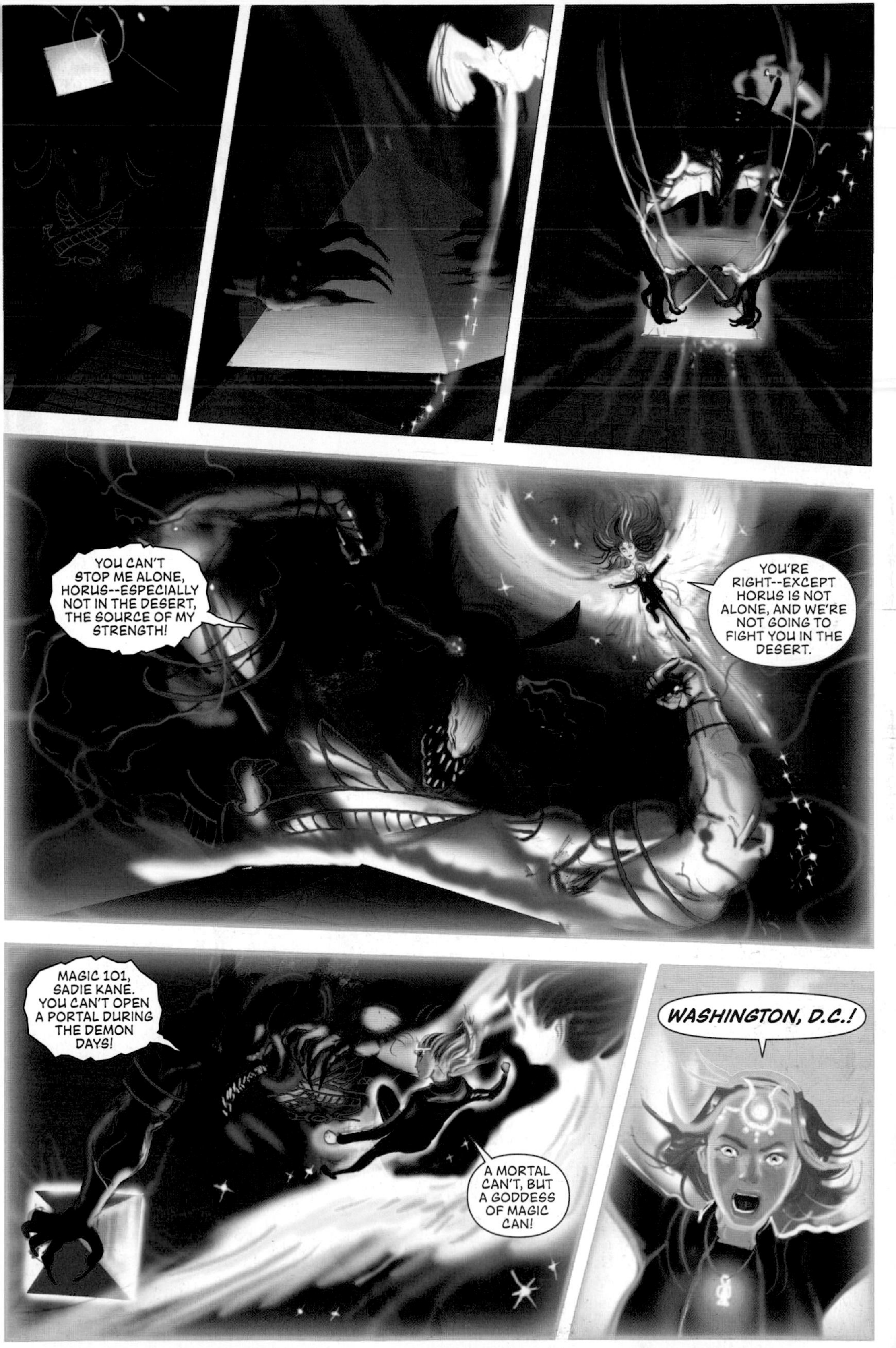
YOU CAN'T STOP ME ALONE, HORUS--ESPECIALLY NOT IN THE DESERT, THE SOURCE OF MY STRENGTH!
YOU'RE RIGHT--EXCEPT HORUS IS NOT ALONE, AND WE'RE NOT GOING TO FIGHT YOU IN THE DESERT.
MAGIC 101, SADIE KANE. YOU CAN'T OPEN A PORTAL DURING THE DEMON DAYS!
A MORTAL CAN'T, BUT A GODDESS OF MAGIC CAN!
WASHINGTON, D.C.!

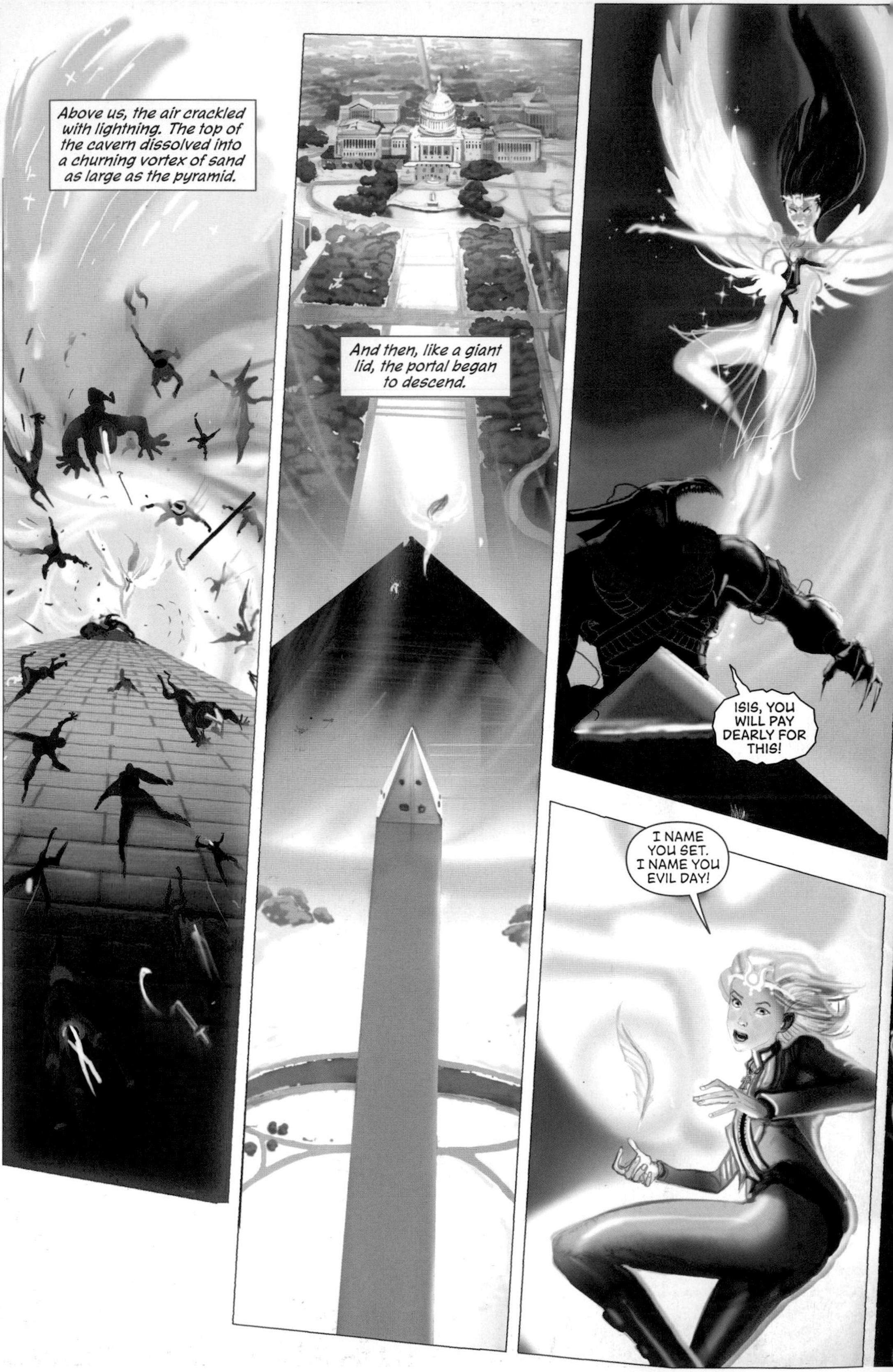
Above us, the air crackled with lightning. The top of the cavern dissolved into a churning vortex of sand as large as the pyramid.
And then, like a giant lid, the portal began to descend.
ISIS, YOU WILL PAY DEARLY FOR THIS!
I NAME YOU SET. I NAME YOU EVIL DAY!

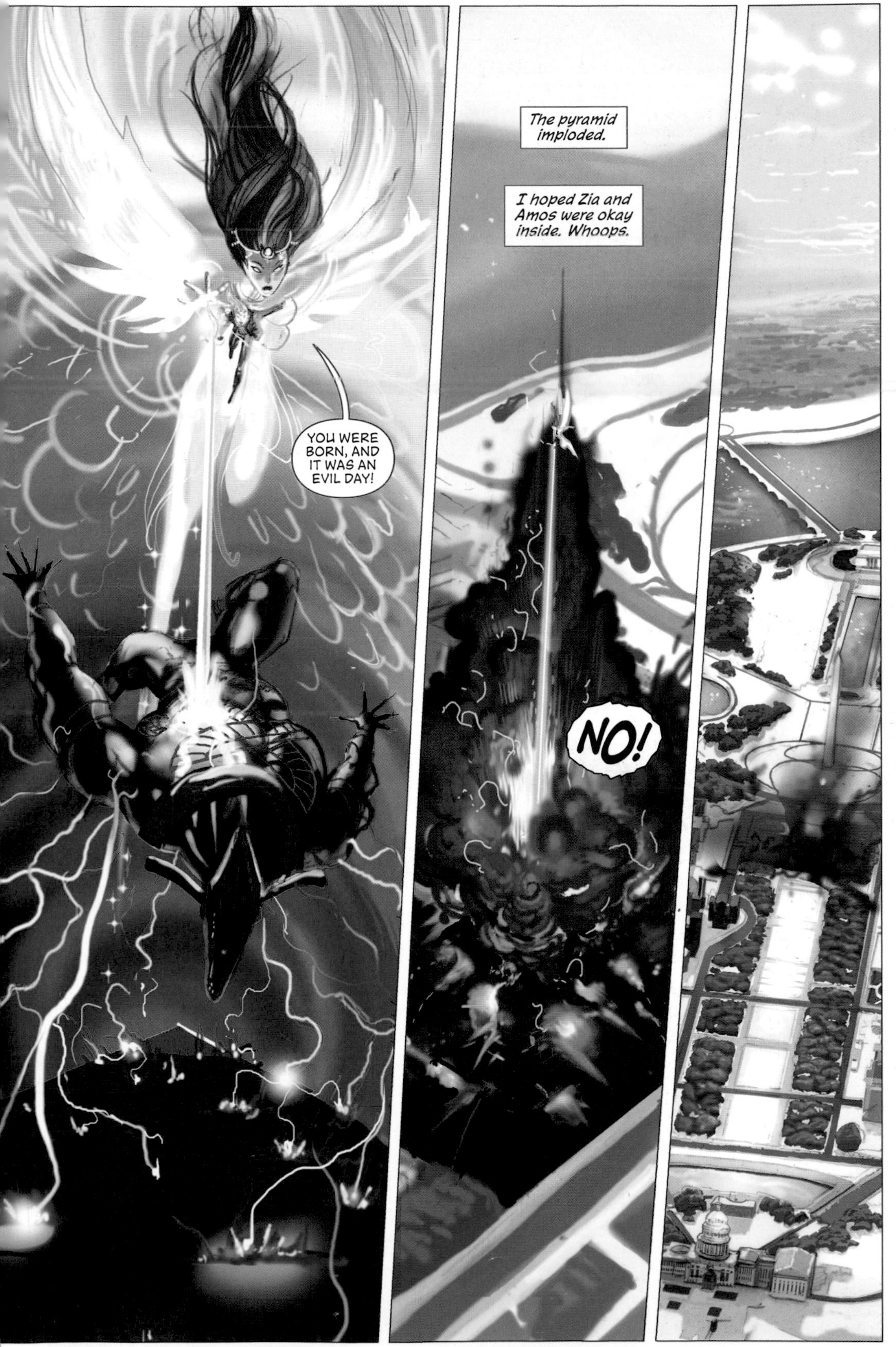
YOU WERE BORN, AND IT WAS AN EVIL DAY!
The pyramid imploded.
I hoped Zia and Amos were okay inside. Whoops.
NO!

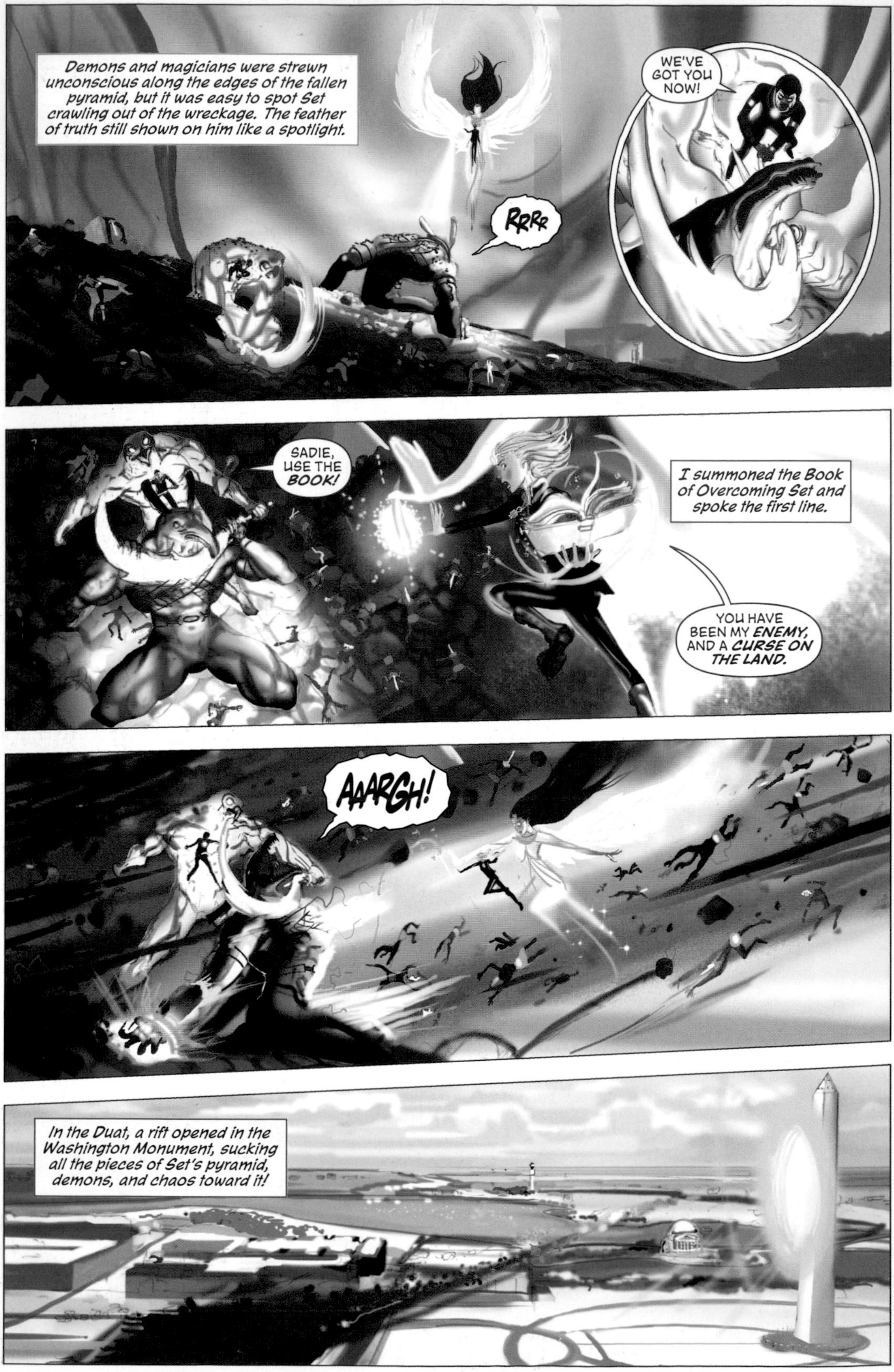
Demons and magicians were strewn unconscious along the edges of the fallen pyramid, but it was easy to spot Set crawling out of the wreckage. The feather of truth still shown on him like a spotlight.
RRRR
WE'VE GOT YOU NOW!
SADIE, USE THE BOOK!
I summoned the Book of Overcoming Set and spoke the first line.
YOU HAVE BEEN MY ENEMY, AND A CURSE ON THE LAND.
AAARGH!
In the Duat, a rift opened in the Washington Monument, sucking all the pieces of Set's pyramid, demons, and chaos toward it!

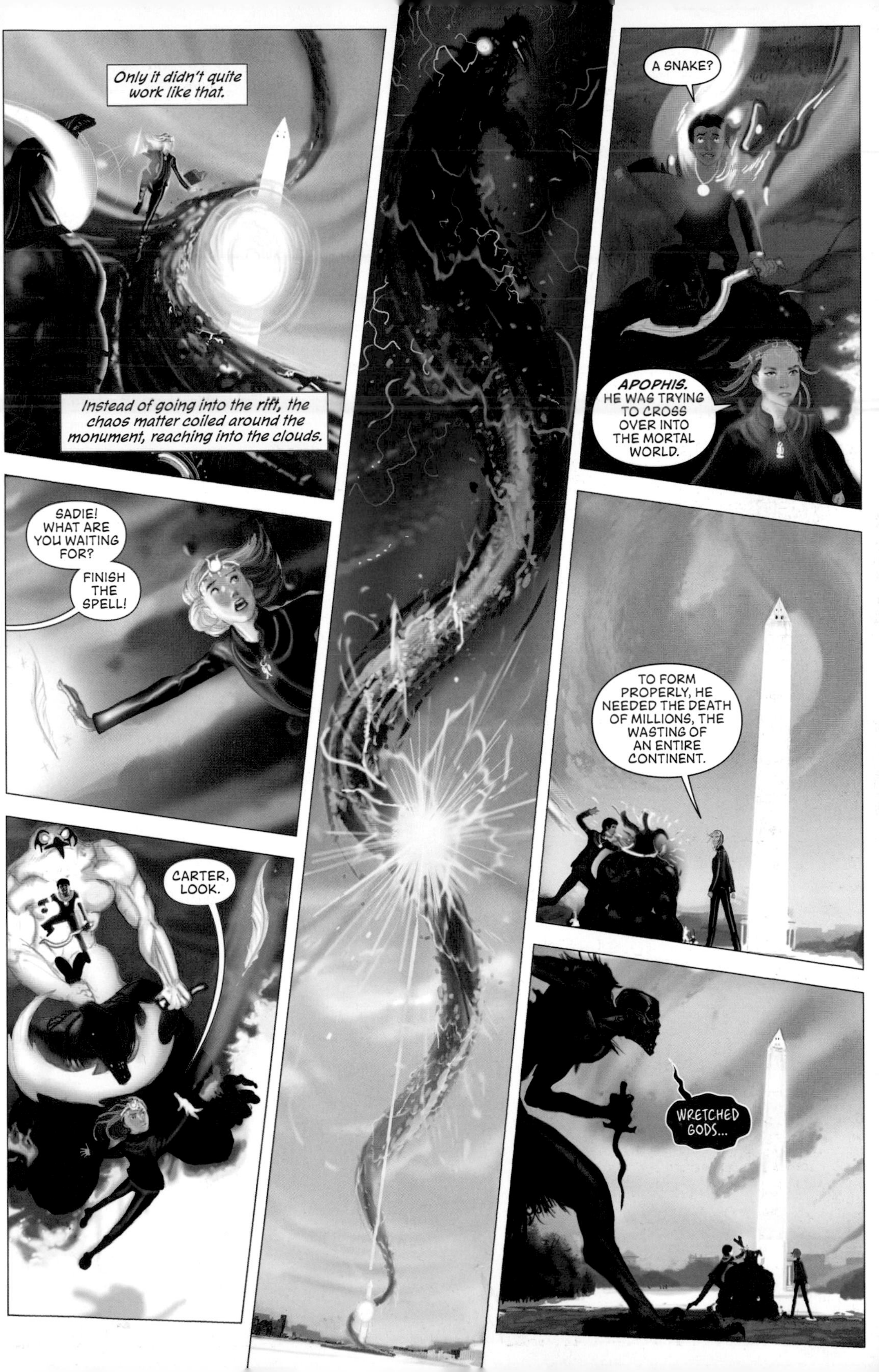
Only it didn't quite work like that.
Instead of going into the rift, the chaos matter coiled around the monument, reaching into the clouds.
SADIE! WHAT ARE YOU WAITING FOR?
FINISH THE SPELL!
CARTER, LOOK.
A SNAKE?
APOPHIS. HE WAS TRYING TO CROSS OVER INTO THE MORTAL WORLD.
TO FORM PROPERLY, HE NEEDED THE DEATH OF MILLIONS, THE WASTING OF AN ENTIRE CONTINENT.
WRETCHED GODS...

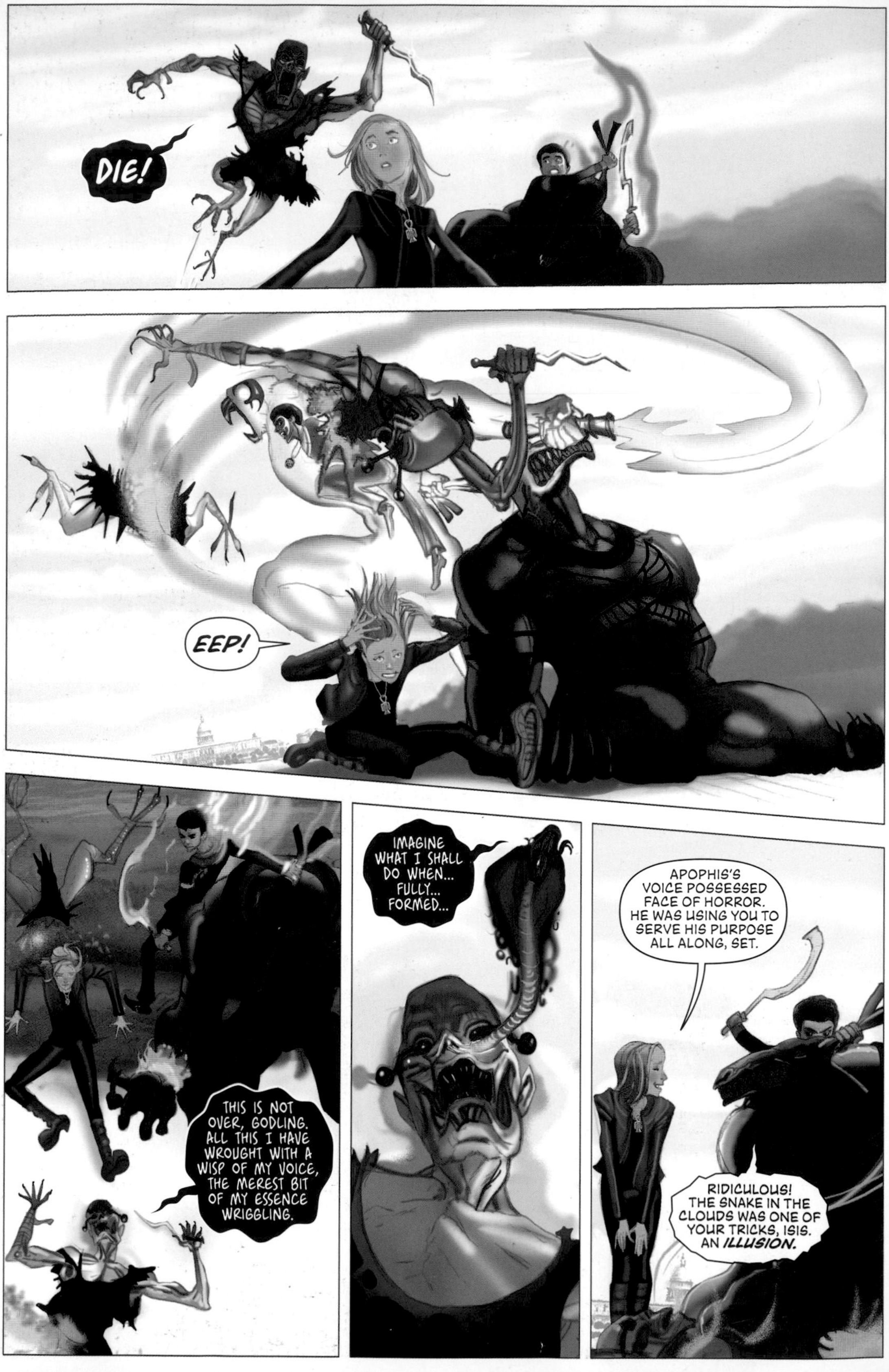
DIE!
EEP!
THIS IS NOT OVER, GODLING. ALL THIS I HAVE WROUGHT WITH A WISP OF MY VOICE, THE MEREST BIT OF MY ESSENCE WRIGGLING.
IMAGINE WHAT I SHALL DO WHEN... FULLY... FORMED...
APOPHIS'S VOICE POSSESSED FACE OF HORROR. HE WAS USING YOU TO SERVE HIS PURPOSE ALL ALONG, SET.
RIDICULOUS! THE SNAKE IN THE CLOUDS WAS ONE OF YOUR TRICKS, ISIS. AN ILLUSION.

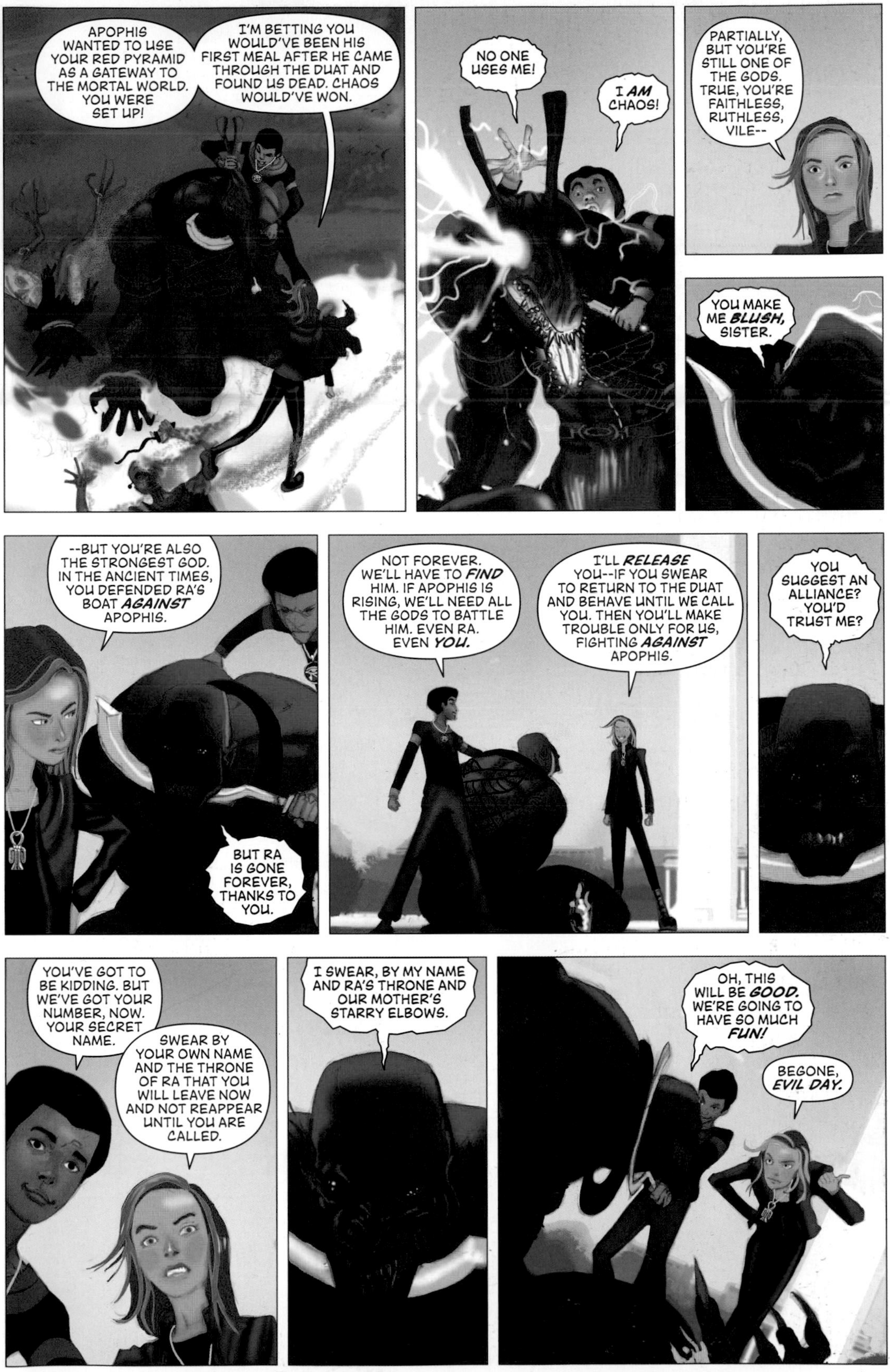
APOPHIS WANTED TO USE YOUR RED PYRAMID AS A GATEWAY TO THE MORTAL WORLD. YOU WERE SET UP!
I'M BETTING YOU WOULD'VE BEEN HIS FIRST MEAL AFTER HE CAME THROUGH THE DUAT AND FOUND US DEAD. CHAOS WOULD'VE WON.
NO ONE USES ME!
I *AM* CHAOS!
PARTIALLY, BUT YOU'RE STILL ONE OF THE GODS. TRUE, YOU'RE FAITHLESS, RUTHLESS, VILE--
YOU MAKE ME *BLUSH,* SISTER.
--BUT YOU'RE ALSO THE STRONGEST GOD. IN THE ANCIENT TIMES, YOU DEFENDED RA'S BOAT *AGAINST* APOPHIS.
BUT RA IS GONE FOREVER, THANKS TO YOU.
NOT FOREVER. WE'LL HAVE TO *FIND* HIM. IF APOPHIS IS RISING, WE'LL NEED ALL THE GODS TO BATTLE HIM. EVEN RA. EVEN *YOU.*
I'LL *RELEASE* YOU--IF YOU SWEAR TO RETURN TO THE DUAT AND BEHAVE UNTIL WE CALL YOU. THEN YOU'LL MAKE TROUBLE ONLY FOR US, FIGHTING *AGAINST* APOPHIS.
YOU SUGGEST AN ALLIANCE? YOU'D TRUST ME?
YOU'VE GOT TO BE KIDDING. BUT WE'VE GOT YOUR NUMBER, NOW. YOUR SECRET NAME.
SWEAR BY YOUR OWN NAME AND THE THRONE OF RA THAT YOU WILL LEAVE NOW AND NOT REAPPEAR UNTIL YOU ARE CALLED.
I SWEAR, BY MY NAME AND RA'S THRONE AND OUR MOTHER'S STARRY ELBOWS.
OH, THIS WILL BE *GOOD.* WE'RE GOING TO HAVE SO MUCH *FUN!*
BEGONE, *EVIL DAY.*

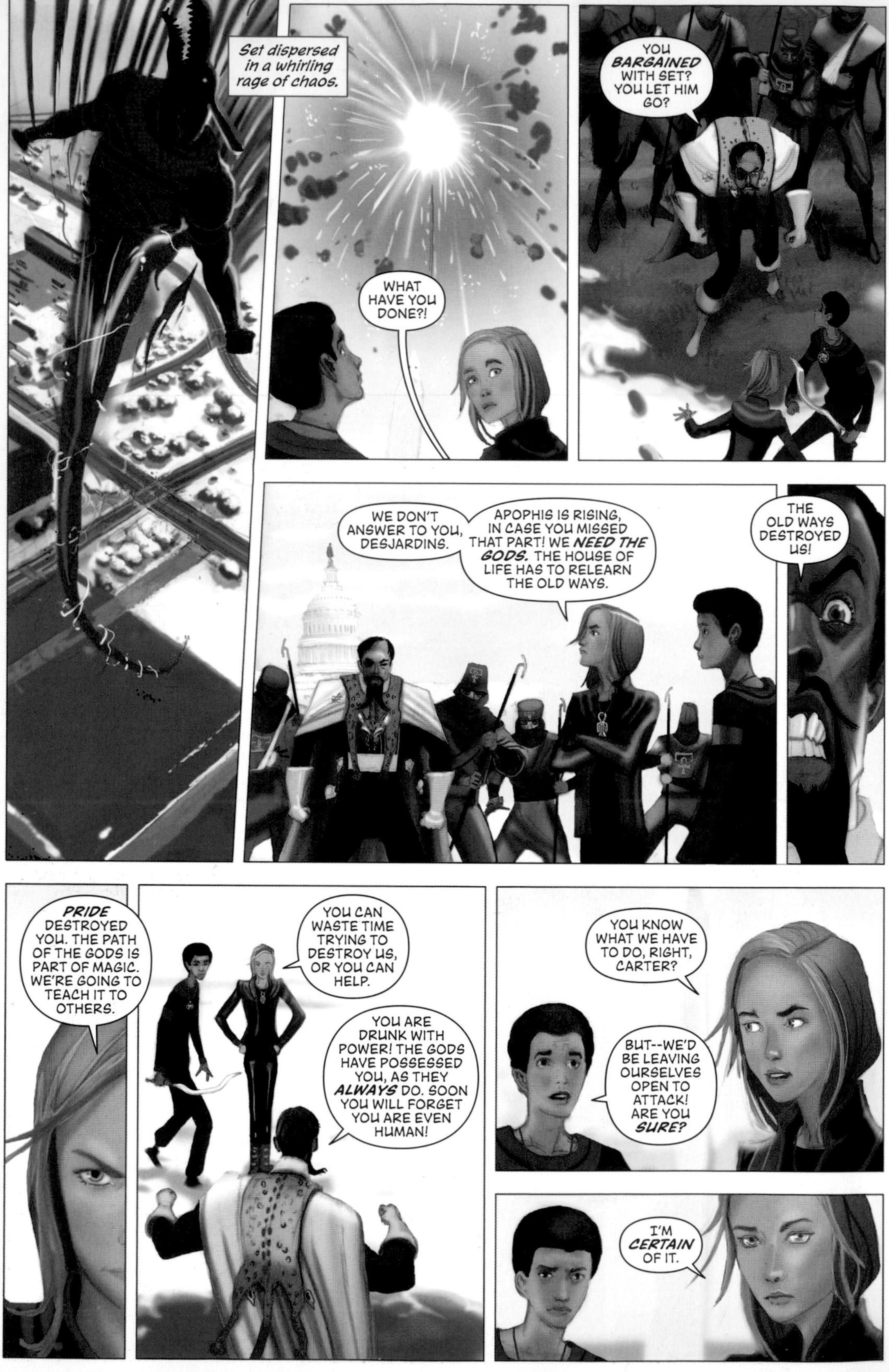
Set dispersed in a whirling rage of chaos.
WHAT HAVE YOU DONE?!
YOU BARGAINED WITH SET? YOU LET HIM GO?
WE DON'T ANSWER TO YOU, DESJARDINS.
APOPHIS IS RISING, IN CASE YOU MISSED THAT PART! WE NEED THE GODS. THE HOUSE OF LIFE HAS TO RELEARN THE OLD WAYS.
THE OLD WAYS DESTROYED US!
PRIDE DESTROYED YOU. THE PATH OF THE GODS IS PART OF MAGIC. WE'RE GOING TO TEACH IT TO OTHERS.
YOU CAN WASTE TIME TRYING TO DESTROY US, OR YOU CAN HELP.
YOU ARE DRUNK WITH POWER! THE GODS HAVE POSSESSED YOU, AS THEY ALWAYS DO. SOON YOU WILL FORGET YOU ARE EVEN HUMAN!
YOU KNOW WHAT WE HAVE TO DO, RIGHT, CARTER?
BUT--WE'D BE LEAVING OURSELVES OPEN TO ATTACK! ARE YOU SURE?
I'M CERTAIN OF IT.

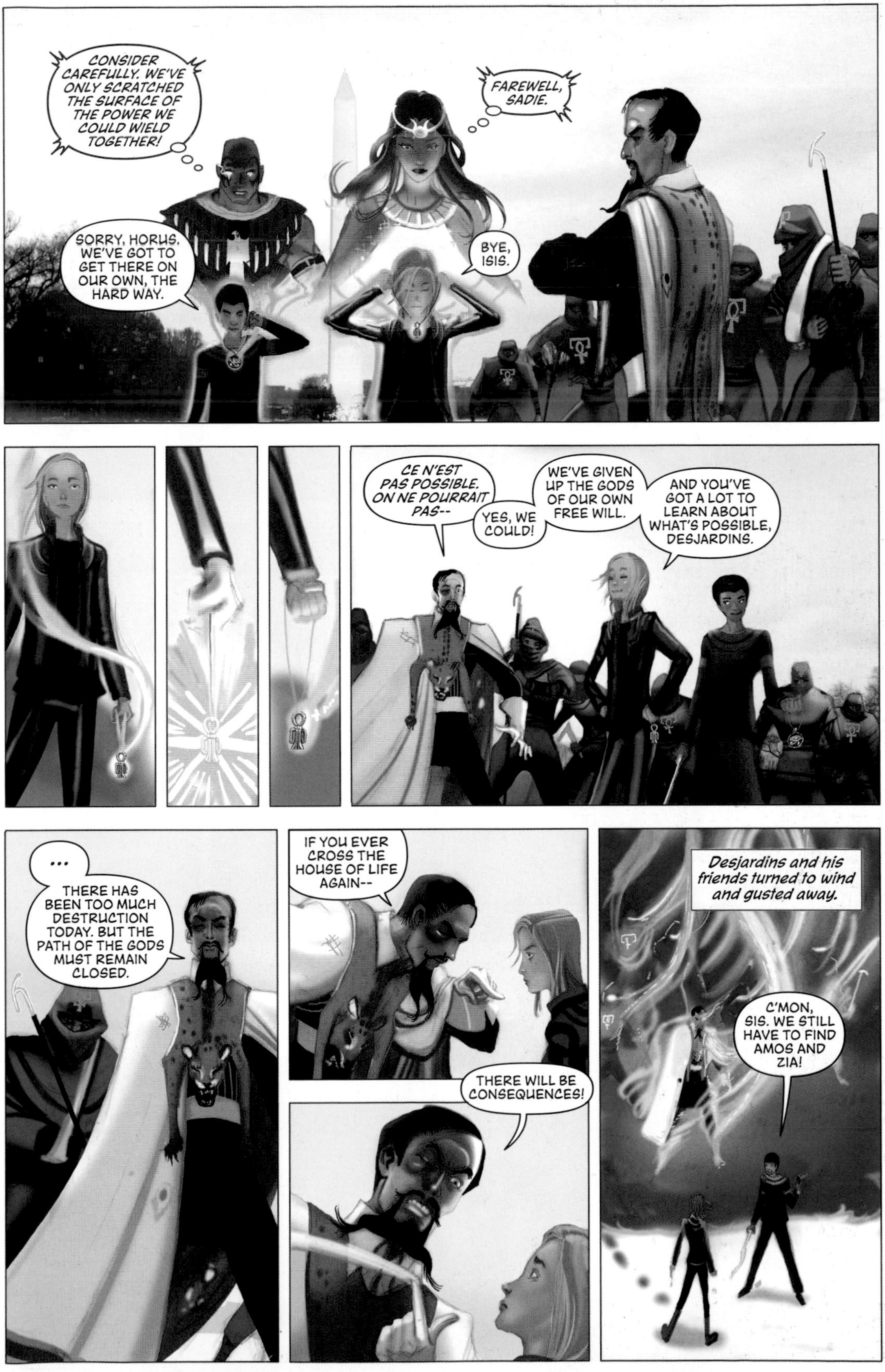
CONSIDER CAREFULLY. WE'VE ONLY SCRATCHED THE SURFACE OF THE POWER WE COULD WIELD TOGETHER!
FAREWELL, SADIE.
SORRY, HORUS. WE'VE GOT TO GET THERE ON OUR OWN, THE HARD WAY.
BYE, ISIS.
CE N'EST PAS POSSIBLE. ON NE POURRAIT PAS--
YES, WE COULD!
WE'VE GIVEN UP THE GODS OF OUR OWN FREE WILL.
AND YOU'VE GOT A LOT TO LEARN ABOUT WHAT'S POSSIBLE, DESJARDINS.
...
THERE HAS BEEN TOO MUCH DESTRUCTION TODAY. BUT THE PATH OF THE GODS MUST REMAIN CLOSED.
IF YOU EVER CROSS THE HOUSE OF LIFE AGAIN--
THERE WILL BE CONSEQUENCES!
Desjardins and his friends turned to wind and gusted away.
C'MON, SIS. WE STILL HAVE TO FIND AMOS AND ZIA!

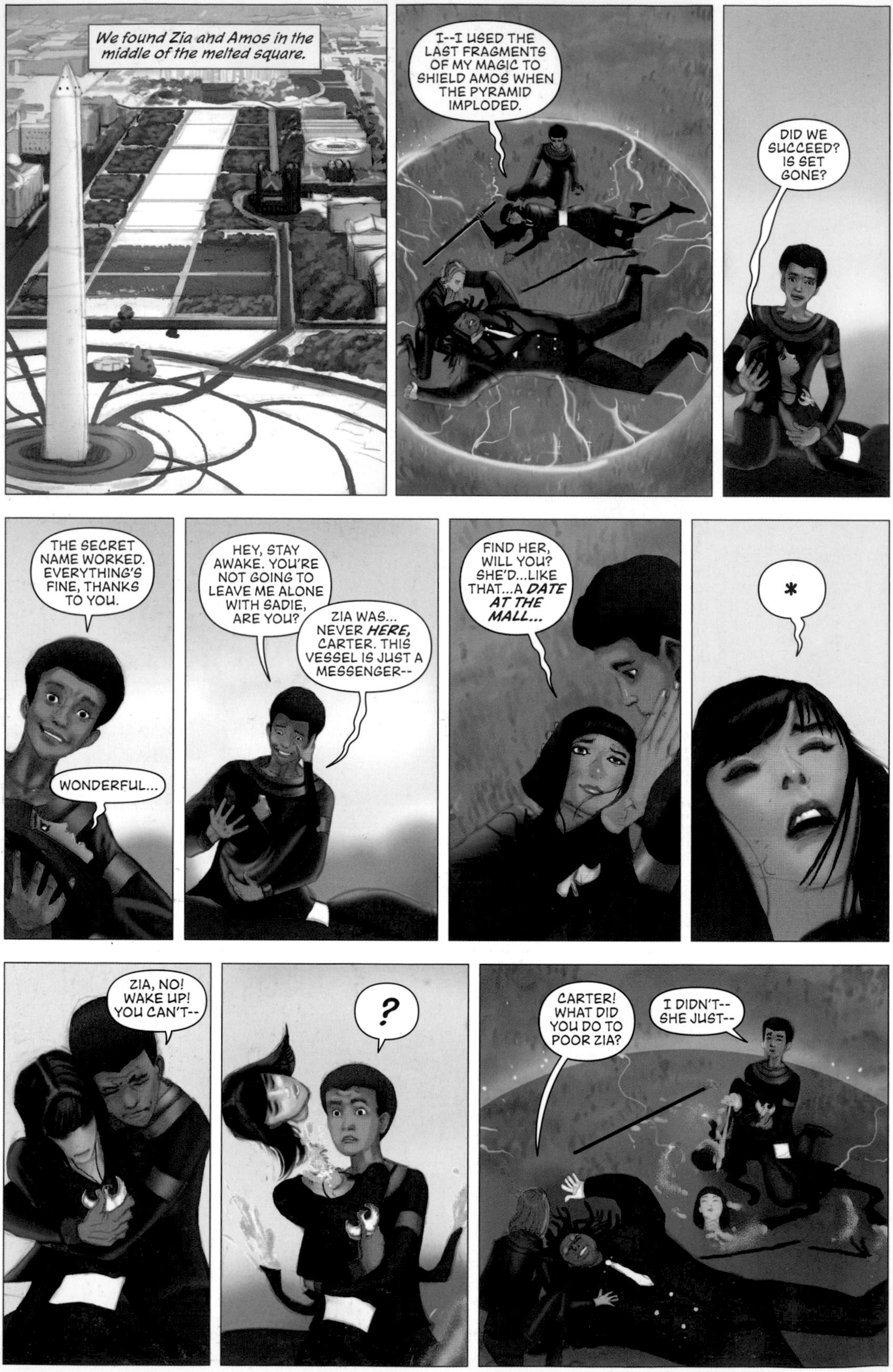
We found Zia and Amos in the middle of the melted square.
I--I USED THE LAST FRAGMENTS OF MY MAGIC TO SHIELD AMOS WHEN THE PYRAMID IMPLODED.
DID WE SUCCEED? IS SET GONE?
THE SECRET NAME WORKED. EVERYTHING'S FINE, THANKS TO YOU.
WONDERFUL...
HEY, STAY AWAKE. YOU'RE NOT GOING TO LEAVE ME ALONE WITH SADIE, ARE YOU?
ZIA WAS... NEVER *HERE,* CARTER. THIS VESSEL IS JUST A MESSENGER--
FIND HER, WILL YOU? SHE'D...LIKE THAT...A ***DATE AT THE MALL...***
*
ZIA, NO! WAKE UP! YOU CAN'T--
?
CARTER! WHAT DID YOU DO TO POOR ZIA?
I DIDN'T-- SHE JUST--

LOOK, CARTER!

THAT LIGHT-- IT'S JUST LIKE THE SHABTI IN MEMPHIS!

REMEMBER WHAT THOTH SAID? "SHABTI MAKE EXCELLENT STUNT DOUBLES." THAT'S WHAT SHE WAS.

ISKANDAR MUST'VE HIDDEN THE REAL ZIA...

HE KNEW SHE'D BE IN DANGER WHEN THE SPIRIT OF NEPHTHYS JOINED WITH HER IN *LONDON!*

THEN... THE REAL ZIA IS ALIVE...

...AND THAT BLUE LIGHT'S PROBABLY REPORTING *BACK* TO HER! WE SHOULD *TRACK* IT!

CARTER, I'M NOT SURE IF NOW'S THE BEST TIME.

WE'RE PRACTICALLY IN THE PRESIDENT'S BACKYARD.

IF WE DON'T GET OUT OF D.C. SOON, WE'RE GOING TO HAVE TO ANSWER TO SOME HEAVILY ARMED COMPANY!

The evening news would eventually attribute our adventures to a rare occurrence of the northern lights. But all the cameras could show was a big square of melted snow on the mall, which kind of made for boring video.

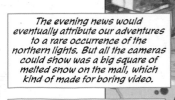

We managed to escape the cameras, and the police. I had just enough magic to turn myself into a falcon and Amos into... a hamster. (Hey, I was rushed!)

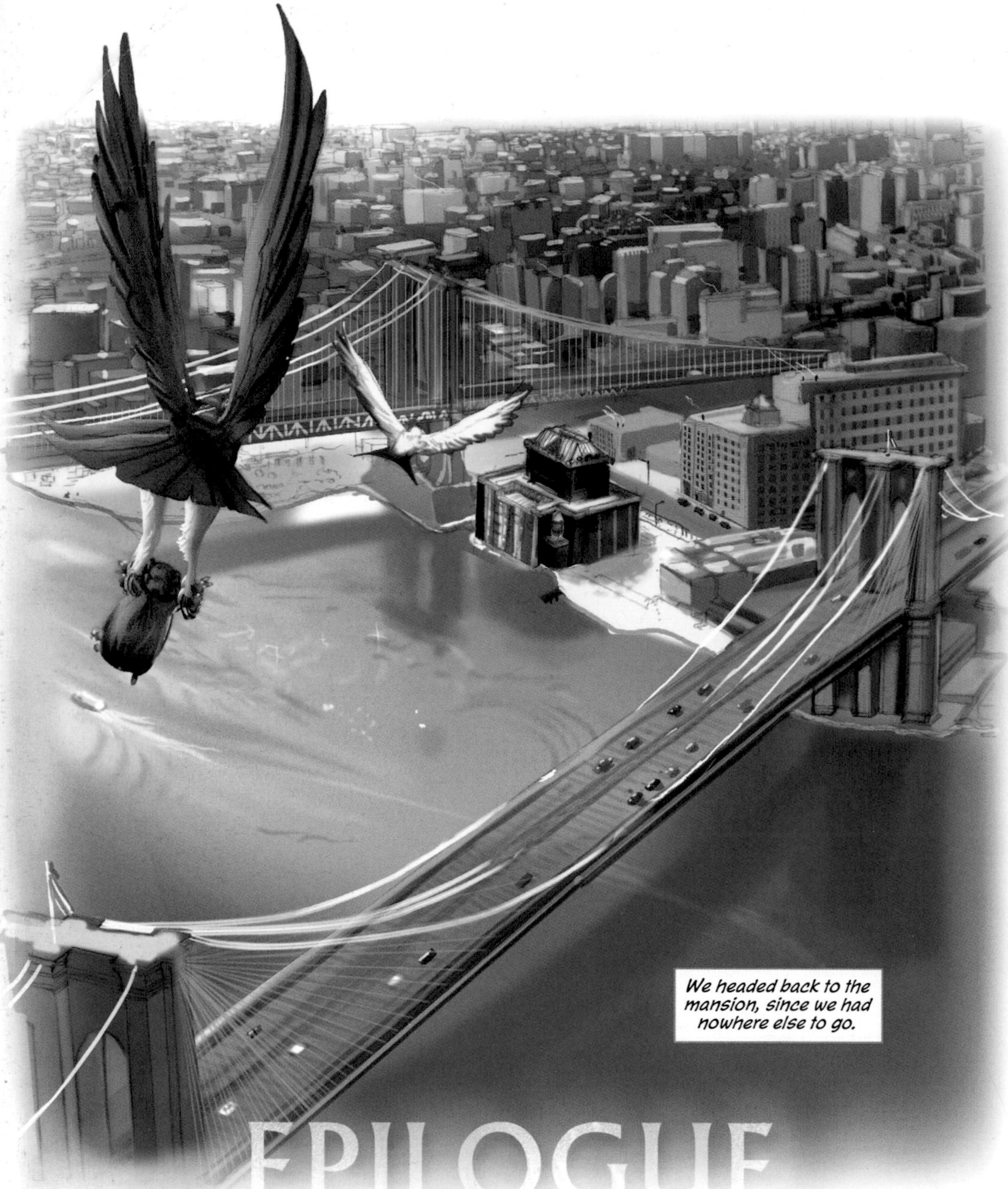
We headed back to the mansion, since we had nowhere else to go.

EPILOGUE

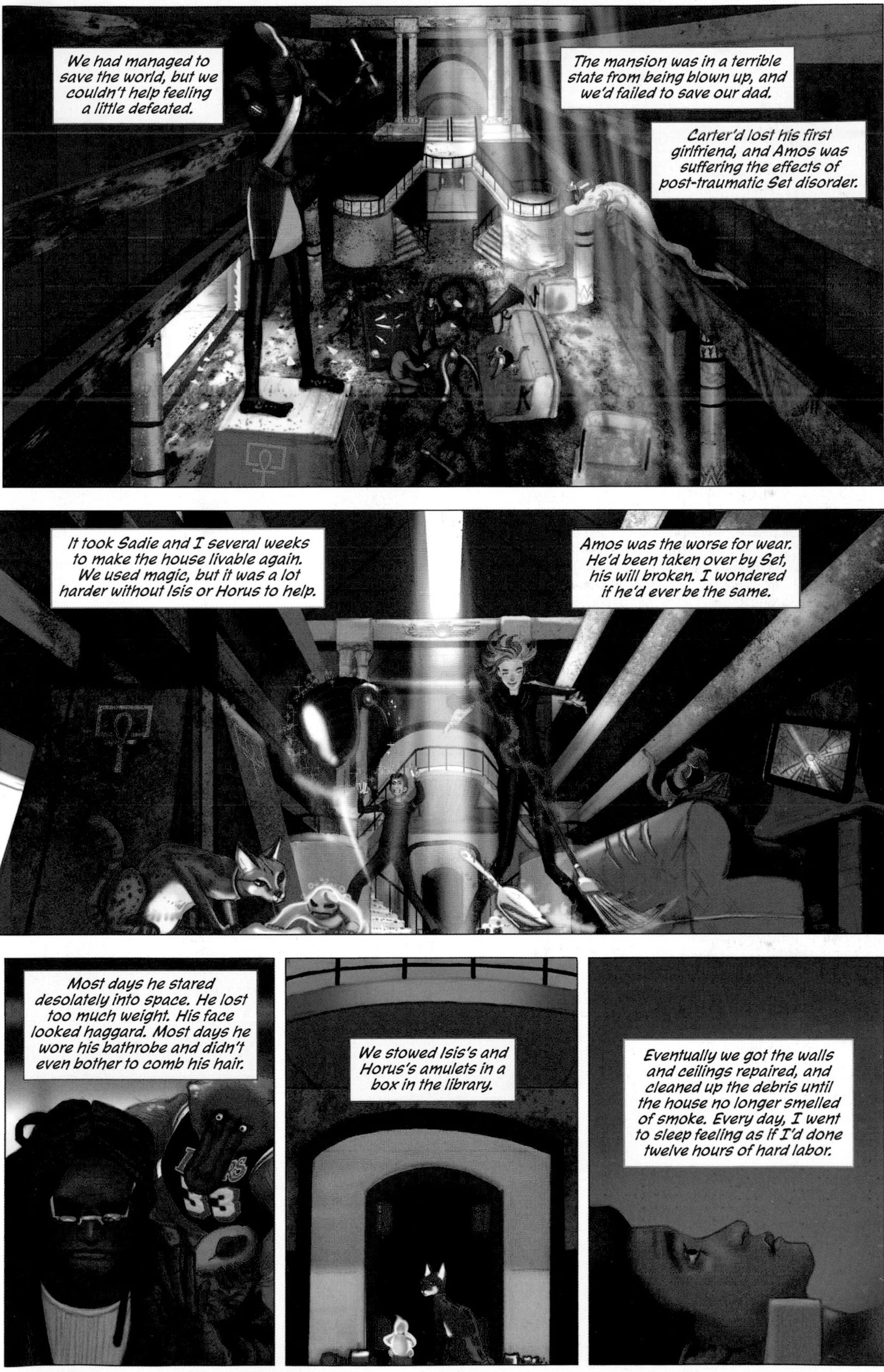
We had managed to save the world, but we couldn't help feeling a little defeated.
The mansion was in a terrible state from being blown up, and we'd failed to save our dad.
Carter'd lost his first girlfriend, and Amos was suffering the effects of post-traumatic Set disorder.
It took Sadie and I several weeks to make the house livable again. We used magic, but it was a lot harder without Isis or Horus to help.
Amos was the worse for wear. He'd been taken over by Set, his will broken. I wondered if he'd ever be the same.
Most days he stared desolately into space. He lost too much weight. His face looked haggard. Most days he wore his bathrobe and didn't even bother to comb his hair.
We stowed Isis's and Horus's amulets in a box in the library.
Eventually we got the walls and ceilings repaired, and cleaned up the debris until the house no longer smelled of smoke. Every day, I went to sleep feeling as if I'd done twelve hours of hard labor.

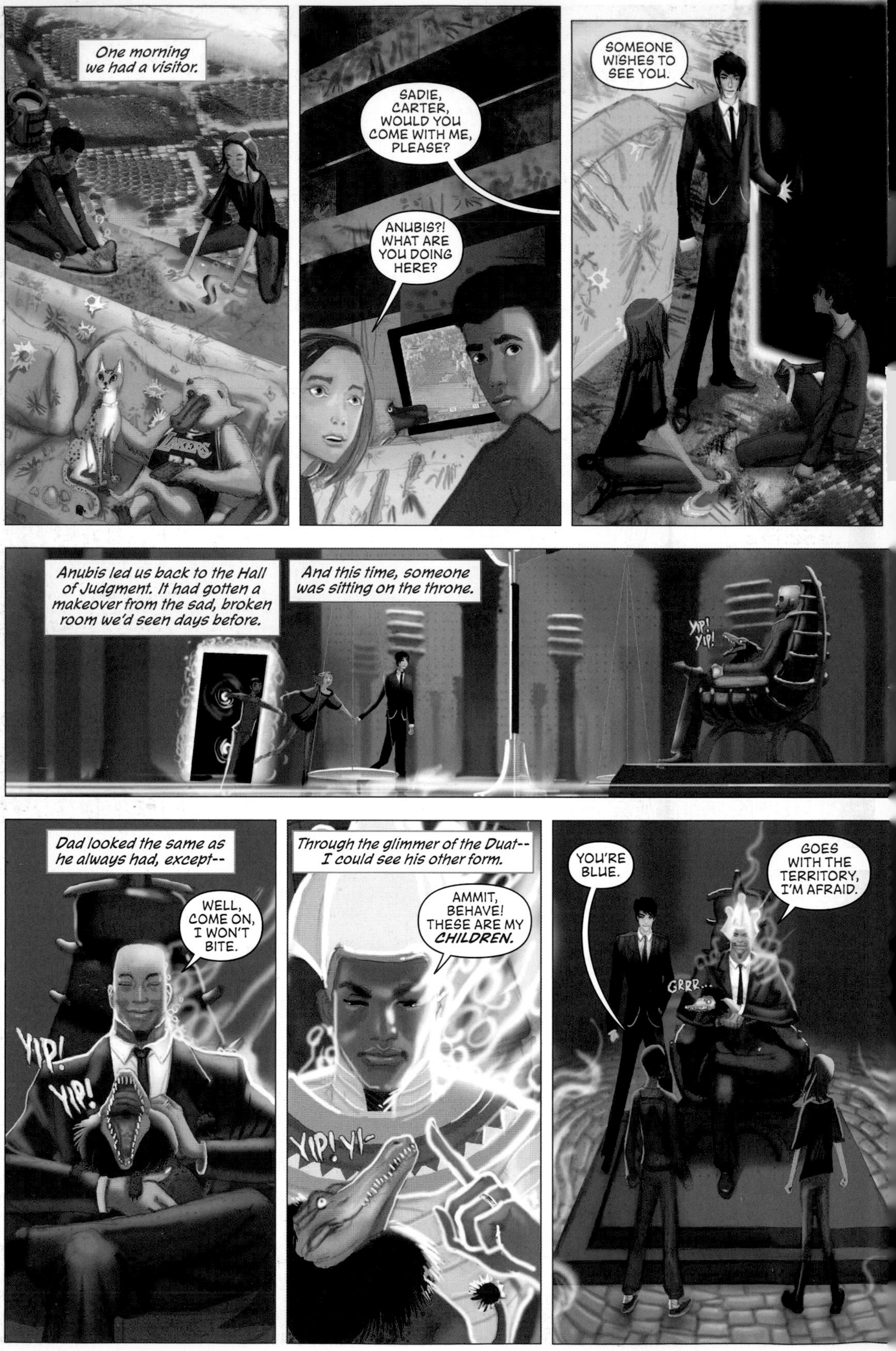

One morning we had a visitor.
SADIE, CARTER, WOULD YOU COME WITH ME, PLEASE?
ANUBIS?! WHAT ARE YOU DOING HERE?
SOMEONE WISHES TO SEE YOU.
Anubis led us back to the Hall of Judgment. It had gotten a makeover from the sad, broken room we'd seen days before.
And this time, someone was sitting on the throne.
YIP! YIP!
Dad looked the same as he always had, except--
WELL, COME ON, I WON'T BITE.
YIP!
YIP!
Through the glimmer of the Duat-- I could see his other form.
AMMIT, BEHAVE! THESE ARE MY CHILDREN.
YIP! YI-
YOU'RE BLUE.
GOES WITH THE TERRITORY, I'M AFRAID.
GRRR...

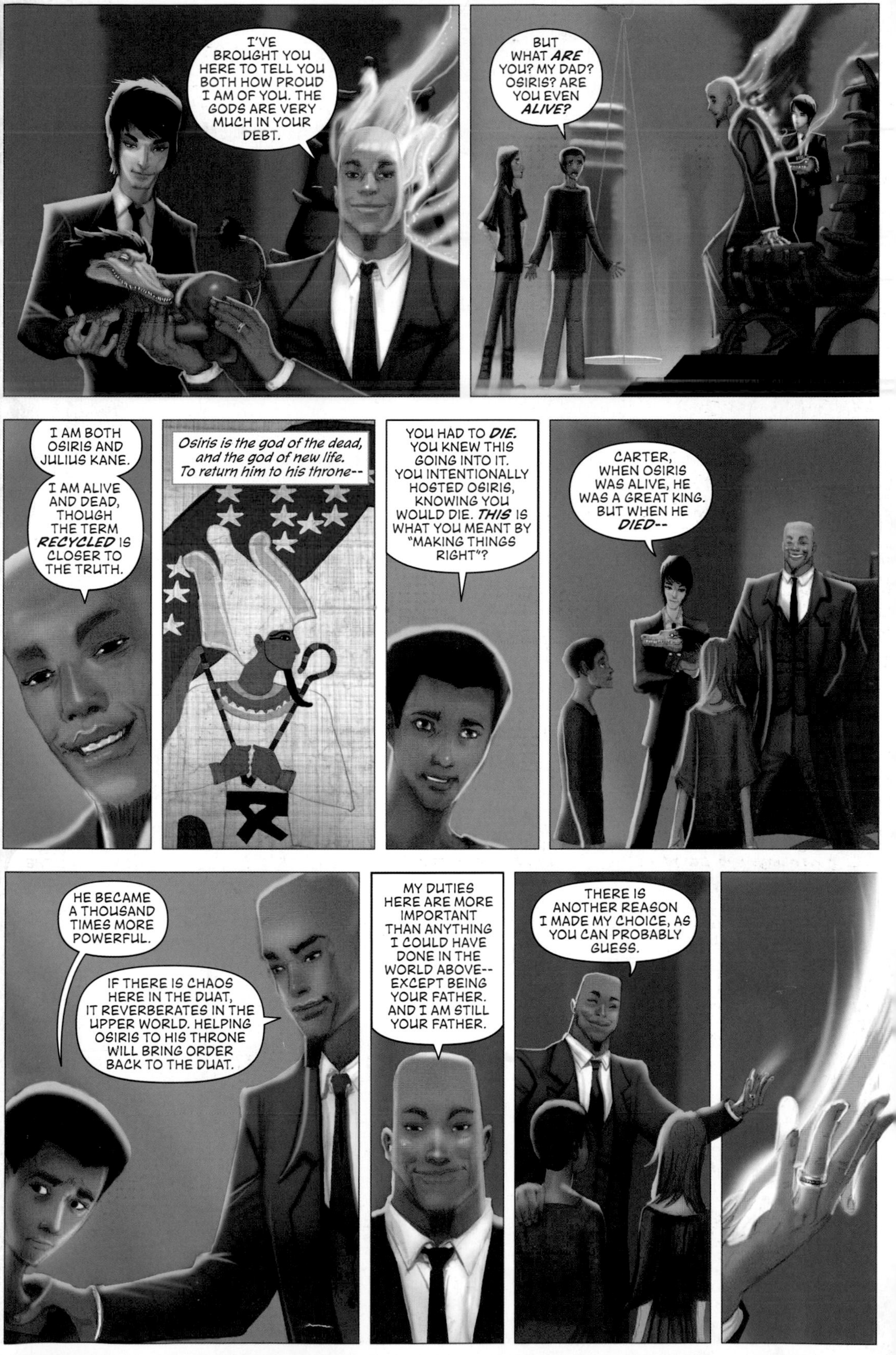

I'VE BROUGHT YOU HERE TO TELL YOU BOTH HOW PROUD I AM OF YOU. THE GODS ARE VERY MUCH IN YOUR DEBT.
BUT WHAT ARE YOU? MY DAD? OSIRIS? ARE YOU EVEN ALIVE?
I AM BOTH OSIRIS AND JULIUS KANE.
I AM ALIVE AND DEAD, THOUGH THE TERM RECYCLED IS CLOSER TO THE TRUTH.
Osiris is the god of the dead, and the god of new life. To return him to his throne--
YOU HAD TO DIE. YOU KNEW THIS GOING INTO IT. YOU INTENTIONALLY HOSTED OSIRIS, KNOWING YOU WOULD DIE. THIS IS WHAT YOU MEANT BY "MAKING THINGS RIGHT"?
CARTER, WHEN OSIRIS WAS ALIVE, HE WAS A GREAT KING. BUT WHEN HE DIED--
HE BECAME A THOUSAND TIMES MORE POWERFUL.
IF THERE IS CHAOS HERE IN THE DUAT, IT REVERBERATES IN THE UPPER WORLD. HELPING OSIRIS TO HIS THRONE WILL BRING ORDER BACK TO THE DUAT.
MY DUTIES HERE ARE MORE IMPORTANT THAN ANYTHING I COULD HAVE DONE IN THE WORLD ABOVE-- EXCEPT BEING YOUR FATHER. AND I AM STILL YOUR FATHER.
THERE IS ANOTHER REASON I MADE MY CHOICE, AS YOU CAN PROBABLY GUESS.

HELLO, CHILDREN.

MOM?

JULIUS TOLD ME HOW MUCH YOU'D GROWN, BUT I CAN'T BELIEVE IT!

She looked a lot like Isis!

MY AMULET-- THE TYET-- DID YOU REALLY... WAS THAT--

YES, MY BRAVE GIRL. MY THOUGHTS MIXED WITH YOURS. I'M SO PROUD OF YOU. AND THANKS TO ISIS, I FEEL LIKE I KNOW YOU AS WELL.

AND CARTER!

CARTER, I'LL BET YOU'RE SHAVING--

MOM.

--DATING GIRLS--

MOM!

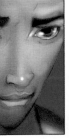

Have you ever noticed how parents can go from the most wonderful people in the world to totally embarrassing in three seconds?

For years I'd dreamed of being back with my parents, but not like this: my mom a spirit, and my dad...recycled.

Still, they looked weirdly happy, so I didn't complain.

YOU HAVE DONE *MA'AT* A GREAT FAVOR, CHILDREN.

AS WE SPEAK, HORUS IS NO DOUBT RECLAIMING HIS BIRTHRIGHT AS KING OF THE GODS.

THE GODS TAKE THEIR DEBT SERIOUSLY. YOU CAN EXPECT A GIFT UPON YOUR RETURN FROM THIS HALL.

BUT FIRST, SOMETHING TO TAKE WITH YOU.

IT IS CALLED A *DJED.* MY SYMBOL--THE SPINE OF OSIRIS.

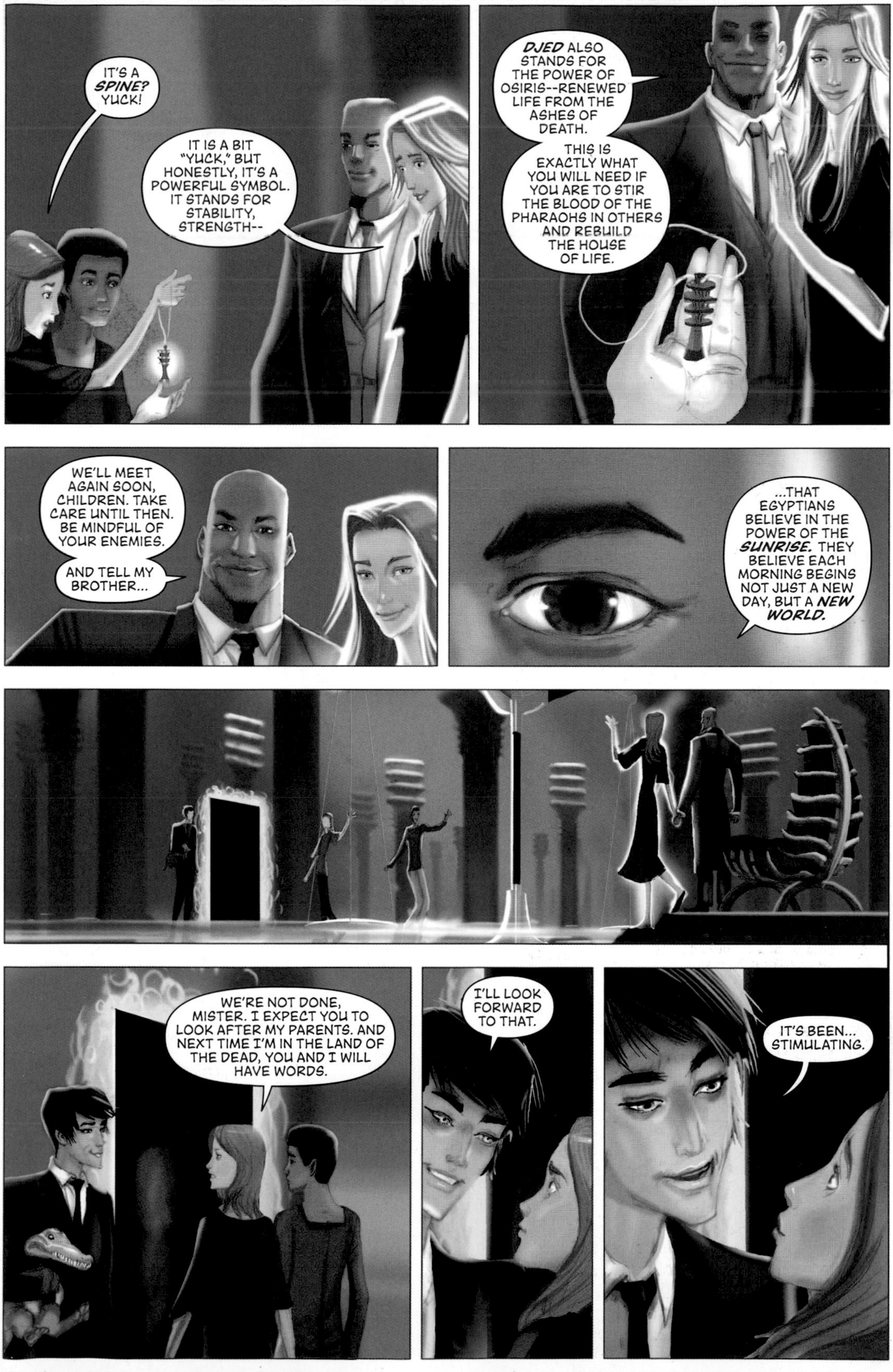
IT'S A SPINE? YUCK!
IT IS A BIT "YUCK," BUT HONESTLY, IT'S A POWERFUL SYMBOL. IT STANDS FOR STABILITY, STRENGTH--
DJED ALSO STANDS FOR THE POWER OF OSIRIS--RENEWED LIFE FROM THE ASHES OF DEATH.
THIS IS EXACTLY WHAT YOU WILL NEED IF YOU ARE TO STIR THE BLOOD OF THE PHARAOHS IN OTHERS AND REBUILD THE HOUSE OF LIFE.
WE'LL MEET AGAIN SOON, CHILDREN. TAKE CARE UNTIL THEN. BE MINDFUL OF YOUR ENEMIES.
AND TELL MY BROTHER...
...THAT EGYPTIANS BELIEVE IN THE POWER OF THE SUNRISE. THEY BELIEVE EACH MORNING BEGINS NOT JUST A NEW DAY, BUT A NEW WORLD.
WE'RE NOT DONE, MISTER. I EXPECT YOU TO LOOK AFTER MY PARENTS. AND NEXT TIME I'M IN THE LAND OF THE DEAD, YOU AND I WILL HAVE WORDS.
I'LL LOOK FORWARD TO THAT.
IT'S BEEN... STIMULATING.

We returned to find that the mansion had been completely repaired down to the smallest detail. Everything we hadn't finished yet--probably another month's worth of work--was done!

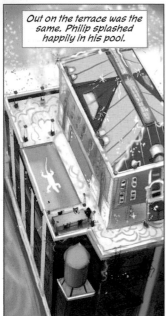

Out on the terrace was the same. Philip splashed happily in his pool.

AMOS, HOW'D THE HOUSE GET FIXED UP? DID YOU DO IT?

IT WAS A GIFT--FROM THE GODS!

Amos was wearing a crisp new suit with matching coat and fedora. His glasses were polished, and his hair freshly braided.

Sadie and I stared at him.

IS SOMETHING THE MATTER?

NO--IT'S JUST THAT YOU'RE LOOKING A LITTLE CLEANED UP TODAY, IS ALL!

YES, WELL, I'VE DECIDED TO GO AWAY... TO THE FIRST NOME.

THEY HAVE THE BEST MAGIC HEALERS THERE.

YOU DON'T THINK THEY'LL TRY TO KILL YOU?

THEY WILL NOT TURN AWAY A PETITIONER SEEKING AID--EVEN ME. I THINK... I THINK I SHOULD TRY.

I MAY BE GONE FOR A WHILE. TREAT THIS AS YOUR HOME. IT IS YOUR HOME.

I THINK YOU SHOULD PERHAPS START RECRUITING. THERE ARE MANY CHILDREN AROUND THE WORLD WITH THE BLOOD OF THE PHARAOHS. TEACHING THE PATH OF THE GODS MAY BE OUR ONLY CHANCE.

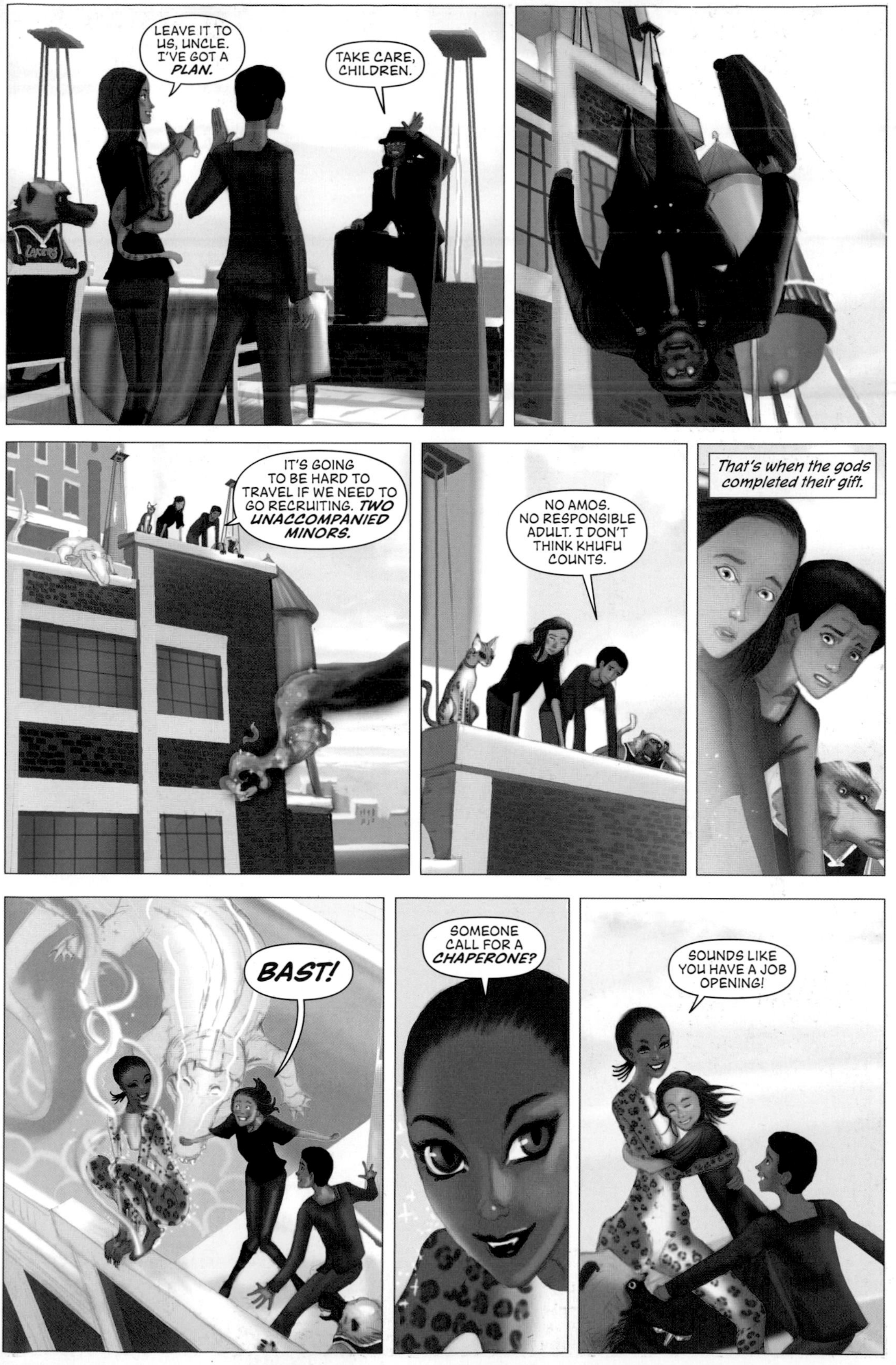
LEAVE IT TO US, UNCLE. I'VE GOT A *PLAN.*
TAKE CARE, CHILDREN.
IT'S GOING TO BE HARD TO TRAVEL IF WE NEED TO GO RECRUITING. *TWO UNACCOMPANIED MINORS.*
NO AMOS. NO RESPONSIBLE ADULT. I DON'T THINK KHUFU COUNTS.
That's when the gods completed their gift.
BAST!
SOMEONE CALL FOR A *CHAPERONE?*
SOUNDS LIKE YOU HAVE A JOB OPENING!

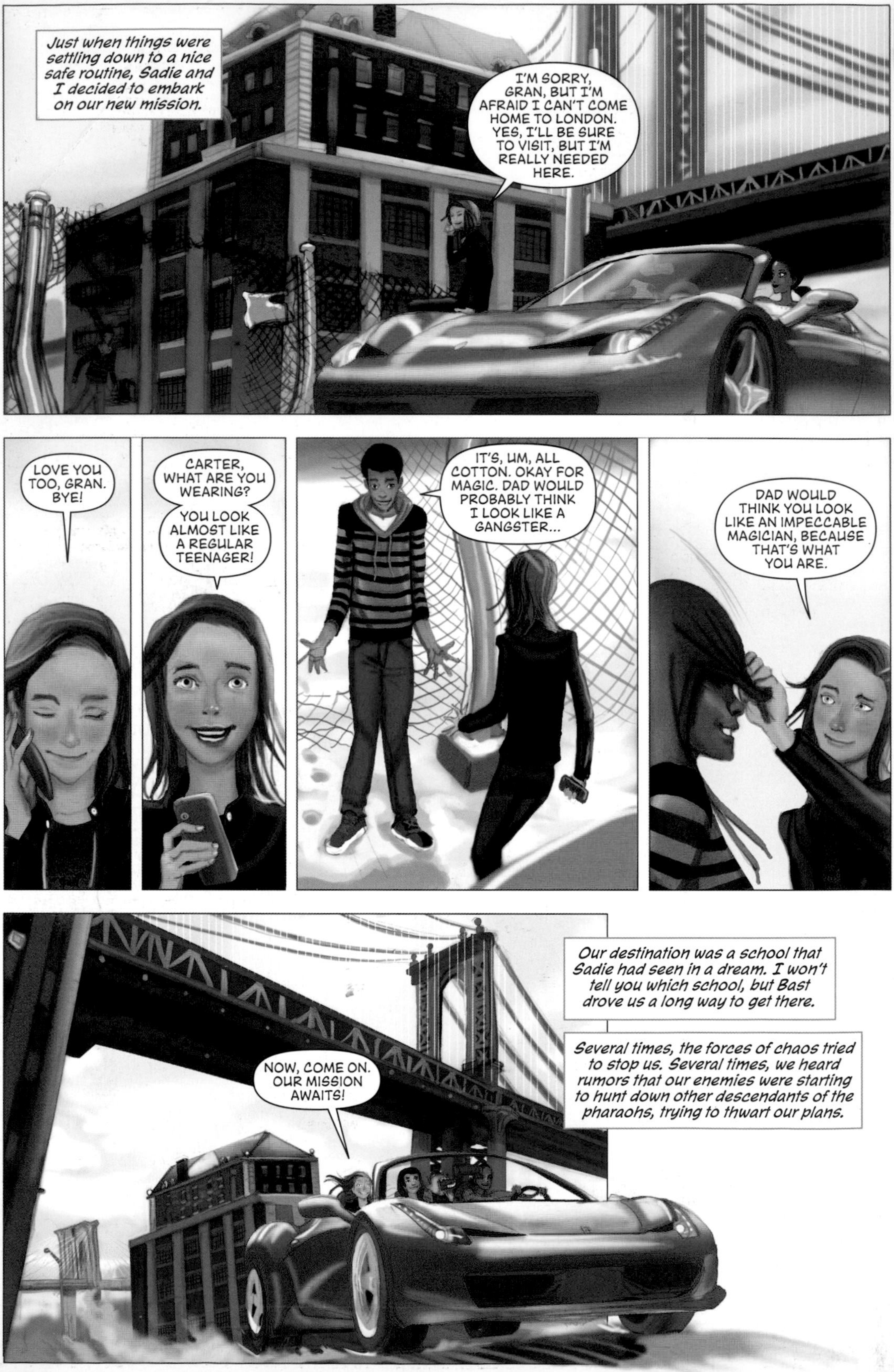

Just when things were settling down to a nice safe routine, Sadie and I decided to embark on our new mission.
I'M SORRY, GRAN, BUT I'M AFRAID I CAN'T COME HOME TO LONDON. YES, I'LL BE SURE TO VISIT, BUT I'M REALLY NEEDED HERE.
LOVE YOU TOO, GRAN. BYE!
CARTER, WHAT ARE YOU WEARING?
YOU LOOK ALMOST LIKE A REGULAR TEENAGER!
IT'S, UM, ALL COTTON. OKAY FOR MAGIC. DAD WOULD PROBABLY THINK I LOOK LIKE A GANGSTER...
DAD WOULD THINK YOU LOOK LIKE AN IMPECCABLE MAGICIAN, BECAUSE THAT'S WHAT YOU ARE.
Our destination was a school that Sadie had seen in a dream. I won't tell you which school, but Bast drove us a long way to get there.
Several times, the forces of chaos tried to stop us. Several times, we heard rumors that our enemies were starting to hunt down other descendants of the pharaohs, trying to thwart our plans.
NOW, COME ON. OUR MISSION AWAITS!

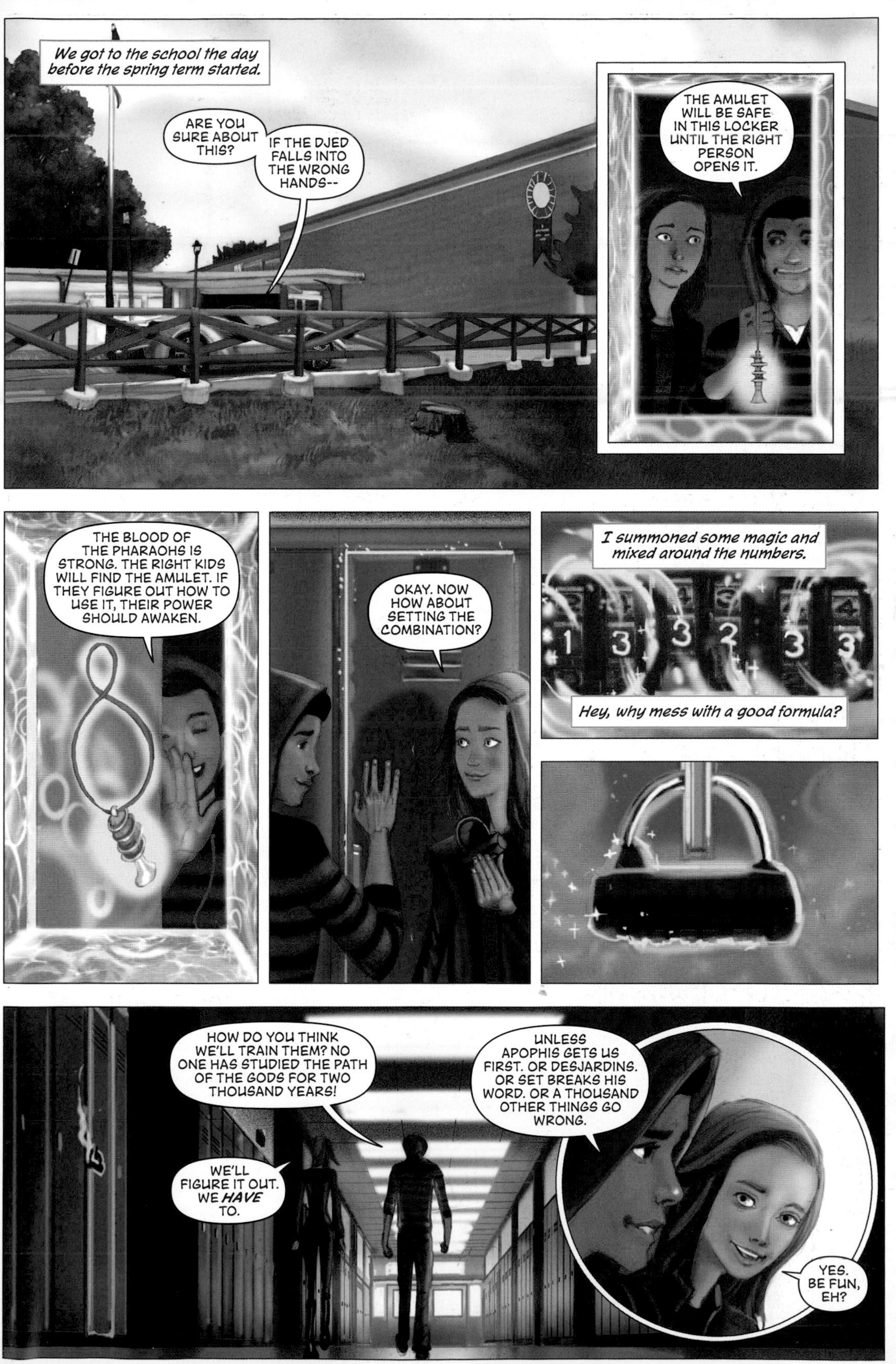
We got to the school the day before the spring term started.
ARE YOU SURE ABOUT THIS?
IF THE DJED FALLS INTO THE WRONG HANDS--
THE AMULET WILL BE SAFE IN THIS LOCKER UNTIL THE RIGHT PERSON OPENS IT.
THE BLOOD OF THE PHARAOHS IS STRONG. THE RIGHT KIDS WILL FIND THE AMULET. IF THEY FIGURE OUT HOW TO USE IT, THEIR POWER SHOULD AWAKEN.
OKAY. NOW HOW ABOUT SETTING THE COMBINATION?
I summoned some magic and mixed around the numbers.
1 3 3 2 3 3
Hey, why mess with a good formula?
HOW DO YOU THINK WE'LL TRAIN THEM? NO ONE HAS STUDIED THE PATH OF THE GODS FOR TWO THOUSAND YEARS!
WE'LL FIGURE IT OUT. WE *HAVE* TO.
UNLESS APOPHIS GETS US FIRST. OR DESJARDINS. OR SET BREAKS HIS WORD. OR A THOUSAND OTHER THINGS GO WRONG.
YES. BE FUN, EH?

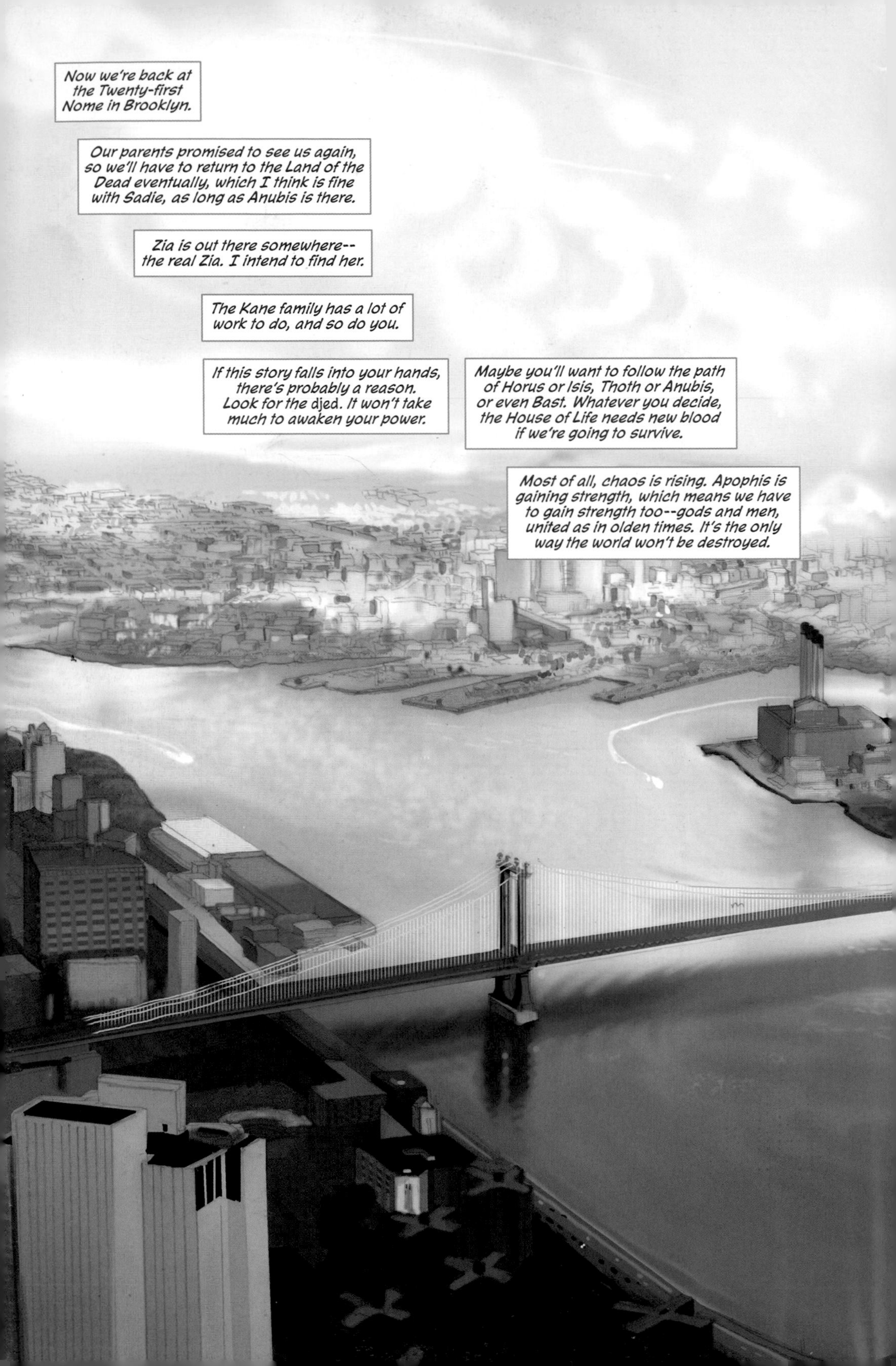
Now we're back at the Twenty-first Nome in Brooklyn.
Our parents promised to see us again, so we'll have to return to the Land of the Dead eventually, which I think is fine with Sadie, as long as Anubis is there.
Zia is out there somewhere-- the real Zia. I intend to find her.
The Kane family has a lot of work to do, and so do you.
If this story falls into your hands, there's probably a reason. Look for the djed. It won't take much to awaken your power.
Maybe you'll want to follow the path of Horus or Isis, Thoth or Anubis, or even Bast. Whatever you decide, the House of Life needs new blood if we're going to survive.
Most of all, chaos is rising. Apophis is gaining strength, which means we have to gain strength too--gods and men, united as in olden times. It's the only way the world won't be destroyed.

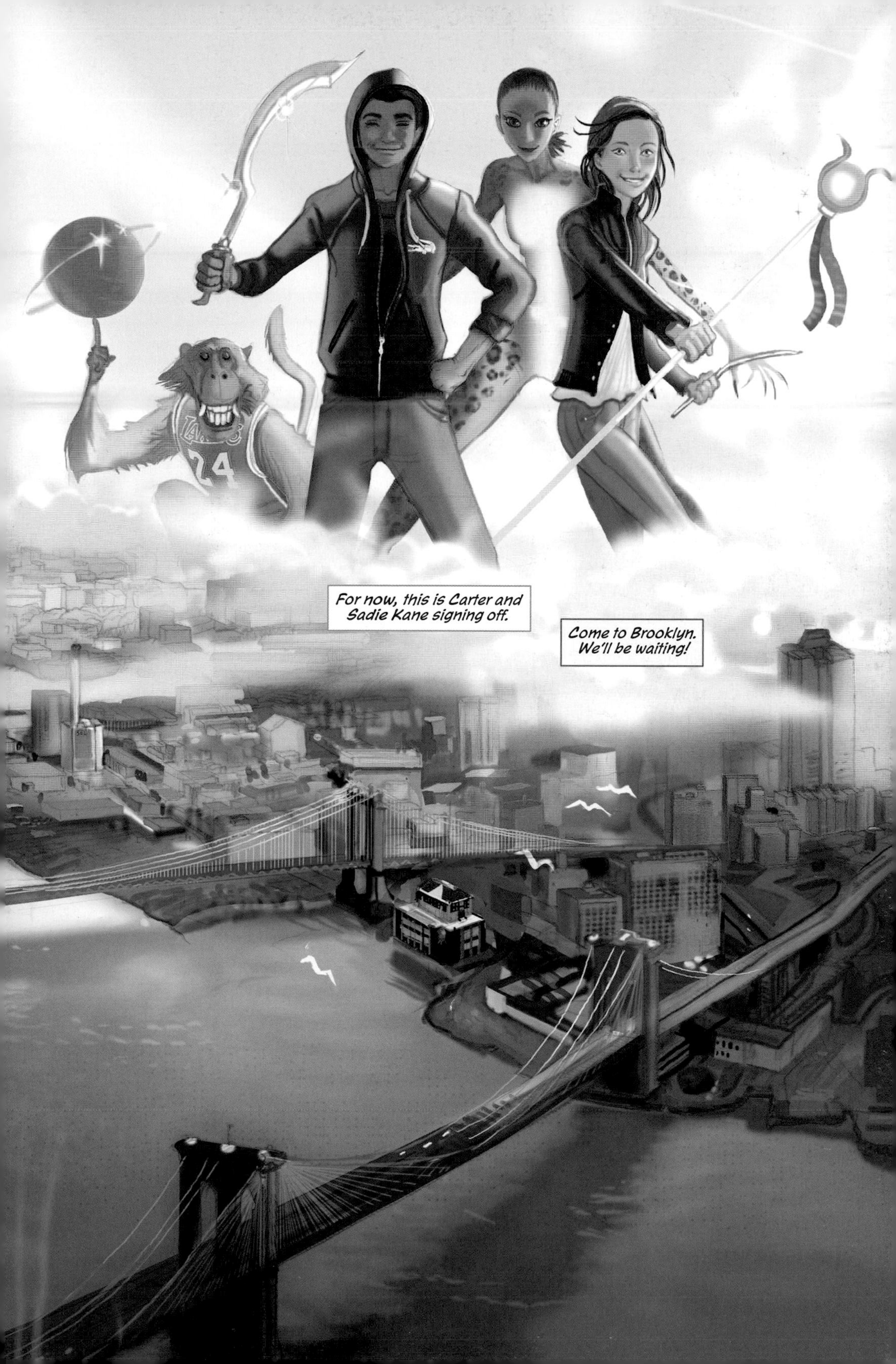
For now, this is Carter and Sadie Kane signing off.
Come to Brooklyn. We'll be waiting!

RICK RIORDAN is the author of the *New York Times* bestselling Kane Chronicles series: *The Red Pyramid*, *The Throne of Fire* and *The Serpent's Shadow*. His other novels include the award-winning five-book Percy Jackson series and the thrilling Heroes of Olympus series: *The Lost Hero*, *The Son of Neptune*, *The Mark of Athena* and *The House of Hades*. Rick lives in Boston, Massachusetts, with his wife and two sons. To learn more about him, visit: www.rickriordanmythmaster.co.uk

ORPHEUS COLLAR is a storyboard artist and illustrator who received his BFA from the Maryland Institute of Art. He has contributed his colouring skills to numerous titles, including *The Amazing Spider-Man* and *Ultimate X-Men*, as well as the storyboards for *Percy Jackson and the Lightning Thief: The Graphic Novel*. Born and raised in Baltimore, Maryland, Orpheus now lives in Los Angeles, California. Visit him at: www.orpheusartist.com

PUFFIN BOOKS

Published by the Penguin Group
Penguin Books Ltd, 80 Strand, London WC2R 0RL, England
Penguin Group (USA) Inc., 375 Hudson Street, New York, New York 10014, USA
Penguin Group (Canada), 90 Eglinton Avenue East, Suite 700, Toronto, Ontario, Canada M4P 2Y3
(a division of Pearson Penguin Canada Inc.)
Penguin Ireland, 25 St Stephen's Green, Dublin 2, Ireland (a division of Penguin Books Ltd)
Penguin Group (Australia), 707 Collins Street, Melbourne, Victoria 3008, Australia
(a division of Pearson Australia Group Pty Ltd)
Penguin Books India Pvt Ltd, 11 Community Centre, Panchsheel Park, New Delhi – 110 017, India
Penguin Group (NZ), 67 Apollo Drive, Rosedale, Auckland 0632, New Zealand
(a division of Pearson New Zealand Ltd)
Penguin Books (South Africa) (Pty) Ltd, Block D, Rosebank Office Park, 181 Jan Smuts Avenue,
Parktown North, Gauteng 2193, South Africa

Penguin Books Ltd, Registered Offices: 80 Strand, London WC2R 0RL, England

puffinbooks.com

Adapted from the novel *The Kane Chronicles: The Red Pyramid*, published in Great Britain by Puffin Books
Graphic novel first published in the USA by Disney•Hyperion Books,
an imprint of Disney Book Group, 2012
Published in Great Britain by Puffin Books 2013
001

Text copyright © Rick Riordan, 2012
Illustrations and jacket art copyright © Disney Enterprises, Inc., 2012
Jacket and graphic novel design by Jim Titus
The moral right of the author and illustrator has been asserted
All rights reserved

Printed in Italy by Graphicom

British Library Cataloguing in Publication Data
A CIP catalogue record for this book is available from the British Library

ISBN: 978-0-141-35039-4